DIARY OF A BODY

Also by Daniel Pennac in English translation

FICTION

The Fairy Gunmother

The Scapegoat

Write to Kill

Monsieur Malaussène

Passion Fruit

NON-FICTION

The Rights of the Reader

School Blues

FOR CHILDREN

Dog

Eye of the Wolf

Daniel Pennac

DIARY OF A BODY

Translated from the French by
Alyson Waters

MACLEHOSE PRESS
QUERCUS · LONDON

First published in the French language as *Journal d'un corps*
by Editions Gallimard in 2012
First published in Great Britain in 2016 by MacLehose Press
This paperback edition published in 2017 by

MacLehose Press
An imprint of Quercus Publishing Ltd
Carmelite House
50 Victoria Embankment
London EC4Y 0DZ

An Hachette UK company

Copyright © Editions GALLIMARD, Paris, 2012
English translation copyright © 2016 by Alyson Waters
Copyedited by Dominique Buchan

This book has been selected to receive financial assistance from English PEN's PEN Translates! programme. English PEN exists to promote literature and our understanding of it, to uphold writers' freedoms around the world, to campaign against the persecution and imprisonment of writers for stating their views, and to promote the friendly co-operation of writers and the free exchange of ideas.

The moral right of Daniel Pennac to be identified as the author of this work has been asserted in accordance with the Copyright, Designs and Patents Act, 1988.

Alyson Waters asserts her moral right to be identified as the translator of the work.

All rights reserved. No part of this publication may be reproduced or transmitted in any form or by any means, electronic or mechanical, including photocopy, recording, or any information storage and retrieval system, without permission in writing from the publisher.

A CIP catalogue record for this book is available from the British Library.

ISBN (MMP) 978 1 78206 098 7
ISBN (Ebook) 978 1 78206 097 0

This book is a work of fiction. Names, characters, businesses, organisations, places and events are either the product of the author's imagination or are used fictitiously. Any resemblance to actual persons, living or dead, events or locales is entirely coincidental.

10 9 8 7 6 5 4 3 2 1

Designed and typeset in Minion by Libanus Press, Marlborough
Printed and bound in Great Britain by Clays Ltd, St Ives plc

FOREWORD

My friend Lison – my dear old, inimitable, and very exasperating, friend Lison – has a knack for giving cumbersome gifts, for example the unfinished sculpture that takes up two-thirds of my bedroom or the paintings she leaves to dry for months in my hallway and dining room with the excuse that her studio has become too small. She turned up at my place one morning, cleared a spot on the table where I had been hoping to eat my breakfast, and dumped a pile of notebooks that had been bequeathed to her by her recently deceased father. Her bloodshot eyes indicated she had spent the night reading them – as did I the following night. Taciturn, ironic, straight as an arrow, with an international reputation as an old sage to which he paid no attention, Lison's father, whom I had met some five or six times in my life, intimidated me. If there is one thing I couldn't possibly have imagined of him, it's that he'd spent his entire existence writing those pages. Totally dumbfounded, I asked my friend Postel for his opinion; Postel had been his doctor for many years (as he had been for the Malaussène family). His answer was instantaneous: Publish it! Do not hesitate. Send this to your publisher and get it published! There was a catch, however. Asking someone to publish a text by a fairly well-known personality who has demanded anonymity is no small thing! Should I feel some remorse for having extracted this favour from such an honest and respectable man in the book business? You will have to judge for yourselves.

D. P.

3 August 2010

My dear Lison,

So, you have returned home after my funeral; you are obviously down in the dumps, but Paris awaits you, with your friends, your studio, a few paintings to be dealt with, numerous projects, among them your scenery for the Opéra, your political passions, the twins' future, life, your life. Surprise! When you get there, a letter from my lawyer R. informs you in legalistic terms that she has in her possession a package for you from your father. Gracious me! A post-mortem present from Papa. You race to get it, naturally. And what an odd gift the lawyer places in your hands: nothing less than my body! Not my body in flesh and blood, but the diary I secretly kept over the course of my entire life. (Your mother was the only one who knew about it, and she learned of it only recently.) Surprise! My father kept a diary! What got into you, Papa, you who were so distinguished, so inaccessible? And your whole life! Not a personal diary, dear daughter; you know my bias against cataloguing our changing moods. Nor will you find anything about my professional life – my opinions, my lectures, or what Etienne pompously called my "battle"; nothing about your father's social life and nothing about the state of the world. No, Lison, the diary of my body, only, truly. You will be all the more surprised because I was not a very "physical" father. I don't think my children or grandchildren ever saw me naked, rarely in swimming trunks, and never did they come upon me flexing my muscles in front of a mirror. I do not think either, alas, that I was particularly cuddly. And as for telling you and Bruno about my little aches and pains, I would just as soon have died – which happened, by the way, but only once my time was up. The body was not a subject of conversation among us, and I left you and Bruno to figure out the development of yours on your own. You shouldn't take this to mean some particular indifference or modesty on my part; born in 1923, I was simply a bourgeois product of my time, one of those people who still use the semi-colon and who never come to breakfast in pyjamas, but appear showered, shaved, and corseted in their work clothes. The body was invented by your generation, Lison. At least when it comes to the way it is used and how it is put on show. But as far as the relation our minds have with it as a bag of surprises and a faecal pump, the silence surrounding it today is as total and utter as it was in my time. If one were to look into the matter, one would find that there is no one more modest than the most naked of porn stars or the most dissected of body artists. As for doctors (when was the last time you had an actual "physical"?), today's don't touch the body at all. They are concerned only with the enigma of cells, the X-rayed, ultrasounded, scanned, analysed body; the biological, genetic, molecular body; the antibody factory. Can I tell you something? The more it is analysed, the more it is exhibited, the less this modern body exists. It is cancelled out in inverse proportion to its exposure. I kept a daily diary of another body, our fellow traveller, our being machine. Well, not exactly daily; do not expect to read an exhaustive diary; it is not a day-by-day account but rather, it moves from surprise to surprise – our body is generous with surprises – from my twelfth to my eighty-eighth and final year, and it is punctuated with long silences, as you'll see, during those stretches of life in which our body allows itself to be forgotten. But each time my body manifested itself to my mind, it found me with pen in hand, attentive to the *surprise du jour*. I have described these manifestations as scrupulously as possible, as best as I could, without any scientific pretence. My lovely love of a daughter, this is my legacy: it is not a treatise on physiology, but my secret garden, which is, in many respects, our most shared territory. I entrust it to you. Why you precisely? Because I adored you. It's bad enough not to have told you while I was alive; so grant me this small posthumous pleasure. If Grégoire had been alive, I would surely have left this diary to him; it would have interested him as a doctor and amused him as a grandson. God, how I loved that boy! Grégoire, who died so young, and you a grandmother today: the two of you make up my bundle of happiness, my provisions for the great journey. Well. Enough effusiveness. Do what you wish with these notebooks: toss them in the dustbin if you find this gift from father to daughter out of place; distribute them to the family if your heart tells you to do so; publish them if you think it necessary. In this last instance, please see to it that the author remain anonymous – especially since he could be anyone – change the names of people and places; you never know who will be offended and why. Do not attempt to publish the whole thing; you won't be able to manage it. In fact, a number of notebooks got lost over the years and several others are simply repetitive. Skip those; I'm thinking, for example, of the ones from my childhood where I counted my press-ups and sit-ups, or those from my youth where I kept track of my sexual conquests like an accountant. In other words, do what you wish with all this, however you wish; it will be well done.

I loved you.

Papa

1

THE FIRST DAY

(SEPTEMBER 1936)

Maman was the only person to whom I did not call out.

64 years, 2 months, 18 days *Monday, 28 December, 1987*

A stupid joke that Grégoire and his friend Philippe played on little Fanny reminded me of the scene at the origin of this diary, the trauma that gave birth to it.

Mona, who likes cleaning things out thoroughly and completely, organised a huge bonfire of junk, most of which was as old as the hills: rickety chairs, mildewed mattresses, a worm-eaten wheelbarrow, bald tyres: call it a gigantic, foul-smelling auto-da-fé. (All in all, less gloomy than a car boot sale.) She was in charge of the boys, who had decided to re-enact Joan of Arc's trial. I was torn from my work by Fanny's howls – she had been recruited to play the role of Saint Joan. All day long Grégoire and Philippe had been singing Joan's praises; Fanny, only six years old, had never even heard of her. They had painted the pleasures of paradise in such glowing colours that Fanny clapped her hands and jumped for joy as the time of the sacrifice drew near. But when she saw the inferno in which they proposed to throw her alive, she rushed to me, screaming. (Mona, Lison and Marguerite had gone into town.) Her tiny hands gripped me in terror, like claws. "Grandfather! Grandfather!" I tried to console her, saying, "There, there," and "It's all over now," and "It's nothing." (It wasn't nothing, it was quite serious, but I had no knowledge of the canonisation project.) I took her on my knee and felt that she was damp. More than that, even: she had soiled her pants out of sheer terror. Her heart was beating frighteningly fast, and her breathing was quick and sharp. I put her in a warm bath. And it was from the tub that she told me, in snatches between ebbing sobs, about the fate those two morons had had in store for her.

And so I found myself gone back to the time when this diary was first created. September 1936. I am twelve years old, almost thirteen, a Boy Scout. Before that I was a Wolf Cub, in a troop with one of those animal names made fashionable by *The Jungle Book*. So, I am a Boy Scout, and this is important, I am no longer a Wolf Cub, I am not a little boy, I am big, I am a grown-up. The summer holidays are coming to an end. I am at a Scout camp somewhere in the Alps. We are at war with another troop who has stolen our pennant. We have to go get it back. The rules of the game are simple. Each of us wears his kerchief on his back, tucked into the belt of his shorts. Our adversaries do the same. This kerchief is called a "life". Not only must we return from this raid with our pennant, but we must also bring back as many "lives" as possible. We also call them "scalps" and we hang them from our belts. The one who brings back the most is a fearsome warrior, a "flying ace", like those pilots from the Great War whose cabins were decorated with as many German crosses as planes they had shot down. In other words, we are playing war. Because I am not very strong, I lose my "life" as soon as the hostilities break out. I fall into an ambush and am held down on the ground by two enemies, my "life" torn from me by a third. They tie me to a tree so I will not be tempted, even dead, to go back into the fray. And they abandon me there. In the middle of the forest. Tied to a pine tree the resin from which sticks to my naked arms and legs. My enemies vanish. The front moves away, and from time to time I can hear shouts that grow ever fainter, then nothing. The vast silence of the woods swoops down on my imagination, the silence of the forest that whispers with every possibility: cracklings, rustlings, sighs, chuckles, and the wind in the trees . . . I tell myself that the animals, disturbed by our games, will now reappear. Not wolves, obviously, I am a grown-up, I no longer believe in man-eating wolves. No, not wolves, but wild boars, for example. What does a wild boar do to a boy attached to a tree? Probably nothing, so I forget about that one. But what if it is a wild sow with her young? Still, I am not afraid. I just ask myself the sorts of questions that arise in a situation where everything can be explored. The more I attempt to free myself, the tighter the knots become and the more the resin sticks to my skin. Will it harden? One thing is certain, I will not be able to get out of these bonds; Scouts know how to tie knots that cannot be unknotted. I feel quite alone but I don't think I will never be found. I know that lots of people come to the forest; we often meet blueberry or raspberry pickers. I know that once the hostilities have ended, someone will come to untie me. Even if my enemies forget me, my patrol will notice my absence, an adult will be told, and I will be freed. So I am not afraid. I grin and bear it. My reason easily masters everything the situation sends to my imagination. An ant climbs onto my shoe, then onto my naked leg and gently tickles it. This lone ant will not get the better of my rational self. On its own, I deem the ant to be inoffensive. Even if it were to bite me, even if it were to get into my shorts, then into my underpants, it would be no big deal; I would be able to stand the pain. It isn't unusual to be bitten by ants in the forest, the pain is familiar, controllable; it is sharp and temporary. This, then, is my state of mind – that of a calm entomologist – until my eyes fall upon a genuine anthill, two or three metres from my tree at the foot of another pine: a gigantic tumulus of pine needles crawling with dark and wild life, a monstrous, immobile swarm. It's when I see the second ant climbing on my sandal that I lose control of my imagination. It is no longer a question of being bitten; I am going to be completely covered with ants, eaten alive. My imagination does not represent the thing in all its detail, I don't tell myself that the ants are going to climb up my legs, devour my penis and anus or enter me through my eyeballs, my ears, my nostrils, that they will eat me from the inside out, winding their way through my intestines and sinuses; I don't see myself as a human anthill tied to this pine tree and vomiting through my dead mouth columns of worker ants busily transporting me crumb by crumb into the terrifying belly swarming upon itself three metres from me; I don't imagine these tortures, but they are all there in the howl of terror I let out now, eyes closed, mouth immense. It is a cry for help that must sheathe the entire forest, and the world beyond – a stridency in which my voice breaks into a thousand shards, and it is my whole body that screams through the voice of the little boy I have once again become. My sphincters scream as immoderately as my mouth, my insides run down my legs, I can feel it as it happens; my shorts are filling up and I am dripping. Diarrhoea mixes with resin, and this increases my terror because, I tell myself, the odour will intoxicate the ants and attract other animals, and my lungs dissolve in my cries for help. I am covered in tears, drool, snot, resin and shit. Yet I can see that the anthill is not concerned with me, that it remains working seriously, steadily on itself, busying itself with countless small things, and that beside these two vagabond ants, the others – no doubt millions – are completely ignoring me; I see it, I am aware of it, I even understand it, but it is too late, my fear is too strong; whatever has grabbed hold of me has no bearing in reality and my whole body is expressing the terror of being devoured alive, a terror conceived only in my mind, without the ants' complicity; somehow I know all that, and later when Father Chapelier – his name was Chapelier – asks me if I seriously believed the ants were going to devour me, I answer no; and when he asks me to admit I was putting on an act, I do; and when he asks if I was amused while my screams were terrorising the hikers who finally untied me I say I don't know; and when he asks aren't you ashamed to have been brought back to your troop covered in shit like a baby, I say yes; he asks me all these questions as he cleans me off with a hose, washing away almost everything with it, without even taking off my clothes – "a uniform, let me remind you, the uniform of the Scouts, let me remind you, and did you wonder for even a second what that pair of hikers would think of the Scouts?" No, forgive me, no I didn't think about it. "But, tell me the truth, you enjoyed playing that little game, didn't you? Don't lie, don't tell me you didn't get some pleasure from it! You liked it, didn't you?" I don't think I knew how to answer his question because I hadn't yet started this diary that, during the entire lifetime that would follow that moment, was determined to distinguish body from mind, to protect from then on my body from the assault of my imagination, and my imagination from the excessive manifestations of my body. "And what will your mother say? Have you thought about what your mother will say?" No, no, I hadn't thought of Maman and as he was asking me this question I even said to myself that the only person to whom I didn't call out for help as I was screaming was Maman; Maman was the only person to whom I didn't call out.

They sent me home. Maman came to fetch me. The next day, I started this diary by writing: I won't be afraid anymore, I won't be afraid anymore, I won't be afraid anymore, I won't be afraid anymore, I will never be afraid anymore.

2

12–14 YEARS OLD

(1936–1938)

Because this is what one is supposed to look like,
this is what I will look like.

12 years, 11 months, 18 days *Monday, 28 September, 1936*

I won't be afraid anymore, I won't be afraid anymore, I won't be afraid anymore, I won't be afraid anymore, I will never be afraid anymore.

12 years, 11 months, 19 days *Tuesday, 29 September, 1936*

The list of my fears:

– Afraid of Maman.
– Afraid of mirrors.
– Afraid of my friends. Especially Fermantin.
– Afraid of insects. Especially ants.
– Afraid of pain.
– Afraid of soiling myself if I'm afraid.

It's stupid to make a list of my fears, I'm afraid of everything. In any case, fear always surprises us. You don't expect it and two minutes later it drives you crazy. That's what happened to me in the forest. Could I have expected to be afraid of two ants? At almost thirteen! And before the ants, when the other Scouts attacked me, I threw myself on the ground without defending myself. I let my "life" be taken and allowed myself to be tied to a tree as if I were dead. I had *died of fright*, really died!

The list of my resolutions:

– You're afraid of your mother? Act as if she didn't exist.
– You're afraid of your friends? Speak to Fermantin.
– You're afraid of mirrors? Look at yourself in one.
– You're afraid of pain? It's your fear that hurts you the most.

– You're afraid of soiling yourself? Your fear is more disgusting than shit.

If there is something more idiotic than making a list of my fears, it's making a list of my resolutions. I never keep them.

12 years, 11 months, 24 days *Sunday, 4 October, 1936*

Ever since they sent me home, Maman has been furious. This evening, she made me get out of the tub before I had finished washing. She forced me to look at myself in the bathroom mirror. I hadn't even dried myself. She held me by the shoulders as if I were trying to run away. Her fingers hurt me. She repeated over and over: "Look at yourself! Look at yourself!" I clenched my fists and shut my eyes. She was screaming. "Open your eyes! Look at yourself! Look at yourself!" I was cold. I clenched my jaw so my teeth wouldn't chatter. My whole body trembled. "We will not leave this room until you have looked at yourself! Look at yourself!" But I did not open my eyes. "You don't want to open your eyes? You refuse to look at yourself? It's always the same nonsense with you. Fine. Would you prefer me to tell you what you look like? What the boy in front of me looks like? What do *you* think he looks like? What do you look like? Want me to tell you? You look like nothing! *Absolutely nothing*!" (I am writing down exactly *everything* she said to me.) Then she walked out, slamming the door behind her. When I opened my eyes, the mirror had misted over.

12 years, 11 months, 25 days *Monday, 5 October, 1936*

If he had witnessed Maman's screaming fit, Papa would have whispered to me: "A boy who looks like absolutely nothing, well, well, now *that* is *interesting*. What, then, must a boy who looks like nothing look like? Like the cut-away diagram of the human body in the *Larousse Encyclopedia*?" (When Papa emphasised a word, it was as if he were pronouncing it in italics.) Then, he said nothing in order to leave me time to reflect. I am thinking of the diagram of the human body in

Larousse because Papa and I used it a lot to study anatomy. I know how a man is built. I know where the splenic artery is, I know every bone, every nerve, every muscle by name.

13th birthday *Saturday, 10 October, 1936*

Maman played the handkerchief trick on Dodo again. Obviously she waited until lunchtime when everyone was there. Dodo was passing around the *zakuski*. Maman asked him to "kindly" put down the plates and pulled him very gently to her, as though she was going to cuddle him. Instead of which she took out the handkerchief. She rubbed it behind his ears, and in the creases of his elbows and knees. Dodo stood very stiff. Naturally, the handkerchief (which Maman showed to everyone!) was not as white. Dodo's nails were not right either. "When you are such a dirty little boy, you cannot play the young lady of the house! Go back and scrub yourself, young man!" Pointing to Dodo, she said to Violette: "Watch him closely, would you? And don't let him forget his navel. I will give you ten minutes." Whenever she is being nasty like this, Maman uses her bubbly, young-girl voice.

When I was little and Violette would wash me, she would describe the filth of Louis XIV's court as if she had just left it. "Oh! So many odours, you wouldn't believe it! Those people used to put on perfume the way we slip dust under the carpet." Violette also likes Napoleon's letter to Josephine (he was coming back from his Egyptian campaign): "Don't wash, I'm on my way." "All that to say, young fellow, that we don't need to smell like a rose for people to love us. But don't say I told you!"

And speaking of cleanliness. One day when I was washing Papa's back with a scrubbing mitt, he said to me: "Have you ever wondered where all this human filth goes? What do we cause to become dirty whenever we become clean?"

I did it! I did it! I let the sheet covering the mirror on my wardrobe fall and I looked at myself! I decided enough was enough. I let the sheet fall, clenched my fist, took a deep breath, opened my eyes, and looked at myself! *I LOOKED AT MYSELF!* It was as if I were seeing myself for the first time. I stayed in front of the mirror for a long time. It wasn't really me inside it. It was my body, but it wasn't me. It wasn't even a friend. I kept repeating: "You are me? You, me? This is us?" I am not crazy, I know full well that I was playing with the *impression* that it wasn't me, but rather some boy who had been abandoned at the back of the mirror. I wondered how long he had been there. These little games that make Maman furious didn't frighten Papa in the least. "My son, you are not crazy, *you are playing with your sensations*, like all children your age. You question them. And you will never stop questioning them. Even as an adult. Even when you are very old. Remember: *All our lives, we must make an effort to believe our senses.*"

My reflection really did seem like a child abandoned in my wardrobe. This sensation is absolutely true. When I let the sheet fall, I knew whom I would see, but I was surprised nonetheless, as if that boy were a statue abandoned there long before I was born. I stayed looking at him for a long time.

And it was then that I got the idea.

I left my bedroom, tiptoed to the library, and I opened the *Larousse Encyclopedia.* I carefully tore out the cut-away diagram of the body using a ruler (no one will notice; Maman only uses the *Larousse* to slip it under Dodo's bottom when we eat in the dining room), came back to my bedroom, locked the door, undressed completely, slid the cut-away man into the mirror frame, and compared the two of us.

The fact is that we have *absolutely nothing in common.* The cut-away man is an adult athlete. His shoulders are broad. He holds himself erect on his muscular legs. I, on the other hand, resemble nothing. I am a pale, feeble child with a sunken chest, so skinny you could slip the post under my shoulder blades (according to Violette). We have, however, one thing in common: we are both *transparent*. You can see our veins, you can count our bones, but none of my muscles are visible. I am nothing but skin, veins, slackness and bones. Nothing is *taut*, as Maman would say. It's true. And as a result, anyone can take my "life", tie me to a tree, abandon me in the forest, clean me off with a hose, make fun of me or tell me I look like nothing at all. And you wouldn't defend me, would you? You would let me be gobbled up by ants, wouldn't you! You would shit all over me!

Well, *I* will defend you. I will even defend you against myself. I am going to build your muscles, strengthen your nerves, deal with you every day, and pay attention to *everything* you *feel*.

13 years, 1 month, 4 days *Saturday, 14 November, 1936*

Papa said: Every object is *first and foremost* an object of interest. Thus my body is an object of interest. I am going to write the diary of my body.

13 years, 1 month, 8 days *Wednesday, 18 November, 1936*

I also want to write the diary of my body because everyone talks about other things. *All bodies are abandoned in wardrobes.* People who write ordinary diaries, Luc or Françoise for example, write about everything and nothing: emotions, feelings, stories of friendship, love, betrayals, endless justifications, what they think of other people, what they think other people think of them, the trips they have taken, the books they have read, but they never write about their bodies. I saw that this summer with Françoise. She read me her diary "in great secrecy," even though she reads it to everyone; Etienne told me. She writes in an emotional state, but she hardly ever remembers *which* emotion was affecting her. Why did you write that? I don't remember. As a result, she is no longer quite sure of the *meaning* of what she writes. I, however, in fifty years, want what I write today to mean the same thing. Exactly the same thing! (In fifty years, I will be sixty-three.)

13 years, 1 month, 9 days *Thursday, 19 November, 1936*

When I was thinking back on all my fears, I drew up this list of feelings: the fear of heights that crushes my balls, the fear of being punched that paralyses me; the fear of being afraid that distresses me all day; anxiety that gives me diarrhoea; emotion (of any kind, even delightful) that gives me goose bumps; nostalgia (thinking of Papa, for example) that brings tears to my eyes; surprise that makes me jump (even a slamming door!); the panic that makes me pee; the slightest little sorrow that makes me cry; fury that suffocates me; shame that shrinks me. My body reacts to everything. But I don't always know *how* it will react.

13 years, 1 month, 10 days *Friday, 20 November, 1936*

I have really thought about it. If I describe *exactly* everything I feel, my diary will be an *ambassador* between my mind and my body. It will be the *translator* of my sensations.

13 years, 1 month, 12 days *Sunday, 22 November, 1936*

I will not only describe strong sensations, great fears, illnesses, accidents, but absolutely *everything* that my body feels (or that my mind makes my body feel). The wind caressing my skin, for example, the sound silence makes inside me when I cover my ears, Violette's smell, Ti-Joe's voice. Ti-Joe already has the voice he will surely have when he is an adult. It is a *gritty* voice, as if he were smoking three packs of cigarettes a day. And he's only three years old! When he is an adult, his voice won't be high-pitched anymore, obviously, but it will be the same gritty voice, with laughter behind the words, I'm sure of it. As Violette says when she talks about Manès' fits of anger: "A person can scream all they want, they have the voice that they have!"

13 years, 1 month, 14 days *Tuesday, 24 November 1936*

Our voice is the music the wind makes when it goes through our body (well, unless it comes out the other end).

13 years, 1 month, 26 days *Sunday, 6 December, 1*

I vomited coming back from Saint-Michel. Nothing makes me angrier than vomiting. Vomiting is like being turned inside out like a sack. Like your skin is being turned inside out. Tugged at. Torn off. You resist, but you are turned inside out. Everything inside comes out. Exactly like when Violette skins a rabbit. The other side of your skin. That's what vomiting is. It makes me ashamed and absolutely furious.

13 years, 1 month, 28 days *Tuesday, 8 December, 1936*

I must always calm down before writing in here.

13 years, 2 months, 15 days *Friday, 25 December, 1936*

Last night, Maman's present to me was a question: "Do you *truly* believe you deserve a Christmas present?" I thought back to the Scouts and I said no. But it was mostly because I didn't want anything from her. Uncle Georges gave me two two-kilo barbells and Joseph gave me a piece of equipment to develop my muscles called a "chest expander". It's made of five rubber cords tied to two wooden handles. You have to hold one handle in each hand and pull the expander as many times as possible. In the instructions you can see a picture of a man before he bought the expander and the same man six months later. You wouldn't recognise him. His rib cage has doubled in volume and his levator scapulae muscles give him the neck of a bull. Yet he only did *ten minutes a day.*

13 years, 2 months, 18 days *Monday, 28 December, 1936*

We played the fainting game, Etienne and I. It was great. One person stands behind you, takes you in his arms, compresses your chest as hard as possible while you empty out your lungs. Once, twice, three times, squeezing with all his might, and when there is no more air at all in your chest, your ears buzz, your head spins, and you faint. It's wonderful. You can feel yourself *leaving*, Etienne says. Yes, or reeling, or flowing out of yourself . . . In any case, it is really wonderful.

13 years, 3 months *Sunday, 10 January, 1937*

Dodo woke me in the middle of the night. He was crying. I asked him why; he didn't want to say. So I asked him why he woke me up. In the end he told me that his friends were making fun of him because he couldn't pee as far as they could. I asked him how far. He said not far. Maman didn't teach you how? No. I asked him if he wanted to pee now. Yes. I asked him if he retracted his foreskin before peeing. He said: what do you mean my foreskin? We went out on the balcony and I showed him how to do it. Violette showed me how, in the bathtub, when I was little. "Retract your foreskin so it doesn't grow fungus!" His little tip came out and he peed really far, all the way to the roof of the Bergeracs' Hotchkiss. It was parked below the house. He peed as far as the width of the pavement. He was so happy that he laughed while he peed. And that sent the stream even farther, in spurts. I was afraid Maman would wake up and I covered his mouth with my hand. He continued to laugh into my hand.

13 years, 3 months, 1 day *Monday, 11 January, 1937*

There are three ways for boys to pee: 1) Sitting. 2) Standing, without retracting the foreskin. 3) Standing, retracting the foreskin. When you retract it, you can pee a lot further. It is absolutely *unbelievable* that Maman didn't teach Dodo how to do this! On the other hand, isn't it instinctive? If it is, why didn't Dodo figure it out for himself? What would I have done if Violette hadn't shown me how? Is it possible that some men sprinkle their feet their whole lives because they never thought to retract their foreskin? I asked myself this question all day while I was listening to my teachers: Lhuillier, Pierral, Auchard. The countless things they know about "the workings of the world" (as Maman would say) without possibly ever having thought of retracting their foreskin! Monsieur Lhuillier, for example, with his attitude of seeming to want to teach everything to everyone, I bet you anything he pees on his feet and wonders why.

13 years, 3 months, 8 days *Monday, 18 January, 1937*

What I like when I am falling asleep is waking up for the pleasure of falling asleep again. To wake up at the exact moment when you are falling asleep is fantastic. Papa is the one who taught me *the art of falling asleep.* "Observe yourself carefully: your eyelids grow heavy, your muscles relax, on your pillow your head at last weighs its weight of a head, you feel that what you are thinking is no longer entirely *thought*, as if you were starting to dream all the while knowing you are not yet sleeping." As if I were walking, balancing on a ledge, about to fall over into sleep? "Exactly! As soon as you feel yourself tipping over into sleep, shake your head and wake yourself up. Remain on the ledge. You will be awake for a few seconds during which you can say to yourself: I'm going to fall back asleep! It is an exquisite *promise.* Wake yourself up again to enjoy the feeling a second time. If you need to, pinch yourself as soon as you feel yourself falling over! Come back to the surface as often as possible and then, *finally*, let yourself go." I can hear Papa whispering his sleeping lessons to me. More! More! Thanks to him, this is what I ask for from sleep night after night.

13 years, 3 months, 9 days *Tuesday, 19 January, 1937*

Maybe that's what dying is. It would be really good if we weren't so afraid of it. Maybe we only wake up every morning to delay the delicious moment when we will die. When Papa died he fell asleep one last time.

13 years, 3 months, 20 days *Saturday, 30 January, 1937*

When I was blowing my nose a moment ago, I remembered that when Dodo was little I tried to teach him how to blow his nose. But he didn't blow. I would put the handkerchief under his nose and say go on, blow, and he would blow air out of his mouth. Or else he didn't blow out at all, he would suck in, inflating like a balloon and nothing would come out. At the time I thought Dodo was an idiot. But it wasn't true. It's simply that man must learn everything about his body, absolutely everything: we learn to walk, to blow our nose, to wash. We wouldn't know how to do any of that if someone didn't show us how. At first, man knows nothing. Nothing about anything. He is as stupid as an ass. The only things he doesn't need to learn how to do are breathing, seeing, hearing, eating, peeing, shitting, sleeping and waking. And yet! We can hear, but we have to learn how to *listen*. We can see, but we have to learn how to *look*. We can eat, but we have to learn how to cut our meat. We can shit, but we have to learn how to use the toilet. We can pee, but when we no longer piss on our feet, we have to learn how to *aim*. Learning is first and foremost learning to *control one's body*.

13 years, 3 months, 26 days *Friday, 5 February, 1937*

"Do you suppose I am an *imbecile* who needs you to emphasise *phonetically* the key words of your *arguments*?" Monsieur Lhuillier asked me in front of the whole class. He did it imitating me, which of course made everyone laugh. "Do you think your history teacher waited for you to come along to decide that the Edict of Nantes was an *onerous error*? And besides, don't you consider the words *onerous error* to be a bit *sophisticated* for a boy of your age? Would you not happen to be a tad *snobbish*, my boy? I would ask you for more *unaffectedness* and to not *overwhelm us with your knowledge*."

I was immensely sad to see Papa being mocked like this because of my italics. (My italics are his, so therefore they were mocking him.) I would have liked to answer Lhuillier by imitating his shrill voice, but I blushed, held my breath to keep back my tears, and said nothing. When the bell rang, panic! To leave the classroom and find them all waiting outside, no! Just the idea of it paralysed me. Literally paralysed. My legs refused to carry me. I remained seated. I no longer had a body. *I had gone back into my wardrobe*. I pretended to be looking for something in my schoolbag and in my desk. How shameful! It was my disgust at this shame that finally gave me the strength to get up. After all, they can make as much fun of me as they want, it doesn't matter. They can beat me up or kill me, I don't give a damn.

But it was Violette who was waiting for me outside. She was running errands and had taken advantage of this to come and get me. "You, my little fellow, are afraid of something. I can see it on your face!" On my face? "Yes, you are as white as a sheet." Am not! "Are too! Our faces speak more than we do. Look at Manès. If he blushes, it lasts the whole day. And I can hear your heart beating." She couldn't hear a thing, but that's Violette for you, she had guessed everything. At home, she made me my afternoon snack (bread, grape preserve, cold milk). I asked her not to fetch me from school anymore. "You want to defend yourself on your own, my little fellow? Yes, it's time. Don't be afraid of anyone. If you come back from school black and blue, I'll take care of you."

13 years, 3 months, 27 days *Saturday, 6 February, 1937*

When I mentioned to Papa that I wasn't a baby anymore and he should no longer speak to me in italics, he answered: "Impossible, my boy, that's my *English* side."

13 years, 4 months *Wednesday, 10 February, 1937*

Maman first thought I was faking it so I wouldn't have to go to school. But I wasn't. I really had tonsillitis. With an amazingly high temperature the first two days. Above 40 degrees Celsius. And the feeling of being enclosed in a bouillon-filled diving suit (so said Violette). The doctor was afraid it might be scarlet fever. Ten days of bed rest.

It starts with a hand that strangles you *from the inside*, making it impossible for you to swallow anything. Even your own saliva. Much too painful! And we produce saliva *continuously*. How many litres in a day? We swallow every one of them because it isn't polite to spit. Salivate, swallow: a bodily function as mechanical as breathing. Without it, we would be as dry as dried herring. I wonder just how many notebooks it would take simply to describe everything our body does without our ever thinking about it. Are its automatic functions *innumerable*? We never pay attention to them but all it takes is for one of them to break down and we can't think of anything else. When Papa felt I was complaining too much, he would always quote the same sentence of Seneca's: "Every man thinks his own burden the heaviest." Well, that's exactly what happens when one of our functions breaks down. We become the unhappiest person in the world. When my tonsillitis first started, I was nothing but my throat. "Man *focuses*," Papa used to say. "Everything stems from this fact! In the eyes of man, nothing exists without its frame. My son, I advise you to break the frame."

13 years, 4 months, 6 days *Tuesday, 16 February, 1937*

For a week my room was turned into an infirmary. In the kitchen, Violette would boil the water for my gargling medicine, and prepare it on Papa's small card table that she had set up near the window with a white tablecloth on it. Sister Saint-Michel had shown her how to make mustard plasters. "Don't be stingy with the seed, my girl," she'd say. (And Violette could have been her grandmother!)

Violette spreads the towel on the tablecloth, pours the flax meal gruel on it, sprinkles the gruel with mustard seed, folds the towel in half, sticks it around my neck, and we're off for fifteen minutes of torture. It itches, burns, a thousand tiny needles stick in your throat, which obviously hurts less than before because all you can think about is this burning. "Exchanging one powerful emotion for another, my lad, that's the trick!" (Thus Papa.) "To forget the bad, aim for the worst!" (Thus Violette.) The worst of the worst was when Sister Saint-Michel painted my throat. She stuck the cotton swab deep in my throat and I immediately vomited on her apron. I called her every name in the book and she didn't want to come back any longer. And Maman was in all her states: "You don't want to get better? Do you want to catch albuminuria? Rheumatism? You could die, you know! It ends up attacking the heart!" When Violette does it, the cotton swab is not a problem:

"Open wide, little man, and keep breathing without shutting the back valve. Don't shut it, I said!" (She means the glottis.) "Therrrrre you go. And don't faint if your pee comes out green. It's the medicine that does that! That's right: the colour of the methylene blue mixed with the yellow of pee makes you piss green …" Lucky she warned me; that's exactly the kind of surprise that could make me pass out.

13 years, 4 months, 7 days *Wednesday, 17 February, 1937*

Poultices, gargling, swabbing, resting, yes, but the best of remedies is falling asleep in the scent of Violette. Violette is my house. She smells of wax, vegetables, burning wood, black soap, bleach, aged wine, tobacco, and apples. When I crawl under her shawl, I am entering my house. I hear her words bubbling up deep in her chest and I fall asleep. When I wake up, she isn't there anymore, but her shawl is still covering me. "So that you won't get lost in your dreams, my little man. Lost dogs always return to the hunter's clothes."

13 years, 4 months, 8 days *Thursday, 18 February, 1937*

My body is also Violette's body. Her scent is like my second skin. My body is also Papa's body, Dodo's body, Manès' body . . . Our bodies are also the bodies of other people.

13 years, 4 months, 9 days *Friday, 19 February, 1937*

My legs still feel like jelly, but my fever is gone. The doctor is reassured. He says that scarlet fever would have already "declared itself." The expression struck me because whenever Violette speaks about her husband, she always says that he was "adorable when he declared himself." (He died in the war, right at the beginning, in September 1914.) Wars are also "declared".

13 years, 4 months, 10 days *Saturday, 20 February, 1937*

"You want more?" More what? "More fever? You want more?" Why would I want more? "So you won't have to go to school, of course!" Dodo is very happy to slip into my bed again. He doesn't stop blathering. "If you want more, you'll have to heat the thermometer, but not on the stove, it could break, better to flick it a little, not the end that you stick in, but the other one, the round one. You flick it gently with your fingernail and it goes up, you can do it underneath the sheets, even if Maman is watching you, but not too hard otherwise the mercury breaks up into little dots, get it?" (He is quiet for a moment, but then starts up again.) "And do you know the blotting paper trick? If you slip a piece of dry blotting paper into your shoe, between the sole of your foot and your sock, you get a fever as soon as you start walking." What *are* you talking about? "I swear!" Who told you that? "A friend."

13 years, 4 months, 15 days *Thursday, 25 February, 1937*

Maman wonders how I can stand Violette's grape preserve. She says she would rather die of hunger than eat one spoonful of "that horror"! She insists that I keep the jar in my room. "I don't want that abomination in my kitchen, understand? Just the smell of it makes me nauseous."

I, however, like everything about grape preserve. Its smell, its colour, its taste, its consistency. Smell, sight, touch, taste: all by itself it is a pleasure for four out of five of our senses!

<u>Its smell</u>: the Isabella grape, which we call a raspberry grape. I can see myself with Ti-Joe, Robert and Marianne underneath the vine arbour. The shade is warm. It smells of raspberry. We are happy.

<u>Its colour</u>. Almost black on a purple background. When I dunk my preserve-covered bread in my milk, it makes a halo that breaks up from violet black to very pale blue, passing through every shade of red and mauve. Magnificent!

<u>Its raspberry taste</u>. But less acidic than raspberries.

<u>Its consistency</u>. Between jam and jelly. It melts but doesn't slide. Violette can do the same thing with blackberries.

<u>Ah! Its temperature as well</u>. If I let the jar stand overnight on my

windowsill and I dunk my jellied bread in very hot milk, the contrast between hot and cold is wonderful.

But what I like most of all is the fact that it is *Violette's grape preserve.* And I am sure that's why Maman doesn't like it.

Question: Do our feelings for people influence our taste buds?

13 years, 4 months, 17 days *Saturday, 27 February, 1937*

A moment ago, in the bathroom, Dodo was rinsing his eyes because of the sandman. Violette told him that the sandman comes by every evening and as a result, as soon as his eyes stung him, he wanted to rinse them. I explained to him that it wasn't the sandman but *sleepiness* that makes our eyes sting. That what we call the sandman is the desire to go to sleep. He answered: "Well, that's the sandman!" Dodo is still *under the sway of imagery.* I am keeping this diary to free myself of that.

13 years, 4 months, 27 days *Tuesday, 9 March, 1937*

Uncle Georges answered my letter. Along with Violette, he's the only adult who answers the questions children ask him. So Etienne knows a lot more than I do.

> My dear boy,
>
> . . . You asked me if I "lost my hair from a fright or from a shock of some kind". . . My boy, I went bald during the Great War and I am not the only one. I woke up one morning with tufts of hair in my helmet, and the same thing the next morning, and the next. I became bald in a few weeks. The doctor called it "alopecia" and said my hair would grow back. Hah! . . .
>
> And now you are asking me if "as a representative of the bald genus" I get "shivers on my skull". Well, it happened to me at least once: when I saw Sarah Bernhardt on stage, just after the war. You cannot imagine the voice she had . . .
>
> As for your questions about "menstruation and all that", I

am incapable of answering you. Woman, my boy, is a mystery to Man; unfortunately the opposite is not true . . .

Juliette and I send our love. And say hello to your mother and come to Paris whenever you want and show us your biceps.

Your Uncle Georges

As far as a woman's period is concerned, what he says is a nice way of letting me understand that these questions are not for someone my age. I was sort of expecting that. In the meantime, Violette explained the main things to me. I had asked her the question because of something Fermantin said about his sister: that she was having her "monthlies" and was "in a foul mood." The rest I am copying from the dictionary: Menstruation: "The process in a woman of discharging blood and other material from the lining of the uterus at intervals of about one lunar month from puberty until the menopause, except during pregnancy."

13 years, 5 months *Wednesday, 10 March, 1937*

I remember a conversation between Uncle Georges and Papa. Papa couldn't get out of bed anymore. He was hardly eating anything at all. Uncle Georges asked him to get a hold of himself. He was begging him even. He had tears in his eyes. "Impossible," said Papa. "I, my dear fellow, have become bald on the *inside*! And the hair isn't growing back in there any more than it is on your egghead." Uncle Georges and Papa loved each other a lot.

13 years, 5 months, 6 days *Tuesday, 16 March, 1937*

Papa warned me! But it's one thing to know about it and something else when it happens to you! I woke up and jumped out of bed. My pyjamas were soaked and my hands were all sticky! There was some on the sheets, too. In fact, there was some all over. My heart beat wildly.

While I was taking off my pyjama bottoms I remembered what Papa had told me. "Ejaculation, my boy. If it happens to you at night, don't be afraid; it's not that you're starting to wet your bed again, *it's the future.* Don't get upset, you might as well get used to it right away, you will be producing sperm your whole life. At first, you don't really control it very well: a little rubbing, pleasure, and, wham, you release everything. And then you get used to it, you learn how to slow down, and in the end you manage to control it."

The pyjama bottoms were sticking to my thighs like gummed paper. Dodo came into the bathroom while I was washing. He had to put his two cents in. He was all excited. "It's nothing, it's just spermatozoids, they're to make babies with, half from boys and the other half from girls!"

13 years, 5 months, 7 days — *Wednesday, 17 March, 1937*

As the sperm dries on my skin, it cracks. It looks like mica.

13 years, 5 months, 8 days — *Thursday, 18 March, 1937*

I don't really remember Papa's face anymore. But his voice! Oh, yes! I remember *everything* he ever said to me. His voice was a breath. He would whisper very close to my ear. Sometimes I wonder if I'm really remembering or if Papa is still whispering inside me.

13 years, 5 months, 18 days — *Sunday, 28 March, 1937*

Once again, the cut-away man is in the mirror frame. Because that is how one should look, this is how I shall look.

13 years, 5 months, 19 days — *Monday, 29 March, 1937*

I did it. I went to Fermantin and asked him to show me some things to develop my muscles. At first he made fun of me. He said I was a hopeless case and would not demean himself. "Even if I do your maths homework for you?" He stopped laughing. "What's happening? You want to have big guns to impress the girls?" (I suppose he was talking about biceps, deltoids, and levator muscles). "You want Roman armour?" (Probably the abdominal muscles: the rectus abdominis and the obliques; and the serratus posterior superior muscle too.) "Well, you will have to do tons of sit-ups and press-ups!" Fermantin is only two years older than I am, but already he is a real gymnast. In team sports like football or dodgeball, the side he is on usually wins. He belongs to several clubs and wants me to go with him. No way. First I have to come out of my wardrobe. No team sports, but I will do pull-ups, press-ups, and sit-ups – whatever a person can do alone. I can also practise with the skipping rope, bar exercises, long-distance running. And he has to teach me to ride a bicycle (Violette will lend me hers), and to swim. Manès has already shown me how, but when I jump into the river I'm happy just to move around like a frog. In exchange for running, bicycle riding, and swimming lessons, Fermantin wants me to write his French compositions and do his English homework. Agreed.

13 years, 6 months, 1 day *Sunday, 11 April, 1937*

In order to do a press-up you need to hold your body at an angle of about fifteen degrees from the floor keeping it very rigid between the toes and your straightened arms, then bend your elbows until your chin touches the floor, and then push yourself back up as many times as the strength of your arms will allow. Your body has to remain taut, your back mustn't curve, and your knees mustn't touch the ground when you bend your elbows, and your chest should just skim it. You can also place your feet on the edge of your bed to make your arms work harder. That is the basic press-up. There are many others. Fermantin did a demonstration for me. In music, this would be called "variations on a theme". The clap press-up: your forearms push your body high enough for you to clap your hands before placing them back on the ground. (Don't try this right away, your head will be the first thing to come down and you'll break your teeth.) The behind the back clap press-up: same thing, but you need to push up harder to have the time to clap your hands *behind* your back. (Don't even think about it. Or else do it on a mat.) Even harder is the spin press-up: your body spins around itself before landing back in its original position. The one-arm press-up, and the three-finger press-up (excellent for mountain climbers' phalanges).

*

NOTE TO LISON

My darling Lison,

The following four notebooks (April 1937–summer 1938) are typical of the ones you can skip. They contain nothing but tables charting the development of my musculature (biceps, forearms, torso, thighs, calves, abdominals . . .). I spent my entire early adolescence measuring myself; tape measure in hand, I had become both ethnographer and noble savage. I can smile at the thought today, but I believe I had really got it into my head to look like the cut-away man in the *Larousse Encyclopedia.* In Saint Briac, where Violette took me to spend every summer holiday since the Scouts had dumped me, I replaced gymnastics with work in the fields and woods. Manès and Marta were amazed that a city kid could become so involved in farm life. They never suspected I chose my chores in strict relation to their muscle-building ability: cutting wood for my biceps and forearms; loading hay for my thigh, abdominal and back muscles; running after the goats and my fervent swimming to expand my chest. These days I am a bit remorseful that I wasn't honest with them about my goals, but Violette was not fooled, and nothing made me happier than sharing a secret with Violette.

You know, Lison, because I never really spoke to you about my childhood, it has suddenly crossed my mind that you probably don't understand very much about my calamitous beginnings: the death of my father, my furious mother, the young body abandoned in a wardrobe, and this thirteen-year-old child who was already writing with the affected gravity of a member of the Académie française. The time has come for me to say a few words to you about all this.

I was born because someone was dying. My father was one of the countless walking dead that the War To End All Wars returned to civilian life. His mind was saturated with horrors, his lungs were destroyed by German gas, but he tried in vain to survive. He fought the most heroic battle of his life during his final years (1919–1933). I was born from this attempt at resurrection. My mother had tried to save her husband by conceiving me. A child would do him good, a child means life! I imagine at first he had neither the strength nor the appetite for such a project. But my mother bucked him up just enough for me to come into the world on 10 October 1923. All for nothing; the day after I was born, my father started dying again. My mother did not forgive either of us – neither me nor my father – for this failure. I don't know what their relationship was like before I was born, but to this day I can still hear the litany of my mother's complaints: he "coddled himself"; he "didn't push himself enough"; he "didn't give a damn about anything" and always "sat on his behind", leaving her "all alone" in this life where she had to "think of everything and do everything" by herself. These insults to a dying man were the daily music of my childhood. My father didn't respond to them. Out of compassion, I am sure: it was an unhappy woman who was insulting him – but also out of exhaustion, a dejection she took to be an underhand form of indifference. That woman did not get what she had hoped for from that man; it doesn't take much more for certain volatile temperaments to live in resentment, scorn and solitude. Yet she stayed. She didn't leave him. People didn't get divorced at the time, or rarely, or less often than today, or not our people, or not her – I have no idea.

My birth did not resuscitate her husband, and so from the very outset my mother considered me a useless object, literally a good-for-nothing, and she left me to him.

And I adored that man. I didn't know he was dying, of course; I thought his languor was the expression of tremendous gentleness and I loved him for it, and because I loved him, I imitated him in every way, to the point that I became a perfect little dying man. Like him, I moved little, I ate little, I made my gestures carbon copies of his very slow ones. I grew without filling out; in other words, I made every effort not to "take shape". Like him, I did not speak much and expressed myself with gentle irony while looking on everything with long gazes overflowing with powerless love. One of my testicles obstinately refused to descend, as if I had decided to live only halfway. When I was eight or nine, an operation put it in its proper place, but for a long time I thought I was "blind" on that side.

My mother called us, my father and me, her "phantoms." "I've had it with those two phantoms!" we would hear her say behind the doors she slammed. (She spent her time fleeing while staying in place; hence my memories of slamming doors.) So I lived my first ten years in the sole company of this evanescent father. He would look at me as if he were deeply sad to have to leave this world, abandoning to it the child who had wrested from him some optimism for the species. It was, however, out of the question for him to leave me unarmed, defenceless. Despite how weak he was, he took it upon himself to educate me. And not just a little, let me tell you! The final years of his life were a headlong race between the extinction of his consciousness and the flowering of mine. Once he was dead, his son would have to know how to read, write, conjugate, count, multiply, think, memorise, reason, know when to keep his mouth shut and his thoughts to himself. That was his aim. Play? No time. And with what body?

I was one of those limp and perplexed children you see at the edge of the sandpit, petrified by the energy of their fellow creatures. "As for him," my mother would say, pointing at me, "he is the shadow of a phantom!"

But what a head I had, dear daughter! And so early! Even before I could read, I knew countless fables by heart. My father and I would discuss their morals in long confabs that he called our exercises in "minor philosophy". And soon he brought in the moralists' maxims, those watercolours of thought that a child can understand at a very young age provided they are annotated in the margins; and this is what he did: he annotated with whispered commentary, because his voice was fading – the last two years of his life he only spoke in whispers – but also, I believe, because he liked to offer me these timeless truths as friendly little personal secrets. As a result, at a very young age I had a broad knowledge that I cherished as the legacy of a unique love. Do you remember when you and Bruno were children, how you would make fun of me because you heard me reciting (as if I were singing to myself while I tied my shoelaces or did the dishes) a phrase from Montaigne, three lines from Hobbes, one of Lafontaine's fables or Pascal's *Pensées* or Seneca's maxims ("Papa's talking to himself! Papa's talking to himself!")? Well, these were bits of "minor philosophy" bubbling up from my childhood.

When I was six years old and supposed to start school, my father wanted to keep me close to him. The chief education officer – his name was Monsieur Jardin – whom my mother had summoned to oppose the idea, was amazed by the level, breadth and variety of our whispered conversations. He gave us carte blanche. Once my father died, my mother delivered me straight into the hands of the state schools, my sitting the entrance exam into year seven having been expedited. You can easily imagine the sort of pupil I was. More than the quality of my knowledge or the fact that I wrote and spoke like a book (all the while whispering like a personal adviser to the prince and emphasising the main points of what I was saying with those exasperating italics), what my teachers especially admired was my impeccable handwriting, which paternal rigour had bestowed on me. "Be legible," my father used to say. "Do not let anyone suspect you of trying to conceal behind indecipherable handwriting an idea you have not mastered." As for break in the playground, you can imagine what my schoolmates would have made of me if the teachers had not taken under their wings the pitiful blindworm I was.

My father's death left me doubly orphaned. Not only had I lost him but, with him, all traces of his existence. As widows sometimes do – whether crazed with sadness or drunk on freedom – the day after he died my mother erased everything that could call to mind his very existence. His clothing was donated to the parish; his personal things went into the bin or up for auction. And so I did become his phantom! Deprived of the slightest tangible souvenir of him, I roamed the house like a shadowless body. I ate less and less, did not speak a word, and developed a terrible dread of mirrors. My corporeality felt so slight that reflections seemed suspect to me. (Sharp little customer that you were, you often pointed out my mistrust of mirrors and photographs, a remnant of that childish terror, I suppose.) At night, even more than during the day, the idea of walking in front of a mirror made my blood run cold. I could not get out of my mind the notion that my image was captured there, but with all the lights out I couldn't see myself in it. In other words, my darling, at ten your father weighed little and was off his rocker. It was then that my mother attempted to "incarnate" me once and for all by enrolling me first in the Wolf Cubs, and then in the Boy Scouts. "Outdoor activities! Team spirit!" (She said this without irony.) They would do me a world of good. A total fiasco, as you know. This is not the kind of milieu in which you can last long when you started out with a single testicle.

No, the person who really gave me shape, gave me body, until I became a "ballsy" boy, the person who shamelessly used her physical skills, was Violette, the woman who did our cleaning, washing and cooking. Violette, Manès' sister, and aunt of Ti-Joe, Robert and Marianne. Our servants lost patience with my mother at unbelievable speed; hardly had they been hired than they ran off, having been accused of every sin under the sun – until the day Violette took things in hand and held on against all odds, because she had secretly adopted the larval child who haunted the house. It was under her wing that I grew. Once the institution of the Boy Scouts had been eliminated – the sole aim of which had been to get me out of Maman's hair – Violette turned out to be the only institution capable of relieving Maman of me for a long time. She would take me to spend all the school holidays – including the long summer months – to the farm that belonged to her brother Manès and her sister-in-law Marta. Violette, who was the only love of my childhood, was nothing but the easiest solution for Maman. You'll see I often mention Violette in this diary, even long after she had died.

So. End of this biographical note. You can go back to the serious things: to the farm, to Manès, to Marta. Summer of 1938. And you'll see, I was in much better shape then.

14 years, 9 months, 8 days — *Monday, 18 July, 1938*

In order to combat my fear of heights, I asked Manès to let me to sleep in the fruit loft (four metres above the ground). Marta agreed. Climbing up is okay, the ladder is vertical and you look upwards. Climbing back down is something else! At first, I hugged the ladder very tightly.

Sometimes I have stayed a full five minutes on the middle bar. Robert, waiting for me below, would yell at me not to look down and to breathe deeply. "Keep your eyes on the upper bars! Or else, just let go of everything, you'll come down faster!"

14 years, 9 months, 19 days *Friday, 29 July, 1938*

Jumping into the grain at Peluchat's, that's something else again! Until last week, I didn't dare; same old fear of heights. Marianne made fun of me: "Ti-Joe can do it! And he's only five!" Robert said "Don't you like the beach?" Robert calls it "going to the beach" because the wheat is as "gold as the sand, unless it's the other way around". We take off our clothes before climbing up the ladder so we won't get grain on them. We're not allowed to jump into the wheat, and grain on your clothes is damning proof. If Manès or Peluchat find one single grain on us, they will tan our hides (according to Robert). The roof is seven metres off the ground, the main beam is five metres off the ground, and the pile of grain is two metres high. We climb up the ladder, run along the beam, and jump. Three metres down! Without screaming! If they were to hear us and catch us jumping *naked* in their wheat, well, they will tan our *two* hides (Robert again). Until last week, I couldn't run on the beam, or even stand up on it. Whereas Ti-Joe prances about before he jumps, I could only crawl on hands and knees and jump with my eyes shut tight. The first time, Marianne pushed me. Fear made me scream. We remained hidden in the wheat without moving for at least five minutes, Robert covering Ti-Joe's mouth and holding on to him to keep him still, because Ti-Joe wanted to jump again right away. But no one had heard my scream. Then I had to jump three times in a row; that was the pledge. Without screaming! And stand up on the beam! And keep your eyes open as you jump. Jumping down three metres, your heart in your throat, the crunching hole your body makes in the grain, the warmth of the newly threshed wheat on your naked skin, its caress is so alive . . . Fantastic! Now

I do it easily. Sometimes just with Ti-Joe. Yet I am still afraid of heights: you can *master* your fear of heights, but it is never completely *overcome.*

14 years, 9 months, 21 days *Sunday, 31 July, 1938*

I am afraid of heights, but I don't give a damn. As it turns out, we can prevent our sensations from paralysing our body. They can be tamed like wild animals. The memory of our fear can even add to our pleasure! The same is true for my fear of the water. Now I can dive into the river as if I had tamed a wildcat. Jump in the grain, fish for trout using my bare hands, feed Mastouf without being afraid of getting bitten, bring the bull back in from the meadow: these are all fears I have overcome. "Your Bridges of Arcola," Papa would have said.

14 years, 9 months, 25 days *Thursday, 4 August, 1938*

Fear protects you from nothing and exposes you to everything! This fact does not, however, prevent you from being careful. Papa used to say: "Prudence is the intelligence of courage."

14 years, 10 months *Wednesday, 10 August, 1938*

Caught two trout, the third got away. Last year I couldn't even hold a live trout in my hands. It disgusted me. I would let it go immediately, as if the living thing were electrocuting me. That said, Robert catches six or seven whereas I get only one or two. The day Ti-Joe starts doing it, there will be no more fish left in the river!

14 years, 10 months, 10 days *Saturday, 20 August, 1938*

Two *conceptions* of pain.

When we were milking the cows this morning, one of them knocked the pail over. Robert knelt down to push the milk into the drain, and got up with the pail in his hand *and a board nailed to his knee.* He had knelt on the nail! He pulled out the board, just like that, and went back to work. When I told him that he had to disinfect it right away, he said, no big deal, it can wait till I'm done milking. I asked him if it hurt: a little. At four in the afternoon, I cut the fleshy part of my thumb when I was slicing bread for an afternoon snack. The blood spurted everywhere, and I was immediately nauseous, my head spun, and I let myself slide along the wall to sit down so I wouldn't faint. That's the difference between Robert and me. If one were to ask Maman where this difference comes from, she would say: "Those people don't have any imagination, that's all!" She often said that about Violette. (When Violette lost her daughter, for example, and didn't cry.) My fainting therefore must have to do with my sublime degree of culture! Oh, sure. Robert, who is my age, lives in harmony with his body, that's all. His body and mind were brought up *together*, they are good friends. They don't need to meet each other again for the first time with each new surprise. If Robert's body bleeds, it doesn't surprise him. If mine bleeds, the shock of it makes me faint. Robert knows he is full of blood! He bleeds because he lives in his body. Like the pig bleeds when you slaughter it. *Whereas for me, every time something new happens, I discover I have a body.*

14 years, 10 months, 13 days *Tuesday, 23 August, 1938*
The ladder in the fruit loft has been replaced by a rope. Mostly to keep Ti-Joe from climbing up there. For the moment, I can only climb halfway up without using my feet.

14 years, 10 months, 14 days *Wednesday, 24 August, 1938*
Ti-Joe is the opposite of what I was as a child. He's completely physical. Nothing like the fat little Buddhas children his age usually are. He's like some kind of spider made entirely of nerves, muscles and tendons. He can be completely still and then suddenly very swift. He never moves slowly. He's so quick that you can't prevent any of the catastrophes that his energy triggers. I bet it will only be three weeks before he climbs up the rope that leads to my loft. Last week he got it into his head to follow

a badger into its hole. Manès freed him by digging him out with a shovel, like you would do for a dog. A very unhappy badger, *but it didn't scratch Ti-Joe!* Or bite him. If Ti-Joe had been a dog, that badger would have torn him to shreds! (Do wild animals understand what childhood is?) Ti-Joe was all dirty but all smiles. Every day, he pulls off a physical stunt of this kind. At night, though, he asks me for a bed-time story like any well-behaved child. He listens, stiff in his bed, eyes wide beneath his black mop of hair (yesterday, we read *Tom Thumb*), and all his emotions can be seen on his face: worry, impatience, shock, compassion, he bursts out laughing and then, suddenly, he is sound asleep.

14 years, 10 months, 18 days *Sunday, 28 August, 1938*

I miscalculated my dive into the river. My dive was too straight, and I heaved myself up too late. As a result, my palms and knees are scraped. I didn't feel much when I was in the water, but when I got out, it hurt like hell! ("Burning" is really the perfect word for this pain.) When Violette told me she was going to clean it with Manès' calvados, I couldn't help asking if it was going to hurt. "Of course," she said, "what do you think? Manès' hooch isn't milk! Give me your leg." I stretched out my leg and held on tight to the chair. "Ready?" (Ti-Joe was watching the whole thing, fascinated.) I gritted my teeth and shut my eyes tight, nodded yes, Violette dabbed the wound, and I didn't feel a thing! *Because she started to howl in my place.* A real howl of pain, like she was being skinned alive! At first I was dumbfounded, and then it made Ti-Joe and me laugh. Afterwards I felt the coolness of the alcohol as it evaporated on my knee. It took part of the pain with it. I told Violette it wouldn't work for the other knee because now I was aware of the trick. "You think so? Give me the other one." This time she let out *another* cry. An incredibly shrill bird cry that pierced my eardrums. Same results. Didn't feel a thing. "That, my little man, is what's called *auditory anaesthesia.*" She didn't shout when she was cleaning my hands and her silence surprised me even more than her howls. The whole thing was over before I had a chance to feel a thing.

So, if we manage to distract the mind from pain, the wounded person doesn't feel it. Violette told me she had figured this out when she was taking care of Manès when he was little. So Manès was afraid of pain? She smiled: "Even Manès was a little boy once."

14 years, 10 months, 20 days *Tuesday, 30 August, 1938*

I found Ti-Joe in my bed when I went to go to sleep. So he had climbed up the rope! I didn't have the heart to send him back down. How could I have done it, anyway? I would have had to tie him up and let him down with the *same* rope. He sleeps like a puppy. He runs and yaps while he runs. And, at the same time, he sleeps like a baby. A bomb couldn't wake him. I have always been a light sleeper. Even if I am exhausted, my mind keeps watch. And that claw that rips my heart from my chest so often when I wake up! "You are just like your mother," Françoise says to me. "You are full of anxiety." It's true. But much less here than at home.

14 years, 10 months, 23 days *Friday, 2 September, 1938*

Violette came upon me when I was naked in the little pool by the river. I was washing up after blackberry picking. My hands and arms were as red as a murderer's. She looked at me: "I see that watercress has grown around your fountain!" (Nobody ever talks about our body hair, except for Violette.) "Is there some nestled under your arms, too?" I raised my arms in the air so she could see for herself. She doesn't know my body anymore. It's been almost three years since she's washed me in the tub. The people who know you best no longer know anything about your private life when you grow up. Everything becomes a secret. And then, you die and everything reappears. Violette is the one who washed his body for the last time.

*

14 years, 10 months, 25 days *Sunday, 4 September, 1938*

Manès advised me to take up boxing. "You are flexible, you are quick, you have good muscles, and when you get bigger you will have a long reach; you need to box." He was army champion when he did his military service. The most interesting thing about this sport is dodging. Manès drew an outline of feet facing each other on the barn floor. We each step into our own feet and I have to try to swipe him with my fists. "Go ahead, hit me, try to touch me." That's the game. I am in my outlines, he is in his, in reach of my fists, and I have to touch him. It's impossible to get to him. At first, I went slowly, but he kept repeating, "Faster! Harder! Faster! Hit harder! Try to touch me! Again! Again!" It's completely impossible. He dodges every blow. Either he pulls back and my fist arrives at the end of its trajectory without having touched him (which hurts my elbow), or else he ducks and I shoot over him (which makes me lose my balance). Or else he pivots on his hips and I hit the air next to him (which forces me to come out of my outlines). Sometimes, he dodges simply by turning his face from one side to the other. Missed again. Came within a hair's breadth, but missed him. And all this while his hands stay behind his back and his feet stay within the outlines. My fists meet only air. If I pretend to start hitting one side in order to hit the other, he dodges it, laughing: "Think you're clever, huh?" It's incredibly exhausting to box with a ghost as your opponent! You lose your breath; your shoulders, elbows, and tendons hurt, you get annoyed, you exhaust yourself. And that's when your opponent decides to counter-attack. In two or three cat-like swipes, Manès grazes my abdomen, my chin, and my nose. He is flexible and fast like you wouldn't believe. Yet Violette says that he has doubled in volume since 1923, the year of his military service and my birth.

14 years, 10 months, 27 days *Tuesday, 6 September, 1938*

Whom can I tell that a five-year-old child can climb up a four-metre rope? No one would believe me. And yet that's what Ti-Joe does every night now. In fact, he is very well behaved. As soon as I've read him a story, he falls asleep. In the morning, he and I punch the sack of bran that Manès attached to my beam. Manès drew his own face on it with charcoal: "Erase me." Those are the instructions. I have to erase his portrait by practising. And the self-portrait looks just like him! His mop of hair, his eyebrows, and his moustache are all it takes: it's Manès all right.

14 years, 10 months, 28 days *Tuesday, 7 September, 1938*

Violette is dead, Violette is dead,

Violette is dead, Violette is dead. It's over.

*

NOTE TO LISON

My dear Lison,

Once again, you can skip the next notebook. You will find in it only the above sentence, repeated ad infinitum. Violette was indeed dead. And according to the boy I was, she should not have died. You see, I was her protector. Any strength I had found in her earlier strength had turned me into her natural protector. Nothing could happen to her as long I was living close to her. Yet she died. She died and I was there. Alone. I was the sole witness to her death. One afternoon when I had caught five trout, following them upstream as she waited for me seated on her red canvas folding chair (she had taught me how to catch trout with my bare hands: slam them against a rock and don't be afraid of water snakes: small animals don't eat big ones), five trout that I'd tossed alive into her basket that afternoon (she was the one who killed them, with one slap against a rock), and she died. Just as I was onto the sixth. I found her, fallen from her chair, suffocating, trying to get air into her lungs like the fish I had just dropped while running towards her, and I shouted her name, I pounded her on the back thinking she had swallowed something wrong, and I unbuttoned her blouse and soaked my shirt in the river to make a cool compress for her, and all that time she was trying to catch her breath, trying to suck in the air that was suffocating her, the air that should have saved her and that now was suffocating her, her eyes looking amazed by this betrayal of life, her hands gripping my arms like a drowning person grips the last branch, unable to speak to me even to say she was dying, nothing but her frozen fingers, her stifled screams, that awful tear in the trachea, that hoarse, blue death, for she was dying, and we both knew it. Violette, please don't die! That's what I screamed, not: help, help! Violette, please don't die, I repeated until the very second when I could no longer see myself in her eyes, when her eyes that were so close no longer looked at anything, that second when she suddenly weighed in my arms her weight of a dead woman. And then, we did not move any longer. Her body was emptied of the air that had suffocated her and I let the day go by. When Robert and Marianne found us, the trout was still alive.

Once Maman had brought me back to the house, I shut myself up in my bedroom and started to fill up a notebook with this single sentence: Violette is dead, repeated ad infinitum. It was the notebook you have in your hands, the eighth of my diary, and once this notebook was filled, I filled up another, that was my goal, all the following notebooks filled with this single sentence: Violette is dead, notebook after notebook, as a way of writing without breathing until my own strength was snuffed out. Judging from my careful handwriting, it was a calm resolution: Violette is dead. My handwriting was the same then as it is today, completely mastered loops, downstrokes and upstrokes: a Third Republic, authoritarian cry, pages and pages of perfect handwriting in the service of horrendous pain. I screamed Violette is dead until exhaustion made the pen fall from my hand. I wasn't tired from writing, I was tired from having nothing in my stomach. I had begun my hunger strike. Maman did not go to Violette's funeral. She talked about the dead Violette as she had about the living Violette. Maman, I thought, was tarnishing the memory of Violette – "I'm not tarnishing anyone, I'm just saying what I think" – and I began my hunger strike so I wouldn't have to live with Maman anymore. I didn't know at the time that my mother did *not* think, that she was a member of the immense cohort of people who, "in their conscience and souls" use the words "opinion", "conviction", "certainty" and even "feeling" and even "thought" for those vague yet tyrannical sensations that serve to reinforce their views. Violette was sly, Violette was vulgar, Violette didn't know her place, Violette probably stole things, Violette was negligent, alcoholic, over-indulgent. Violette smelled. Violette was bound to end up that way, and I no longer wanted to live with Maman. Boarding school or death was my slogan. And the hunger strike was my way of putting the pressure on.

*

14 years, 11 months, 3 days *Tuesday, 13 September, 1938*

"You, a hunger strike? We'll see about that tomorrow." She's wrong. I can do it. It's not so bad, in fact. I don't cheat. I'm not eating anything in secret. When I get too hungry, I drink a glass of water, just like you're allowed to do before communion. At every meal, she serves me the exact same plate of food, like she does with Dodo when he doesn't like what we are having. "Do you expect me to waste food?" She really doesn't understand a thing. It's interesting: someone who thinks she knows everything and who has such a poor understanding of people. But I don't want to bother with her. I won't say Maman ever again.

14 years, 11 months, 4 days *Wednesday, 1 September, 1938*

I went to the toilet for the last time. Now I am truly empty. My stomach (or intestines?) is rumbling because my digestive system is working in vain. When you are really hungry, you sleep curled up in a ball. You close up around your stomach, as if you were compressing yourself to forget this emptiness. During the day, you only think about eating. Your saliva becomes sweet. You could eat absolutely anything, I believe. Dodo wants me to bring him to boarding school with me. He says he won't stay here alone.

14 years, 11 months 5 days *Thursday, 15 September, 1938*

Last night, I chewed my sheet. It wasn't cheating, it was just to have something in my mouth. I think I was still chewing as I was falling asleep. Dodo took advantage to threaten me. He made me swear to take him with me. He said if you don't take me with you, I will bring the best things to eat in here and I will eat them in front of you. We laughed.

14 years, 11 months, 6 days *Friday, 16 September, 1938*

This morning she wanted to kiss me. I jumped out of my bed. I don't want her to touch me. But my head spun and I fell. She wanted to help me up, but I rolled under the bed so she couldn't catch me. She said she wasn't going to send me to boarding school, she was going to have me locked up with the crazies. And she added, "Besides, you're faking! You eat in secret. I saw you!" She repeats that all the time to reassure herself. Dodo told me.

*

14 years, 11 months, 7 days *Saturday, 17 September, 1938*

Food is energy. I have no energy left. Well, none for my body. For my will, I'm all right, nothing has changed. I won't eat again and won't speak again until she has agreed to boarding school. Any boarding school, I don't care which one.

I should not remain lying down. I mustn't sleep. I have to go out. I have to walk. The less you eat the heavier you feel and the longer the distances seem. Outside, I move from one street lamp to the next. When I get to one, I stop to catch my breath, look at the next one, and head towards it. I have to do at least ten street lamps on each walk I take. Ten going, ten coming. Maybe this is how I will walk when I am old. Counting street lamps.

14 years, 11 months, 8 days *Sunday, 18 September, 1938*

She hired a new woman to cook: Rolande. Since she doesn't come into my bedroom anymore, she sends Rolande with my lunch. She has her make my favourite dishes. This morning it was pasta with tomatoes and basil (the sauce from Violette's jars!). This evening, *gratin dauphinois* and curds with grape preserve. I didn't touch a thing. I just leaned over the plates to breathe deeply, with a towel around my head, like for a steam inhalation. The scent of tomato and basil fills you completely. It spreads through all the empty spaces that hunger has dug out in you. The scent of nutmeg, too. You aren't nourished but you feel full. Rolande takes back the untouched plates. She must think she has come to a madhouse. Dodo says I am really terrific.

I helped Violette prepare the tomato and basil sauce in August. "You can't keep the jars too long, my boy, a month and a half, two months at most. Otherwise the basil will make the oil cloudy and give it a bad taste." (I realise now that at the time her voice didn't have much air left in it.) I cried.

*

14 years 11 months, 9 days *Monday, 19 September, 1938*

It's getting hard to do press-ups. I have no strength left in my arms. I can't do more than ten. Before my hunger strike, I didn't even count them anymore. I don't mind that I'm getting skinny, I just don't want to lose my muscles. The problem is, I don't have much fat to lose. Despite my undershirt, my velour shirt, my big sweater, and Papa's blanket, I am cold. Hunger will do that. Your fat melts and you are cold. Violette would not have liked to see me cry so much. "Stop emptying yourself out like that, my boy. You will waste away!" A long time ago, to console me when Papa died, she took me to the fair and I won twelve kilos of sugar at archery. The stallholder was furious. "He's a sharpshooter, that kid, he'll ruin me, that's enough!" I was only ten and a half! We got a ride back and we gave a bag of sugar to the driver. Violette, Violette, Violette . . . I repeated Violette, Violette, Violette, Violette, Violette, without stopping, emptying myself of all my tears. Violette, Violette, Violette, Violette, until her name didn't mean anything anymore.

14 years 11 months 10 days *Tuesday, 20 September, 1938*

This morning I threw my breakfast out of the window. The temptation was too strong. Rolande didn't bring me anything else that day, neither at lunch nor at dinner. I thought of Papa as I looked at my ribs in the wardrobe mirror. Papa probably had to count street lamps, too. In the end he didn't go out at all. I can't visualise his face very well anymore, but I can still feel his hand on my head. It was very big at the end of his skinny, skinny arm. And very heavy. He had to make a terrible effort to lift it up. Most of the time he just put his hand on mine and I brought it to my head. But I had to hold it there so it wouldn't fall off. Or else I would put my head in his lap, which was easier for him. He was never hungry. He stayed at the dinner table for a long time, even after the meal was over and everything had been cleared away. I think he didn't have the strength to stand back up. And he didn't feel like talking. One day, a fly landed on his nose. He did nothing to chase it away. Around the table, everyone was looking at the fly. He said: "I believe it thinks I am already a corpse."

14 years, 11 months, 11 days *Wednesday, 21 September, 1938*

When you don't eat, you don't feel like talking. Even if I wanted to, it would be hard for me to speak. It doesn't cost me anything to be quiet. It's restful. For Dodo, I make little signs with the tips of my fingers, and that's enough for him, he understands. Staying silent for a long time is like cleaning yourself out completely. And then, I don't have any more saliva. My mouth is dry now. I stay in bed a lot.

14 years, 11 months, 13 days *Friday, 23 September, 1938*

I fell down the stairs as I was going to the lavatory. She wasn't there. My arm is bruised, my thigh and my chest as well. I hurt everywhere, especially when I breathe. I can only take in a little bit of air at a time. Breathing tears my lungs like wrapping paper. Rolande carried me to my bed. The bruises scared her. And so did, especially, the lump on the back of my skull. "Oh. My goodness! It's not possible! Oh my goodness! It's not possible!" she kept repeating. She called the doctor. Nothing is broken but I may have cracked a rib. When the doctor left my bedroom, I heard screaming. He screamed that it was "unacceptable". Rolande answered that all the same, it was not her fault. She kept repeating "All the same!" "Where is the mistress of the house?" "How should I know?" I fell asleep. Uncle Georges was the one who woke me up. He didn't go back to Paris after the summer holidays. He is staying with Joseph and Jeanette until the end of September. He is butterfly hunting with Etienne . I talked to *him.* I explained about boarding school. He thought it was a good idea. "You'll make a lot of friends." Rolande came to let him know that Madame had come home. They shut themselves up in the living room, but they were arguing so loudly that I could hear some words, even some entire sentences. Uncle Georges' voice: "You are completely insane!" Her voice: "He's *my* son!" Uncle Georges' voice:

"He's Jacques' son!" Her voice: "Jacques was not a father!" His voice very angry: "He is my nephew and you can count on me to be an uncle!" Her voice, shriller and shriller: "How dare *you* tell *me* how to raise my son? In my own house! My own house!" The living-room door slammed, then the door to her bedroom. Everything was quiet for a long time, and then I fell back asleep. Once again, it was Uncle Georges who woke me. He said: "I'll take care of boarding school, you'll go to the same one as Etienne . And now what would you like to eat? What do you want most?" I answered a bowl of cold milk and a piece of bread with grape preserve. When he brought me my tray, he told me never to do that again. "You don't fool around with your health. Your body is not a toy! Eat up and get dressed, I'm taking you to Joseph and Jeanette's."

3

15–19 YEARS OLD

(1939–1943)

From now on, whenever an adult suggests that I "take matters into my own hands," without lying, I can promise I will.

15 years, 8 months, 4 days *Wednesday, 14 June, 1939*

I think we did something really stupid in the dormitory. And it was my fault. An experiment. I wanted to verify the role our five senses play in the waking-up stage; it was scientific. Whenever we wake up, it's always because of a signal from one of our five senses. Hearing, for example: a slamming door wakes me up. Sight: I open my eyes the second Monsieur Damas turns on the dorm light. Touch: Maman always woke me up by shaking me; the shaking was pointless, by the way; as soon as she touched me, I would wake up with a start. Smell: Etienne claims that at Uncle Georges' the smell of hot chocolate and toast is enough to pull him out of his sleep. All that was left for us to test was the sense of taste. Can stimulating taste wake someone? That's how our experiment started. Etienne put a little salt in my mouth and that woke me up. The next day, I slipped some very finely ground pepper between his lips with the same result. I then wondered what would happen if we stimulated *all five senses at the same time*: hearing, touch, sight, smell and taste. What kind of waking-up would that result in? Etienne christened our experiment "total wake-up." He positively wanted to be the first one to "attempt the mission." Since I also wanted to go first, we tossed a coin and I won. So he had to wake me up by doing five actions simultaneously: calling me, shaking me, dazzling me with light, placing salt in my mouth, and making me smell something pretty strong. For the sense of smell, Etienne went down to the staff storage room to steal a little of the ammonia they use to clean the bathroom tiles. We did the experiment this morning, fifteen minutes before the regulation wake-up. All five senses at once. Malemain shook me, Rouard slid a spoonful of vinegar into my mouth, Pommier dazzled me with an electric lamp, Zafran stuck an ammonia-soaked cotton ball under my nose while Etienne shouted my name in my ear. It seems I let out a terrible scream and remained paralysed, my eyes wide open, as tense as a bowstring, unable to utter a word. Etienne tried to calm me down while the other boysran back to their beds. When Monsieur Damas arrived I was still in the same state. My spell lasted over half an hour. They called for a doctor. The doctor said I was in a "cataleptic state" and had me carried to the infirmary. His theory was that I might be epileptic and he recommended keeping an eye on me. After the doctor left, Monsieur Damas referred the matter to Monsieur Vlache who summoned Etienne to ask him what *really* happened. Etienne swore to god he knew nothing about it, that he heard me shout as if I were emerging from a nightmare and that he had tried in vain to bring me back to my senses. Vlache dismissed him, without seeming to believe him. As for me, I don't remember a thing. I was very surprised to wake up in the infirmary, rather groggy, with the impression of having been run over by a steamroller.

Therefore, if you stimulate at the same time all five senses of someone who is sleeping, you can kill him.

16 years *Tuesday, 10 October, 1939*

Greasy hair. Dandruff (very visible if I wear a dark jacket). Two red pimples on my face (one on my forehead and one on my right cheek). Three blackheads on my nose. Swollen nipples, especially the right one, very tender if I press on it. A sharp pain, like it's being pierced with a needle. What must it be like for girls? I put on ten kilos and grew twelve centimetres in one year. (And gained a longer reach in boxing, Manès was right.) My knees hurt, even at night. Growing pains. Violette said that the day all that would stop, I would start to shrink. My reflection in the big mirror in the shower room. *I don't recognise myself.* Or, more accurately, I have the feeling I grew without me. And so my body becomes an object of curiosity. What surprise will there be tomorrow? Your never know where the body's surprises will come from.

16 years, 4 months, 27 days *Friday, 8 March, 1940*

Etienne claims that Brother Delaroué touches himself while he's in charge of us during study hour. What we do under our sheets he apparently does under his desk. This doesn't seem either normal or abnormal to me; it just seems *out of place*, but no doubt it is rather common. The idea of tossing off in public would not occur to me, but it is conceivable that a certain amount of danger adds to the intensity of the pleasure. Etienne says that Brother Delaroué pulls something out of his satchel, a photograph perhaps, not a magazine in any case, it's much smaller than *Paris-Plaisirs*, and that he looks at whatever it is and touches himself on the sly. That might be true, but it's impossible to check because Brother Delaroué always puts his enormous satchel on his desk, like a wall between us. Etienne is insistent: "But I swear it, with his right hand, look!" So he's right-handed. It is almost impossible to toss off with any seriousness with your left hand if you are right-handed. Take it from an expert.

16 years, 5 months *Sunday, 10 March, 1940*

Rouard K.O.'d me in the corner of the ring. Since I hadn't dropped my guard and the ropes were holding me up, he didn't realise my state right away and he kept on punching me until I genuinely collapsed. It was the first time I was K.O.'d. (And the last, I hope.) An interesting experience. First of all, I had the time to admire Rouard's dodges: bending of the knees, torso and neck; he slid beneath my guard and bounced back up like a spring. I was still off balance, admiring his speed and realising I was buggered-up when his fist caught me under the chin. I heard a kind of "plop" as if my brain had become liquid. While he was hitting me I could still hear what was going on around us, but didn't understand anything anymore. He has *unplugged me*, is what I thought. Because in this semi-unconscious state I was thinking fairly clearly, I was even reasoning; time had stopped, and I said to myself: That's a great counter-punch, very violent! Obviously, in a counter-punch the shock is produced by the momentum and the weight of our *two* bodies. And also: That will teach you to think you are the fastest. I knew, as I was falling, that I was fainting. The loss of consciousness itself only lasted seven or eight seconds.

16 years, 5 months, 1 day *Monday, 11 March, 1940*
Side effect of being K.O.'d: pressure from the inside of my eyes this morning. As if someone were trying to push them out of their sockets. It was gone by the end of the day.

16 years, 6 months, 6 days *Tuesday, 16 April, 1940*
In the cafeteria this evening, hard-boiled eggs on a cowpat of spinach. Malemain reminds us that the lawn was mowed earlier in the day. Which is true. He says this every time we have spinach. Even if I don't believe it – that they are making us graze on their grass – Malemain's remark influences my gustatory perception to the point of giving an absolutely green taste to this purée of boiled spinach – the taste of the green scent that floats in the air above freshly mown grass. The quintessence of plant life. It is, I am certain, the taste that spinach will have for me until the end of my days. The taste of Malemain.

16 years, 6 months, 9 days *Friday, 19 April, 1940*
Brother Delaroué is definitely touching himself during study hour. He had, in any event, the necessary materials in his satchel: postcards of naked ladies. He doesn't have them anymore. While I lured him into the laundry room to show him a leak (which I had created), Etienne stole them from him. Obviously, the poor man can't complain about this theft and this makes him look like a lost animal: a mix of fury,

shame and suspicion on his face. Etienne and I have decided to use these ladies to our advantage. There are one hundred and twenty-five of them! Since we know there will be an inspection of the dormitory under one pretext or another, we have hidden them in the chapel where no one will go looking for them. From time to time, we select one to be the sole object of our love. Each of us has his own. And we love her. Until the next one.

Do girls do the same thing with pictures of men? The bodies of Christ or Saint Sebastian artistically stripped of their clothing and being tortured – do these send girls into raptures?

16 years, 6 months, 15 days *Thursday, 25 April, 1941*

The question of breasts. (Women's.) I don't think there exists an object of adoration more ravishing, more moving, and more complex than women's breasts. Maman often said to me: "You gave me an abscess on my breast." She was talking about the time when she breastfed me. It was a very short period of her life but she would talk about it as if, years later, she was still suffering. At first I wondered – I was really little – what an abscess was (*a collection of pus in a tissue or an organ*); I tried to imagine an abscess on a breast. Although I couldn't manage it – picturing a purulent breast was beyond my capacities – I felt genuine sadness. I wasn't sad for Maman but for women's breasts in general. That part of their body that was so poignant had to be very fragile for a baby's toothless mouth to be able to transform a nipple into a purulent abscess! Yet when Marianne showed me her breasts and let me touch them, they didn't seem fragile. On the contrary, they were small and firm; the areolas were very wide, a pale pink, like a bishop's skullcap. The nipple shone like a mother-of-pearl button. True, Marianne was only fourteen. So her breasts must still have been developing. If I can judge from the postcards in our divine harem, breasts change a lot with age. They grow bigger and softer. The areola seems to shrink proportionally; the nipple pushes out more and seems less shiny, more fleshy. Etienne lent me his butterfly magnifying glass to look more closely. They grow softer and take on all kinds of shapes. But their skin still seems just as delicate, especially the skin on top that connects the breast to the thorax. I find it unbelievable that such a beautiful part of the female body can also be *functional*. It's a sacrilege that these marvels are used to feed nurslings who suck greedily at them and slobber all over them! In short, I adore women's breasts. In any case, I adore those of our one hundred and twenty-five lady friends, that is, the breasts of *all* women, whatever their size, shape, weight, density, colouring. It seems that the hollow of my hands is made to receive women's breasts, that my skin is soft enough for the softness of their skin. Not much more time will pass before I confirm this!

16 years, 6 months, 17 days *Saturday, 27 April, 1940*

Montaigne, Book III, chapter 5:

> . . . what has the act of generation, so natural, so necessary, and so just, done to men, to be a thing not to be spoken of without blushing, and to be excluded from all serious and moderate discourse? We boldly pronounce kill, rob, betray, and that we dare only to do betwixt the teeth. Is it to say, the less we expend in words, we may pay so much the more in thinking?

16 years, 6 months, 18 days *Sunday, 28 April, 1940*

What is extraordinary when I pleasure myself is that instant I call the tightrope walk: the second when, just before coming, I haven't yet come. The sperm is there, ready to gush forth, but I hold it back with all my might. The rim of my glans is so red, my glans itself is so swollen, so close to exploding that I let go of my penis. I hold back my sperm with all my might, watching my penis vibrate. I squeeze my fists, eyelids, and jaws so tightly that my body vibrates as much as my penis. This is the moment I call the tightrope walk. My eyes roll behind my eyelids,

I inhale in short little breaths, I push away every exciting vision – the breasts, bums, thighs, silky skin of our female friends – and the sperm stops in this eruption column, right on the edge of the crater. It's true, it reminds you of a volcano about to erupt. You cannot let this lava go back down. If something surprises us, for example, if Monsieur Damas opens the door to the dorm, it really does go back down. But it mustn't. I am almost sure that making our sperm do an about-face is bad for our health. As soon as I feel it going back down, my thumb and my index finger make a ring around my rim and I play with keeping it right on the edge, bubbling up (lava, yes, or sap, so similar to a taut and knotty branch is my dick in those moments!). You have to be very careful, very precise, it's a question of a millimetre, maybe less. My entire dick is so sensitive that my glans could explode simply if someone were to blow on it or if the sheet were simply to skim it. I can hold back the eruption once, twice, and each time it's a delight. But the absolute delight is that instant when, at last, I lose the battle once and for all and the sperm submerges everything and flows hot onto the back of my hand. Oh, what a marvellous defeat! That, too, is difficult to describe, everything inside that passes outside and at the same time all that pleasure that engulfs you . . . This eruption is all-engulfing! It's the tightrope walker's fall into the molten crater! Oh, the bedazzlement in the darkness! Etienne says that it is an "apotheosis."

16 years, 6 months, 20 days *Tuesday, 30 April, 1940*

The opprobrium heaped on this apotheosis of sensation can be seen clearly in the ugliness of the words used to speak about it: "to wank" sounds ridiculous; "to flog the bishop" sacrilegious; "to masturbate" is disgusting (there is something spongy about this verb, even in Latin) and "to touch yourself" doesn't mean anything. "Did you touch yourself?" asks the confessor. How could I wash otherwise? Etienne and I talked this over with our friends for a long time. I think I have found the perfect expression: to take matters into our own hands. From now on, whenever an adult suggests that I "take matters into my own hands" I can, without lying, promise I will.

16 years, 6 months, 24 days *Saturday, 4 May, 1940*

A Game of the Goose! Great idea! This is what we have decided to do with our one hundred and twenty-five female friends. Use the prettiest of them to illustrate an erotic Game of the Goose. More precisely, the "Game of the Goose of Defloration". That's what we'll call it. After moving through sixty-three squares, the one who *wins* will have the right to *lose* his virginity. "You are the winner. Climb aboard." You have to pay to play. The money will go into a common kitty. The club will be made up of eight players so that the kitty will increase sufficiently. Malemain, Zafran, and Rouard will belong and are enthusiastic about the idea. The final game is to take place after our baccalaureate orals, right before the summer holidays. The winner will get the entire kitty with the obligation to use it for one thing alone: losing his virginity. And a written report will be required. Amen. The symbol of the game will be the face of Mona Lisa, her enigmatic smile open to every possible interpretation.

THE GAME OF THE GOOSE OF DEFLORATION

Rules for Playing

The game is played with two dice.

<u>Here's what happens when you land on certain squares – on:</u>

2 Wait till you grow up. Skip 3 turns.

4 When she looks at your underwear, your mother is shocked by suspect stains. She takes you to the doctor who fits you out with a device to prevent wet dreams. Go back to **3** and skip 2 turns.

6 Monsieur Damas catches you red-handed. You must take cold showers. Go back to **5** and skip 2 turns.

8 You have committed the sin of lust in your heart. Go confess at 7 and skip 1 turn.

10 Your fantasies have got the better of you. Go wash your dirty laundry discreetly on **9**.

12 When by chance your uncle Georges sees your soiled underclothes, he congratulates you: you have become a man. Roll the dice two more times and move ahead the number of squares indicated by the total.

<u>Next, if you land on square number:</u>

15 (On this square is a picture of Mona Lisa's enigmatic smile.) She's smiling at you! Take another turn.

19 To attract girls, you have to be very strong. You go to the gym. Pay 3 and skip 2 turns.

21 Mona Lisa smiled at you, but her smile was ironic. Go back to square 17 and think your dark thoughts.

23 To attract girls, you have to be a good swimmer. Take swimming lessons. Pay 4 and skip 1 turn.

27 You tried to kiss Mona Lisa, and she slapped you. Go brood over your disappointment on square **13**.

29 To attract girls, you need to know how to dance. Take dancing lessons. Pay 5 and skip 1 turn.

33 Mona Lisa thinks you are dirty. Go back to square **11** and wash.

39 Mona Lisa thinks you have a terrible haircut. Go to the barber on square **31** and pay 1.

41 Love is blind. Skip a turn as you wait to get back your clear-sightedness.

43 You have a coated tongue and bad breath. Purge yourself and skip 1 turn.

45 Mona Lisa doesn't like your clothes. Go and get a suit made on square **37** and pay 10.

47 You have an acne flare-up. Take care of it and skip 1 turn.
51 Mona Lisa thinks you are an ignoramus. Go back to square 1 and get yourself an education.
53 You are wasting precious time making yourself handsome. Skip 1 turn.
57 Don't tell anyone what she did to you. She is thrilled, and so are you. Roll again.
59 Love gives you wings. Roll again.
61 Monsieur Damas catches you playing this game. Everyone back to square 1.
63 You won! Slip inside her! And take all the money in the kitty!

In order to win, you have to land exactly on square 63. If the dice make you go beyond, move backwards by counting as many squares as there are too many points.

16 years, 7 months, 2 days *Sunday, 12 May, 1940*

Sometimes in the dormitory when anxiety wakes me up in the middle of the night (often because I am dreaming about Papa or Violette), I slowly calm myself down by allowing myself to be permeated by the feeling that all the other sleeping boys and I form but a single body. One huge sleeping body breathing in unison that dreams, moans, sweats, scratches itself, wriggles, sniffs, coughs, farts, snores, has wet dreams and nightmares, awakes with a start, then immediately falls back to sleep. It's not a sense of camaraderie at those moments, but rather the impression that, from an organic point of view, our dormitory (there are sixty-two of us) forms one body. If one of us were to die, the big common body would go on living.

*

NOTE TO LISON

As an aside, Lison, I was writing those words the day after the German invasion of 10 May. The Second World War. Humankind was at it again. That day, I swore to myself, in memory of Papa, that I would not have anything to do with it. As you will see, circumstances dictated otherwise.

*

16 years, 8 months, 13 days *Sunday, 23 June, 1940*

We come across people who are stooped over, their eyes empty, their movements lethargic. Some are completely lost. Literally. Ragged, flea-ridden, badly shaved refugees roaming the streets of a city with which they are unfamiliar. I cannot conceive that just last month they were living a normal life in Paris. Bodies adrift . . .

The next day

The last match of the Game of the Goose has been put off *sine die*: Rouard lost his brother at Dunkirk. He loved him very much. Problems of our virginity will just have to wait for better times.

16 years, 9 months, 14 days *Wednesday, 24 July, 1940*

Mérac. I scraped my chest, the bottom of my feet, the inside of my arms and thighs against beech bark. Literally skinned alive. Because of Ti-Joe. He had got it into his head to steal a baby crow from its nest, but the bird's parents proved hostile to this adoption plan. Because Ti-Joe refused to let go of his prey, they set upon him. He was holding the fledgling against his chest with one hand and trying to chase the parents away with the other. And all that, a good six metres up, straddling a branch! At the foot of the tree, Marta was screaming at him to let the bird go, and Manès left to get his shotgun to shoot the crows. In other words, all were defending their offspring. Not doubting that Manès would shoot, I rushed up the tree to Ti-Joe. I climbed the first three metres like a monkey or a utility worker, holding onto the branchless trunk with my hands and the soles of my feet. I was coming back from catching crayfish, so I was barefoot and in my bathing trunks. Climbing up was no problem. I had the impression I was clasping a living body in my arms. Coming down, Ti-Joe's weight pulled me backwards and I glued myself to the trunk. But because Ti-Joe was strangling me with his left arm (he did not want to let go of his new friend), I loosened my grip on the tree a little bit to speed things up. It was during this phase of the operation that, rubbing against the bark, I was skinned alive. Especially when I tried to slow us down because we were approaching the bottom a little too quickly. When we touched down I was bleeding and the little crow was dead, obviously suffocated by Ti-Joe's affection. Marta was screaming: "What's next? Barely seven years old and he's got into more mischief . . ." Naturally I got a good daubing with alcohol to clean the scrapes. Without auditory anaesthesia this time around. Marta is not Violette. While I was digging my nails into my palms, Manès was planning to give a hiding to his last-born, and this last-born was now busy burying his victim. But Manès gave up, a hint of pride in his voice: "At any rate, he's not afraid of a damn thing, that little twerp." As a result, I am sleeping naked, sheets and blankets tossed aside, legs spread, all my nerves on fire. From now on this will be how I represent hell: a flameless, perpetual combustion, eyes open onto the endless night. The torment of Marsyas.

16 years, 9 months, 23 days *Friday, 2 August, 1940*

In any case, what a joy it is to climb trees! Especially beech trees or oaks. Your entire body comes into play. Your feet and hands haul you out of your ordinary condition. How quickly we learn to grip! How precise our gestures are! It's not so much that we are going higher, it's not mountain climbing (I think I would be scared of heights if I were mountain climbing), it's moving freely through the leaves! Where are we? Neither on the ground nor in the sky: we are at the heart of the explosion. I would like to live in the trees.

16 years, 11 months, 6 days *Monday, 16 September, 1940*

When my head grows heavy from poring over books, I go and hit the punching bag. Manès replaced his caricature with Laval's. "Go for it! Erase him!" (Thick hair, drooping eyelids, pouty lips with a cigarette stuck in the corner, a very good likeness!) The hemp scrapes my knuckles, so I bind my hands with a pair of socks.

16 years, 11 months, 10 days *Friday, 20 September, 1940*

Mérac. Tennis, in the barn. I drew a line on the back wall at the height of a net. Since the liming and the flooring are crooked, the ball bounces unevenly; nothing is better for our reflexes. If I add together jumping into the grain with Ti-Joe and the others, running after stubborn goats and the farm work I do with Robert who never grows tired, my stays here are equal to commando training.

17 years, 1 month, 14 days *Sunday, 24 November, 1940*

Manès sliced his calf with a scythe that was lying under the straw. Hygiene according to Manès and Marta: as always, alcohol to clean the wound, but, to bind it, a spider web absolutely black with manure that Manès went to collect in the stable. "It's absorbent," he says in his typically laconic way. Obviously you can't talk to him about tetanus. "This is how we've always done it, and nobody ever died." I can manage to believe that the spider web has some astringent, even healing, properties. But manure? The fact is that these plasters have not yet killed anyone in the family.

17 years, 2 months, 17 days *Friday, 27 December, 1940*

When he came to visit at Mérac, Uncle Georges asked me if I might like to be a doctor. "This is the path your cousin Etienne has decided to follow." Not me. The body's disorders, no thank you! That's where I started out, if you recall! And as far as trying to heal other people . . . First you have to waste a lot of time curing them of the stories they tell themselves about a body they only look at from a moral perspective. I wouldn't have the patience to explain to Aunt Noémie that it is not a matter of understanding whether or not she "deserves" her emphysema. "So what *are* you interested in?" my dear uncle asks me. Observing my own body because it is an intimate stranger to me. (This, of course, I don't tell him.) No matter how advanced it is, medical science will never manage to eliminate any of this feeling of foreignness. In other words, I am "botanising" like Rousseau did on his walks. "Botanising" until the day I die, and only about myself if I am to hope that someday it will *be of use to* someone else. As far as a profession is concerned, that's something else entirely. In any case, it won't be mentioned in this diary.

17 years, 5 months, 8 days *Tuesday, 18 March, 1941*

Etienne and I had a serious disagreement last night over Voltaire and Rousseau: he in the role of the scoffer and I as defender of Rousseau. What I retain from this dispute is not our respective arguments (truth be told, we barely have the intellectual means with which to argue), it is Etienne 's reflex: he grabbed the long ruler from the blackboard to stick one end of it in my stomach and the other in his. Every time one of us, propelled by the strength of our convictions, walked towards the other, the ruler would sink into both our abdomens. Painful! If we backed up, the ruler would fall and that would put an end to the discussion. Now, that's what I call "measuring one's words"! A system to be patented.

17 years, 5 months, 11 days *Friday, 21 March, 1941*

The way desire sneaks up on me sometimes when I least expect it. In the excitement of certain things I read, for example. The engorgement of cavernous bodies by the stimulation of neurons. I read and I get a hard-on. And I am not talking about Apollinaire or Pierre Louys, who kindly offer us these gifts, but about Rousseau, for example, who would have been quite surprised to see me get a hard-on while reading his *Social Contract*! A little orgasm that engages only the mind.

18 years, 9 months and 5 days *Wednesday, 15 July, 1942*

I didn't write anything in here while I was studying for my baccalaureate exam and during this preparatory year. Ablation of the body. I boxed, hit a tennis ball, and swam to relax. Helped Manès in the fields a couple of times. Three calves and six lambs born. Still incapable of killing the pig. But not of eating it. The poor beast came over to me for me to pet him while I was working. This stubborn faith that animals have in humankind.

18 years, 9 months, 25 days *Tuesday, 4 August, 1942*

Tennis: hammered the three de G brothers. None of them won more than two games out of the six sets in three matches. The whole thing started out with their attempt to humiliate me. Correcting me on the proper way to refer to aristocratic families, the eldest brother told me that one does not say the "*de* G.'s", but rather simply the "G's"; a proper upbringing requires the *de* to be elided. "Everyone knows that, for Pete's sake!" Fine. And another thing. I had neither shorts nor tennis shoes, and it was not "acceptable" for me to play in my "togs" even if it was on a private court (theirs, as it happened). They therefore lent me the requisite uniform: shorts, short-sleeved shirt, the whitest tennis shoes ever. I held up my shorts (intentionally too big?) with a bit of laundry cord I found in the "outhouse" and I proceeded to beat them mercilessly. The highest of the high beaten by the lowest of the low! This resulted in my forfeiting any affection I could possibly have obtained from their sister, to whom I was not indifferent. Too bad. I avenged Violette, who – the three brothers were unaware of this – had worked for their family when she was young and had been fired for having "de-virginised" a first cousin when he was thirty-two! (You can't make that stuff up!)

The thrilling sensation during these games of having nothing but my body to pit against their arrogance. Not even a skilled body: no-one taught me how to play tennis. Manès' barn and watching other players were my only professors. Hitting a tennis ball without having taken lessons is to feel one's body adapt to circumstances without the help of the *proper motion.* I make too many gestures, most of them incorrect, aesthetically unpleasing, and wasteful of energy (irregular rhythm, jack-knife jumps, uncoordinated body, limbs akimbo, clownish acrobatics), but the fact that my movements owe nothing to having learned the game gives me an intense sensation of physical freedom and constant renewal: never the same movement twice. I take advantage of whatever surprise my eyes transmit to my legs and my racquet. None of my shots is prepared in advance, none resembles the one that precedes it or corresponds to the academic movements of my distinguished adversaries. Consequently, I am totally unpredictable and all my shots disconcert them, because the one that comes is never the one they expect. They protest and roll their eyes, both exasperated and condescending, especially when faced with some of my horribly weak shots, as if I weren't fighting according to the rules of war. My speed, flexibility, skilfulness, and reflexes amaze me (oh, the certainty of the perfect shot the microsecond I hit the ball!) and, more than anything, I am tireless; I return everything they send my way. This free use of my body enchants me. My antics demoralise my adversaries, and to see their composure dissolve thrills me. It's not my victory that enthrals me. It's the look on their faces in defeat. At Valmy we already had no manners. (And I still don't wear underpants.) My pledge: to live my life, in every sphere, exactly the same way I play tennis!

19 years, 15 days *Sunday, 25 October, 1942*

The scene takes place in a café. You are with a young woman, a student like you. You are making sheep's eyes at each other. Suddenly she takes the plunge: "Show me your hand." Just like that, she takes your hand and examines your palm extremely attentively, as if all she needed to know about you depended on your lines: lifeline, heartline, headline, fateline, what else? By now, there are many young women who have studied the lines on my palm. And not a single conclusion of one woman has been the same as another. They are all clairvoyant, but not a one sees the same thing. Is this infatuation with superstition a sign of these terrible times? Is everything lost except the stars? My selection criterion: choose the girl who will throw herself headlong into my hands.

19 years, 1 month, 2 days *Thursday, 12 November, 1942*

Saw the Krauts marching in step. Abominable version of a single body.

19 years, 2 months, 17 days *Sunday, 27 December, 1942*

My inability to dance. Françoise, Marianne and a few other girls tried to teach me how, and last night, at Hervé's Violaine, a splendid girl and our host's sister, tried yet again. "Just let yourself be led." Nothing doing. Very rapidly I lose the rhythm, and my body is nothing but a deadweight in my partner's arms. A few grotesque hops to try to get back on the beat wind up discouraging me completely. Dance is one of the rare domains where my body and mind remain irreconcilable. More precisely, the lower half of my body: my hands can keep time with no problem, but my feet simply refuse to follow. A paraplegic orchestra conductor, that's what I am. As for my head, as soon as things get complicated, it begins to spin. And since dance is by nature a gyratory, twirling art, one cannot dance without circling around oneself. Dizziness, nausea and the colour draining from my face. "What's the matter, don't you feel well?" I'm perfectly fine, dear Violaine, but come, let's talk for a moment, and here I am trying to explain the thing to the beautiful Violaine who says, "Come now, *everyone* knows how to dance!" Everyone except me, apparently. "It's because you don't *want* to!" Oh really! And why would I deprive myself of that skill, my beauty, when I can see all the advantages it affords my friends? "You don't let yourself go. You're too cerebral, you are not *wild* enough." Not wild enough? Bring us a bed, for god's sake, right this second! Instead of which I hear myself explaining to Violaine that the phenomenon is incomprehensible to me as well, given that in other circumstances that require arms and legs – boxing, for example, or tennis – my four limbs are in perfect harmony and my schoolmates used to fight to be on my dodgeball team where I proved to be completely unbeatable, and I hear myself saying to this amazing young woman that at fifteen I was a dodgeball superstar and I tell myself shut your trap while I elaborate on the merits of dodgeball, a game so complete, demanding such physical aptitudes, a perfect synchrony of arms, head and legs that one day it will become, without a doubt, my dear Violaine, a team sport next to which football will look like a distraction for penguins, but what has got into you (I say to myself), you moron? Not content with having been no more than a bag of cement in the arms of this beauty whom you are hoping to lie on top of, here you are boring her to death with dodgeball, "a game requiring so much strategy, so many tactics, dear Violaine," but shut your mouth, you ass (I say to myself), this game was a game of massacre where two pimple-faced teams spent their time teasing each other and throwing balls in one another's faces; well, the beautiful Violaine will have gotten her fill of savagery with this, and if it is true that you excelled at dodgeball, this is not the kind of advantage that will get this girl in your bed, and in fact the girl in question makes herself scarce, declaring that your exploits have made her thirsty and she is going to get a drink.

19 years, 2 months 19 days *Tuesday, 29 December, 1942*

Still, she came to me. That same evening. And it was worse than dancing. I was in my bedroom at Hervé's, late at night; the household was asleep at last, and I was sitting at a sort of chessboard table, occupied with writing the pathetic story of trying to dance, when the door opened behind me so quietly that I only heard it close, which made me turn around. And there she stood in her nightgown – white organdie or some fabric of that kind – that left one shoulder bare like a Greek tunic, a thin strap knotted on the other shoulder with a tiny bow whose two loops looked like butterfly wings. She did not say a word, she wasn't smiling, she gave me a hard stare, and I, too, was entirely unable to speak; her well-rounded shoulders, long, pale, slender arms, her hands hanging by her thighs, barefoot, out of breath, high, full breasts, her nightgown draped on their tips, falling straight down and forming a space between her nakedness and the fabric. My eyes sought the outline of her hips, her belly, her thighs, the general shape of her body, but the small lamp next to me created no transparency; it would have needed to be behind her to sketch her outline. At first I thought only about that: the bad placement of the lamp that dulled the promise of transparency; it would have been different had the lamp been behind her; we were both motionless. I didn't even get up, I didn't make the slightest move towards her, and she remained standing, the door having closed behind her, and I was seated, in three-quarter profile, one hand remaining on the table, closing the notebook clumsily. The ink is going to dry on the tip of my fountain pen, I said to myself; I was thinking about that: that I couldn't put the cap back on the pen while trying to make out Violaine's outline beneath the opaque fabric whose whiteness was now dazzling me, and then I saw her left hand sliding up along her chest, her fingers unfolding when they got to her shoulder, her thumb and index finger grasping the thin strap, which she tugged on gently to untie the knot, and the nightgown fell to her feet with all the weight of the fabric, revealing her naked body, and I don't think I will ever see a more beautiful body of a woman than the one that appeared suddenly in the golden light of the lamp, my god what beauty, what beauty I repeated to myself, if the light had been shut off forever I would have died with the memory of this beauty. I think I almost cried out without, however, getting up, absolutely paralysed by surprise and rapture, what beauty, what perfection, and I think I felt gratitude; no one had ever given me such a gift, I thought as well, but without moving an inch; she is the one who moved, she went to lie down on the bed; she did not signal to me to join her, did not hold out her arms to me, did not speak or smile; she was waiting for me to come to her, which I did at last, and as I stood near the bed, I couldn't take my eyes off her; you need to undress, I told myself, it's your turn, which I did, clumsily, discreetly, ungenerously, turning my back to her, sitting on the edge of the bed, hiding myself more than offering myself, and when it was done I slipped in next to her, and nothing happened, I did not stroke or kiss her because something had died inside me, or did not want to be born, which comes down to absolutely the same thing, because my heart was pumping my blood everywhere except where it was expected; my blood lit my cheeks on fire, splattered the sides of my skull, beat wildly at my temples, but not a drop came between my legs, nothing between my legs. I wasn't even telling myself you don't have a hard-on. I felt nothing between my legs, I was thinking only about that, this non-existence between my legs. I have to say she was of no help to me, not one word from her either, not one movement, until she suddenly got up and I heard the door close again behind her.

19 years, 2 months, 21 days *Thursday, 31 December, 1942*

The Violaine fiasco has made me take stock. At home for a spell, naked in front of my wardrobe mirror, I am counting up the things I have mastered since childhood regarding the systematic building of my body. No doubt, my orgy of press-ups, sit-ups, and physical exercises of all kinds has made me a boy who resembles something – in this instance, the cut-away man from the *Larousse Encyclopedia* that is still in the mirror frame. On comparing, all my muscles are where they should be, perfectly visible: big pectorals, biceps, deltoids, abdominals, brachio-radials, hamstring muscles, and if I turn around, flexors, calf muscles, gluteus muscles, latissimus dorsi, brachial muscles, trapezii, everything is there. The cut-away man is my spitting image, a real success, I could spend my life in front of the mirror. I, who used to resemble "really nothing," now look like the guy in the *Encyclopedia*! Let me add that I am no longer afraid. Of anything. Not even of being afraid. Not a single fear that cannot be mastered by exercising the same will that sculpted this body. Try to steal my "life" from me, just to see, try to attach me to a tree! Yes, yes, my boy, but this masterpiece of physical and mental equilibrium came to naught when you stretched out next to the beautiful Violaine. My poor fellow, you *truly* resemble nothing at all. Go back to your gymnastics and your precious studies, work on your body and your exams, the only thing you're good for is "maintaining yourself" and "becoming someone". My god, this feeling of *non-existence* that the flaccidity of one's penis leaves a man with! Yet how many times did I take it in hand! How many times did my desire sculpt it? Truly, how many times? One hundred? One thousand? Venous branch that a simple thought sufficed to engorge! How much sperm has been drawn from the depths by this virgin's formidable eruptions! It must be possible to calculate that as well. Litres? Litres spilled to play the "man" in front of postcards swiped from poor Brother Delaroué. And finally, this dead body in bed with Violaine. Not even able to dance. Grotesque in foreplay, non-existent in action. What paralysed you, monsieur, if not that fear you boast of having vanquished? That's what I was saying to myself, more or less confusedly, naked in front of my mirror this morning, faced with the Larousse cut-away man. And next time? What will happen next time? In what *state of mind* from now on will your body dare to approach a woman's body? That's what I was saying to myself this morning and what I am writing now with the cut-away man in front of my eyes. And suddenly I notice this detail: *there is nothing between his legs either!* No representation of his rod or his testicles! The two closest muscles named are the psoas and the pectineus muscles, which have nothing to do with it. The cut-away man has nothing between his legs! The penis is not a muscle, granted. An organ? A limb? The fifth limb? What is its nature? Spongy. A blood sponge. Well, nothing at that place on the cut-away man represents the circulation of blood! The entire body is irrigated all the way to the groin, but nothing about the vascularisation that pulses life into the member that begins it all. Nothing between the legs. Apparently, the penis is banished from the Larousse family. A shameful body part. A trick of the Holy Spirit. Deal with it. Monsieur Larousse is a eunuch.

19 years, 2 months, 22 days *Friday, 1 January, 1943*
A detail that I forgot to write down. Maman, opening the door to my bedroom and catching me naked in front of the mirror: "What's going on, you think you're handsome?"

19 years, 2 months, 24 days *Sunday, 3 January, 1943*
Penis: rod, member, cock, dick, prick, bone, dangler, jigger, John Thomas, dong, knob, tool, pisser, etc. Testicles: family jewels, balls, nuts, parts, knackers, marbles, gonads, goolies, apples, danglers, swingers, etc. A lexical profusion to name this genital equipment that the physiologist is reluctant to represent.

19 years, 3 months, 4 days *Thursday, 14 January, 1943*
Unexpected epilogue to the Violaine affair. It begins by a shouting match on the street with Etienne , who finds my attitude towards the sister of his friend "unspeakable." "To lure this girl into your room and not touch her, do you realise the humiliation? And then, how do *I* look to her brother Hervé now? I'm the one who invited you, after all!" Etienne is beside himself and I am about to slam my fist into his face. Luckily one of his sentences stopped me. "It's true she is not all that pretty, but that's all the more reason! You should have realised that ahead of time, it wasn't the first time you'd seen her! She's been talking to Hervé about you for months! And now she's been crying for days! You're within a hair's breadth of being murdered, old man, and I'm doing everything I can to calm Hervé down." Not pretty? Violaine? No, Violaine thinks she's ugly, her face unattractive, too flat, a fish face according to her, and her skin too dark, her own brother says so. "Don't you think she's a little on the ugly side?" Violaine? Ugly? No, I don't think so. Definitely not! My god, that magnificent person is persuaded

that she was repudiated because she is ugly! And it's my fault! Hurt to the point of tears! Violaine, alone in front of a mirror of suffering! Just like me! Shame, panic, ignorance, and loneliness in both camps then?

19 years, 3 months, 6 days *Saturday, 16 January, 1943*

This evening in a laudable attempt to break the ice between us, Etienne pointed out the paradoxical humour of the situation: a brother furious that his sister was not dishonoured! Ah, modern times! And so I told him everything. Practical as always, he concluded: "A virgin's fiasco? Do what everyone else does, go to a whorehouse, it's an excellent pedagogical experience!" Have you been? "No." What about Rouard? "No." And Malemain? "He said he hadn't wanted to because the whore was a Pétainist."

We left it at that.

*

NOTE TO LISON

My dear Lison,

A contextual note now. "Meanwhile . . .", as they used to say in the comic strips of your childhood, the bombings in the Old Port in Marseilles, on 3 January to be precise. A bomb in a whorehouse reserved for the German troops, another in the dining room of the Hôtel Splendide. So many casualties. Next, a series of round-ups, in which my friend Zafran disappeared; the dynamiting of the Panier by the Germans: fifteen hundred buildings destroyed and my left eardrum damaged for a while. At the end of January a militia was formed and in February the hunt for forced labour began. To those who were depressed by this situation, Etienne would explain that, on the contrary, he saw in it a watershed of the war. The Krauts were getting worked up; it was the beginning of the Nazis' end. He was right.

*

19 years, 6 months, 9 days *Monday, 19 April, 1943*

A big free-for-all in the cafeteria caused by Zafran's disappearance. Malemain, who was pleading his case, was trapped in an ambush. I punched fast and furious to get him out of there. I imagine my sexual humiliation had given me the strength of ten. Ladies and gentlemen, beware of the virgin who has been found lacking! He is a potential killer. At least that's one domain in which my body obeys me. Aided by my knowledge of the cut-away man, I gave myself the fearsome pleasure of striking where it hurts. The thrill of the fight without fear! Rouard, with his eighty kilos, didn't do so badly either. I will probably be expelled. Will have to study for the exams on my own. If they allow me to take them . . .

19 years, 6 months, 13 days *Friday, 23 April, 1943*

Met up with Etienne on the train taking me home, with the explanation for my expulsion in my pocket. Etienne , as serious as possible, as if he had just read the information in the medical textbook that he has open on his lap, asks the three other passengers in our compartment – two men and a woman – if they know that the nerves and arteries on which our genitalia depend are called the "pudendal nerve" and the "pudendal artery", from the Latin word *pudere*, "to be ashamed". Eyes are raised from the newspaper, turned away from the landscape, the passengers shoot each other questioning glances, and no, they confess with an embarrassed smile, they did not know. Etienne , whose tone of voice is becoming curt, says that in these times of national revolution, that fact is absolutely disgraceful. He looks at the cover of the textbook, reads aloud the name of the author, and decrees that to consider the reproductive organs as objects of shame when Marshal Pétain is exhorting us every Sunday to repopulate France is a deliberately unpatriotic attitude! "And you, monsieur, who seem not to be interested in the question," he asks me as if we didn't know each other, "what do you think about this?" I feign surprise before shyly proposing, while looking searchingly at the other passengers, that the aforementioned nerves and arteries should be renamed the Nerve of National Recovery and the Artery of Family Values. No one suspects the hoax; they appear to contemplate the matter and then, as seriously as you can imagine, they agree. The lady even offers other suggestions.

What times we live in!

19 years, 6 months, 16 days *Easter Monday, 26 April, 1943*

Fermantin and two other guys came to the house to sign me up. Fermantin doesn't know I've been expelled from school; he thinks I'm on holiday. Maman greets him joyously and sends him to my room. In his uniform, under his militiaman's beret, he looks like something out of the *commedia dell'arte*, but without the humour. I was in the middle of studying for my exams and, in one of those "bouts of posturing" that make me laugh in other people, I declared to my old friend that I would never enter the militia, and that I even considered his suggestion an insult. He turned towards his two associates (I didn't know them; one of them was also in uniform) and said: "An insult? No. This, on the other hand, is an insult!" And he spat in my face. Fermantin has been spitting on everyone since he was a little boy. I was one of the few who had not yet been on the receiving end; as a result, although his spit surprised me, it did not startle me so I managed to keep my cool. I did not flinch, did not even try to avoid it. I heard the "*ptooey*", I saw the spit coming, I felt it plop onto my forehead then run down the middle of my nose and my left cheek, quite similar, I must say, to a splash of lukewarm water. I did not wipe it away. I concentrated on the sensation – quite banal – rather than on the symbol, reputed to be humiliating. If I had flinched, they would have massacred me. Saliva doesn't drip as fast on skin as water does. It has a soapy consistency; it travels in fits and starts. It dries without really evaporating. One of the other guys, the one who was wearing the uniform (he and Fermantin were armed), said that in any case they were only recruiting men. I did not react. I felt the remains of the spit trembling on the left corner of my lips. For a second I thought I could collect it with a flick of my tongue and return it to the sender but I abstained. I had postured enough. "We shall meet again," said Fermantin without taking his eyes off me. As he was backing out of my room with his finger pointed at me, he repeated theatrically: "We shall meet again, you pussy." I am writing these words before getting back to work. Tomorrow, I'm heading for Mérac.

4
21–36 YEARS OLD
(1945–1960)

Mona's loving punctuation:
Entrust me with this comma so
I can make an exclamation mark out of it.

NOTE TO LISON

My dear Lison,

You will notice a gap of two years following Fermantin's assault. That's because he and his little buddies came to find me at Mérac to beat me up, if you can believe it. Luckily, Ti-Joe had caught sight of them (he was all of nine years old then, but already had all the quick-wittedness you knew him to have) and warned me in time so I could get away. After which, of course, there was no solution other than for me to go underground. It was Manès who got me into the Resistance. I didn't know he and Robert had joined. Manès pretended to say a lot of bad things about it, and he was someone you took at his word. Because he didn't say anything good about the Occupiers either, he held on to his reputation as a solitary recluse who should be left alone. Manès' belonging to the Party was one of the biggest surprises of my life. In fact, he was a Communist till the end, despite the Berlin wall, despite Hungary, despite the Gulag, despite de-Stalinisation, despite everything. Manès had a fairly one-track mind.

If I never spoke to you about this period of my youth, it's because after all I was only a member of the Resistance out of expediency. If it hadn't been for Fermantin's little gang, I would in all probability have simply continued to punch my sandbag and dip into my books until the fighting ended, to excel at my studies, collect diplomas, solve a problem: that was the tribute I owed to the memory of my father. Certainly not go to war! He would have cursed me! "What distresses me the most about humankind," he used to say, "is not that it spends its time killing each other, it's that it survives." I needed the impact of that spittle to throw me into turmoil. My enlistment in the Resistance is based on the laws of ballistics, nothing more.

To cut a long story short, from the spring of '43 through to the spring of '45 (enlistment in de Lattre's army), I dropped my studies and stopped keeping this diary. The trace that our writing leaves behind us does not go well with life in the underground. Too many friends fell because of what they had written! No diaries, no letters, no notes, no address books, no traces. Especially during the liaison missions I was in charge of during the final six months!

For that entire time, I lost interest in my body. As an object of observation, I mean. Other priorities had taken over. Staying alive, for example, or making sure that tasks and missions were carried out, and keeping myself in a state of heightened vigilance during the interminable weeks when nothing happened. The life of an underground soldier is a crocodile's life. One remains motionless in one's hole until the very second one jumps out of it to strike, then disappears just as quickly to begin the waiting again. The idea is to not let one's guard down between strikes, to keep one's cool, increase one's exercises, and remain on the lookout for every eventuality. Outside threats muzzle the body's small surprises.

I don't know if anyone has ever studied the question of the health of Resistance fighters, but it is a subject worth looking into. I saw very few sick people among my comrades. We had all imposed hunger, thirst, discomfort, insomnia, exhaustion, fear, loneliness, confinement, boredom, injuries on our bodies: they did not grumble. We did not fall sick. From time to time we would suffer from dysentery or from a chill that was quickly warmed away by the necessities of our service, nothing serious. We slept with empty stomachs, we walked on sprained ankles, we were not a pretty sight, but we did not fall sick. I don't know if this observation is true of Resistance fighters in general, but in any event, it's what I noticed in my network. This was not the case for the lads who had been forced into Compulsory Work Service. They fell like flies. Accidents in the workplace, depression, epidemics, infections of all sorts, the self-mutilation of the ones who wanted to escape decimated units. These free labour forces paid with their health for work that only required their bodies. For us, it was our minds that were mobilised. Whatever name one gave to it, whether the spirit of revolt, patriotism, hatred of the Occupier, desire for revenge, a taste for battle, political ideals, fraternity, or the prospect of liberation – whatever it was, it kept us in good health. Our minds put our bodies in the service of the greater fighting body. Obviously this did not prevent rivalries; each political faction was preparing for peace in its own way and each had its own idea of what a liberated France would look like in its fight against the invader. But the Resistance, as diverse as it was, always seemed to me to form but a single *body*. Once peace returned, the larger body returned to each of us his batch of personal cells and thus his own contradictions.

During those last weeks of the war I met Fanche, whom you loved so much. She wasn't a doctor, but she used her innate surgical skills in an abandoned brickyard where we piled up our wounded. As you know, it's thanks to her that I did not lose my arm. But what you don't know is that I taught her Violette's auditory anaesthesia technique and she used it successfully. She shouted so loudly when she changed our bandages that pain was forced to the back of our brains. And you also don't know that despite her square head, her slightly slanted eyes, her Gallic accent, Fanche was no more Breton than you or I. She was Conchita, the daughter of Spanish refugees in Brittany, renamed Françoise out of gratitude to our French Republic. Fanche is the masculine nickname that her Breton childhood friends gave her to celebrate her skills as a tomboy.

*

21 years, 9 months, 4 days *Saturday, 1 July, 1945*

In the name of the provisional Government of the French Republic and by virtue of the powers vested in me . . .

What was I crying over during the ceremony? I hadn't cried since Violette's death, except in pain recently because of my mashed-up elbow. In short, I cried my heart out during the whole ceremony, cried continually without the help of sobs, as if I were emptying myself out, without making a single gesture to wipe away my tears. I was still emptying myself out when He decorated Fanche and me. Far from taking offence, He gratified me with a manly: "Now you are entitled to it!" Even though I was as sticky as gummed paper, He embraced me heartily. He did not wipe away his tears either. This is real heroism! After a two-year hiatus, I want to write about tears first. This morning, I really shed *all the tears of my body*. It would be more accurate to say that my body shed all the tears accumulated by my mind during this unbelievable slaughter. The amount of self that tears eliminate! By crying, one empties oneself infinitely more than by pissing, one cleanses oneself infinitely better than by diving into the cleanest, clearest lake; one lays down the burden of one's mind on the arrival platform. Once the soul has been liquefied, one can celebrate one's reunion with one's body. Mine will sleep well tonight. I cried out of relief, I believe. It's over. In truth it has been over for a few months, but I needed this ceremony to close the episode. Finished. That's it. He decorated the end of my *resistance*. Hail to the tears!

21 years, 11 months, 7 days *Monday, 17 September, 1945*

I have gone back to preparing for my exams. I immediately rediscovered all the physical sensations of intellectual work. The vibrant silence of books, the downiness of their pages beneath my fingertips, the acrid scent of glue, the reflections of ink, the weight of my motionless body, the tingling in my legs that have remained crossed for too long and which makes me suddenly jump up to hit my punch bag, dancing and striking, giving straight lefts and rights, right or left cross, stiff jabs, hooks, uppercuts (I am unable to stretch my left arm completely, of course, but it can still manage hooks and uppercuts), my head buzzing with poems recited to the beat of boxing, my brain repeating again and again phrases offered through centuries while my legs dance, my fists strike, my sweat drips, the coolness of water drawn from the washtub, sprinkle yourself, dry yourself, put your shirt back on, get to work, to work, and stillness once again, that sensation of gliding above the lines! The peregrine falcon focuses on the broad field of the printed page. Hide yourselves, dear ideas, my prey and my pasture, not only am I going to eat you up but I will digest you, flesh of my mind! Goodness! Where am I going? Let's stop here for this evening, my eyelids are heavy with sand and my pen is talking nonsense. Let's sleep. *Let us lie down on the earth and sleep.*

21 years, 11 months, 10 days *Thursday, 20 September, 1945*

I allowed myself a break to reread a good part of this diary. (Ti-Joe is the one who returned my notebooks to me the other day. He had hidden them – "Without reading a thing, I swear!") I rediscovered Dodo with astonishment, very emotionally. Dodo, whom I had invented when I was living with Maman to keep me *physical* company. Dodo, my imaginary little brother whom I taught how to pee. Dodo, whom I taught how to eat what he didn't like. Dodo, whom I taught endurance. Dodo, to whom I taught the secrets of sex – jerk me off, my little Dodo, my sap is rising! Dodo, whom I silently raised against proud, lying, and pontificating maternal imbecility. I cannot say that Dodo was me, no, but he was a convincing exercise in embodiment. I felt I had barely existed, between my dying father and the lies my mother called "life". Life *is not* this, life *is not* that . . . As imaginary as it was, Dodo's small feverish body (I could hear him breathing in his sleep next to me when fear made him leave his bed to come into mine) was far more real and concrete than "life" according to holy Mother. As I write this, I realise that during these past years, Pétain's voice was the exact replica of my mother's. What this trembling voice implied about life when he spoke about the Nation stemmed from the same static, age-old, frightened, hypocritical and laughable lie. Deep down, it is Dodo who went into the Resistance, Dodo who was decorated. At least I feel certain he will not boast about it.

22 years, 3 months, 1 day *Friday, 11 January, 1946*

The taste of coffee after all these years of chicory! Black, strong, bitter coffee. That bite *in* the mouth that prompts a tiny clicking of one's satisfied tongue as soon as a mouthful is swallowed. That burning sensation behind the sternum that stimulates and awakens you, speeds up your heartbeat, and plugs in your neurons and, incidentally, often tastes terrible. It seems to me that coffee was much better before the war. But why would it not be as good today? Nostalgia for a former time?

22 years, 5 months, 17 days *Wednesday, 27 March, 1946*

The question of nightmares. I haven't had very many these past two years. Now that peace has returned, they are back on the offensive. I don't find them to be a product of the mind, but rather the cerebral excrement of my organism. I've made a resolution to tame them by writing them down. I keep a notebook at the foot of my bed, and as soon as I wake up, I write down the nightmare. This habit has two effects on my dreams. It structures them like narratives and eliminates their ability to frighten me. They are no longer objects of fear but rather of curiosity, as if they knew I was waiting for them in order to write them down and they considered that to be a literary homage, the imbeciles! As sinister as they remain, they have lost their nightmare quality. This very night, during one of the most terrifying, I clearly thought: Don't forget to write that down when you wake up. This one happened to be about the Rosans gendarme's torn-off arm writing in the sky.

22 years, 6 months, 28 days *Wednesday, 8 May, 1946*

The first anniversary of the Victory. It's as if all the ills I was spared during those months of fighting suddenly flared up to celebrate it: coryza, colic, insomnia, nightmares, anxiety, bouts of fever, holes in my memory (misplaced my watch and my wallet, lost Fanche's address, my notes on Suetonius, all my other schoolwork, etc.). In other words, my body is going off the rails. It's as if all of a sudden it were renewing ties with the feverish child I used to be. (It's nothing, Violette would say, just nerves.) The fact is, this morning when I woke up I was completely on edge, my nose stuffed, my bowels liquefied, a lump in my throat, and a temperature of 38.2 degrees Celsius. Catching a cold under three blankets and getting diarrhoea after an excellent stew: could my body be rebelling against comfort? As for anxiety, two hours of work sufficed to dissolve the lump obstructing my throat; translating good old Pliny calmed me down. On the other hand, dysentery has worn me out completely, and I can barely hit my punching bag. Long live war, the requirement for good health? In any event, during the two years I was in the *danse macabre*, the world was on edge instead of me.

23 years *Thursday, 10 October, 1946*

Went to Fanche's when I got to Paris. Tomorrow is my interview with the government. Fanche asks me if I have a place to sleep. A hotel in the 14th arrondissement. "As long as I'm alive, my petard, there will be no hotel for you, especially on your birthday." (Well, well, she remembers this detail!) She accompanies me to the home of half a dozen musicians living in a requisitioned apartment on boulevard Rochechouart. They drink, they laugh a lot, they ration very little, and they reason even less. In other words, they let loose. And it's good. At one point, they all head out to a cellar nightclub. Fanche knows a shelter that has been turned into a fantastic club on rue Oberkampf: Come on! I hesitate. I'm tired. I can still feel the train journey in my body. No way am I going to compromise my interview tomorrow. If I mess up, I'll have no choice but to go back from where I came. No thanks, I'm going to sleep. Fanche shows me a bedroom, a bed. "Do you want to have a bath?" A bath? In a real bathtub? Is that possible? I'm putting back together a body that's been pulverised by a seventeen-hour train ride. After the bath, I immediately fall asleep, naked and warm. I wake up in the middle of the night. Someone has slipped under my sheets. A body as naked and warm as mine, all plumpness, as feminine as possible, just a few spoken words, "Shhhh, don't move, let me," before I am swallowed up, my penis immediately unfurling in her mouth as it takes on authentic, praiseworthy and durable flesh, while two hands stroke my belly, sliding up to my chest, outlining my shoulders, going back down along my arms and hips, turning me over as if I were in the hands of a potter, grabbing my arse that fits trustingly in them and is gently kneaded, while tender, fleshy lips and a soft, moist tongue go to work, oh! Don't stop, please, don't stop, but obviously I feel a flood rising and my belly hollowing, hold back my boy, hold back, don't destroy this eternity, and how does one hold back an erupting volcano, what can one use to hold it back, it's not enough to squeeze my fists and eyelids shut, to bite my lips, to rear up beneath a horsewoman whom I above all do *not* want to unseat, everything is useless, murmurings, stop, gently, wait, stop, stop, my hands push back her shoulders, wait, wait, but her shoulders are so soft, so full that my fingers linger there, the traitors, like the paws of a kneading cat now, and I know I cannot hold on, I know it, and the well-brought-up boy says suddenly to himself, not in her mouth, *it's probably just not done*, I'm even sure of it, not in her mouth, but she pushes my hands away and holds me there while I come so deep inside of myself, she keeps me in her mouth and drinks, slowly, patiently, resolutely, totally, the sperm of my virginity.

Once it's over, she slides over to my ear and I hear her whisper: "Fanche told us it was your birthday; I thought this would be an acceptable gift."

23 years, 3 days *Sunday, 13 October, 1946*

The name of my birthday present is Suzanne. She comes from Québec, is a specialist in explosives, a bomb disposal expert as a matter of fact, which is also a *labour of patience and precision*. Thanks to her, my interview went well. I was bursting with vital energy. There are sleepless nights and sleepless nights. Because, as Suzanne calmly explained at the communal breakfast table the next day, we spent the entire night "in love"; it was not just a matter of satisfying a simple "mouthful", after my turn "came", her turn "came", then mine again, then both of ours, this time a synchronous explosion, and one or two more "trips around the block", because, as she said about me, "that guy! Amazing how much love he had stored up!" I am putting quotation marks around the words she spoke with her Québec accent, and I am dreaming of that accent that has crossed centuries and oceans. As the whole table was laughing, I had a sense that Louise Labé had written her poetry with Suzanne's accent, and perhaps so had Corneille, whose *Polyeucte* Fanche parodies in this regard: "Desire grows as the object of desire withdraws."

23 years, 4 days *Monday, 1 October, 1946*

I love the flesh of accents!

23 years, 5 days *Tuesday, 15 October, 1946*

There is something physical, almost animal, primitively sexual even, about the confrontation between the old office chief and the young job candidate. At least that's the feeling I came away with after my last interview. Two males observe one another. The old, dominant one and the young climber. There is no affability in this sniffing-out of knowledge and intentions. What exactly do you know? Where exactly are you going? the boss's snout asks. What trap are you laying for me? asks the candidate's muzzle. Two generations face off: the one that is dying and the one that is replacing it. It's never nice. Despite appearances, knowledge and diplomas play very little part in all this. It's a battle of the balls. Are you worthy of perpetuating the caste? That's what interests the boss. Do you deserve to keep on living? That's what the candidate wants to know. Grunt, grunt, in a smell of rancid sperm and fresh cum.

23 years, 16 days *Saturday, 26 October, 1946*

A while ago, after making love, lying on my stomach sweating, emptied out, calm, already half-asleep, I felt cool drops falling on my back, thighs, neck and shoulders at irregular intervals. A slow and delicious dripping, all the more delightful since I did not know when or where the next drop would fall, and each one allowed me to discover a precise point on my body that had remained, it seemed to me, untouched until then. Finally I turned around: kneeling above me, a glass of water in hand, Suzanne was sprinkling me from her fingertips, concentrating as if she were hovering over a mine. Her skin, studded with freckles and beauty spots, is a starry sky. With a ballpoint pen, I traced the month's night sky: Ursa Major, Ursa Minor, etc. "Your turn now," Suzanne said to me. "Let's see what your 'skies and heavens' look like." But there is nothing on my skin, back or front; not a single beauty spot, nothing. A blank page. Which upsets me, and which she translates in her own way: "You are brand-new."

23 years, 3 months, 11 days *Tuesday, 21 January, 1947*

Suzanne has left, gone back to her Québec. Wars end for everyone. We celebrated this wrenching separation with dignity:

A scratch on the right cheek.

A trace of a bite on the left earlobe.

A lovebite on the neck, to the right, where the artery throbs.

Another on the left, beneath the chin.

A trace of a bite on the upper lip, swollen and bluish.

Four parallel scratches about one centimetre from each other, going from the top of the sternum to the left nipple.

Similar gashes on the upper back.

A lovebite on the right nipple.

A rather deep bite on the thumb pad.

Balls painfully wrung out.

And, the ultimate signature: the trace of a kiss in the right hollow of my groin: "When the lipstick has disappeared, you'll have to start to live again."

Once again, Fanche tends to my wounds. By telling me, for example, that Suzanne did not only slip into bed with me because it was my birthday. No? "No, my petard, it was on orders that she went to take your virginity." No kidding? "No kidding! You perturbed us. And a chaste liaison agent is extremely rare. With so many dangers and so much tension, most of you found yourselves in bed as soon as your mission was accomplished. Liaison officers exorcised the demons of war by screwing like rabbits. Everyone, men and women, needed vital energy and arms to hold them! But not you. Everyone knew it. We had our suspicions: Priest? Virgin? Impotent? Cold fish? Burned by love? These were the questions everyone asked about you. Suzanne went to find out 'in the field'. The last exploit of the Resistance, my petard!"

*

NOTE TO LISON

Fanche had called me "my petard" ever since that afternoon in March 1945, after the battle of Colmar, when a piece of shrapnel from a mine almost tore off half of my left arm. I was driving down a road, one elbow resting on the car door, carefree, as if the war had already ended. Fanche called all her wounded by the name of the weapon that had injured them. "My petard" because of that landmine; "my burst of gunfire" for Roland, who had escaped an ambush carrying his guts in his hands; "my bathtub" for Edmond, who had survived an exhaustive interrogation. My petard: She never used another name for me after that.

*

23 years, 3 months, 28 days *Friday, 7 January, 1947*

After every cold, I wake up with a stuffed-up nose. Dry, but stuffed. Especially the left nostril, blocked by a growth on my nasal mucous membrane and that I can feel quite well with the tip of my index finger if I push deep enough. I sleep with my mouth open and wake up parched, like a dried-out carcass. Could I be allergic to the Paris air?

23 years, 4 months, 9 days *Wednesday, 19 February, 1947*

Is it Suzanne's departure, or Chapelin's continuous barrage of oppositions to all my suggestions, or is it that idiot Parmentier who exasperates me with his obsession with quotas? Whatever it is, something is giving me bitter heartburn. As a child I already had the ailments of an old man. These ailments accompany you your whole life and end up defining your character. Could I be *bitter*, and in a few years, will I have become *embittered*?

23 years, 5 months, 21 days *Monday, 31 March, 1947*

I ate in dribs and drabs, slept badly. Nothing goes in and nothing comes out. Almost ceaseless pains in the oesophagus. I let it drag on and now I'm worried. Etienne thinks I should see a doctor. It's a good idea, especially to keep my anxiety away. The gastroenterologist whom he recommended to me can see me in two weeks at the Cochin Hospital. The antacid tablets help a little. No news from Suzanne.

23 years, 5 months, 30 days *Wednesday, 9 April, 1947*

Still five more days to wait. Such a waste of time, my God! And still nothing from Suzanne. "What are you expecting from that girl?" Fanche asks me. "She opened the doors to life for you, my petard. All you need to do now is go in!" I'm waiting for my appetite to return. My sexual appetite, among others. And an appetite for living. But instead it's my childhood fears that are coming back to me. In the form of hypochondria! For what I am feeling – and it's pointless to try to hide it from myself any longer – is an irrational fear of cancer. Hypochondria: a mental imbalance that leads to a hypertrophic perception of physical symptoms. A kind of persecution madness in which we are both persecutor and persecuted. My mind and my body are playing tricks on *each other*. A new sensation, incidentally, and thus an interesting one. Am I a hypochondriac by nature or is it just a passing phase? Stomach cancer: being eaten alive from the inside by the digestive organ itself! Mythical terror!

23 years, 6 months, 2 days *Saturday, 12 April, 1947*

I can no longer stomach myself.

23 years, 6 months, 4 days *Monday, 14 April, 1947*

The appointment lasted seven minutes. I came out of the gastroenterologist's office completely terrified. I only retained a quarter of what the doctor said to me. I would be incapable of describing his office. An odd sideration of one's ability to think. "You are lucky. A patient had to cancel. I can take you in three days." Is that the truth, or did he tell me this white lie so as not to have to say it was urgent? Instead of listening to him, I examined his face. Tersely, precisely, he stated that in three days he would send a tube down into my stomach to see what was going on. There was absolutely nothing else to be interpreted on his face besides that information, but my hypochondria lent to each of his features some sordid hidden thoughts. You are becoming nuts, my poor boy; you're reacting as if this doctor were an S.S. spy!

23 years, 6 months, 6 days *Wednesday, 16 April, 1947*

I am unable to read. Unable to concentrate on anything at all. Work is the only thing that manages to absorb my attention just slightly. Even so, this morning Josette found me to be distracted, and Marion thought I seemed anxious. The antacid tablets no longer afford me any relief. My nerves are shot. I'm sure that the die is cast, that I am tasting this wine, these olives, the mashed potatoes for the last time as a non-sick person, even though they won't go down – and that I will never again see Luco's chestnut trees flower. Since when do you care about chestnut trees, you imbecile? You always considered them to be unimaginative! It's true, but the certainty of approaching death would make anyone fall in love even with a cockroach. Fear of illness is more frightening than illness itself! I can't wait for the diagnosis so I can move on! Faced with inevitable cancer, I will know how to act! I even dream up a few heroic poses for myself. Meanwhile, my hands are damp, my fingertips tremble ever so slightly, and I experience episodes of panic that turn my constipation into diarrhoea, like when I was twelve years old. *I won't be afraid anymore, I won't be afraid anymore, I'll never be afraid anymore . . .* Hah! Could it be that I have learned nothing? That this diary, which I began in order to exorcise this sort of panic, has served no purpose? Will I have to live until the end with this spineless brat who would shit in his trousers at the slightest scare? Stop snivelling, will you! Look at yourself from the outside, you stupid idiot. You survived a global massacre and a marvel of a woman finally opened the door to the ladies' chamber for you!

23 years, 6 months, 7 days *Thursday, 17 April, 1947*

I underwent the *gastroscopy* in a state of total abdication. I laid down my arms at the hospital. Blind faith, with no illusions about the results. Calm fatalism. The whole time that the gastroenterologist, flanked by his student, was pushing that tube down my throat, then shoving it into my oesophagus to finally explore my stomach all the way to the pylorus, I fought off my horror of vomiting by thinking of the sword-swallower I had seen as a child one day when Papa took me to the circus. The doctors chatted away as they explored me. They checked my pipes while they talked about their upcoming holidays. Fine. Let life continue when it stops! Good news: the exam revealed only an ordinary irritation of the oesophagus. Bad news: I need to see him again for the results of a blood test. Treatment: gastric demulcents and diet. No more meat with gravy. (This doctor doesn't seem to me to have the slightest awareness of the rationing!)

23 years, 6 months, 18 days *Monday, 28 April, 1947*

My tests came back absolutely *normal.* Nothing is wrong with me! Which causes mixed feelings: jubilation tempered by the shame of having been so afraid. But relief won the day, and I went to the restaurant with Estelle. I ordered an andouillette, sautéed potatoes, and a bottle of Brouilly. Until now, no heartburn. A lovely stroll with Estelle in the Jardin des Plantes. My body is mine again. Oh, yes, Montaigne, *the beautiful light of health*!

23 years, 6 months, 28 days *Thursday, 8 May, 1947*

A passer-by asks me how to get to Trocadéro. Instead of telling him, I answer spontaneously, with Suzanne's Québecois accent, that "I am not from here, I'm from Québec, don't know Trocadéro." When Suzanne would imitate a French accent, *my* accent, she showed me the physiology of our French language. Her face shrank, she raised her eyebrows, lifted her chin, lowered her eyelids halfway, and stuck out haughty and pouting lips: "You damn French, you're always speaking with pursed lips, as if you were shitting golden eggs on our poor heads!"

*

23 years, 6 months, 29 days *Friday, 9 May, 1947*

An accent, Suzanne would say, expresses the way we eat a language. "You, Frenchman, pick at your food; I, on the other hand, stuff my face!"

*

NOTE TO LISON

Months of silence after the hypochondria episode. The pleasures of life returned to me, the excitement of a budding career and political sparring took precedence over this diary. After the trick it had just played on me, my body receded into the background. And of course, life was in full swing right after the war.

*

24 years, 5 months, 19 days *Monday, 29 March, 1948*

After we make love, Brigitte asks me if I keep a diary. I say no. She does. I ask her if she will write about our night. "Perhaps," she says, with the false modesty of girls who, once they have confessed the main thing, believe they are keeping their secret safe by being stingy with details. Of course you'll write about it, I thought, and this is precisely why I myself do not keep that sort of diary. What I recall about our night is first and foremost a persistent sensation of painful tension on my frenulum, almost a tear. That's all I need to set down here. The rest, more agreeable, is of no concern in a diary.

24 years, 6 months, 6 days *Friday, 16 April, 1948*

I went to see a certain Dr Bêk, recommended to me by Uncle Georges, about those huge balloons that block my nostrils (especially the left one) for weeks after each cold. They are polyps and there is nothing to do about them. Is this an ailment from which I will suffer my whole life? "With the present state of medical science, young man, there is no doubt about it." Really nothing can be done? "Try not to catch cold in autumn and spring." How? "Avoid public places: the metro, cinemas, churches, museums, railway stations, lifts . . ." He rattles off this list the way one would dictate a prescription and he ends with this recommendation: "And refrain from oral contact." (In other words, avoid human beings.) What about an operation? "I don't advise it; polyps are not ton-sils, they grow back systematically." Old Doctor Bêk at least sent me off with one piece of good news: nasal polyps rarely turn out to be cancerous, unlike those that might one day be found in one's bladder or intestines.

24 years, 6 months, 14 days *Saturday, 24 April, 1948*

My cleric has lost his skullcap: my frenulum gave way in the end and my torn penis covered Brigitte and me in blood. After having examined herself, Brigitte announced: "Looks like we've switched places."

24 years, 6 months, 21 days *Saturday, 1 May, 1948*

So: abstinence. In any case, Brigitte's skin is rather coarse-grained. I don't think I would be able to spend all my nights against coarse-grained buttocks. My life with her, perhaps; my nights against her bum, no.

25 years

Sunday, 10 October, 1948

Orgasms from deep inside the body, orgasms from the tip of the dick. With Brigitte now, I manage to come because I have to. A polite orgasm, a tiny pleasure reduced to the region that produces it, a concession of the glans to the following refrain: because one must fuck, let's fuck, and because one must end, let's come. An orgasm of principle, without the mind's engaging the entire body. Tough luck, whispers an edifying voice inside me: to empty yourself out, you first have to fill yourself up, my boy. Love; fill yourself with love, love with all your heart, and you will come to your heart's content. This advice was contradicted last evening by a woman of the night on rue de Mogador whom I gave myself for my birthday. She was so generous with her time, so convincing in her art, and so enthusiastic with her body that mine, including my head, literally exploded, like it had with Suzanne.

25 years, 2 days *Tuesday, 12 October, 1948*

Birthdays remind me of the time when Maman would ask me what I thought I "deserved" as a present. I can still hear her saying, with a pedagogical intent that emphasised each syllable and those big eyes popping out of her head to signify that nothing escaped her: "In your opinion, what have you deserved for your birthday?" Yet she was so thoughtless, so unmindful of the needs of others. I would purposely cough as I blew out the candles. Like Papa. What I really would have loved for my birthday: a good case of tuberculosis!

25 years, 3 months, 6 days *Sunday, 16 January, 1949*

I spent what seemed to me a considerable amount of time flushing out what I thought was a bit of leek stuck between my upper right incisor and its neighbouring canine – first with my fingernail, then with the corner of a business card, and finally with a sharpened matchstick. But there was no piece of leek. It was an erroneous message that my gums were sending me, themselves misled by some previous irritation. And this isn't the first time! My gums are delusional!

25 years, 3 months, 12 days *Saturday, 22 January, 1949*

There's no point in kidding myself any longer: I don't desire Simone. And the feeling is mutual. Our bodies are not in harmony. Sooner or later this physical incompatibility will win out over our complicity. We are already at a stage of compensation. The perfect understanding that we appear to have and that makes us such a "public" couple hides our sexual fiasco from us. A child must never be made to suffer from this misunderstanding.

25 years, 3 months, 14 days *Monday, 24 January, 1949*

In bed I try to apply to Simone the method I'd taught Dodo for eating what he didn't like. Alas, the transposition is impossible. My imaginary little brother was supposed to think very hard about what was in his mouth and nothing else, to identify every constitutive element of his mouthful, and not come up with one of those fanciful representations that children make based on the consistency of the food rather than on its taste. Rice pudding is not vomit, spinach is not *caca*, etc. Well, in bed, everything, or almost everything, is a matter of consistency, and so this method does not work. The more I know what I am holding in my arms, the less I am able to accept it: the dry skin, the sharp collarbone, the humerus that I can immediately feel behind the biceps, the chest that is too muscular, the hard stomach, the rough pubic hair, the tight little buttocks, too small for my hands; in other words, this athletic body unfailingly makes me dream of its opposite. And what's worse, I absolutely *must* fantasise in order to consummate. Otherwise: flaccidity, lame excuses, dismal night, and a bad mood in the morning.

25 years, 3 months, 22 days *Tuesday, 1 February, 1949*
And then, I don't like the way she smells. I love her but I cannot stand the smell of her. In love, there is nothing more tragic.

25 years, 3 months, 25 days *Friday, 4 February, 1949*
Montaigne: "She smells sweetest who smells not at all." Indeed? Where are you, Violette? Your scent was my cloak. But Montaigne was not speaking about you. Where are you, Suzanne? Your perfume was my flag. He was not speaking about you either.

25 years, 4 months *Thursday, 10 February, 1949*
Simone and I have "everything we need to get along", except for the fact that our bodies don't communicate. We get along, but don't form one body. To tell the truth, it's less her body that first attracted me than her way of being: her gaze, the way she walks, the tone of her voice, the somewhat abrupt grace of her gestures, her thin elegance, that plump smile on her uncertain face, all of that (which I took to be her body), because it was in perfect accord with what she said, thought, read, kept

to herself, seemed to foretell a total accord between us. And now I find myself in bed with a tennis champion made of sheer muscles, tendons, reflexes, self-control and reserve. What would it have been like if boxing and physical exercise hadn't made me muscular as well? Abdominal muscles against abdominal muscles, we reject each other. And if from now on I were to aim for a soft obesity? Allow my body to bloat until it unctuously absorbed hers all the while penetrating it? She would give herself to me, basking in the folds of my body. Pauline R., when Fanche asked her why she only liked very fat men, had replied, with trembling eyes and voice: "Ah, it's like making love to a cloud!"

25 years, 4 months, 7 days *Thursday, 17 February, 1949*

This morning our bed is barely ruffled.

25 years, 5 months, 20 days *Wednesday, 30 March, 1949*

Toothache: the temptation of pain. I shot straight up in bed this morning, awakened by a raging toothache. After it made me leap in the air, the damn thing seemed *interesting* to me. A cavity electrocutes you. It is the pain closest to an electrical discharge. Like any electrocution, it creates a shock. The tongue is wandering around the mouth without thinking, and suddenly, two or three thousand volts! It's extremely painful, but momentary. An isolated lightning bolt in a stormy sky. The pain is not diffused; it is strictly contained within its perimeter of harm and disappears almost immediately. To the point that, after having created the surprise, it then creates doubt. And the dangerous game of verification begins. Our tongue goes to explore very circumspectly the sides of the suspected tooth with the precision of a mine-clearing expert, before then venturing on to the chipped ridge and sliding into the gulf as carefully as a slug groping with its antennae. No matter how vigilant you are, you get another electrical discharge that sends you jumping to the ceiling. And so you have been warned. The only thing is that it's not easy to retain for long the knowledge of a pain that is so fleeting.

You go back. Another electric shock! The mollusc immediately curls up. A cavity is such a tease!

25 years, 5 months, 24 days *Sunday, 3 April, 1949*
Caroline is a toothache. The searing intensity of her nasty comments is instantaneously forgotten, so that once you've been struck, you wonder if it happened at all. Such a sweet girl! Such a gentle voice! Such pale skin! Such blue eyes! Such Botticellian hair! So you go back again. You verify. And you come home snivelling. She did this to me, she did that to me. So many victims. Caroline is one of those toothaches produced by our insatiable need to be loved. Unmasked, she acts like a bad tooth: "I was such an unhappy child." She poses as an innocent cavity: "It's not my fault, men's nastiness made me what I am." And her countless victims play dentist. I'll be able to cure you, me, me, I'll know how! A charming cavity. So many of us! Trust my salves, my love, my drill, I know you're not like that deep down. And our tongue cedes to the fascination of the abyss. I predict that this girl will have a dazzling political career.

25 years, 5 months, 25 days *Monday, 4 April, 1949*
With these thoughts about dear Caroline, this is becoming another, more personal diary. Question: when my body produces an enlightening metaphor about my peers, do I have the right to extend what I'm writing to what could pass as a personal diary? Answer: no. The main reason for this taboo? Caroline most likely keeps a personal diary in which she mixes reality with the sauce of her desires. And then, other metaphors would suit her temperament: a tick, for example, that feeds surreptitiously on your blood and that you flush out too late. Or the staphylococcus aureus, sound asleep between two destructive awakenings. No, no, no extension to the personal diary allowed!

*

25 years, 6 months, 3 days *Wednesday, 13 April, 1949*

For the first time in my life, I went to see a dentist (recommended by Uncle Georges). As a result, I have a puffiness that won't allow me to show myself at work. I exchanged an intermittent electrocution for a lasting pain, a brazier whose fuel is my upper left maxilla, raised to the highest degree of incandescence. "If it hurts, take this." I took "that" and it still hurts. The pain began with the anaesthetic shot itself. I found myself with a needle stuck perpendicularly in the crater of my molar and, the entire time my torturer was moving his syringe to inject his drug, my body remained stiff as a board. "It won't be fun but it'll be quick." It was neither fun nor quick. Once the liquid was injected, the dentist began to perforate my jawbone with a drill that resonated in my skull as if it were a coalmine where an entire penal colony was slaving away with pickaxes. All that fuss to extract some minuscule grey filaments from the depths of the earth. "Look, that's your nerve. I'll make you a bandage and we'll deal with your crown once everything is healed over."

He advised me to brush my teeth a bit more regularly. No less than two minutes morning and night. From top to bottom, right to left. Like the American soldiers from S.H.A.P.E.

25 years, 6 months, 9 days *Tuesday, 19 April, 1949*

Tough negotiations with M&L, and suddenly I detected a strong odour of shit that was so unexpected and brutal that I gave a start. Apparently, my interlocutors didn't smell a thing. A smell that was there, nonetheless! It's acidic, it's smothering, indeed it "grabs you by the throat", and it is as excremental as it can be. As if I had fallen into a septic tank. That horror follows me all day long, in gusts, while no one around me is affected by it. In the office, the metro, at home, a door opens and closes on sordid latrines whose stench suffocates me. An olfactory illusion, that's my diagnosis. I did not fall into a septic tank, I *am* that septic tank saturated by a stench that, fortunately, I don't export. An illusion of an odour in an airtight septic tank, at least it's no more than that. I spoke about it to Etienne to get it off my chest. He asked me if I had been to the dentist recently. Yes, your father's, last week. "An upper molar?" Yes, the left one. "No need to look further, he perforated a sinus and now you're hooked directly into your nasal fossae. It'll take a few days until it heals." Nasal fossae? What do they open onto? Our soul smells like shit? "You didn't know?" Etienne explained this *sui generis* stench to me. It's not that our soul is foul-smelling, it's that our sinuses, which are often infected, produce an odour of pus, in other words, organic rotting, which our olfactory apparatus takes full advantage of if a dentist's drill goes slightly off track. It happens all the time and isn't serious. This direct connection to the inside of our head acts like a magnifying glass on the smells of personal rot. (On the outside, the stench abates as it is diffused.) As for the smell, it is quite real, it is not an illusion: a concentrate of putrefying cells.

25 years, 6 months, 15 days *Monday, 25 April, 1949*

Six days spent smelling like shit without anyone else noticing. Even while I was presenting my thesis. The jury was oblivious. First-class honours with distinction. While I was swimming in my cesspit. A kind of Lady Macbeth.

25 years, 7 months, 4 days *Saturday, 14 May, 1949*

The tailor's quick movements to take my measurements with his tape measure. Length of the arms, legs, waist size, collar size, shoulder width. Precise, neutral brushing between my legs. (I ask myself fleetingly what I *feel*.) But the tailor is not interested in this body. In fact, he doesn't touch me at all. Nothing like a doctor palpating you. His hands sticking in needles measure a volume, sketch out a shape. It is the social man who leaves his shop, the man clothed in his function. My body feels strangely naked in this new suit.

*

25 years, 7 months, 5 days *Sunday, 15 May, 1949*

The tailor asked a question I didn't understand. Does it hang to the right or the left? He had to explain what he meant. Once he had, I had to think about it. More to the left, I think. Yes, more to the left. My penis has a tendency to roll to the left. I had never considered that before.

26 years, 5 months, 2 days *Sunday, 12 March, 1950*

It's been months since I've written in here, as always when something important happens to me. In this instance, it was love at first sight. It wasn't urgent to write about it, but rather to experience it. Lovelorn suffocation! It's not easy to describe if you don't want to drown in sentimental sop. Luckily, love has everything to do with the body! Three months ago, then, at a party at Fanche's. The apartment is full. The doorbell rings, I'm closest to the door, I open it. She says simply: "I'm Mona," and I stand there, blocking her, lost in an instantaneous, unconditional, definitive love. It's madness what tribute desire pays to beauty! This Mona, without a doubt the most desirable apparition that exists, is immediately promoted to the most intelligent, nicest, most refined, kindest and best companion among women! A superlative perfection. My heart melted. She could have been the stupidest, nastiest, most ordinary, most rapacious, taciturn, lying, slutty, damned bourgeois woman or beggar – even if I had learned all that from her case file, my heart would have believed only what I was seeing with my own eyes. My life was waiting for her and her alone! What was standing before me in the doorway and what, all things considered, seemed in no hurry to come in either, belongs to me! Woman with a capital W! *My* woman! Possessive adjective! Eternal certainty! Our entire culture flows from our glands to our heart the instant we are struck by love at first sight: every tuppenny love song and every high-class opera – the first time Romeo sees Juliet, the first time the Comte de Nemours gazes at the Princesse de Clèves, and all the virgins and Venuses and Eves by Cranach, Botticelli and company – all that astounding quantity of love has come to the fore, from the gutter and the museums, from magazines and novels, from advertising photos and sacred texts. Song of songs of songs, the entire sum of desires accumulated in our youth, magnified by our ardent masturbation, all that teenage wanking in the void to pictures and words, all those designs of our passionate souls – all of that makes our hearts swell and sets our minds on fire! Ah! The bedazzlement of love! Oh, the clairvoyant man of a moment! Who remains standing in the doorway like a fool. Fortunately, my coat was hanging nearby. I grabbed it and for the past three months Mona and I have not left our bed where we have contemplated each other from near and far, for now and forever.

Nacre, silk, flame and pearl, the perfection of Mona's cunt! Simply to mention the essential – for there is also the hunger in her gaze and the infinitesimal velvet of her skin, the tender weight of her breasts, the supple firmness of her bum, the appropriate contour of her hips, and the perfect slope of her shoulders, all fitting perfectly in my hand, all made to measure for me, all at the ideal temperature, made for my nostrils and my taste buds – oh! The flavour of Mona! – there must be a God for a door to open on a man's so perfect complement! A God must at least exist for all our parts to fit so perfectly together! In a natural progression, first our hands and lips got to know each other; then we tamed, caressed, titillated, masturbated, and attuned our genitals to one another, before allowing them to inspect and swallow each other, to skilfully draw out the note of pleasure until we hit that high C. And now they devour each other and work like mad at every little thing without our say-so, blindly, in the stairwell or the doorway, in the cinema, in the basement of that antique shop, in the cloakroom of that theatre, under the copse in that park, at the top of the Eiffel Tower, if you please! I said "our bed", but all of the greater Paris area has become our bed, from the Seine to the Marne! We wear out our bodies until our thirst is slaked; we prepare them and lick them clean like the bottom of a pot, like the back of a spoon; we contemplate them in all their glory and in all their exhaustion, with the dumb tenderness of a drunkard who translates it all into terms of love and future and children. I'm in favour of everything, progeny and all, as long as Mona doesn't leave my bed; grow and multiply, why not, if pleasure doesn't suffer because of it and if the addition is called happiness? So, I'm fine with a ton of kids, as many as we want, one kid for each time we have sex if necessary, and we'll rent a barracks to house this army made by love! That seems to sum up what I feel. I could let my pen go on and on if a stark-naked emergency in my bed weren't whispering to me that this is not a time for commemoration, but a time for action, again and again! Not a matter of celebrating time that has passed, but of honouring time that doesn't pass!

26 years, 7 months, 9 days *Friday, 19 May, 1950*

Yesterday afternoon, Ascension Day, Mona and I did it six times. Six and a half, even. Longer and longer. That radiant – literally – sense of exhaustion. Like torches that end up with dead batteries after having given off all their light. Mona gets up and falls back very softly at the foot of the bed. She laughs: "I don't have any skeleton left." Usually she says she can't feel her legs. We've beaten our own record.

26 years, 9 months, 18 days *Friday, 28 July, 1950*

How much the body benefits from the energy of love! Everything, absolutely everything does me good right now. My bosses think I am inexhaustible.

26 years, 10 months, 7 days *Thursday, 17 August 1950*

As far as an orgasm is concerned, our vocabulary couldn't come up with anything more evocative than "to keel over". It's true, we keel over! And yet, if one is to believe the *Littré* dictionary, in the nineteenth century, "to keel over" signified a failure, a false step in one's social climb. "This young man keeled over." No entry of this verb at the time had to do with pleasure. It simply designated the shipwreck of bourgeois hopes.

26 years, 11 months, 13 days *Saturday, 23 September, 1950*
Mona's loving punctuation: Entrust me with this comma so I can make an exclamation mark out of it.

27 years: birthday *Tuesday, 10 October, 1950*
Mona and I have found our perfect animal mate in each other. Everything else is literature. Let's skip over the gracefulness of her gait, the light of her smile, our complicity in everything; let's skip over everything that would belong in an ordinary diary, simply to arrive at the statement of our satisfied animality: I have found my female and ever since we have been sharing the same bed, coming home means returning to my lair.

27 years, 29 days *Wednesday, 8 November, 1950*
One cannot live with a stuffed nose. I snore. Mona hasn't said anything to me about it, but it's obvious. And I know from my long experience sleeping in dormitories that someone could easily suffocate a snorer with his pillow. Allow myself to be repudiated for snoring, me? Never! First thing in the morning, I made an appointment with Dr Bêk to have him extract the polyp in my left nostril. Who cares if the disgusting octopus grows back in a short while; all I ask from the operation is for it to allow me to breathe freely for six months. "Are you sure? Having a polyp extracted is no fun! But my nephew will help us." The nephew in question is an enormous Senegalese fellow about twenty years old, as wide as he is tall, who is finishing his philosophy degree at the Sorbonne and earning his living helping out this "uncle" by mutely doing the office work. "Please pay my nephew" is the last sentence patients hear as they leave Dr Bêk's office. The nephew hands you the bill, pockets the money, gives back any change and stamps the receipt without a smile or a word. In my case, his "help" consists of immobilising my

head, one hand on my forehead the other under my chin, keeping my head against the imitation-leather back of a surgical armchair while the uncle orders me to hold on to the armrests and "if possible" not to move. And then he introduces a long pair of curved forceps (called "Politzer forceps") in my left nostril, raises his investigating eyes to the sky, feels around, and then his gaze locks: "Ah, I've got the bastard! Take a deep breath!" And the doctor pulls mercilessly on the polyp, which resists with all the fibres of its being, forcing a scream of surprise from me, which is immediately suppressed by the nephew's enormous hand, less to prevent me from shouting than to keep up the morale of the waiting room, which has been filled to bursting since dawn thanks to the doctor's fame. Ligaments crunch in the echo chamber of my skull. Ah! The filthy beast won't let go! The whole thing has become strictly personal between the polyp and the doctor, the former grabbing the sides of its cave with all its tentacles and the latter going at it so fiercely that the muscle in his forearm is stretched to breaking while I am suffocating in the nephew's hand and it's exactly as if Dr Bêk were attempting to extract my entire brain through my left nostril. No one knows how long this eternity lasted during which I held in all my life's breaths; my lungs were on the point of bursting, my fingers drilled into the armrests down to the metal, my legs projected out into space in the shape of a paralysed victory V, and my inner ear – crunching, tearing, screaming of flesh – resonated from the titanic combat as it gave up my skull's living matter to the madman with his bulging eyes, his swallowed lips, who was then sweating all the water in his head such that his misty eyeglasses little by little caused him to go blind. He couldn't have worked harder if he had been pulling out my tongue.

"Ah! That's it! Here it is! I feel it! It's coming! Yesssss!" A bloody geyser accompanies the orgasm of victory. "It's something else, isn't it?" exclaims the doctor as he contemplates the bit of flesh that's dripping at the end of his forceps. Then he says to the nephew, in a distracted whisper: "Clean him and pack him up." He's talking about me. What's left of me.

"Who did that to you?" Tomassin asked me when I sat down at my desk. My swollen nostril with a bloody piece of cotton wool poking out of it and my eye half closed in a reflex reaction make me look as though I've undergone some serious torture. And since the other nostril is blocked by the pressure exerted by the first one on the inner wall of my nose, I am breathing with my mouth open; my lips are dry, and I can only express myself in the labials of a seriously drunk man. Tomassin would gladly have sent me home (less out of compassion than for his own personal hygiene), but we had a meeting with the Austrians and could "not afford to put the contract at risk". Alas, as I was bending over to kiss the gloved hand that the Baroness von Trattner (the minister's wife, Gerda) was holding out to me, my cork popped and the geyser of blood that splattered on the Venetian lace seriously compromised the contract in question. *Verzeihen Sie bitte, Baronin!*

27 years, 5 months, 13 days *Friday, 23 March, 1951*

Easter week. Honeymoon. According to Mona, Venice, which is pure spectacle, is a paradise for the blind. You don't need eyes to feel completely sighted. This capital of silence is the sonorous city *par excellence.* Between the footsteps of the tourists and the determined clicking of Venetian heels, the flight of pigeons in the squares and the mewling of the gulls, the unique call of each market – flower, fish, fruit and flea – the little bells of the vaporetti, the staccato of the pneumatic drills, the Venetian accent that is less rhythmic and more lagoon-like than the other Italian dialects, everything in this place is addressed to the ears. Cannaregio doesn't echo like the Zattere; no street or square offers up the same sounds. Venice is an orchestra, Mona says, forcing me to identify our excursions by their sounds, with my eyes closed and my hand on her shoulder. She makes me promise that if one of us loses our eyesight one day, we will come to live here together. And, the icing on the cake: the *acqua alta* gives us an excuse to walk in puddles.

27 years, 5 months, 14 days *Saturday, 24 March, 1951*

Yesterday it was Venice through hearing; today, it's Venice through smell, still with closed eyes. "Imagine you are blind *and* deaf," Mona says. "You'd have to be able to recognise each *sestiere* with your nose in order not to get lost!" So, we sniff. Mona, whose sense of smell goes back to the twelfth century, claims that the Rialto smells of fish, the streets that lead to San Marco smell of luxury leather, the Arsenal of rope and tar. And when I beg to visit a museum or two, she argues that museums can be found in books, that is, in our own library.

27 years, 5 months, 16 days *Monday, 26 March, 1951*

Seeing Etienne admiring himself in a mirror, I realise I've never *really* looked at myself in one. Never an innocently narcissistic glance, never a mischievous freeze-frame that makes you delight in your reflection. I have always reduced a mirror to its functions. It acted as inventory-taker when as a teenager I would check the development of my muscles; it has a sartorial function whenever I need to match tie, shirt and jacket; and its role is to be vigilant when I shave in the morning. But the vision of the whole doesn't grab my attention. I don't go through the looking glass. (Am I afraid of not being able to come back out?) Etienne *really* looks at himself. Like everyone, he dives deep into his image. Not I. The elements of my body constitute but don't characterise me. In sum, I never really looked at *myself* in a mirror. It isn't a virtue; it has more to do with distance, the irreducible distance that this diary is trying to overcome. Something about my image remains foreign to me, to the extent that sometimes I am startled when I come upon it unexpectedly reflected in a shop window. Who is that? No one; relax, it's only you. Ever since I was a child, it has taken me a bit of time to recognise myself and I can never catch up. As far as a reflection goes, I prefer Mona's gaze. How do I look? "Great, you're perfect." Or Etienne 's before we go into a meeting. I look okay? "Yeah, okay. You won't drive the women mad with lust, but you will persuade the court."

27 years, 7 months, 10 days *Sunday, 20 May, 1951*
In truth, I would be incapable of saying *what I look like.*

28 years, 3 days *Saturday, 13 October, 1951*
I thought I had conquered my fear of heights when I was a child, but I can still feel it there, lurking in my testicles, as soon as I am near a precipice. A small battle must then be waged. I had the experience again just yesterday, on the cliffs in Etretat. Why does this fear first manifest itself in me by a strangling of the testicles? Is this true for other people? In my case, in these moments, my balls are the centre of everything; a bottleneck that diffuses fear in powerful upward and downward thrusts, as if my balls were replacing my heart in order to push a geyser of sand through my veins that abrades my whole circulatory system: arms, torso, legs. The explosion of two balls of sand. In the past this fear would paralyse me.

28 years, 4 days *Sunday, 14 October, 1951*
I asked Mona if ovaries are also sentries of vertigo. She said no. My testicles, however, were once again strangling themselves when I saw her walk to the edge of the cliff. I had vertigo in her place. Empathetic balls?

As I was experiencing these things, the story of a hiker who fell from a cliff came back to me. He takes a false step, slips a few metres on fallen rocks and topples over into the void. Horrified, his friends continue to scream when he has ceased being afraid. He believes his terror left him the second he knew he was finished. For the rest of his life, he remembered this loss of hope as the very experience of beatitude. It was the branches of a tree that saved him in the end. And his fear returned with the hope that he would come out alive.

28 years, 1 month, 3 days *Tuesday, 13 March, 1951*

After lunch in the cafeteria, Martineau burps discreetly, his fist in front of his mouth. Once again I notice that someone else's burp, which gives me direct access to the fermentation going on in his stomach, bothers me more than his farts, the smell of which seems less intimate, more universal to me. In other words, I feel more *indiscreet* smelling someone's burps than sniffing a fart.

28 years, 2 months, 17 days *Thursday, 27 December, 1951*

Bruno's birth. Unto us a babe is born. He's come to stay *as if he had always been here*! I am speechless. My son is an object of *familiar amazement.*

28 years, 7 months, 23 days *Sunday, 27 January, 1952*

Becoming a father means losing an arm. For the past month I have had only one arm, the other one carries Bruno. One-armed from one day to the next. You get used to it.

28 years, 7 months, 23 days *Monday, 2 June, 1952*

I woke up with a lump in my throat, short of breath, my lungs constricted, my teeth clenched, and my mood dark for no particular reason. This is what Maman used to call "having anxiety". "Leave me alone, I'm having anxiety!" How many times did I hear her say those words when I was doing nothing other than living the life of a too-well-behaved child at her side? She would frown, and her eyes would grow dark with anger (her eyes that were so blue!) and her face would look – how can I describe it? – as if she were gazing at herself nastily from the inside, without worrying about the effect it was producing on the outside. I would ask Dodo: "What have you done to Maman now?"

28 years, 7 months, 25 days *Wednesday, 4 June, 1952*

One of the strangest manifestations of my anxiety attacks is the tic I have of chewing on my bottom lip from the inside. I've done this as far back as I can remember. Despite my resolve never to do it again, I indulge in it with meticulous cruelty at each new offensive. As soon as I experience the first symptoms, the inside of my lip seems to be anaesthetised and my premolars *enjoy* tearing off strips of what seems to be dead skin. This happens without pain, as if I were peeling a piece of fruit. My incisors play for a few seconds with these strips of myself, and then I swallow them. This self-devouring goes on until my teeth arrive at a depth of my lip where the flesh becomes sensitive to the bites. Then comes the first pain, and the first blood is drawn. A limit has been reached. I have to stop. But I have a strong desire to tickle the wound, either by deepening it with tiny bites that exacerbate the pain until my eyes fill with tears, or else by compressing the injured lip with a sucking motion that makes it bleed even more. The game then consists of inspecting on a handkerchief or on the back of my hand the quality of the red of that particular blood. It is a strange sort of torture that a guy who is not particularly inclined to masochism has been inflicting on himself since childhood. I curse myself the whole time that the wound is healing, while experiencing a vague fear of having reached the point beyond which this tortured flesh will refuse to heal. Since when have I been performing this little ritual of hysteria with its dash of suicidal tendency? Since I lost my baby teeth?

29 years *Friday, 10 October, 1952*

My birthday! A day to remember! Brandishing Bruno to show him to the guests as if he were the eighth marvel of the world, I fell with him on the staircase. I tumbled headfirst and rolled all the way down to the bottom of the steps. Eleven of them, to be exact. Instinctively I folded over Bruno. As I rolled, I held his head against my chest, protecting him with my elbows, my biceps, my back; I was a shell closed around my son and we rolled to the bottom of the steps in a great concert of screams. All the guests had arrived. I felt the sharp edge of the stairs against the back of my hands, the bones in my pelvis, my shoulder blades, my ankles, my spine, but I knew, all while rolling, my chest hollow and my abdomen pulled in, that Bruno was perfectly safe against me. I instinctively transformed myself into a human shock absorber. Bruno was as safe as he would have been had he been wrapped in a mattress. Yet I never did judo, I never learned how to fall properly. A spectacular expression of paternal instinct?

29 years, 2 months, 22 days *Thursday, 1 January, 1953*

Celebrated New Year's Eve last night at R.'s. Cigars were handed out. A discussion ensued about the relative merits of Cuba, the Philippines, and I don't know what other tobacco-producing countries. My opinion was asked for. But, watching those connoisseurs as they cut their fat cigars with solemnity, I could not help thinking that the anus, as it severs the turd, acts like a cigar cutter. And in both instances, the same determined expression appears on one's face.

29 years, 5 months, 13 days *Monday, 23 March, 1953*

I didn't think a baby could come into the world smiling. Yet this is true for Lison, who was born this afternoon at ten past five: chubby, smooth, relaxed, with the smile of a fat, bald little Buddha gazing at the world with the obvious intention of comforting it. My first reflex when faced with a newborn – and this had already happened with Bruno – is not to look for family resemblances, but rather to seek signs of temperament on this brand-new face. My little Lison, beware of this father of yours who from the outset has attributed to you the ability to bring peace to the world.

29 years, 7 months, 28 days *Sunday, 7 June, 1953*

There is a difference between a purely tender caress and one to which you merely consent in order to stop tears from flowing. In the first instance, the baby senses it is the centre of love; in the second, the baby wants to hurl itself out the window.

30 years, 1 month, 4 days *Saturday, 14 November, 1953*

Where does Mona find her ease when she handles babies? I am always afraid of breaking them. Above all because, whenever I am holding Lison in my arms, Bruno stamps his feet with impatience to take her place. A shortcoming of the French language: I was *manchot* when I carried Bruno, and I'm *manchot* when I carry both Bruno *and* Lison. Whether you have lost one arm or two, we only have one word in French: *manchot.* The one-legged (*unijambiste*) and the legless (*cul-de-jatte*) are treated better, as are the one-eyed (*borgne*) and the blind (*aveugle*).

30 years, 3 months, 18 days *Thursday, 28 January, 1954*

I have a dream that I am unable to recount. Anxiety wakes me at five in the morning. More precisely, I know that anxiety is waiting for me the moment I awake. I am still asleep, but I sense I am going to be torn from sleep by the forceps of anxiety, my heart squeezed like a baby's head. Oh, not this time, no! I don't want it to happen! No! With a deft twist, my heart rends itself from those forceps and my body escapes anxiety, diving back into sleep with the effortlessness of a porpoise, and sleep's very nature has changed or, rather, its texture has changed and sleep has become a simple fabric of familiar well-being, a refuge in which obtuse anxiety will be unable to reach me; it is a sleep that UNDERSTANDS EVERYTHING: My body has just dived into Montaigne's *Essays.* And on that note, I wake up and immediately realise I had taken refuge in the fluid substance of the *Essays*, the very material of that book, of that man!

*

NOTE TO LISON

An interruption of two years. Once again, keeping a diary yielded to constructing the social person: professional advancement, political battles, all sorts of debates, articles, speeches, meetings, journeys to the four corners of the earth, conferences, colloquia, raw material for those Memoirs that, thirty years later, Etienne absolutely wanted me to write. Mona didn't see things the same way as I did: "Save the world, save the world," she would say, "but do it far from the babies!" In fact, Bruno often criticised me because he felt like an orphan during that time. No doubt our falling out stems from this.

*

32 years, 4 months, 24 days *Monday, 5 March, 1956*

When I went to pick up Ti-Joe as he was leaving prison this morning, I suddenly recalled the moment he was born. Or rather, more precisely, the moment I *saw him* being born! I watched his birth "live", literally, as he shot out from between Marta's thighs, his eyes and fists squeezed shut as if he were plunging into life already unequivocally determined to do battle with it. I was ten years old, and until now had completely repressed this image. But seeing him this morning, ejected from the doorway of the house of detention (a slit cut out of the immense black metal sheet of the gate, which itself was embedded in the red rock of the outer wall), immediately brought to mind his appearing between Marta's thighs. Marta had been screaming loudly, which is what caused me to open her bedroom door in the first place. Violette, not particularly worried by her buxom sister-in-law's wails, chased me away: "What are you doing here? Go! Beat it!" I slammed the door, then ran straight outside to the bedroom window and saw Violette, beaming despite her bloody hands as she brandished all of Ti-Joe, Marta sweating in a swampy bed, and Ti-Joe blackish and reddish, wailing in turn with all his might. Suddenly I was pulled away from the window by some immense power and found myself face to face with a livid Manès reeking of hooch, who asked me, as if my life depended on my answer: "So, is it a guy or a girl?" It was a guy. But he was so tiny that as soon as he had been baptised Joseph (in honour of Stalin), he became Ti-Joe, Little Joe. The prison gate closed behind him and Ti-Joe looked right and left to check out his prospects in freedom. Then he saw me on the pavement opposite, opened his arms wide to me, and laughed.

32 years, 5 months, 1 day *Sunday, 11 March, 1956*

Bruno spent part of the morning with his tongue hanging out of his mouth, like a dreaming dog. When I asked him the reason for this "exhibition", he answered as seriously as could be: "My tongue gets bored inside, so from time to time I take it out." My little boy still experiences himself as if he were a scattered puzzle. He is getting to know the parts that constitute him as if they were casual acquaintances. He is quite aware that it is his tongue, I don't doubt it for a second, but he can still pretend it is a foreign body and take it out for an airing as if it were a dog. His tongue, but also his arms, his feet, and his brain – he has been talking a lot with his brain recently: "Keep quiet, I'm talking to my brain!" – all these pieces of him still have the ability to delight him. In a few months, he will no longer say this sort of thing, and in a few years he won't want to believe he ever did.

32 years, 6 months, 9 days *Thursday, 19 April, 1956*

Ti-Joe made me aware that whenever I sneeze, I literally say "ACHOO". He takes this to be a sign of my conventionalism. "You and your good manners! You are so well-mannered that if your bum could talk, it would say 'fart'."

32 years, 10 months *Friday, 10 August, 1956*

As I watch the children carefully brushing their teeth, I must confess that I don't follow any of the instructions Mona and I have burdened them with: three times a day, *without thinking about anything else,* first the upper teeth – from top to bottom, please! – then the lower ones – from bottom to top, please! – in front and behind, and finally a long, circular motion, methodical and patient, for at least three minutes. The only thing of all that that has survived in me is the nightly brushing, quick and disorderly, just so I don't have to inflict the after-taste of my dinner on Mona. In other words, I don't like to brush my teeth. It doesn't matter that I know that plaque will get me in the end, and that as I grow older my teeth will become loose and my smile will turn yellow, that one day or another this little wall will have to be assaulted with a pneumatic drill, and that dentures are surely in my future; none of this changes a thing: the prospect of brushing my teeth always immediately makes me think of other, more pressing tasks: rubbish to take out, phone calls to make, one last project to close . . . It's as if procrastination, which I conquered a long time ago in every other sphere, had set up camp for good when it comes to dental hygiene. Where does this come from? From boredom and, in this instance, real metaphysical boredom. Brushing my teeth is the antechamber to eternity. Only Mass bores me more.

33 years, 18 days *Sunday, 28 October, 1956*

Mona and Lison having gone out, I spent the entire day alone with Bruno. Other than during his comatose nap, he wriggled about, *producing constant movement*, and I had the feeling that no adult anywhere in the world, however young, strong, physically fit, or tireless, no adult at the height of his nervous and muscular strength could produce, in one day, half the energy expended by the body of this very small boy.

33 years, 4 months, 17 days *Wednesday, 27 February, 1957*

I wasn't dressed warmly enough when I left the house this morning. The cold pounced on my shoulders and penetrated me. When it is extremely hot outside, I have the opposite sensation. Winter invades us; summer absorbs us.

33 years, 4 months, 18 days *Thursday, 28 February, 1957*

My sole ambition is to find myself at the perfect temperature.

33 years, 5 months, 13 days *Saturday, 23 March, 1957*

I woke up in a foul mood, with a bitter taste in my mouth. Clearly I am incapable of resisting food, whether the company I am in is pleasant or tiresome. In the first instance, I eat out of enthusiasm, in the second, out of boredom; in both cases I eat and drink too much, without a real desire to do either. And the next day I am punished for it: my awakening is bitter, my mouth and mood filled with gall. As for last night, I suspect the culprit to be a bellyful of dry sausage on buttered bread and three whiskies before dinner. The butter and dry sausage didn't make it through customs. Nor did the ton of cassoulet that came next. (How many times did I take more? Twice? Three times?) This matutinal bitterness is then exposed to my higher authority, which scolds me once again for not knowing how to control myself. With the pre-dinner drinks, I eat like a mechanical sparrow. The small plates call out to me to dig in. I eat a bite and talk, eat a bite and talk. A sparrow. This relationship between food and boredom – or enthusiasm – goes back to my early childhood, when Maman would make me play the "young hostess", in other words, when I would pass around the pre-dinner snacks to the guests without being allowed to take any. The penalty for this goes back a long way too: this morning I awoke with the taste of cod-liver oil in my mouth.

33 years, 5 months, 14 days *Sunday, 24 March, 1957*

This evening, my shit was heavy and sticky. Two flushes were not sufficient to unstick the crap from the ceramic or to erase the brown traces from the bottom of the bowl. Out came the toilet brush. And then: revelation. In my childhood, I didn't know what a toilet brush was used for. I thought it was some kind of ornament, with its porcupine head perpetually plunged in its immaculate little dish. It was familiar to me and literally meaningless. Sometimes, I would turn it into a toy, a sword I would brandish while sitting on the throne. My ignorance stemmed from the fact that small children's turds don't stick – or just barely – to the bowl. They slide down by themselves and disappear in the torrent without leaving a trace. The remains of angels. No need for the brush. And then, one day, matter wins out. It resists. Matter *forms a callus.* You don't pay attention to this – no one ever looks at the bottom of the bowl – until the adult in charge makes you see the thing and demands you clean it up.

So when did I first use the brush, an action that is so often obligatory for me these days? The event is not recorded in this diary. Yet it was an important day in my life. A loss of innocence.

This sort of gap confirms my prejudice against diaries: they never manage to seize on anything truly decisive.

33 years, 6 months, 11 days *Sunday, 21 April, 1957*

At the zoo in Vincennes. As Lison, Bruno, Mona and I were day-dreaming in front of a chimpanzee couple busy delousing each other ("What're they doing, Papa?"), I thought of that animal expression of intimacy that almost every woman I've ever known wears when she is on the hunt for blackheads. The skin of my chest pinched between two thumbs so that the comedo is gently expelled by the meeting of the fingernails. Mona's expression when she does this! As for me, I glance rapidly at the white worm with the black head on her nail and submit to this delivery with the dreamy stoicism of my friend the chimpanzee.

33 years, 6 months, 13 days *Tuesday, 23 April, 1957*

It's the oxidisation of the sebum on contact with the air that gives the comedo its black head. This greasy mass of cellular debris remains impeccably white as long as it is protected by the dermis. As soon as it pierces this layer, it turns black. Ageing is nothing but this pervasive phenomenon of oxidisation. We are rusting. Mona removes my rust.

33 years, 6 months, 21 days *Tuesday, 1 May, 1957*

I thought back to those greasy adolescent outbreaks as I was washing my hair this morning. Ever since I was a teenager, if I wait one day too long to wash my hair, I feel it is foreign to my skull, a dishcloth that has fallen by chance onto my head. In other words, I wash my hair in order to forget about it.

33 years, 9 months, 5 days *Monday, 15 July, 1957*

As I was peeing in the cafeteria toilet today, while my foreskin was filling up and I was eliminating its contents before opening the floodgates, I recalled once again that at twelve or thirteen I could not control the flow very well. Lack of maturity? An act of resistance against Maman? An animalistic marking of territory? Why does the man who uses public latrines systematically piss next to the target? Once Maman had stopped calling my attention to my floods, I began to hit the bull's-eye.

33 years, 9 months, 8 days *Thursday, 18 July, 1957*

Ti-Joe likes to tell this story about a man pissing:

STICKY STORY OF THE MAN AT THE PUBLIC URINAL

A man is standing in front of a urinal, his hands at his side, paralysed, clearly incapable of making the slightest gesture. His neighbour, busy buttoning his own fly, politely asks what the matter is. The man, very embarrassed, shows him his paralysed hands and asks if he would be kind enough to open his fly for him. The other man, a good Samaritan, obliges. Then the man, more and more embarrassed, asks if he would continue his kindness and take out his penis. The other man does it, very embarrassed as well, but he does it. And naturally, caught in the spiral of this kindness, he finds himself obliged to hold the dick of the poor disabled man so that he doesn't sprinkle on his feet. The other man pisses heavily, with a relief that brings tears to his eyes. Once everything is finished, the man with the paralysed hands asks his benefactor if he wouldn't mind . . . could you possibly . . . shake it dry, please? And so it goes: shake it dry, put it back in place, close my fly. Once it's all packed up, the man warmly shakes the hands of his benefactor who, dumbfounded to see the hands that he had thought were paralysed functioning properly, asks what kept him from carrying out the business himself.

"Oh, nothing at all, but if you only knew how the whole thing disgusts me!"

33 years, 11 months, 4 days *Saturday, 14 September, 1957*

Ran into a guy on boulevard Saint-Michel. Impossible to remember his name. Impossible to put a name on that vaguely familiar face. Impossible to recall the reasons why it was familiar. Who is this man to whom, if I am to believe him, I was once very close under unforgettable circumstances? I told Fanche about our meeting and described the man, and she said: "Why, that's Roland! He was one of my wounded, at the same time as you, right before the end of the war, don't you remember?" She gave me loads of details: a dynamiter! He escaped an ambush with his guts hanging out – but still I couldn't piece him together. My amnesia empties him of his substance. He's nothing but the shape of a man in some lost spot of my memory. And, of course, his real name means no more to me than his Resistance alias. This happens to me quite often, and always has. Something in my brain isn't doing its work. Memory is the least reliable tool in my toolkit. (With the exception of Papa's aphorisms and the maxims he made me memorise, which are completely indelible.) "At least," Fanche says in the end, "if the Krauts had tortured you, *you* wouldn't have given anything away."

34 years, one month, 25 days *Thursday, 5 December, 1957*

My fellow-creatures, my brothers, are all busy picking their noses in their cars at the red lights – just like me. And all of them, if they sense they are being watched, stop what they are doing as if they had been caught red-handed in some dirty act. Such an odd sense of modesty! It's a very healthy occupation, nonetheless – it's even quite relaxing to pick your nose at a red light. The tip of the fingernail explores the nostril, finds the bogey, feels its edges, gently unsticks it, and manages to extract it. The thing is that it mustn't be gooey or it's a real problem to get rid of it. But when it has the soft, elastic consistency of pizza dough, it's such a pleasure to roll it endlessly between your thumb and index finger!

34 years, 1 month, 27 days *Saturday, 7 December, 1957*

What if the bogey were merely a *pretext*? A pretext to play with that cartilage toy, the tip of our nose? What was that driver thinking about? What was I thinking about before I noticed him? Nothing that I can remember. Some vague daydream while waiting for the light to turn green. That's what this cartilage is good for: helping us wait patiently for life to start up again. This hypothesis was confirmed this evening as I watched Bruno sitting quietly in the bathtub, busy twisting his foreskin around his index finger, with the same *lack of expression* on his face as the driver at the red light. Our foreskin, the tip of our nose, our earlobes are, strictly speaking, nothing more than transitional objects. They have no specific function, and so do not serve the symbolic purpose of a doll or a security blanket. They are content to keep our fingers busy when our minds are elsewhere. A discreet reminder of materiality for a wandering mind. This lock of hair I twirl as I read *Crime and Punishment* whispers to me that I am not Raskolnikov.

34 years, 4 months, 22 days *Tuesday, 4 March, 1958*

A dead pigeon on top of the sewer grate. I turn my eyes away, as if I could "catch something" just by looking at it. Sheer figment of visual contamination! There is something particularly infectious about the image of a dead bird. The foreshadowing of a pandemic. Hedgehogs, cats, or dogs crushed by cars, horse carrion, and even the corpses of men, don't have the same effect on me. As a child, fish were too alive in my hand, and this pigeon in the gutter is too dead.

I'm keeping an eye on the eggs as they cook to soft-boiled while Lison draws, her hand grasping a pencil stub. Once the drawing is finished, she shows it to me and I cry, oh! such a lovely drawing, without taking my eyes off the second hand of my watch. "It's a man screaming in his head," the artist tells me. And that's what it is: from the head of a worried man springs forth another, howling, man drawn with two ovals and a few lines that tell the whole story. Children's drawings are like soft-boiled eggs: a unique masterpiece each time, but so plentiful in this world that neither the taste buds nor the eye lingers over them. But if you isolate one of them – this Sunday breakfast egg or this man screaming in his head – you concentrate wholly on the flavour of the egg or the meaning of the drawing, and both of them then emerge as primal miracles. If every hen but one were to disappear, nations would fight to possess the last egg, for nothing in the world tastes better than a soft-boiled egg, and if there remained only one single drawing by a child, what wouldn't we read into it!

Lison is at the age when a child involves his or her entire body in the act of drawing. The whole arm draws: shoulder, elbow, and wrist. The total surface of the page is required. *The Man Screaming in his Head* unfurls on a double sheet ripped out of a notebook. The howling head springs forth from the worried (or sceptical?) head and takes up all the available space. The drawing is expanding and expansive. In a year, learning how to write will get the better of this massive scale. The line will impose its laws. Shoulder and elbow united, wrist immobile, the gesture will be reduced to the oscillation required by the minute loops of handwriting. Lison's drawings will suffer on account of this surrender, to which I myself owe my perfectly legible clerk's penmanship. Once she learns how to write, Lison will start to draw little things floating on the page, sketches that are as atrophied as the feet of long-ago Chinese princesses.

34 years, 6 months, 10 days *Sunday, 20 April, 1958*

Watching Lison draw, I relived the experience of learning how to write. My father brought back from his war a huge mass of watercolour sketches in which he had captured everything that had not been affected by heavy shelling: entire villages during the first months, then isolated houses, then bits of yards, clumps of flowers, a single flower, a petal, a leaf, a blade of grass, a portrait of the soldier's shrinking environment that said everything there was to say about war as total annihilator. Only images of peace. Not a single battlefield, not a single flag, corpse, boot, or gun. Nothing but the remnants of life, coloured crumbs, shards of happiness. He had notebooks-full. As soon as I was able to hold a pencil, I would amuse myself by outlining these sketches. Far from getting angry, Papa guided me: his hand on mine, he helped me give the most precise outline possible to the reality his paintbrush had sketched. From drawing, we moved on to writing. His hand still guiding mine, he made me outline letters after having me outline daisies. This is how I learned to write: going from petals to upstrokes and downstrokes. "Trace them carefully; they are the petals of words!" I never found those notebooks of watercolours that disappeared in my mother's great auto-da-fé, but sometimes I still sense my father's hand on mine in the childish pleasure I feel as I carefully shape my letters.

35 years, 1 month, 18 days *Friday, 28 November, 1958*

Manès was killed by a bull, crushed against the stable wall. When Ti-Joe told me the news, even before I felt grief, I felt the impact physically: his twisted ribs, his exploded ribcage, his burst lungs, his amazement, and, Manès being Manès until the very end, his final flash of fury. Ti-Joe's funeral elegy: "It was bound to end that way; he was always beating his animals."

35 years, 1 month, 22 days *Tuesday, 2 December, 1958*

I was struck hard, like Proust with his famous madeleine, after Manès' funeral (where Fanche, Robert, and I had to play an official role among the various members of the Resistance Party present). Once we were back on the farm, as Robert was uncorking the bottles, Marianne placed before me a slice of bread with grape preserve and a bowl of cold milk, claiming it was "snack time" and that I had to "recuperate". The bowl, the bread, the brotherly company of Robert and Ti-Joe, Marianne's expressions as she quoted Violette ("Right, my little fellow!") would have been enough to carry me back to those moments of my childhood, but the true voyage happened on the jellied bread itself, with that raspberry grape preserve concocted by Violette for my "afternoon snack". I dipped the bread in the cold milk, not really out of a desire to (I don't digest milk very well anymore), but to play the game of memory with Marianne. The scent of slightly mouldy raspberry, the gradations of red, mauve and blue on the white of the milk, the first cool, spongy mouthful, the crisp crust, the slightly granular velvet of the jam between the teeth and the palate – not really jelly, no longer really jam – the flow of memory through the instantaneous harmony of all these elements immediately gave me a true sense of *having been this mouthful* so much so that I still was! I finished my bread and milk, turning down the alcohol Robert was handing me ("Stop with that milk. Have a real drink."). Ti-Joe shouted, "It's true! Look how he loves his grape jelly! So you didn't just eat it to make Violette happy? You really liked it?" Of course, I answered. Didn't all of you? "No way!" And so a new light was shed on an entire gastronomic part of my childhood. Whereas I thought Manès and Violette had favoured me ("No one touch the grape jelly, it's for the little one, he needs to recuperate!"), in reality I was the one thanks to whom the stock of detested preserves was disposed of. And whenever it happened that I would offer some to one of them, their terrified refusal ("No thank you. If Manès were to find out . . .") was nothing but the expression of cowardly relief. Today they all admitted that they hated Violette's grape preserve with its "smell of vomit" and its "aftertaste of dust". "No doubt about it," said Robert.

"If the Krauts had made us eat it, we would have told them everything!"

But didn't Violette like it? I asked.

Who knows. One day, I went into the kitchen by chance the first time she was trying out the recipe ("Open wide and taste this!") and I had shown such rapture – and then such faithfulness in this rapture – that she had never dared stop making it.

35 years, 1 month, 23 days *Wednesday, 3 December, 1958*

A history of taste could never be divorced from a treatise on the power of association.

35 years, 1 month, 24 days *Thursday, 4 December, 1958*

While we were still at Manès' funeral, Fanche said to me: "You, my petard, could disguise yourself as an Apache, a Pygmy, a Chinese man, or a Martian, but I would still recognise you by your smile." And then we wondered about those emanations from a body that are one's shape, one's way of walking, voice, smile, handwriting, gestures and gesticulations, the only traces left in our memories by those whom we truly looked at. Fanche said about her brother, who had been blown to bits in his fighter plane: "Lips, mouth, yes, they can be blown to pieces, but one's smile, no, that's impossible." She also remembers her mother from her minuscule handwriting and speaks very emotionally about the perfectly formed loops of her cursive "r"s and "v"s.

What remains in my mind of my own mother is the image of a gaze that demands a settling of accounts: "Did you deserve your life?" Two exophthalmic eyes and a shrill voice. She thought her eyes were piercing; they were merely bulging; her voice she believed to be natural; it was simply strident. The memory of those eyes and of that voice reminds me less of a person than of an attitude: the nasty, obtuse authority that she employed to "do good" by studding her kindness with petty moral precepts as foul-smelling as farts from the soul. Yet she was a good-looking woman, with blonde curls, a luminous gaze, a dazzling smile:

all the photographs attest to this. I said to Fanche: "Don't trust my smile. It's my mother's."

*

35 years, 1 month, 25 days *Friday, 5 December, 1958*

My mother's body was never found. It probably disappeared under the rubble of the tunnel on boulevard National on 27 May, 1944. She had gone into the city to collect her rents. The Allies bombed that afternoon. The sirens screeched, and the whole population moved towards Saint-Charles station, which was very close to her apartment building. We think she must have taken refuge in the tunnel with the others. Unfortunately, the Allies were aiming at the station and the tunnel collapsed under the shelling. So many people died or disappeared. Ironically, the apartment building was the only one in the area left standing. Two months later, a letter from Uncle Georges told me that Maman had disappeared. And that I had inherited that apartment building.

35 years, 6 months, 22 days *Saturday, 2 May, 1959*

I glance at Lison, who is totally motionless, but surprisingly animated from the inside. She smiles at me and, still without moving, says: "My body isn't dancing, but my heart is." Oh, my Lison! Happiness for no reason except the happiness of being alive. I still experience this happiness from time to time as well, an inner jubilation that makes my heart dance on certain days when I force my body to be still. For example, at our wrap-up meetings when Bertholieu, with his ancient pince-nez half hidden by his enormous eyebrows talks to us about "diffraction" and "lines of convergence, gentlemen." Dance, my heart, dance!

36 years, 4 months, 11 days *Sunday, 21 February, 1960*

A rainy day yesterday. Bruno played Cowboys and Indians with the little figurines Uncle Georges gave him for his birthday. A whole hour of attacks and counter-attacks, offensives, strategic withdrawals, peace pipes, broken ceasefires, stunning breakthroughs, attacks from the rear that always end in bloody defeat for the cowboys, every single one of them slaughtered. An hour of extreme agitation in an almost motionless body. The adult in me watches him play with the amazement of an ethnologist: was I like this when I was eight? What sensations would I feel if today I were to start playing Cowboys and Indians for an hour or two?

I tested this in the afternoon. While Mona took the children to the small zoo ("No, Papa's not coming with us, he has work to do"), I sat cross-legged on the floor. I had barely set my troops up for battle when, by means of a cramp, my body manifested the feeling of wasting precious time. I am too big to play with toy soldiers. Too bulky to encase myself in an imaginary box. And during this time, at the zoo, the children were enchanted by the hall of mirrors. "I was, too," said Mona when she came home. "As if I were a little girl again!"

36 years, 7 months, 3 days *Friday, 13 May, 1960*

When Ti-Joe says he is going to pee, invariably the same words come out of his mouth: "Okay, I'm going to wash my hands at the base of a tree." Today after lunch, a strange impulse made me take his words literally. I passed my hands through my own stream. As far as I know, I'd never done this before, even as a child. I was surprised by the warmth of my urine. Almost a sense of actual burning. We are like alcohol stills, perpetually boiling. With no more consistency than jellyfish, we propel ourselves by pissing hot liquid. Food for thought: what got into me to do this experiment today, at the age of thirty-six, after having negotiated a very big contract with our German suppliers?

36 years, 10 months, 1 day *Thursday, 11 August, 1960*

At Mérac, which Ti-Joe, Robert and Marianne sold to us (thanks to which Robert could finally buy his garage), the water-heater and shower finally breathed their last. So I now can give the children the joys of a quick wash like in the olden days, in the big zinc tub in which Violette used to scrub me thirty years ago (it was waiting patiently for the next generation in the shade of the laundry room). I go at it the way she did, with a watering can, a bar of soap, and a washcloth, hunting down rolls of flesh, folds, all the nooks and crannies where filth likes to hide, and where sweat irritates the skin with prickly heat. Lison and Bruno stamp their feet, howl, protest that "it's wet" or "it's cold" or "it stings" as I must have done at their age, but I continue, showing no mercy at their shortness of breath and their chattering teeth, because it is not my childish suffering to which I relate here, but to Violette's gestures, the pitiless precision of her hunt for grime behind my ears, in my bellybutton, between my toes, with cold water and not a whit of worry if this soaping-down stung my eyes or irritated my nostrils; at first I would protest, but soon I would be thrilled to spin around beneath her efficient hands, pretending to run away after being rinsed off, and enjoying the slap-slap of the wet soles of my feet on the laundry room's cement floor, screaming at being followed by a big ghost of a sheet, and caught, and rubbed dry then rubbed down with camphor, then sprinkled with talcum powder if my bottom was red enough to necessitate it – and I am making my offspring endure all of this, and they don't seem too happy about it, I must admit. Lison is saying, hurry, hurry, hurry, sucking in air through her tightly closed lips, while Bruno has officially called for the water heater to be repaired, and I am wiping them down with flannel and soap, each time amazed by the density of these tiny bodies, as if I were manipulating raw energy, all the energy of their two existences yet to come amassed in this compact child's flesh beneath such soft, smooth skin. They will never have this density again; their features will never be as sharp, the whites of their eyes never so white or their ears so perfectly drawn, and the grain of their skin will never be so tightly woven. Human beings are born in hyperrealist style, only to distend over time, ending up in a very vague pointillism before being scattered in the dust of abstraction.

36 years, 10 months, 2 days *Friday, 12 August, 1960*

As a child, I had no *consistency.*

36 years, 11 months, 7 days *Saturday, 17 September, 1960*

Yesterday at dinner, old General M. L., who had been wounded at Verdun, commented about the testicle he had lost: "It's the only thing I left in the Douaumont ossuary." Nevertheless, he fathered one of those large families for which military men seem to have a knack. "If it hadn't been for the war," he said mathematically, "I would have had twice as many children!" His wife did not react.

36 years, 11 months, 21 days *Saturday, 1 October, 1960*

In the park, Bruno and a little boy his age are obeying the laws of that time-honoured ritual: they are comparing biceps. Two little arms bent at right angles, two clenched fists, two biceps straining, two faces theatrically tensed with effort. We spend our lives comparing our bodies. But once we are no longer children, we do it furtively, almost shamefully. When I was fifteen, on the beach, I assessed the biceps and abdominal muscles of the boys my age. At eighteen or twenty, I evaluated that swelling under the bathing trunks. At thirty or forty, men compare their hair (to the distress of the bald). At fifty, their waistlines (don't get a pot belly), at sixty, their teeth (don't lose any). And now, in those meetings of old crocodiles who are our regulatory authorities, it's the back, the walk, the way of wiping one's mouth, of getting up, putting on one's coat, in sum: age, simply age. So and so looks much older than I do, don't you think?

5

37–49 YEARS OLD

(1960–1972)

It is out of the question that I become a specialist in the field of my own illnesses.

37 years, birthday *Monday, 10 October, 1960*

During an exceptionally soporific meeting about distribution problems, I gave in to the temptation of verifying if yawning is contagious. I pretended to yawn, in a remarkable splitting of my face, followed by a quick "Excuse me", and my yawn spread to about two-thirds of the participants, until it came back to me, causing me to *really* yawn!

37 years, 3 days *Thursday, 13 October, 1960*

Bruno, for his part, noticed that yawning makes him deaf. When his teacher bores him, he yawns, not so as to demonstrate that he is bored, but so as not to hear his teacher. He says that when his jaws open wide, his ears buzz as if a strong wind were blowing through them. "So I listen to the wind." He adds that sneezing, on the other hand, makes him blind. He observed that his eyes close the second his nostrils explode. He claims he cannot yawn and sneeze at the same time. Blind and deaf, but each in turn. This is exactly the kind of observation I could have written down at his age if I had taken pleasure in my body rather than feeling the need to dominate it.

37 years, 4 days *Friday, 14 October, 1960*

I learned something from the yawning experiment at the offices of G.L.R. This time around, I yawned, but at the same time I pretended to *conceal* my yawn. I yawned without opening my mouth, jaws clenched, lips pulled taut. And I saw how this yawn, just like yesterday's, spread around the room, along with the attempt to conceal it. In certain circumstances, then, learned behaviour can spread just as naturally as reflex behaviour. (And by the way, the quick crackling in my ears when I yawn is like the sound of silver foil around a chocolate bar.)

37 years, 7 days *Monday, 17 October, 1960*

When I told Ti-Joe about my experiments with the spreading of yawns, he told me that, in regard to contagion through mimicry, he has been interested for some time in what he calls "variations in opinions of complicity." Two hours later, he demonstrated what he meant in the restaurant where we were having lunch with three of the partners from Z. Addressing everyone at the table, Ti-Joe declared: "Yesterday, my wife (he is obviously not married) took me to see the latest Bergman. It's really . . ." and then, rather than finishing his sentence, he stopped speaking and on his face appeared a look of disapproval, almost one of disgust (nostrils pinched, lips pursed, eyebrows knitted, face squinched, etc.), an expression that immediately began to appear on the faces of our three companions. Once it was clearly formed on all their faces, Ti-Joe finished his sentence, exclaiming with a broad smile: "It's really . . . *brilliant*, don't you think?" This manifestation of enthusiasm instantly and drastically changed the topography of the faces. They suddenly opened up, smiling, illuminated by expressions of complete and utter approbation.

37 years, 13 days *Sunday, 23 October, 1960*

The first thing that can be read on our faces when we are in the company of others is the desire to belong to the group, the irrepressible need to *be part of it*. Of course, this may be attributed to upbringing, to a follow-the-leader attitude, to weakness of character (that's what Ti-Joe is tempted to think); but I see in it an archaic reaction to ontological loneliness, a reflexive movement of the one body to incorporate itself within the common body, instinctively refusing solitude and exile, even for the time of a superficial conversation. When I observe us, no matter how many we are, in public places where we converse – meeting rooms, parks, restaurants, hallways, subways, lifts – it is the ability to say "yes" with our bodies that strikes me. It turns us into a flock of birds mechanically nodding "yes, yes", like pigeons walking side by side. Unlike what Ti-Joe believes, this superficial joining of the group does not damage our inner dignity at all. Some critical thinking will follow; it may even be at work almost immediately. But first, we instinctively sacrifice ourselves for the sake of the cohesion of the group before going on to kill each other. In any case, this is what we make our bodies say.

37 years, 6 months, 2 days *Wednesday, 12 April, 1961*

Looking down on an impeccable turd, all in one piece, perfectly smooth and formed, dense without being sticky, with a smell but not a stench, cleanly severed and of a uniform brown, produced with a single push causing a smooth exit, and leaving no trace on the toilet paper, I have the sense of a satisfied craftsman: my body did its job well.

38 years, 7 months, 22 days *Friday, 1 June, 1962*

Lison is in tears. Her brother swore at her. Lison is particularly sensitive to insults. Words have real meaning for her. It turned out that Bruno had said: "Go shit yourself." I scolded Bruno and asked him where such a totally physical insult had come from. "From José." "Which José?" A friend from school. A little pied-noir fresh off the boat from Algeria with his tragedy, his family, his accent, and his vocabulary. I bet it won't be ten years before this vocabulary will completely revamp our catalogue of insults. "Go shit yourself" has an entirely different dimension from that of "arsehole" or "bugger off". The imperative of the verb "to shit" combined with a reflexive pronoun is a lethal weapon. What could be worse than reducing one's adversary to being nothing more than his own shit and whom one commands to defecate on himself?

38 years, 8 months, 7 days *Sunday, 17 June, 1962*

Another ultra-physical insult of José's, who came to play at our house: "May your bones die!"

39 years, 3 months, 4 days *Monday, 14 January, 1963*

A sleepless night caused by anxiety. I woke with a lump in my throat, a heavy chest, and throbbing nerves. Got out of bed early and went to work on foot, making an enormous detour to get there: République, grands boulevards, Opéra, Concorde, Tuileries, Louvre, Pont des Arts . . . At first my footsteps were purely mechanical, my body weight falling on each foot, from one exertion to the next: Frankenstein's monster out on a ramble, short of breath with staring eyes, until little by little *it* dissolved, my jaws and fists unclenched, my limbs became softer, my gait more limber, my lungs filled with air, my mind separated from my body, and I put on the suit of my social self. Then the citizen and "boss" made his legendary, galvanising entrance at the office: "Good morning, everyone, how's it going?"

40 years, 7 months, 13 days *Saturday, 23 May, 1964*

I went with the children to the Luxembourg Gardens this afternoon. Out of the corner of my eye, I saw a woman on the tennis court sniff her underarm. She was on her way to the changing room, her racquet under one arm, and zip! she made that quick little pigeon gesture to check out what it smells like under her wing. And, in one of those miraculous moments of empathy that make us all members of the same species, I knew exactly what she felt: the charm of a familiar smell that is instantly decoded as an odour to be fought off. One can take pleasure in one's sudations, yes, but in their smell? No! Ten to one as soon as she crossed the threshold of the changing room, she went to slather her underarm with any old deodorant, a deodorant that made her smell like anyone else.

In secret we revel in the fumes we hide from other people. This duplicitous game is also true of our thoughts and this duplicity is the most important thing in our lives. When we get home, my tennis player and I, we will both, in our separate beds, enjoy one of those long farts that ages ago we learned how to make waft up to our nostrils with our sheets.

40 years, 7 months, 14 days *Sunday, 24 May, 1964*

I literally devoured Mona with my nostrils and my tongue last night. I plunged my nose in her armpit, between her breasts, thighs and buttocks, inhaled deeply, licked, became sated with her taste, with her smell, just like when we were young.

41 years, 2 months, 10 days *Sunday, 20 December, 1964*

In the restaurant where the children and I were celebrating Mona's birthday, Bruno asked us to explain an enigmatic sentence that he'd read in the restroom: "Please do not throw sanitary napkins in the toilet." Two questions tormented him: 1) Aren't napkins sanitary by nature? And 2) Who would be crazy enough to throw a napkin in the toilet? A shadow of a smile crossed Lison's lips. "What!?" shouted Bruno. Like a coward, I left it to Mona to explain both the sentence and the smile.

41 years, 7 months, 25 days *Friday, 4 June, 1965*

Testicles can contract out of fear for others; I had already noticed this in Etretat: Mona had made me dizzy when she drew too close to the edge of the cliffs. My balls reminded me of their capacity for empathy again this morning when I was witness to a bicyclist being hit by a taxi. The cyclist had run a red light; there was no way the driver could have avoided him. Crash! He flew through the air and fell flat on his face: broken leg, two or three ribs crushed by the kerb, his scalp gashed, his cheek scraped, and my balls contracting as he hit the ground. It could only have been an empathetic fear because, after all, the poor guy did not fall on me. I concluded that balls are altruistic, capable of fearing for the life of another. Testicles: seat of the soul?

41 years, 7 months, 26 days *Saturday, 5 June, 1965*

I thought again last night about my flying cyclist. While I was turning him on his side and sponging off his blood as we waited for the ambulance to arrive, he asked me several times if his watch had broken.

42 years, 3 months, 19 days *Saturday, 29 January, 1966*

Dined at Chevrier's, who returned to headquarters after two years in Peru *ad majorem buxidae gloriam*. He brought back an impressive collection of small, rectangular ex-votos, no bigger than a thumb, engraved with hands, hearts, eyes, lungs, breasts, backs, arms, legs, intestines, stomachs, livers, kidneys, teeth, feet, noses, ears, and the rounded bellies of pregnant women. Ex-votos without prayers, just the organ that needed healing engraved on a metal plate, heavy or light, precious or less precious. Not a single genital, male or female. The majority, Chevrier told me, were of hearts, eyes, and hands. When asked if I believed in them, I said no. But this didn't stop me from taking a pair of eyes without thinking twice when he said I could choose one.

42 years, 3 months, 20 days *Sunday, 30 January, 1966*

When it comes down to it, I said to myself in the dark during a short bout of insomnia, I would rather be blind than deaf. Not being able to hear . . . is that like spending one's life in an aquarium, watching everyone else live their lives? No, better not to see them and continue in darkness to hear them speak, move, blow their noses, etc. To hear Mona breathing, the house creaking, the clock in my library ticking, to listen to silence itself. And with that thought, I fell back to sleep and had the following dream: I am lying on an operating table. Parmentier is leaning over me, wearing a surgeon's white coat, a white cap, and a mask that prevents me from seeing him smile. His assistant secures my eyes with a complicated piece of equipment that keeps my eyelids open. Meanwhile, Parmentier lights a Bunsen burner on which he begins heating up a small brass receptacle. I realise that this is some sort of initiation rite, or rather, an ordeal: Management wants to know if I am worthy of becoming one of the "top brass"; Parmentier must therefore pour boiling oil from the brass receptacle into my eyes and *I must not lose my sight at any cost.* Fortunately, I have the ex-voto that Chevrier gave me in my house. I look for it, blind, groping my way, completely terrified, bumping into the furniture. I look for it but I cannot find it. I wake up with a start and immediately change my mind: better deaf than blind!

42 years, 4 months *Thursday, 10 February, 1966*

So, no cunts or phalluses on the walls of South American churches. My highly scornful secularism gets a good laugh out of this. Yet there is no phallus, either, on the *Larousse* cut-out man that I've religiously held onto since childhood, or in the very secular science book we had in eighth grade and that was supposed to deal with human physiology. I have forgotten the name of the author (Dehousseaux? Dehoussières?), but not my fury when I discovered that *every* human system was described – circulatory, nervous, respiratory, digestive – except the reproductive system!

43 years, birthday *Monday, 10 October, 1966*

I dreamed last night about an obelisk that was rising so slowly that I was the only one who could perceive its movement. To tell the truth, I couldn't really perceive it, but I was certain the erection was taking place. The obelisk was lying down, pointing east, and it began to stand millimetre by millimetre, *millennially*. I stared at it, fascinated by my confidence that one day, even if it took my entire lifetime, I would see it oscillate on its base, remain still at last, and point to the sky like the hands of a clock pointing to noon. Don't wake up, do *not* wake up before it is standing. I had decided to sleep until it was perfectly vertical. Its rise was so slow that the night promised to be the longest of my entire life, and I thrilled to this slowness, never letting my eyes leave the obelisk, and that night was my life itself, and my life was the patience totally devoted to watching the obelisk rise up. And indeed, I awoke at the precise second when, after a wavering hesitation, the obelisk at last stood straight up on its base. I immediately recalled the words Ti-Joe had uttered during my birthday dinner: "You are forty-three years old, and forty-three is your shoe size! This will be a steady, stable year for you! Your feet will stand on solid ground!"

43 years, 2 months, 20 days *Friday, 30 December, 1966*

For the past two weeks, the second toe of my right foot has been adorned with a kind of cyst I've never seen before. Is it the beginning of a corn, a wart, a callus or a bunion? Whatever it is, it is painful to the touch and, for the first time in my life, I have to choose my shoes accordingly. We never know the precise word for the pains we suffer. We have only generic words at our disposal: "pimple", "rheumatism", "heartburn", "corn".

43 years, 2 months, 25 days *Wednesday, 4 January, 1967*

I learned that it is indeed a corn. So this is what is called a "corn". I seem to remember having corns when I was in the Resistance: too-narrow shoes.

43 years, 3 months, 5 days *Sunday, 15 January, 1967*

A father's body. A friend of Bruno's was staying with us last weekend, and Bruno told him that he had never seen me come to breakfast in my pyjamas. "Papa is always impeccable: shaved, combed and wearing a tie as soon as the sun comes up." These indiscreet remarks, though slightly ironic, annoyed me, and I told my son, with as much seriousness as I could muster, that Mona and I had in fact just decided to spend our next family holiday in a nudist colony. "Didn't I tell you?" The effect of this little joke was immense: Bruno turned bright red, put down his toast and walked out of the kitchen with an expression of biblical shame. His friend followed. It was like Shem and Japheth walking backwards to cover their father's nakedness. There is always too much of the body or not enough. Ever since Noah's time, it's been the same story.

43 years, 5 months, 19 days *Wednesday, 29 March, 1967*

My precious polyps. I expelled one this morning when I sneezed. It had been blocking my left nostril since my last cold, for over three months. Leaning over my handkerchief, I sneezed as hard as I could. Not one of those open-mouthed sneezes that empty your lungs and fill the house with a joyful explosion, but a purely nasal sneeze, mouth closed and all the air pressure concentrated in the nostril that needed to be unblocked. Usually, nothing can unblock a nostril in which a strong-minded, fully-formed polyp is thriving. The air comes up against the obstacle, flows back in, and seals your ears hermetically. It's as if your brain were swelling, bouncing against the insides of your skull until it settles back to its original shape. And you find yourself completely dazed. I sneezed *nevertheless.* (When it comes to sneezes, past experience never wins out over hope.) I sneezed with premeditation. I closed my mouth and eyes and blocked my other nostril. I allowed my longing to tickle my mucous membrane, climb up through my nose, fill my lungs; I spread my handkerchief as much as possible to prevent whatever was discharged from scattering, and I sneezed with all my might through the left nostril (with the well-known energy of despair). And miracle of miracles, my nostril unblocked! I felt a soft impact in the hollow of my hand, a long column of misty air rushed out and, wonder of wonders, the route was clear as I inhaled as well! For the first time in weeks, the air is circulating freely in my nostril. I opened my eyes on the handkerchief spotted with red in the centre of which was sitting what I at first thought was a big blood clot. But when I touched it, it turned out to be fleshy. I did not faint. I did not tell myself that I had just lost a part of my brain. I rinsed the thing in water, and it revealed itself to be comparable to a scallop: soft and dense, with a pinkish blush, slightly translucent and discreetly fibrous; 21 millimetres long, 17 wide, and 9 high. So there you are, old polyp! Unbelievable that such a monster could have been lodged in my nostril! The good doctor Bêk (how old must he be now?), to whom I went to show it, literally jumped for joy. Spontaneous expulsion of a polyp? Why, that is extremely rare! I've never seen anything like it! He kept it to analyse it and didn't charge me for the consultation. He was as happy as if I had offered him a giant pearl.

43 years, 8 months, 24 days *Tuesday, 4 July, 1967*

I've been pushing myself too hard recently: boozy dinners, late to bed and early to rise, relentless work, writing two articles and a lecture, dealing with family, friends, colleagues, clients, the Ministry, attentive to every moment, reacting immediately to everything, authority, affability, conviviality, efficiency, self-control for a week or ten days, in an excess of energy-guzzling in which my body has had to follow, uncomplainingly, the flag waved by my mind on an endless Arcola Bridge.

This morning, not a trace of energy remained. I realised it as soon as I opened my eyes. No impulse to do anything. After "pushing myself too hard", I am now tempted to "pull back". Everything today required willpower; everything demanded a decision. Not those decisions that follow one another naturally during ordinary days, but one decision per action, each action needing its own decision, each decision its own effort, with no dynamic link to the preceding one, as if I were no longer fuelled by personal and continuous energy but rather by some generator outside the house that has to be started – with a crank! – every time there is a new decision to make.

The most exhausting thing is the mental exertion it takes to hide this fatigue from everyone around me. I need to be as affectionate as ever with the family (who have become strangers because of this exertion), just as professional with everyone else (who have become unduly familiar to me). In other words, I have to work at my reputation for equanimity, watch over the equilibrium of my statue. If I don't rest, if I don't give my body its proper dose of sleep, the generator itself will break down and I will lose my grip. Every day the world will weigh more heavily on me, and then anxiety will worm its way into my fatigue and it will no longer be the world that seems too heavy for me, but myself in the world, an impotent, vain, lying self: that's what my anxiety will whisper in the ear of my exhausted consciousness. And then I'll yield to one of those fits of anger that will leave my children with the memory of a father who had dangerous mood swings.

43 years, 8 months, 26 days *Thursday, 6 July, 1967*

As expected: anxiety attack. Anxiety is different from sadness, concern, melancholy, worry, fear, or anger in that it has no identifiable cause. A sheer state of nervousness with immediate physical consequences: difficulty breathing, jitters, clumsiness (I broke a bowl at breakfast), bursts of fury at whomever I come across, repressed swearwords that poison the blood, lack of desire, and thoughts as difficult to come by as breath. I cannot concentrate on a thing, I am totally befuddled with half-made gestures, half-formed sentences, half-formed thoughts, nothing carried through or out, everything bounces back in, anxiety is constantly referred back to the heart of anxiety. It's no one's fault, or else it's everyone's fault, which comes down to the same thing. I am stamping my feet on the inside, angry at the whole world because I am only me. Anxiety is an ontological illness. What's the matter with you? Nothing! Everything! I am alone like the rest of humanity!

*

Woke up bloody. The hollow left by my head in the pillow is full of dark blood about to coagulate – so much of it that the kapok couldn't absorb it all. I must have had a bloody nose while I was sleeping. I get up quietly so as not to wake Mona. I filch the pillow and toss it into the dustbin. The sheets are not stained. In the bathroom, confirmation: my cheek is black and sticky with dry, crackled blood. My left nostril is filled with blood clots. I wash my face quickly, blow my nose, then shower, and that's it. Two hours later in the board of directors meeting, another nosebleed, still from the left nostril. The blood flows almost continuously and my shirt is spattered. I begin my presentation again, with my nostril stuffed with cotton wool, and then haemostatic gauze, which Sabine went to get at the local pharmacy. She also bought me a clean shirt. At 2.00 in the afternoon, it started up again, this time in the middle of negotiations with the Rs, at V.'s, while we were having coffee. A veritable waterfall! Practically splashed my neighbours! Another haemostatic pack, another new shirt, this time graciously presented to me by the maître d'hôtel. (That's what I call service!) Back in the office, a fourth nosebleed at 6.00. Visit to the ENT emergency room in the Necker-Enfants Malades Hospital, which Etienne swears has the best doctors in Paris. A houseman with transparent eyes *packs* me. This involves stuffing a frightful quantity of material in your nostril until all your sinuses – protesting with every ounce of their energy – are plugged. It's unimaginable just how hollow a skull is! A thin bony crust around countless caverns, galleries, fossae, anfractuosities, the one more innervated than the next! The ordeal was so long and painful that I had to keep myself from punching the houseman in the face. They could warn you, for God's sake! I have tears in my eyes. "There now, finished," he says. But, just when I am getting into bed, another nosebleed: the compressed gauze was gorged with blood, which also flowed into my throat. Back to the hospital. Another doctor. "Who did this packing job?" I dodge the question, but specify that because the nosebleeds occurred every four hours, this one came right on time. Was his colleague aware of this regularity? I don't recall having mentioned it to him. "That's annoying; we will need to repack you and keep you overnight for observation." The prospect of this second packing does not enchant me, but when it comes to pain I prefer apprehension to surprise. My curiosity makes it more bearable, that is, as bearable as a ball of needles that is crammed into your nostril the same way gunners of old used to stuff their cannons. I had a fleeting vision of Pierre Bezukhov wandering among the Russian artillerymen at the Battle of Borodino. And a vision of an Orwellian rat busy digging a tunnel in the nose of a torture victim to reach his brain. Basically, controlling pain is accepting reality for what it is: rich in vivid metaphors. How long can metaphors be diverting? That is the question. Doctors should have to warn their patients: "Ladies and gentleman, a packing is equal to three minutes and forty-eight seconds of a pain so intense that you will want to climb the walls, but not a second longer; I can manage it in three minutes and fifteen seconds, stopwatch in hand. Fasten your seatbelts!" And the doctor would start counting backwards, like astronauts announcing the blast-off: "No more than twelve seconds . . . five, four, three, two, one . . . There, finished. We'll just keep you overnight."

Mona brought me my pyjamas, my toiletries, and some things to read. All the adult beds were occupied, so I am sharing a room with child patients (one with an ear infection, one who was bitten by a dog) who are making it completely impossible for me to read. The old man with a tumescent conk is an amazing source of amusement. So, adults can fall ill too? So ill that they need to share a room with children in a hospital! In answer to their questions, I give them a problem about the leaky taps in my skull to solve. Knowing that these taps produce 20 centilitres of blood every four hours, calculate the total quantity that has dripped in twenty-four hours. In addition, given the fact that the adult human body contains on average five litres of blood, how long will it take for the patient to empty himself of all his blood, down to the last drop? Go on, get to work! I don't want to hear a pin drop. As I had hoped, they fell asleep while trying to figure this out; I can begin reading again. And I come across a confession of Thomas Hobbes that fits me like a glove, in which he says that fear has been the single greatest passion of his life.

After one last packing, the morning intern sends me home, and he is as optimistic as if he were setting me up in a brand-new life. I had barely stepped through the door, however, when a syrupy discharge left an unmistakable metallic taste in my mouth and throat. Four hours later, I was back in the emergency room for a fourth packing. (Who says we get used to pain?) And this time, the houseman is sceptical: "I am doing this just to be sure, monsieur, but you are not bleeding." Doctor, I am bleeding *inside* every four hours. "Monsieur, it's only an *impression*, you are having an epistaxis, like the majority of children; you're a bit behind for your age, but it's no more serious than that; the packing stopped the haemorrhaging, you are not bleeding anymore."

Home again. Where the bloody "impression" continues as before, with the same regularity. Etienne sends me to see one of his friends in an emergency clinic. In between two nosebleeds that emptied me out completely, the friend confirms the specialist's diagnosis: "You are not bleeding; it really is just an impression, probably caused by your own panic; don't worry, sleep, it will pass." I am not worrying, I am etiolating. I am etiolating and Mona is becoming alarmed. She decides to pull out the packing to check for herself. She wants to calculate the quantity of blood lost. Another haemorrhage: I fill up a soup tureen. Again from the left nostril. Four hours later, another bowlful. We go back to the hospital and shove these bowls in the doctor's face and ask him if these are *impressions*. Which is pointless, because it isn't the same doctor as before. And yet another packing under the pretext that the previous one must have been done incorrectly. "It's a bit trickier than it seems, monsieur, but don't worry, epistaxis is a completely benign ailment."

Monday morning my body goes back to work in its impeccable boss's suit. Every four hours I isolate myself to bleed in peace, like you do to urinate. I lose my strength along with my blood. And as my strength ebbs, so does my morale. An irrepressible sadness follows each haemorrhage. It's as if melancholy were filling the empty space left by the lost blood. I feel as if death were stealing over me. Slowly but surely, death is replacing life. I would have very much liked to spend another ten years or so with Mona, to see Bruno grow up, to console Lison the first times her heart is broken. My dying melancholy focuses on this: Lison's love life. I don't want her to suffer. I don't want some bastard to take advantage of her slightly clumsy gracefulness, her feverish way of looking at the world, her stubborn search for a truth in happiness. At the same time as I am overcome by this anguish, a sort of peace descends on me, I let go, I drift in the current, carried along by my own blood. Death, I say to myself, death is a peaceful falling asleep . . .

The next day, I no longer have the strength to go to the office. Mona tells Ti-Joe, who immediately takes me to the Saint-Louis hospital where he knows a male nurse who is in cahoots with a bigwig ENT facial surgeon who, astonished by the amount of blood I have lost over the last two days, declares that the diagnosis was wrong – it is indeed an epistaxis, but a *posterior* epistaxis demanding emergency surgery under general anaesthesia. Mona's hand leaves mine at the door to the operating room.

When I wake up, my head is a pumpkin riddled with arrows. I am terribly on edge. My body, apparently immobile, cannot keep still. I am ceaselessly wriggling about inside myself, as if I were inhabited by someone else who, according to Mona, has been raving deliriously. This feeling of being possessed is a common reaction to morphine, my nurse explains to me and I ask her to stop the morphine. "Impossible, monsieur, you will be in too much pain!" If that's the case, we'll start it up again. Once the morphine is eliminated, the pain escalates and as it does, each one of my nerves follows it with the greatest interest. I am

Saint Sebastian and the archers are aiming solely at my face. They are shooting me between the eyes. When their quiver is empty, the torture turns out to be bearable as long as I remain immobile. Given my low haemoglobin level, the surgeon wants to keep me here for about ten days, to get me back in shape so I won't have to have a transfusion. He asks me to forgive the Academy of Medicine for this mistaken diagnosis. What can you do? A posterior epistaxis is very rare and medicine is not always an exact science. As far as any diagnosis is concerned, he adds, you always have to leave room for some doubt, like for dessert at the end of a meal. Sadly, young housemen only learn this on the job, as they go.

43 years, 9 months, 8 days *Tuesday, 18 July, 1967*

Had to stay ten days in the hospital, half of which I spent sleeping and the other half writing the above. At first, the huge gauze moustaches that went through the inside of my nose and came out of my nostrils made me look like an old-time Turk. Now I am being pumped full of iron. I read, I wander listlessly down the hallways, I learn the names of the doctors and nurses, I rediscover the pace and customs of boarding school, I renew my ties with cafeteria "gastronomy", I let myself go, and I rest, freed from all impatience. The only drawback that adds despair to my illness is the ugly stripes on my pyjamas. (Mona says the shop didn't have any other sort.)

My roommate is a young fireman who was clubbed by the police during the protests earlier this month. He was attempting to intervene between the police and the protesters. Since he was not in uniform, policemen broke some of his teeth, dislocated his jaw, fractured his nasal septum, smashed one of his eye sockets, and broke a few ribs, a hand, and an ankle. He cries. He is so afraid. He cries out of terror. I am unable to calm him down. The quacking voice that comes out from below my bandages works against the wisdom of my comforting remarks. His parents and his fiancée, a young woman drowning in her tears, are not of much help either. It's his friends from his brigade who bring him back to life. Every evening, about half a dozen firemen turn up in our room, dressed as Breton, Alsatian, Savoyard, Provençal or Algerian women, in a kind of folkloric happening enjoyed by all the nurses on our floor. There are bagpipes, fifes, tambourines, ululations, local dances, butter cookies, couscous and sauerkraut dishes, Kronenberg beer, mint tea, and white wine from the Savoie region. Everyone has such a good time that at first we fear it will all be too much for our little fireman (his jaws and his ribs make it torture for him to laugh), but he ends up being revivified by it all.

43 years, 9 months, 17 days *Thursday, 27 July, 1967*

Home from the hospital. Celebrated in bed with Mona. But my haemoglobin count is 9.8 instead of 13. I was afraid my red corpuscles were not repaired sufficiently to irrigate my erectile tissue. But that was without taking into consideration Mona's tropical hospitality. I had a magnificent erection! We even beat our own endurance record.

I get hard but something else occurs at the end: a flood of tears by way of an orgasm! Irrepressible sobs punctuated with apologies that intensify my sobs. The same thing happens at work, where I have to leave in the middle of a meeting to go and cry my heart out in my office. Grief with no reason, a pure pain of being, washes over me in unexpected waves that are as destructive as the breaking of a flood barrier. This post-operative depression is apparently totally normal: the liquefaction of my soul after the emptying-out of my blood. What's the solution? "Rest, monsieur, lots of rest, you've been through the mill, you need time to recover. Eat calf's liver, monsieur, a lot of calf's liver rich in iron, and horsemeat and blood sausage, and rest. Don't eat too much spinach, it is overrated, there's no iron in it, avoid strong emotions, practise some sport instead, set your body back on the road of life!"

So here I am at Mérac, where my tears begin to dry up. Long hikes overcome my last, despondent weeping. Lying together in the grass, Mona and I offer ourselves the sunsets we knew before we had children. Then gardening, all the kids (Marianne's children and our teenagers), fricasséed meadow mushrooms, music, the list of small joys that fuel our survival instinct is endless.

43 years, 10 months, 1 day *Friday, 11 August, 1967*

My clothes make me itch furiously around the waist. Insect bites? Invisible chiggers, sly spiders, silent gadflies, ticks waiting in ambush – would they have taken advantage of our splendour in the grass? I check: no tick bite, but rather a band of tiny spots with translucent heads. They begin at the right side of my groin and run along my back to the level of my right kidney. Diagnosis: shingles. In other words, a varicella virus that was playing Sleeping Beauty in my body and that depression reactivated as a nervous inflammation. Apparently it's not unusual. It cannot be cured. It is one of those ailments for which they will find a cure some day, but for now, one just has to wait it out. In short: an epistaxis leads to anaemia that provokes a depression that revives a virus that plays out as shingles. What else can I expect at this point? A legendary case of tuberculosis? A tenacious cancer? Leprosy, where my toes will turn to dust?

43 years, 10 months, 3 days *Sunday, 13 August, 1967*

Unbelievable. Who would have expected one more thing? This time, it's *meadow dermatitis.* In an allergic reaction to some plant or other, the fingers of my right hand are covered with a ton of tiny, atrociously itchy small pimples. At first I thought I thought it was a new attack of the shingles, but no, it's meadow dermatitis. Such a lovely name.

Ti-Joe, to whom I recited my series of woes, declared decisively: "Don't be so upset; there's worse out there." And to illustrate this, he offers me one of his great tales. "Do you know the story about a man and his frog?" I don't. "It's a long one, I'm warning you. Do you think you have enough strength left to hear it to the end?"

THE STORY OF A MAN AND HIS FROG

There was a guy who was born with a little frog on his head, see? A real frog, alive and everything, that was part of the guy, stuck by the skin of its ass to the top of the guy's head. Whenever the barber does his job, he is careful, he goes around the frog. The frog never bothered the guy. It's not that he is particularly fond of it, but he was born with it and grew up with it, and since he's happy with who he is, he never made a big deal about it. It was just normal. So normal that no one ever made the least little comment about the frog: not his parents, his friends at school, his girlfriends, not his children, his colleagues at work, the barber, no one.

Until one day at breakfast when, looking over her coffee cup, his wife says to him out of the blue: "Hey, darling, are you going to keep that little frog your whole life?"

Dumbfounded, the chap asks his wife why she asked him that.

"No reason, just to know, that's all."

Her answer doesn't satisfy him, seeing that during the twelve years they have lived together she has never made the slightest allusion to the frog.

"So why this morning?"

She puts down her coffee and looks her husband in the eyes.

"What's the problem? Is talking about the frog taboo?"

The man with the frog looks back at her. "Not at all. But since no one has mentioned it to me until now, I can show some legitimate surprise when I hear you approach the subject this morning." (He's a man who talks like that – a little like you, he's educated.)

"There are loads of subjects that people haven't talked about before talking about them for the first time," the wife answers (she's sort of like Mona.)

In other words, it's the kind of conversation that, first thing in the morning, ruins the rest of your day. Luckily, the kids burst into the kitchen (they have two children, let's call them Bruno and Lison). They have to be given their breakfast and taken to school, which the man does every morning on his way to work.

In the car, he's in a nasty mood. Behind the frog, who's behaving nicely, he sees in the rear-view mirror the two children whispering, as if they had a difficult decision to make. They definitely look as though they're up to something. Finally, the boy takes the plunge: "Hey, Dad, could you drop us off at the corner before we get to school?"

Well, every parent has gone through this, the day when the kids don't want to be dropped off right in front of the school because it's childish. But that day, the man with the frog is in no state to think in simple terms.

"What's going on? Is it because of my frog?"

Of course, he immediately regrets what he's just said, which only adds to his bad mood.

Once he's dropped the kids off at the corner, the man with the frog, totally upset now, goes to work. He's got a good job, he's risen fast. He's the type who doesn't complain, works hard, has a good head on his shoulders, too. Really, a guy like you. As soon as he gets there, his secretary tells him that the big boss has come from New York just to see him. Oh! Really? The man with the frog grabs two or three files, the most urgent ones, just in case, and goes up to see the boss. (You still with me?) The chief (pay attention! It's a huge international company!) asks him to sit down in the nicest way, tells him how happy he is with him, and how for the last fifteen years he has had "nothing but praise for his work, from the point of view of financial growth as well as for the atmosphere you create with your teams," and so on and so forth, I'm giving you the shortened version, "you are an exceptional worker," and all that jazz, until he tells him why he asked him there: for a promotion. He's offering him a promotion. Head of Personnel. And not just for the local branch, but on an international scale. HR manager of the whole consortium. Twelve times the salary. Really something important, promotion to the stars. The man with the frog is both surprised and thrilled, he thanks him profusely, he won't regret it, thank you, Monsieur le Président, really, thank you so much.

"There's just one little thing," the boss says.

"One little thing, monsieur?"

The boss makes a little dismissive sign, as if it were a trifling detail, nothing to be alarmed about.

"Your little frog."

"My frog, Monsieur le Président?"

Now, the boss treads gently, stating he has nothing against the frog, nothing personal in any case, he had always known him with his frog, and he understands that he is attached to it, "you are attached to it, aren't you? Since birth, I suppose? And it never harmed your work in any way . . . But, well, at this point in your professional career, you are not only representing yourself, my friend, nor even the Company, but the Group, and at this level I'm afraid that your frog would be . . . I mean, with the Japanese, for example . . ."

"I understand, monsieur."

"You understand? Good. That's another one of your fine qualities. You don't rush into things. As for me, I would understand perfectly if it were impossible for you to make this sacrifice. In any case, the operation is entirely benign. You can call Dr

So-and-So and use my name. He'll take care of everything, but think about it for a while and give me your answer, let's say, at the end of next week. Agreed?"

That evening the man with the frog goes home with, let's say, mixed feelings. Filled with joy by his boss's proposal but a tad choked up about the frog. Normally, he would have come home with a bottle of champagne, but now . . . His wife doesn't seem to be in good shape either, and the kids are keeping out of sight. A bad day for all four of them. Everyone goes to bed right after dessert. Lights out. Silence. "Are you asleep?" "No." "Neither am I." And then the man with the frog tells his wife his dilemma. "Oh, my poor darling, that must be awful for you! On the other hand, twelve times your salary . . ." "I know." They spend the night talking about it.

The next morning, the decision has been made: shoot the frog. The next day, the opposite decision: save the frog. And on and on like that until the day when, on his way to the office, the man with the frog suddenly brakes, skids into a turn, and goes, foot on the accelerator, to the surgeon's. (Are you listening? Well, listen up, the end is coming fast.)

The surgeon received as surgeons do.

"Please, sit down. What can I do for you?"

And the frog, who until now had not said a single word, answers: "Oh, not much really, doctor. I had a tiny pimple on my bum, and look what it's become!"

43 years, 10 months, 7 days *Thursday, 17 August, 1967*

Bruno's comment during one of Lison's moody moments: "You got the curse, or what?" Lison, who possibly did have her period, which is sometimes painful, remained mute from shock. And Bruno blushed.

A historical invariant, these jokes made by smart alecs about girls' periods. They sense some female mystery from which they are excluded, so they toss a term of abuse at the girl who has become a woman when they feel they are still far from being a man. This is the revenge all boys share.

Menses. Is it because I read up on them so early? Is it because of my family's silence, which denied their very existence? Is it because I heard dirty jokes about periods from my older friends? Or because they never got in the way of Mona's and my lovemaking? Whatever the reason, I had no interest in turning them into the satanically repugnant thing that until my youth was the historical norm in our civilisation, and I felt kindly towards them. When I understood that women had periods and why, and that in addition, they lived considerably longer than men despite repeated childbearing and the exhausting effects of male domination; in short, when I added all these elements together, I attributed to menstruation the virtue of allowing women to live longer than men. I still harbour this superstition today, although to my knowledge it is not based on any scientific fact. It's because, very early on, I thought of blood as a fuel. I believed that every month girls renewed a portion of this fuel, thus purifying all the contents of their reservoir; whereas with men, blood circulates in isolation inside a body that consequently stagnates (thus my violent epistaxis). This idea persuaded me that women's periods were the chief guarantee of female longevity. I never could shake this belief. I don't doubt its fundamental stupidity, but to this day I have not been able to find anyone to prove that stupidity to me. The world of my childhood was a world of widows, and this was in keeping with my thoughts on the matter. Today things haven't changed, judging by all these old women without old men. As far as I know, these widows did not murder all their husbands, and the wars, as devastating as they have been, cannot alone explain this enduring human feature: on average, women live longer than men. And *I* say that it's thanks to women's periods.

I think about this every time I come across tampons in the bathroom drawer or in Mona's toiletry bag when we travel. It's not that I contemplate them with joy or affection, but these cartridges of the future, perfectly lined up in their box with their tiny safety fuses, without fail remind me of my belief: thanks to their periods, women live longer than men.

43 years, 10 months, 8 days *Friday, 18 August, 1967*

According to Mona, if I won't let go of this belief, it's simply because I have no desire to be a widower: "You'd rather I be the one crying at your grave. That's so like a man! Always disguising your fears as virtues." Again according to Mona, women started living longer when they stopped dying in childbirth, that's all. The fact that they live longer today is simply a way of making up for lost millennia.

44 years, 5 months, 1 day *Monday, 11 March, 1968*

We never shake hands, Decornet and I, when we run into each other in the hallways at work – just a nod of the head, hello goodbye. He always manages to have both hands doing something: one holding the umbrella, the other his raincoat; a toolkit *and* a cup of coffee; an office chair *and* a telephone; a typewriter *and* a plant of some sort.

Today I learned the real story from Sylviane: Decornet loathes shaking hands. In fact, he loathes all physical contact. This gentle giant, who looks like Jacques Tati's twin, lives in constant fear of *catching something* – a germ, a virus, a contagious illness. He washes his hands twenty to thirty times a day and always carries with him a tiny flask of disinfectant in case, horror of horrors, the flesh of someone else should happen to touch his flesh. He then is forced to use all the tricks in the book to clean the filth without being seen. How much time will he keep himself locked in this box without giving in to the ritual of the handshake? As for me, I've never had this sort of phobia; I have always been certain that the enemy that will kill me is already in place. And

I wonder with a certain amount of curiosity which part of my body will be the first to fall to pieces.

44 years, 5 months, 12 days *Friday, 22 March, 1968*

It was again Sylviane who told me that one of the secretaries in accounting just left her husband because he would always eat what he picked out of his nose, even at mealtimes. A psychiatrist would have a field day with this habit left over from childhood. And with this wife who asks for a divorce for a reason that is so patently not the real one.

44 years, 6 months *Wednesday, 10 April, 1968*

On the inside of my right forearm, at the spot where the skin is the most tender, I discovered three tiny, bright red spots in the exact shape of the Summer Triangle. They reminded me of those lover's games I played with sweet Suzanne, my gift for my twenty-third birthday, my Québecoise. Whatever became of her? I couldn't help joining those three spots with a ballpoint pen.

44 years, 6 months, 17 days *Saturday, 27 April, 1968*

The dermatologist told me that they were minuscule angiomas known as *ruby spots* and that they will multiply with time. A consequence of ageing, he said, by way of explanation: the skin ages by lighting up. And he continued, somewhat sadly, that for centuries the Chinese had read the future in the distribution of these ruby spots on the body, but that this practice had no doubt been banned since the Cultural Revolution.

44 years, 6 months, 23 days *Friday, 3 May, 1968*

"Skin ages." This harmless phrase hit home. "Saggy-skinned old hag," Maman would say when speaking about someone she didn't like (did she ever like anyone?). Saggy-skinned old hag, old bag, old fool, old bastard, old fart, old ruin, old thing, old fossil, old pig, old fogey, dirty old man: words, language, these ready-made expressions illustrate how difficult it is to enter old age with a light heart. *When* do we enter old age, by the way? At what moment do we become old?

May, 1968

Are the streets suddenly writing a diary of the body?

44 years, 9 months, 24 days *Saturday, 3 August, 1968*

This morning, in Marseille, my first impression of summer: the speed at which I got dressed. In no time at all: briefs, trousers, shirt, sandals. Summer is here. It's not my clothes themselves, as light as they are, that gave me the sense of summer joy; it is the speed with which I got into them.

Getting dressed in winter takes me so long; it's like a knight putting on his armour. Every part of my body requires a matching protective fabric: my feet are very picky about the wool of my socks; my torso wants the triple protection of a vest, a shirt, and a jumper. Dressing myself in winter is a matter of finding a balance between my inside temperature and all the outside temperatures: out of bed, out of the bedroom, out of the house . . . It's a question of marinating in a sauce of the perfect temperature; there is nothing more disagreeable or more reprehensible than being too hot in winter. This wintry harnessing requires considerable time and attention. "To *throw on* some clothes" is a summer expression. In winter we *put on layers* of clothes. And there is their weight as well. Well before its heat-retaining qualities, it is the weight of my winter coat that protects me from the cold.

(From the standpoint of the amount of time they spend getting dressed, toreadors are the only ones who get dressed in summer as if it were winter. A toreador never just *throws on* some clothes. What a job.)

*

44 years, 9 months, 26 days *Monday, 5 August, 1968*

"At the age of thirty-five, I still loved," Montesquieu wrote in his *Pensées*. I was thinking about that while Mona and I were making love. What did he mean? That he *still* had the ability to fall in love as in his early youth? Was he simply stating that his virility remained intact? In that case, what are we to think about the word "still"? Was it normal, in the eighteenth century, not to be able to get an erection after thirty? That's what I was thinking about in Mona's arms, as my desire was rising rapidly, and suddenly, the mountain climber fell, came crashing down . . . Just like during my first attempts. "The gentleman's penis's mind is elsewhere," said Mona, who has always been interested in this male mystery. As for me, I've once again reached the limits of this diary: the border between body and mind. From the panic at being too young to the terror of being too old, through the impotence that killed Pavese and sent Stendhal's Octave de Malivert to die for Greek independence, mind and body accuse one another of impotence, in a terrifyingly silent tribunal.

44 years, 9 months, 29 days *Thursday, 8 August, 1968*

Took the children to the seaside, to the little beach at Cagnes. I had not gone swimming in a long time. I swam under water, as long as I used to at the age of twenty. Under water I would gladly give up breathing and all the other obligations of the surface. That complete caress of my skin by the sea's skin could have become my sole passion: learning how not to breath, living the life of a porpoise, leading a weightless existence in this silkiness, opening my mouth at times to nourish myself. But we make choices that reduce our most powerful passions to simple ideas of happiness. I only need to know that I feel good under water to avoid going swimming. That's what I was thinking this morning, under the Mediterranean, before gaining a foothold back on shore. Gaining a foothold! What a joke! As soon as I get out of the water, the pebbles put me out of joint like one of those small wooden toys – most often giraffes – that children make topple over by pushing on their base. And while I find myself down on all fours, Bruno and Lison, barefoot like me, are playing volleyball with other teenagers, galloping around as if they were running on sand.

44 years, 10 months, 2 days *Monday, 12 August, 1968*

This morning, I walk towards the sea after having turned down the ridiculous translucent plastic sandals that Mona offered me. I manage to hold myself as straight as possible on the pebbles, a little stiff perhaps, with a slight arch in my back, pretending to walk dreamily like a chap enjoying the view before deciding to dive in. The soles of my feet, in accord with my ankles, are testing the back of every pebble – consistency, temperature, surface, roundness – transmitting this information to my knees, which then inform my hips, and the system works, *I am walking*, until the sum of information to be transmitted becomes such that my brain gets lost and the unexpected pebble, pointier than the others, orders it to send my arms out to stop me losing my balance. And this is how, arms windmilling around, I find myself reincarnated as Violette! I don't think of Violette, I don't imagine Violette, I don't remember Violette, I *am* Violette, rocking back and forth on the stones when we used to go fishing. I am the old, shaky body of Violette, Violette is walking inside me – not with me, *inside* me. I am totally possessed, and delightfully consenting. I am Violette with her tottering walk towards the folding stool, which I would always move back two or three yards to tease her. "At my age, you won't be able to stand up on pebbles either," she would say, "but I will always be able to hold a live fish in my hand! Except that when you are my age, I will be dead." Oh, Violette! You are here! You are here!

44 years, 10 months, 3 days *Tuesday, 13 August, 1968*

Deep down, it makes me glad to think that our *habitus* leaves more memories than the way we look in the hearts of those we loved.

44 years, 10 months, 5 days *Thursday, 15 August, 1968*

Still at the beach. I am reading, stretched out on my towel. "I'm going in," says Mona. I watch her walk towards the water. Ah, the wonders of the female body, that continuity that nothing interrupts! And Mona never wears those two-piece bathing suits that slice women into five parts.

45 years, 1 month, 2 days *Tuesday, 12 November, 1968*

After a dinner during which he was completely silent, Bruno goes to bed without a word and, on his face, an absence of expression that is meant to be "expressive". This happens often these days. Teenagers. They want to have features that allow them to avoid the drudgery of verbal expression. They work at making silence meaningful. They parade their faces as if they were a radioscopy of their soul. Unfortunately, the faces say nothing. Barely blank canvases on which a father's oversensitivity is reflected. What did I do to my son to deserve such gloominess? asks the father who is infantilised by this kind of puzzle. It wouldn't take much for him to shout: It's not fair!!!

Bruno's expression reminds me of the short film by the Russian film-maker Kuleshiv, or Kuleshov, in which we see a close-up of man's face filmed from the front, alternating with various other shots (a plate of soup, a dead girl in a coffin, a woman on a divan). The man's face is completely inexpressive, but, depending on whether he is "looking at" the plate of soup, the girl in the coffin, or the woman on the divan, the viewer thinks he is wearing an expression of hunger, grief, or desire, respectively. Yet it is always the same shot of the same face, completely inexpressive.

Speak, my son, speak. Believe me, it's still the best thing we've come up with to make ourselves understood.

*

45 years, 1 month, 7 days *Sunday, 17 November, 1968*

Trying to decipher Bruno's limited facial expressions so that one day he will have a lexicon that will allow him, when the time comes, to read the face of his own son.

Shoulder shrugging, associated with a variety of pouty faces:

1) Yeah, so?

2) I don't give a damn.

3) I have no idea.

4) We'll see.

5) No concern of mine.

Shaking of head side to side, raised eyebrows, gazing straight ahead 30 degrees above the horizon, and a soft sigh:

Now I've heard it all! (*And if the sigh is louder*) What a load of crap!

Quick nods of the head, avoiding the other person's gaze:

Whatever you say.

Eyes looking anywhere, fingers drumming on the table:

Yeah, I've heard that one a hundred times.

Tiny, almost imperceptible smile, eyes gazing at the tablecloth:

Just because I'm not saying anything, doesn't mean I don't have anything to say.

Half-smile:

If I really wanted to, I could annihilate you with my sarcasm.

The role the eyes play:

Eyes to the sky: misunderstood son.

Eyes wide open: incredulous son.

Eyelids closing slowly: Exhausted son.

The role the lips play:

Pursed lips: repressed anger

Twisted lips: scorn

Distended lips: fatalistic sigh

The role the forehead plays:

Vertical wrinkles of pointless concentration: I'm trying to understand you, but . . . no, I just don't get it.

Horizontal wrinkles of ironic astonishment: Oh, yeah? Really? You're kidding, right?

Smooth forehead: Beyond all expression.

And so on.

45 years, 1 month, 8 days *Monday, 18 November, 1968*

Staff meeting at the end of the day. I gather up my few employees and I notice that they are not so few. My dear colleagues have gone from seventeen to thirty-four. Have I been promoted? No, it's not that my staff has doubled in size, it's that there are two of each of them. Two Chevriers, two Annabelles, two Raguins, two Poirets . . . I am seeing double! Exhaustion is making me see double. No doubt about it: two Félixes, a double Decornet . . . As if each one of them had arrived flanked by a translucent guardian angel. If I make an attempt at visual accommodation, the angel returns to its person, as if it were afraid of my frown. But as soon as my muscles relax, the angels taunt me again. Two Sylvianes, two Parmentiers, two Sabines . . .

45 years, one month, ten days *Wednesday, 20 November, 1968*

The ophthalmologist diagnoses the beginning of long-sightedness. Seeing double because of lack of visual accommodation: it's classic. He suggests two sessions of eye exercises in order to "strengthen my eye muscles" and to postpone the moment when I will have to wear glasses. Are they inevitable? Indeed they are, and almost always in one's forties. Well, let's go straight to glasses then. A discussion ensues. He doesn't understand why I don't want to gain two or three years. I respond with some wise reasoning: Because if there is an age for glasses, why postpone it? He insists. I add: I have no time for exercises, and I'm also too lazy to do them. The real reason lies elsewhere, but I keep it to myself: I have absolutely no desire to put myself in anyone's hands to do exercises on any part of me.

45 years, 1 month, 19 days *Friday, 29 November, 1968*

It takes me a long time to choose my glasses. Not because of the (countless) frames the optician suggests, but because I cannot discover what is unique about my face. Even though I try on pair after pair, I am incapable of figuring out if one pair suits me better than another. I have absolutely no opinion on the matter. The salesman is extremely patient, handing me the mirror with every new frame. He is a tall, thin young man with a prominent Adam's apple and cheekbones; he chose to divide his narrow face with thin, black-framed glasses that make him look decisive. In this regard at least, the lad knows himself. His face speaks to him. Mine says nothing to me. I am going to let you choose for me, I say to him. This little game whets my curiosity; I am going to find out what sort of face I have for this stranger who sees all sorts of faces go by all day. He looks at me, contemplates more than hesitates, and chooses a pair that has no frames. "There," he says, "it's as if you weren't wearing glasses at all."

None of this prevents Lison and Mona from finding that these glasses *go* very well with my face. Later, Bruno says laconically: "I'm not surprised that you chose that model!" He expects me to ask him why, which of course I don't do. That nasty little game the two of us play. With him, I become a teenager again, but the kind of teenager I never was.

45 years, 1 month, 19 days *Friday, 20 November, 1968*

"Those glasses really do go well with your face," Mona repeats before I set them on the night table as I close my book, then shut off the light. These glasses *go* well with my face. Why do we use the verb "to go" in this instance? To go, well or badly, in the case of one's health or mood is understandable. "How's it going?" "It's going just fine." The verb retains its ambulatory character. We move in sync, in concert with our health and our moods. But aesthetically? Why do we employ the verb "to go"? The question becomes diluted in the sleepiness that is overcoming me.

"It is the sea gone away with the sun . . ." Luckily, Rimbaud did not ask himself this sort of question.

45 years, 1 month, 20 days *Saturday, 30 November, 1968*

Falling asleep: dissolving ourselves. Waking up: finding our effervescence once again.

45 years, 3 months, 1 day *Saturday, 11 January, 1969*

Lison slices her finger while she is eating shellfish. Ti-Joe grabs it authoritatively and plunges it in finely ground black pepper. The blood coagulates instantaneously, and Lison doesn't feel the slightest pain. And tomorrow you won't even see a scar. I ask Ti-Joe who taught him that. "Who do you think? Violette, of course!"

45 years, 5 months, 9 days *Wednesday, 19 March, 1969*

Seventeen hours of negotiations. I am not going to say a word for the next three days. What is most exhausting in this sort of sporting event is not the effort you make to keep the information from all the different dossiers in your mind, nor the faultless attention you pay to one another's arguments, nor the backsliding on a point you believed was already settled, nor even the time that passes with no respite in sight; no, the most exhausting thing is the burden of self-control for all these priapic temperaments. Because, being who they are, they always have a hard-on. In fact, it is this permanent erection that got them where they are today, to this level of power. The bulge in their trousers exhausts them when they don't have the freedom to take out their dicks to hammer home their convictions. They wear themselves out in tactful circumlocutions while fantasising about sticking it up each other's bums. In their own offices, it's another story: they can ejaculate without consequences on their subordinates, but here . . . Political stars are intrinsically priapic. It is by means of that energy that power is achieved, or by its exact opposite: the glacial impotence of a Salazar, resolute virgin. When Khrushchev bangs his shoe on the table at the U.N., he is not simply having a temper tantrum, he is disgorging: it's his way of giving himself a moment of respite. I understand him: in seventeen hours, my feet have doubled in size.

46 years, 2 months, 29 days *Thursday, 8 January, 1970*

I could tell right away from the very peculiar way Chevrier started looking at me at lunch while we were talking about Geneva in front of our calves' liver that a bit of parsley was stuck somewhere on my lower lip. Which made me think back to a certain Valentin, who had impressed me no end when I was studying for my exams. He was a fount of knowledge with his enchanting digressions on courtly love, on the Renaissance poets, or on the *Carte de tendre*. But he did not understand this sort of look, and he ate like a real pig. At the end of a meal, we could read what he had eaten in his beard. It was absolutely disgusting. And a harbinger of the vagrant he would become: years later, he wound up in a psychiatric ward! Valentin, the Valedictorian!

46 years, 3 months, 11 days *Wednesday, 21 January, 1970*

I can no longer read the name of the rue de Varenne across the street! Nor, as I walk, the other names on the other signs. Even if I squint, it's useless: the letters are blurry. Even the biggest, brightest letters on advertisements resist me. So, now I'm short-sighted, too! I'm more upset by this than when I learnt I was long-sighted. That first sign of my eyes ageing seemed benign to me. Any magnifying lenses could remedy the problem. This is something else entirely; I feel as if I am . . . *threatened*. A primitive feeling? An ancient instinct? A shrinking of my hunting territory? Something like that. My gaze no longer dominates the savannah. Before, I would decipher the horizon, follow my prey in the distance with my eyes; soon I will be reduced to spotting the cockroaches on the walls of my den. All the great outdoors will be blurry. Our ancestors must have felt this sort of fear, trying to conceal it as long as they could from the young people; but the young ones tested the old ones, waiting for the inevitable moment when the hunter becomes prey. This is how kingdoms fall.

Still, the ophthalmologist explains to me, it's no more serious than long-sightedness. "In your case it's a normal outcome: your eye muscles worked too hard in order to compensate for the deficiencies of seeing close up; they became fatigued, and now it's your distance vision that is suffering as a result. In fact, this should have happened earlier. Your vision has held up well! In any case, it's as easily corrected as long-sightedness. You need another pair of glasses, for distance. Or, if you'd prefer, a single pair of bifocals."

46 years, 3 months, 25 days *Wednesday, 4 February, 1970*

I see clearly. My glasses do the accommodating for me. Soon a time will come when I will be nothing but a central brain aided by all kinds of prostheses. Given the foreseeable progress of robotics, what will remain of my original self in thirty years? I doze off while speculating about this idiotic idea.

46 years, 8 months, 7 days *Wednesday, 17 June, 1970*

As trying they are, my insomniac nights remind me of my very old thrill at falling back to sleep. Every awakening is a promise of falling asleep. Between two stretches of sleep, I float.

48 years, 6 months *Monday, 10 April, 1972*

I was awakened this morning by a whistling similar to that of a pressure cooker forgotten on the stove. I thought it was coming from outside and fell back asleep. Woke up again an hour later to the same whistling. High-pitched, continuous, a pipe, a steam-whistle, something like that. I complained about it to Mona. "What whistling?" Can't you hear it? "No, I can't." Are you deaf? She pricks up her ears. A whistling, like steam escaping, very shrill, no? I get up, open the window and listen to the street. Yes, it's in the street. I close the window, and the whistling is still there! Just as loud. Mona, really, can't you hear it? Really, she can't. I close my eyes. I concentrate. Where can it be coming from? I go to the kitchen to make my coffee, the whistling is there, but I still can't identify the source. I check the gas line, the pilot on the water heater, the air-tightness of the windows . . . Going back to our bedroom with the coffee pot in my hand, I open the door to the landing: the sound is there, like everywhere else, with a stubborn constancy, a line drawn with a ruler between my two ears. And then I recognise it. It is one of those whistling sounds I hear in my head sometimes after a meal. But those whistles are short-lived. They are born and die like shooting stars. Some trajectories are longer than others, but in the end they all fade within the infinite space of my skull. This time, no. I cover my ears: the whistling is indeed there, in my head, settled permanently between my two ears! Panic. Two or three seconds of wild imaginings: what if it were to last forever? The idea of hearing this sound my entire life, without being able to shut it off or modulate it, is totally terrifying. "It will pass," says Mona.

And indeed it did: the sounds of the streets, the soft hiss of the metro, the hubbub of the hallways, the conversations about work, the ringing of the telephone, the negotiations that follow; Parmentier's protests, Annabelle's litanies, that particularly annoying heated exchange between Raguin and Garet about operating costs, Félix's interminable diatribe during lunch, all this urban and professional noise gets the better of my shooting star, and it disintegrates.

But when I got home this evening and the door to our apartment closed on me (Mona was at N.'s and Lison in her studio), the whistling was there, stretched between my two ears, identical to what it had been this morning. The truth is, it had not left me during the day. It had just been covered over by the sounds of public life.

48 years, 6 months, 4 days *Friday, 14 April, 1972*

The ENT doctor whom Colette recommended is, of course, the best in his field. After waiting for forty-five minutes, the best of ENT's gives me the news in four bullet points:

1) I am suffering from tinnitus.
2) Fifty per cent of cases can never be cured.
3) Fifty per cent of patients with permanent tinnitus choose suicide.
4) This good news will cost me one hundred francs; please pay the front office.

Sleepless night, obviously. One chance in two of having permanent tinnitus, in other words a radio always turned on in your head, whose sole programme that I produce is a constant whistling; for others it is a screeching sound, or a drumming noise, or the sound of carillons, castanets, or a ukulele. All I can do is *be patient.* Wait until it passes or until it has been confirmed, and see if the programme stays at the stage of a whistling or if an entire orchestra takes over my skull.

48 years, 6 months, 5 days *Saturday, 15 April, 1972*

I refuse to go digging around in medical libraries. I refuse to gather information on tinnitus. It is out of the question that I become a specialist in the field of my own illnesses.

48 years, 7 months, 12 days *Monday, 22 May, 1972*

These past few days Mona has found me to be so anxious that she thinks I should "see someone". In our circles, the words "see someone" only apply to one category of doctors: psychiatrists.

48 years, 8 months, 7 days *Saturday, 17 June, 1972*

The neuropsychiatrist I went to see yesterday seemed to be more worried about the ENT specialist's health than mine. "Truth be told, monsieur, it would have been better if my *colleague* had come to see me. His case seems much more worrisome than yours." Permanent tinnitus, she said, is so common that it would be the primary cause of death if it caused half the people who suffer from it to commit suicide.

And having said that, she changes the subject and asks me how long it has been since I have been breathing without thinking about the polyps blocking my nasal passages. My goodness, forever, I believe. "No, monsieur, not forever." She claims I have simply forgotten the beginnings of a chronic ailment that I cannot do much about, and that gives me a slight nasal twang and the sensation of breathing through a straw. But I manage. My brain has got used to it just as it will get used to this tinnitus that it will soon place in the category of silence. "In reality, at the moment it is the element of surprise that is affecting you the most; the newness of this tinnitus, and the fear that it will be permanent is what's terrifying you. But," she concludes, "no one lives in a permanent state of surprise."

And she tells me more about her specialisation, which consists precisely in convincing her patients that they will get used to that which, for the moment, they find unbearable. The series of ailments and traumatisms that she goes on to enumerate is so impressive in its variety and monstrosity that, in comparison, my tinnitus starts to look like a friendly pet. I leave her full of prescriptions for sleeping pills and what Aunt Huguette used to call "calmatives".

"Come back to see me if you continue to be afraid."

48 years, 11 months, 22 days *Monday, 2 October, 1972*

Minister G., incensed by one of poor Berthelot's jokes, climbs up on his high horse and dangerously lowers his voice:

"Do you have any idea to *whom* you are speaking?"

Berthelot, blushing with embarrassment, withdraws into his shell. And I recall little José's expression: *Go shit yourself,* Minister Arsehole.

"Well!" hisses the Minister, looking daggers at me. "If your *boss* finds it amusing . . ."

No, Monsieur le Ministre. What amuses me is simply the scatological reflex that such manifestations of statuary arrogance provoke in me. You would like us to imagine you as a Roman bust, but statues bore me to tears and the idea of a pigeon shitting on one makes me smile. A smile of idiotic contentment, I grant you, but what other kind of smile do we ever have when we've taken a good shit?

49 years, birthday *Tuesday, 10 October, 1972*

Just as the psychiatrist had predicted, three months have gone by and I have grown accustomed to my tinnitus. Most of our physical fears share a trait with rancid smells: we forget them once the wind has blown them away. We graze calmly in the pasture of our everyday life, but freeze like does at bay as soon as our bodies speak. Then, once the fright has passed, we go back to the pasture wearing predator expressions.

49 years, 20 days
Monday, 30 October, 1972

Our illnesses are like those jokes we think we are the only ones to know, whereas everyone has heard them before. The more I talk about tinnitus (pretending to try to find out what the word means in order to hide the fact that I am suffering from it), the more I meet people who are afflicted with it. For example, yesterday Etienne said to me: "Thanks a lot for asking me that question; it made me conscious of mine again!" He also said that one gets used to it without too much trouble. And then corrected himself: "I mean, one manages to live with it." Nonetheless, one is deprived of silence. Like me, he started out being terribly afraid. He uses the same image I do: "I had the impression I was plugged into a radio and the thought of living the life of a stereo speaker was not particularly appealing to me."

49 years, 28 days *Tuesday, 7 November. 1972*

My tinnitus, *my* heartburn, *my* anxiety, *my* nosebleed, *my* insomnia. In sum, my properties. Which are shared by several million of us.

6

50–64 YEARS OLD

(1974–1988)

May the span of my life be returned to me.
May my cells slow down.

50 years, 3 months *Thursday, 10 January, 1974*

If I were to make this diary public one day, I would do so first and foremost for the sake of women. In exchange, I would like to read a diary a woman had kept about her body. Just to lift the veil of mystery a tiny bit. What does this mystery consist of? For one thing, that a man knows nothing about what a woman feels regarding the shape and weight of her breasts; and women have no idea what men feel regarding the bulk of their penis.

50 years, 3 months, 22 days *Friday, 1 February, 1974*

It seems like an eternity that Mona has been collecting soaps, face creams (which she calls "fake dreams"), face masks, lotions, unguents, shampoos, powders, mascaras, eyeshadows, foundations, blushes, lipsticks, eyeliners, perfumes, in other words, just about everything the cosmetic industry offers to women in order for them to look more like their ideal. Whereas *my* sole toiletry item is a bar of Marseille soap that I use for both shaving and washing myself from head to toe, including my navel, glans, asshole, and even my briefs, which I then immediately hang out to dry. The territory around our bathroom sink is fully occupied by Mona's troops: brushes, combs, nail files, tweezers, eye pencils, sponges, cotton balls, powder puffs, tubes, little jars and atomisers; they fight an endless battle that I have always interpreted as the daily quest for perfection. Mona putting on her make-up is like Rembrandt endlessly retouching his self-portraits. It is less a fight against time than the perfecting of a masterpiece. "Some masterpiece," cries Mona, "unless you mean 'The Unknown Masterpiece'!"

50 years, 3 months, 26 days *Tuesday, 5 February, 1974*

As for me, after a shower, without which I cannot wake up, my first clear-headed meeting is with my shaving brush, a daily pleasure that dates back to when I was fifteen. In my left hand is my bar of soap, in my right, the shaving brush soaking in the warm water in which I have previously plunged my face. I slowly prepare the lather, which must be neither too watery nor too stiff. Then, a thorough daubing until I obtain a perfect whipped-cream half-face. After that comes the shaving itself, which consists of giving my face back to itself, and of finding my pre-beard, pre-foam face as I cast a wide net, from the skin of the throat that has been carefully stretched to the edges of my lips, going over cheekbones and jaw, careful not to miss the rogue hair that escapes my handiwork with the complicity of the skin sliding away as I roll over the jawbone. The real pleasure comes from the crackle of the beard hair under the razor, from the broad swathes of skin the razor reveals, and also from this daily morning challenge: to get the better of *all* the foam, without leaving the least little droplet for the towel with which I dry my face afterward.

51 years, 1 month, 12 days *Friday, 22 November, 1974*

There are days when I could stroll across all of Paris three times after work! Thrilled by my well-oiled gait, supple ankles, stable knees, firm calves, and solid hips, why should I go home? Let's walk some more, revelling in this body on the move. It is the happiness of my body that lends beauty to the landscape. Lungs well-aired, mind open to everything, the rhythm of my pace guides the rhythm of words, which come together in small, contented sentences.

51 years, 9 months, 22 days *Friday, 1 August,1975*

Sometimes I am startled when, blowing my nose, the pad of my fingers shows through the damp Kleenex, and I mistake the pink spot I see for diluted blood. Surprise doesn't have the time to make me afraid; relief comes almost immediately: it's just the tip of my finger! This never happened to me before my epistaxis.

52 years, 2 months, 4 days *Sunday, 14 December, 1975*

Last night, in deep discussion at dinner with the Rs – the subject is of no importance – I was scoring points that were indisputable (mostly to counteract the boredom of being there), and I was a hair's breadth from getting everyone to agree with me, when all of a sudden, I couldn't find the word I was looking for! My memory froze. A trapdoor opened beneath my feet. And rather than resorting to a circumlocution – to inventing something – I instead foolishly tried to find the missing word, I questioned my memory with the fury of a plundered homeowner; I ordered my memory to give me back *le mot juste*! I searched for that damn word with such obstinacy that when, vanquished, I finally opted for the circumlocution, I had forgotten the subject of the conversation. Fortunately, it had already moved on to something else.

52 years, 2 months, 8 days *Wednesday, 17 December, 1975*

Like me when I was his age, Bruno is flustered by the question a tailor asked him about which way it hangs. Obviously he doesn't know what the tailor is talking about. And because of this, I realise that I never taught my son anything about his body. Ti-Joe, who was having dinner with us, claimed that it was, nonetheless, a matter of the utmost importance. Bruno raises his head from his plate and says: Really? And Ti-Joe told him the following story:

THE STORY OF A MAN WHO DIDN'T KNOW IF IT HUNG TO THE LEFT OR TO THE RIGHT

"Doctor," a patient says to his family doctor, "I have a pain that goes from my little finger up to my shoulder, then goes down through my sternum and abdomen and stops at my knee; the pain is unbearable."

"I see," the doctor replies without hesitating. "There is only one cure: ablation of the testicles."

The patient of course hesitates, but the pain becomes absolutely unbearable and in the end he agrees to the operation.

A few months later, an import event causes our man to order a new suit from a well-known tailor. "Does it hang to the left or to the right?" the tailor asks.

"I haven't the slightest idea," the customer answers, terribly embarrassed by the situation.

"Well, think about it," the tailor advises, "because if I were to make your trousers without being sure about this, you would soon feel an unbearable pain from your little finger up to your shoulder, then down through your sternum and abdomen, stopping at your knee."

52 years, 9 months, 25 days *Wednesday, 4 August, 1976*

Before slipping into sleep, I very distinctly saw, resting on a butcher's block, a brain tinged with blood. Something made me think it was my own brain, and this thought caused me inexpressible joy, which I can still feel now. This was the first time, I believe, that I have seen my brain in this way. And I wondered if, were a cannonball to have ripped off one of my feet, or a hand, or torn out an organ, and jettisoned it far across the battlefield among all the other human remains, I would have recognised it just as easily as I recognised my brain in the butcher's shop.

*

52 years, 9 months, 26 days *Thursday, 5 August, 1976*

Ti-Joe and I are drinking a cup of coffee at a pavement café. At the next table, a barber is telling his friends that he is going on holiday. Ti-Joe overhears this and asks me, as seriously as can be: "Doesn't it shock you that a barber can go on holiday while hair continues to grow?"

53 years *Sunday, 10 December, 1976*

Another year older. How did it happen? Where have the last years gone? For example, the past ten years during which apparently all of my cells, except those of my heart and brain, renewed themselves? I refused to have any official celebration – just gifts from the children. No special dinner, no friends, no one but Mona; another night on our life raft, which has become heavier but is still afloat. Mona, having anticipated this moment of melancholy, had planned the evening well ahead of time: two tickets to see Bob Wilson's production of *Einstein on the Beach.* Five hours long! A symphony of slowness. This was exactly what I needed: for the span of my life to be returned to me, for my cells to slow down. I was instantly spellbound by the way the giant locomotive inched its way onto the stage, by all the actors' endless toothbrushing, and by the phosphorescent platform that took a good thirty minutes to go from horizontal to vertical in a half-light where it is the only thing we can see. And I recognised that platform: it was the obelisk that, on the night I turned forty-three, rose up in my dream with record slowness!

53 years, 1 day *Monday, 11 October, 1976*

As a counterpoint to *Einstein on the Beach*, a couple sitting in front of Mona and me demonstrated another concept of a span of time. They were not a young couple, but neither were they chance lovers; not a seducer trying to impress a recent conquest, no; they were two travellers of a unique love who, like Mona and I, had moved beyond the stage of showing off their "culture" to each other and who had probably hired a babysitter for the evening. They had come with a thermos of coffee and a little basket of snacks, which proved that they knew exactly what kind of performance they were dealing with, that they were solidly ensconced in love, in time, in society, and in taste in general and on this day in particular. The wicker basket was charming. Nor were they a couple at the end of the road who had come to the theatre to fill a shared loneliness. Without a doubt, had they been in the Papal Palace in Avignon, they would have curled up together under a single blanket. In fact, the woman rested her head on her companion's shoulder as soon as the bright light of the theatre had given way to the disquieting boreal glow of the stage. Everyone was swallowed up in Bob Wilson's time span and the couple faded in the halo of my own enthralment. I barely saw the man when, with a slight shrug of his right shoulder, he set his companion upright again. Charmed by the entrance of the locomotive, the interminable brushing of teeth, the phosphorescent platform, and Philip Glass's two-note violin, I lost all sense of time, the awareness of my body, and the awareness of everything around me, whatever it was. I would be incapable of saying if I was sitting comfortably or not. My cells must have stopped renewing themselves. At what moment in this eternity did the woman offer her neighbour a cup of coffee, which he refused with a quick shake of his head? When did she try to make a comment, which was immediately and irrevocably shushed? At what point did she wriggle about on her backside until she elicited that exasperated "Will you stop it!" that made one or two heads turn in her direction? I had only a peripheral awareness of these brief episodes spread over several hours, until the moment when the man yelled out a sentence that, for a few seconds, moved the performance from stage to audience by making the wicker basket fall and sending the woman into headlong flight: "Get the hell out of here, you stupid fool!" That's what the woman's agreeable companion shouted. And she fled, knocking over everything in her path, then falling down in the aisle, getting up, pushing her way through as if swimming upstream;

it was one of those routs that make you trample on everything: spectators, handbags, glasses (someone shouted "My glasses!"), and even small children, had there been any in the audience.

53 years, 2 days *Tuesday, 12 October, 1976*

What I wrote down yesterday has no place in this diary. Does one good!

53 years, 1 month, 5 days *Monday, 15 November, 1976*

Ti-Joe, who is fond of anecdotes, told me he had seen his friend R. D. pee discreetly on the car of the policeman who was giving him a ticket. It was raining and, while the cop was making out his report, concentrating on protecting his ticket book from the rain, R. D. peed to his heart's content on the open door of the squad car, his prick hidden by a flap of his raincoat. Obviously such control of the sphincter when faced with the law in action elicits admiration. I would be incapable of doing what he did. Not because I would be afraid to, but because I never find this sort of thing funny. Conspicuous farters, pissers and burpers exasperate me more than sneaky ones. The barracks, locker rooms, cafeterias, and team buses where this endless show of virility flourishes are not for me. Most likely this has to do with my being an only son. Or having been in boarding school too long. Or else I am at peace with my own sneakiness . . .

53 years, 1 month, 10 days *Saturday, 20 November, 1976*

Out of the blue, Bruno asked me if I had been there when he was born. From his tone of voice, I feel that it is not his own curiosity that leads him to ask this question, but the times we live in. (Our times are very suspicious when it comes to this sort of subject.) In fact, no, I was not there when either Bruno or Lison was born. Why? Was I afraid? Not curious? Because Mona hadn't asked me to be? Because I had no appetite to see bodies quartered? Because I adored Mona's cunt? I have no idea. The truth of the matter is that the question didn't even come up; in my time, it just wasn't done; you did not watch your wife giving birth. But today's times demand answers, especially for questions that aren't supposed to be asked. Am I one of those husbands who let their wives lie alone on their beds of pain? This is what my son is asking me behind his staring eyes. Absolutely not, my boy, I am afraid of heights for your mother. I am horribly affected by her migraines and her stomach aches. Her body has always been of keen interest to me, and while you and your sister were coming into this world, I was wringing my hands in the classic manner in the waiting room of the maternity ward. I am as empathetic as possible when it comes to your mother. And I was very curious about your birth, and Lison's. So? Could it be that Ti-Joe's birth, Marta's screams on her clammy bed, the cavernous and sticky opening of her cunt, Manès' ashen face and his smell of rotgut – did all that make me forever inured to childbirth? Perhaps. But at the time you were born, I had no memory of that. A batch of deeply repressed images.

I don't say any of this to Bruno, but it all moves very quickly through my mind before I hear myself answer Bruno: See you being born? No, why?

"Because Sylvie is pregnant and I plan on being there to greet my son."

I get the message loud and clear.

*

NOTE TO LISON

My dear Lison,

Rereading now that heated exchange between your brother and me fills me with shame. That "No, why?" that I meant to be clever simply served to widen the gap between us. Not only did I not try to fill that gap, but it seems I even felt a kind of pleasure in widening it, to the extent that it became like the open grave of our relationship. Bruno annoyed me. I chalked it up to incompatibility. Different temperaments, nothing more, I would say to myself. And I left it at that. This kind of paternal shameful act is the stock in trade of psychoanalysis. I should have taken the time (and energy) to answer Bruno.

So much the more because, rereading this diary, I can find no description of Mona pregnant. It seems that the thing concerns the body, nonetheless! Well, no. Not the slightest allusion to it. As if Bruno and you were the fruits of parthenogenesis. A before, an after, but no Advent. And worse, I realise that, even on reflection, I have no memory of her two pregnancies. That is what I should have said to Bruno. No memory of your pregnant mother, my boy, sorry. I, too, am amazed by this, but it's a fact. And I should have thought about it a little with him. It must not be rare for the men of my generation. (One more area in which I am not unique.) In those days, a woman was on her own during gestation, surrounded only by other women. Men seemed stuck back at the beginning of the Neolithic period, barely conscious of their active role in procreation. A woman was said to be expecting a child as if her pregnancy was thanks to the Holy Spirit. The woman, by the way, wasn't merely "expecting", she was actively working towards giving birth; it was the man who "expected" something, and who cheated on his wife to pass the time. And for five hundred years the shadow of the Council of Trent veiled the image of pregnancy: artists were not allowed to represent a pregnant Virgin, or even show her breastfeeding her baby. One does not paint this, one does not sculpt it, one doesn't look at it, one doesn't take it into account, one doesn't remember it, one erases it from one's memory and one makes it sacred. We are ashamed of our animal nature! As Tartuffe would have said, "Hide this belly upon which I dare not look." The Virgin is not a mammal! This was so deeply embedded in the Catholic unconscious of my generation that it overflowed into my own unconscious, despite my declared atheism. My mind was cast in the same mould as others of my time.

On the other hand, Mona says that we made love very late in her pregnancies when you and Bruno were on the way. Chastity was not our strong point, and if I don't remember Mona pregnant today it is, she says, in order to atone for our lovemaking games, which she in fact remembers quite well! She was the one who put a stop to our trysts, at a precise date in her pregnancy, beyond which she was "perfecting the final product" (*sic*).

So you see, Lison, when you were born, we had not yet entered the era of the pregnant man that your generation inaugurated: a spectacular role reversal carried out by a wombed father, a mimetic absorption of the figure of the mother to the point that, if you recall, your friend F. D. writhed in pain as his wife was giving birth and Bruno claimed to be much more gifted than Sylvie at bottle-feeding.

Finally, and above all, what I would have said to Bruno had our conversation really taken place was that, from the second I took you and him in my arms, *it seemed to me that you had always existed!* That's where the astonishment lies: our children date back to eternity. Hardly are they born, and we can no longer imagine ourselves without them. Of course we remember a time when they did not exist, when we existed without them, but their physical presence sends roots into us so suddenly and so deeply that it seems to us they have existed forever. This feeling is true *only* in regard to our children. No matter how close or how beloved anyone else is, we can imagine their absence, but not the absence of our children, no matter how newly born they are. I would have loved to discuss all that with Bruno.

*

53 years, 2 months, 16 days — *Sunday, 26 December, 1976*

Saw Kurosawa's *Dersou Ouzala.* I felt a premonitory anxiety as soon as Dersou emerged from the tundra. I thought to myself that this skilled hunter, this living part of nature, this old, shrewd human animal *will lose his eyesight.* That is what will happen to him. His eyesight will grow weak, he will be surrounded by a vast blur, he will no longer be able to aim well, and he will go from hunter to hunted, and he will die from this. His character, to me and to the other people in the audience, was extremely sympathetic, and I spent the whole of the film in a painful state of powerless empathy waiting for the inevitable to arrive. And of course what was bound to happen happened: Dersou's vision grew weak and he was killed by hunters who stole the state-of-the-art rifle that his friend, the master surveyor, had given him to compensate for the loss of his visual acuity. I don't like being able to predict what happens in a film. Sometimes I have left the cinema because I know how a film will end. I go and read in a café and wait for Mona. Most of the time she confirms my intuition, eliciting in me a mixed feeling of victory tinged with disappointment. But with Dersou Ouzala, something else occurred. My certainty didn't come from a weakness in the script; it fed on the memory of my own impression on the day when, six or seven years ago, I realised I could no longer see in the distance. That day, I was Dersou.

53 years, 5 months, 2 days *Saturday, 12 March, 1977*

In the shower, the following chronology came to mind: Until I was eight or nine, Violette would "give me a good wash". From ten years old to thirteen, I pretended to wash myself, from fifteen to eighteen I spent hours at it. Today, I take a shower before running off to work. When I am retired, will I dissolve in my bath? No, we become our habits, and it's the shower that will wake me up as long as I am able to stand. When the time comes, I will be currycombed by some nurse during those hours when visitors are not allowed. And finally, I will simply be laid out.

*

53 years, 7 months *Tuesday, 10 May, 1977*

Grégoire was born today. My *grandson* was born, for goodness sake! Sylvie is very tired, Bruno is very fatherly, Mona ecstatic, and I . . . Can one use the term "love at first sight" to speak about the birth of a child? I don't believe anything in my life ever moved me as much as meeting this tiny stranger who was so instantly familiar to me. I left the hospital and walked alone for three hours without knowing where I was going. The impression that Grégoire and I had exchanged a meaningful glance and signed a pact of eternal affection persists. Will I become gaga? This evening, champagne all around. Ti-Joe, ever himself: "Doesn't it disgust you to sleep with a grandmother?"

53 years, 9 months, 24 days *Wednesday, 3 August, 1977*

Since the moment Grégoire was born, Bruno and Sylvie have been exhausted, like all young parents. They suffer through restless, vigilant nights, fitful sleep, disturbed routines, paying attention to every moment, worrying about every little thing, fits of rushing about (misplaced bottles, too-hot milk, too-cold milk, damn! no more milk, damn, the nappy isn't dry yet!). But they were expecting all that. Their culture has prepared them for it so they think they know it instinctively. Especially Bruno. But the real cause of their exhaustion lies elsewhere. What this supposed parental instinct has hidden from them is the formidable disproportion of forces at play. Babies develop an energy that cannot be compared to ours. Next to these expanding lives, we seem like old beings. Even in their greatest flurries of activity, young adults have to be sure to conserve their energy. Not babies. They are pure predatory energy; they shamelessly feed like animals. Unless they are sound asleep, they are never at rest. And so the parents hardly get any sleep at all. Sylvie is worn out; Bruno, trying to play the model father, is a bundle of nerves; they feel as though they are being eaten alive by the sole object of their attention. Without admitting it to themselves – ye gods, they would never admit such a horror – they miss those not-so-long-ago times when "in our circles," as Maman would say, even though she didn't have a "circle", children were handed over to the domestics. Happy centuries when the children of high society sucked the teats of the people dry! Wasn't I myself raised by Violette? At the same time, obviously, Grégoire melts their hearts. After all (but even that, as modern parents, they cannot admit), the little fellow is the incarnation of their love: they were two who greeted him in the labour room, and now they are three, forever more. Those translucent little fingers, those rosy cheeks, those chubby arms and calves, that peaceful belly, those folds, those dimples, that solid little angel's behind, that entire compact, inflatable thing is the fruit of their love! What a look in his eyes! What silent divinity does the gaze that newborns rest on you without batting an eyelash belong to? On what do they open, these eyes with their very black pupils, and their steady irises? What are they seeing *on the other side*? Answer: all the questioning to come. The insatiable appetite to comprehend. Once their bodies have been devoured by their newborns, young parents fear that their minds will be consumed as well. Their exhaustion stems from their certainty that it will never end. But hush . . . Grégoire's eyelids are closing . . . Grégoire is falling asleep. Sylvie places him in his cradle with biblical care. For the supreme ruse of this omnipotent being is pretending to be the most fragile of all.

53 years, 10 months, 16 days *Friday, 26 August, 1977*

Coming back from a stroll with Lison and Robert and Etienne's children, I did not jump over the fence. That was the first time I did not jump over that fence. What held me back? The fear of "acting young" in front of young people? The fear of tripping as I jumped? A sudden lack of confidence, in any case. In what? My body? Did I doubt my impulse? The body speaks. What is it saying? That the prime of life is dwindling away.

*

For two days now, Grégoire has been fiddling with his ears with tremendous concentration. Despite my efforts to reassure Sylvie (all the babies I know play with everything that sticks out: toes, nose, rolls of flesh, prepuce, tongue, first teeth, ears . . .), she has diagnosed the beginning of an ear infection. "We must take Grégoire to the paediatrician *immediately*. An untended ear infection can be very dangerous, Father. Your friend H. became deaf from one!" Lift, car, lift, paediatrician. Who says, "No, no ear infection, don't be alarmed, madame, all babies do this sort of thing at that age, it's completely normal." But he forgets to explain why. Why do ten-month-old babies finger their ears with monomaniacal ardour when those ears do not itch? So here we are, my daughter-in-law and I, busy asking ourselves this question very seriously while Grégoire is napping. Since we don't come up with any convincing answer, we decide to study our own ears in a deliberately regressive spirit of discovery, the idea being to learn what Grégoire has been *feeling* for the last three days. In order to do this, we have to go back and join Grégoire in his babyhood, question our ears with the innocence of our ten months. So we pull on our earlobes as if they were chewing gum (their elasticity is in fact very relative), we go around the rim (Sylvie's is not as wide but much more finely outlined than mine), we knead our tragi (mine is thicker than Sylvie's, and especially hairy . . . hmm . . . since when? Since when have these stiff hairs formed a sort of Mohawk at that triangle of flesh that I didn't know was called the "tragus" until we began our research?), we explore the depths of the concha – "If Bruno were to see us," Sylvie whispers, eyes closed, moving with her fingers from the concha to the rounded pinna – and all of a sudden, eureka! She's found it! "I know! I found it! Close your eyes, Father!" (Which I do.) "Fold your ears, like a cocker spaniel." (Which I do.) "What do you hear?" Sylvie asks, tapping with her fingertips on the back of my pinna. The beating of a drum, I say; I hear my daughter-in-law playing the drums on my pinna and it echoes furiously inside my skull! "Well, that's what Grégoire's just discovered! Music, Father! Percussion!" We verify this hypothesis as soon as Grégoire wakes up from his nap. No doubt about it, it is indeed the *back* of the pinna that the music-loving little Curious George first slaps with both his hands, then taps with his spread fingers, the way one drums on a table with one's fingers. And then, with the appalling lack of attention of a new learner, he attempts to bring a plastic tractor up to his mouth and I suggest to Sylvie that we go down to the garage to get a taste of the car, just to see what it's like.

55 years, 4 months, 17 days *Tuesday, 27 February, 1979*

A little coffee-coloured spot on the back of my hand as I write. A very diluted brown colour. I clean it with the tip of my index finger. It resists. I add some saliva; it doesn't budge. A paint stain? No, soap and water do nothing. Nor does a nailbrush. I have to face facts: it isn't a spot on my skin, it's something that was produced *by* my skin. An age spot that has risen from the depths. One of those that stud old faces and that Violette used to call "cemetery flowers". When did it grow there? Whether I am signing papers in the office, eating, or writing here at my desk, the back of my hand is almost always in my sight and I never noticed this spot! Yet this sort of flower doesn't pop up from one second to the next. No, it intruded on my privacy without piquing my curiosity; it calmly rose to the surface and for days I have been seeing it without noticing it. Today, some particular state of consciousness truly showed it to me. Many more will bloom on the sly and soon I will no longer remember what my hands looked like before all these cemetery flowers.

55 years, 4 months, 21 days *Saturday, 3 March, 1979*

Some changes in our bodies make me think of those streets we have walked down for years. One day a shop closes, its sign disappears, the premises are empty, it's put up for rent, and you wonder what was there before, that is, the previous week.

55 years, 7 months, 3 days *Sunday, 13 May, 1979*

Ti-Joe, whom I compliment on the surprisingly long presence of the lovely Ariette at his side (but what business is it of mine?), lets me ramble on. Then, once I have finished praising long relationships, he says in all seriousness: "A man's member leaves no more traces in a woman than does a bird passing in the sky." It's impossible to read in his eyes the meaning he assigns to this proverb that seems almost Chinese to me.

56 years, birthday *Wednesday, 10 October, 1979*

At twenty, stretching was like flying. This morning, I felt as though I was being crucified as I stretched. The need to limber up. I recall the prediction of that gym teacher (Desmile? Dimesle?) who told us when we were in high school that our muscles would be rusty before their time if we didn't exercise every day . . . Perhaps. In the meantime, when I see the state of my athletic friends who used to amaze me with their performance (Etienne is now crippled with rheumatism, his fingers and collarbones have been broken several times, his rugby man's shoulders ravaged by capsulitis), I consider that I was right to resist the religion of record-breaking and the diktat of constant training. Such onanism! I have always despised sport as a religion of the body. Boxing was a kind of playful dancing, an art of dodging. And then, I almost always boxed by myself; for the most part, I would hit a punch bag. And when playing tennis, I played against a wall. As for sit-ups and press-ups, they were exercises for my embodiment. They offered a body to the translucent boy who had been the phantom of his father. Winning a game of dodgeball, exhausting a nasty opponent in the ring, ridiculing a stuck-up person at tennis, cycling up a steep hill: these were all ways of avenging Papa, while keeping him at a distance, in the stands, sitting in the place of honour. Sports were never a physical necessity to me. In fact, I stopped all that the day I met Mona.

*

56 years, 9 months, 27 days *Wednesday, 6 August, 1980*

I heard this joke a while ago at the café where I was having coffee, from the man sitting next to me at the counter (he had had more than one pastis): No women, said the doctor to his patient. No women, no coffee, no cigarettes, no alcohol. And if I do that, I'll live longer? I don't know, said the doctor, but time will go by much more slowly and seem longer.

56 years, 9 months, 29 days *Friday, 8 August, 1980*

Chickenpox at Mérac; blisters – those spots with rings around them – rained down on the tribe of children like a swarm of locusts. Not a single escapee: they moan, they fall asleep, they wake up, they complain that it itches, they are forbidden to scratch; Mona and Lison, playing war nurses, are fighting on every front. There's Philippe, Pauline, Etienne 's grandchildren, and three of their friends. I immediately cabled Bruno to tell him to send us Grégoire so he could take advantage of this natural vaccination, but Bruno refused in a telegram, the conciseness of which spoke elegantly. Text: *You're joking, I suppose?* Signed: *Bruno.* "Too bad," said Mona. "Chickenpox in a group is a game, all alone it's a punishment."

I can't help picturing Bruno choosing those four words with care. How old do you have to be before you get over the fact that your father is still alive?

56 years, 10 months, 5 days *Friday, 15 August, 1980*

How many sensations have I not yet experienced? At a concert in church, a woman with bare arms, her elbow resting on the back of the empty chair next to her, was tugging dreamily and gently on her underarm hair. I tried it. Not unpleasant. If the spot were more accessible, it could easily become a tic.

57 years, birthday *Friday, 10 October, 1980*

A charming birthday present from Lison. We were dining all together, Mona, Ti-Joe, Joseph, Jeannette, Etienne and Marceline, etc. Sitting across from me, Lison was participating in the conversation with a *joie de vivre* that seemed multiplied tenfold by some external force. She was full of enthusiasm. Some good genie must be inside her, exhausting her a little, judging from her drawn features. After dinner, I summoned her into my library. (We have always used the solemnity of the paternal summons as a game. Daughter, join me in the library! Lison takes on a sheepish air and I the posture of a commander as I shut the door behind us.) Sit down. She sits. Don't move. She stares at her feet. I look over the bookshelves and pick out *Doctor Zhivago.* I look for the passage I want to read to her, ah! Here it is! Part nine, chapter three. Yuri Zhivago's diary. He is writing it in Varykino; it's the end of winter; spring is on the way. Listen. Lison listens.

> I believe Tonia is pregnant. I told her and she doesn't believe it but I feel sure of it. The early symptoms are unmistakable to me, I don't have to wait for the later, more certain ones.
>
> A woman's face changes at such a time. It isn't that she becomes less attractive, but her appearance is no longer quite under her control. She is now ruled by the future which she carries within her, she is no longer alone.

I look up from the book. Lison says: "Well, that's what I call one sharp cookie of a father!" We fall into each other's arms.

*

NOTE TO LISON

So, my darling, your father, who has no memory of your mother's pregnancies, guessed his daughter was pregnant when Fanny and Marguerite were barely begun! To what sort of instinct to we owe this kind of prescience? You know, you could just as easily fob this diary off on *La nouvelle revue de psychanalyse.* Our friend JB would have a field day with it.

*

We remain chatting another hour or two in the library.

"You're the age Violette was when she died," Lison says to me.

"How do you know?"

"It's written on her tombstone."

My god, I never went back to Violette's grave. Even on All Saints Day. Not once.

"Is anyone putting flowers on her grave?"

"Ti-Joe is. Every year. I used to go with him sometimes when I was little."

Yet I have a tendency to calculate in my mind the age at which people died whenever I read an obituary or walk through a cemetery. During Violette's funeral in the Mérac cemetery, I wandered among the graves to flee my grief, calculating ages and saying the names of the dead aloud, certain that they would be pleased to hear themselves called by name once more, and that their ages would be made known for eternity. François Franceschi, 49 years old; Sabine Haudepin, 78 years old; Amédée Brèche, 82 years old. To each his egg timer, Violette used to say as she plunged eggs into boiling water. There were children, too. Some had lived no longer than the time it takes to cook an egg. Baby Salvatore, 3 months. All those names engraved on unpolished granite or polished marble . . . Violette's stele was not ready. Maritain, the gravedigger, had covered the coffin with heavy dirt. It had rained all week; I still have the scent of this dirt in my nostrils. No stele and therefore no date. The date arrived when the stele did. Why did I never go back to the cemetery? Why wasn't I even tempted to? Uncontrollable grief? I don't think so. More likely it was so I wouldn't know how old Violette had been. So I wouldn't know how long she had lived. She was a *character*, wasn't she?

I look at Lison. I am about to tell her that I would like to be buried next to Violette, but I refrain from doing so.

"What's the matter, Papa?"

"Nothing, my darling. Do you want a girl or a boy?"

In shops in our fancier neighbourhoods, it's rare these days to hear someone using a deliberately *physical* racist slur. Yet this morning at the bakery, when Ti-Joe and I were buying croissants and brioches while we were taking care of Fanny and Marguerite when Lison was away, two very proper women and an old Arab man stood in line in front of us. Behind us, the queue stretched to the door. (It is a very well-known bakery.) On the other side of the counter was the woman who owned the place, wearing a pink smock, one of those shopkeepers who use the conditional to mark a certain courtesy: "Pray, tell me what you *would* like." "*Would* you desire anything else?" Once the two women had been served, it was the old Arab's turn. He wore a djellaba and babouches, and had a heavy accent and that indecisiveness that comes with old age. And the conditional flew out the window. "So, what do you want? Can't you make up your mind?" His answer was difficult to decipher. "What?" The man pointed to a palmier pastry, turning to face the one he wanted. The pink woman took advantage of his looking away to pinch her nose with her left hand and, with her right, make a gesture as if she were waving away a stench. She grabbed the pastry with a metal tong, wrapped it up in a flash, and told him how much he owed as she tossed the packet down in front of him. The customer lifts his djellaba to look for some change in his trouser pocket. Not finding the exact amount, he digs around some more to get out the rest, can't find any, searches in another pocket, takes out an old pair of glasses. "Hey! We haven't got all day! Can't you see there are people behind you?" She waves her hand again, gesturing at all the other customers. He panics. Change falls to the floor. He bends down, gets up, and desperately spreads his change on the fake marble counter. She picks out the correct amount. He leaves the shop, eyes lowered. And then, she shouts to everyone in the shop: "Those Arabs! Not only do they come suck our blood, but they leave their smell behind them!" Total silence. Probably an appalled silence, but silence nonetheless (mine included). Until

Ti-Joe raises his voice: "It's true, those Arabs are revolting!" (Pause.) "You really have to be revolting to want to suck Madame's blood!" (Pause.) To the young businessman behind us: "Honestly, monsieur, would *you* suck Madame's blood?" The businessman pales. "No? I understand, because given what comes out of her mouth, her blood must really be something else!" Now everyone is terrified. Ti-Joe says to another customer: "And you, madame, would *you* suck her blood? No? And you, monsieur? Well, that's because you aren't Arabs!" As a result, not a drop of blood circulates in the single body of all the customers. Their faces are afraid of being struck, because Ti-Joe's words are physical. I am about to stop the massacre when Ti-Joe, very smoothly, turns to the owner and says in the sweetest voice imaginable: "My dear madame, you *would* be doing us an immense favour if you were to sell us four of your croissants and four of your brioches."

58 years, 29 days *Sunday, 8 November, 1981*

Man is only truly afraid for his body. As soon as someone grasps that you could really *do* to him what he has *said* to you, his terror becomes unspeakable.

58 years, 1 month, 5 days *Sunday, 15 November, 1981*

Mona and I were babysitting last night for Grégoire and his friend Philippe, both four and a half years old. In addition to feeding them dinner, making them brush their teeth, telling them a bedtime story, turning off the lights at nine o'clock on the dot, and leaving their bedroom door ajar with the hall light on, we had to give them their bath. While I was drying them, I noticed that Grégoire was a lot heavier than Philippe. And yet they are both the same size. Just to check, I weighed them both. Surprisingly, with barely 50 grams difference between them (and Philippe was heavier), they weigh almost the same: just over 17 kilos. Grégoire is not heavier, but infinitely *denser* than Philippe. Poor Philippe! I am convinced that this lack of density will lead to a life of uncertainty, permanent doubt, volatile convictions, latent guilt feelings, recurrent anxiety, in short, considerable self-consciousness; whereas Grégoire, with both feet solidly on the ground, will have the easy fate of a tank. The pain of existence for Philippe, and a stable hedonism for Grégoire. A question of density. No matter how Mona tries to convince me that this observation of mine is not based on any facts, this morning again the memory of these so tragically disproportionate masses reinforced my certainty in the matter.

58 years, 6 months, 4 days *Wednesday, 14 April, 1982*

After hours of negotiations with Toshiro K., who is Japanese, I wonder how old he is. He is so skinny that his brown kimono seems like bark around a twig. His gestures are as slow as a sloth's and his pen seems like a log between his fingers. Contradictory impressions: this man, who seems no longer to have the strength to live also seems to have all the time in the world. His silences are lengthy, and the extreme slowness of his speech and gestures have brought back to life the image of my father who seemed to raise a mountain every time he brought his spoon to his mouth. Four years of war and German gas had emptied him of his substance as completely as an entire century has emptied this ancient Japanese man. It was as if my father had come to sit at the negotiating table; he settled into Toshiro K.'s silences. Get out of here, Papa, you're disturbing me. I imagine him pressing against the kitchen sideboard, but the sideboard doesn't budge a single millimetre. Monsieur Toshiro K. allows me to watch my father exhausting his last strength in this domestic battle. Papa, please, your son is negotiating. Papa is now sitting at the family dining table. Maman and I cannot take our eyes of the fly that has settled on his nose. "It is already mistaking me for my corpse," he says, without making a move to chase the fly away. Maman gets up from the table, knocking over her chair. She screams: "You're awful!" He whispers: "No, no." The little boy I am kisses the hand that is held out to him. Monsieur Toshiro K. is waiting. Papa is slowing down the negotiations. In the plane coming home, my colleagues praise me for my patience with the elderly Japanese man.

58 years, 6 months, 5 days *Thursday, 15 April, 1982*

My father with his body made of bark. No lungs, fleshless muscles, distended cables. And I, a child with flabby, limp limbs, would wander through the house imitating his extreme slowness and knocking against the furniture as if I were his young ghost, and my poor mother would flee from us, terrified by those two inconceivable beings.

59 years *Sunday, 10 October, 1982*

Since late summer, an itch, sometimes fierce, beneath my left shoulder blade. It seems to come from a vertebra, but manifests itself in particular when I've had too much to eat. I have waited for it to become recurrent before mentioning it in here.

59 years, 1 month, 8 days *Thursday, 18 November, 1982*

The morphology of hiring. I have just hired a clerk with holes in his C.V. like a moth-eaten coat. But the sly look in his eyes, beneath his Neanderthal brow, inspired confidence in me. Bréval (with his love of psychomorphology) would have preferred to hire the handsome, slender fellow with his symmetrical skull and superior qualifications, who had been warmly recommended by the Minister himself. But, as soon as he opened his mouth, I realised that the good-looking chap, with all his smugness, was a total neophyte. And I didn't hesitate for a moment between a brand-new skeleton and one that had survived from Palaeolithic times.

59 years, 1 month, 14 days *Wednesday, 24 November, 1982*

On the pleasure of scratching oneself. Not only for the orgasmic ascent that ends in the climax of relief, but also and especially for the thrill of locating, to the nearest millimetre, the precise spot of the itch. This, too, is "knowing thyself". It is extremely difficult to indicate to someone else the exact *point* that needs to be scratched. In this domain, we are always disap*point*ed. As often happens, someone else will simply miss the *point.*

59 years, 1 month, 15 days *Thursday, 25 November, 1982*

We can scratch ourselves until we come, but tickle yourself as much as you like, you'll never make yourself laugh.

59 years, 3 months, 12 days *Saturday, 22 January, 1983*

I am teaching Grégoire how to eat what he hates. Today it was braised chicory, which Bruno stubbornly insists on serving him in order to "educate his palate." So I instructed Grégoire on how to examine patiently the taste of braised chicory. In other words, how to become interested in something that disgusts him, just as I had done in the past with Dodo, my imaginary little brother, so I could manage to swallow them myself. Eat them while *truly tasting them*; really try to understand what they taste like. You'll see, it's *interesting* to know why we don't like something. (In this sort of exercise, I'm amazed to find myself speaking in italics, like Papa did.) Ready? Set? Go! First a tiny bite, then the meticulous description of its specific taste, in this instance the bitterness that puts off the majority of children (with the exception of Italian children, perhaps, who enter into the culture of the *amaro* at a very young age). Then, a second bite, a little bigger this time, to verify the accuracy of the previous description, and so on and so forth (without going as far as taking a whole mouthful, thinking you will reduce the time of torture and thereby making yourself retch). Grégoire managed to finish his plate with an entirely intellectual satisfaction. He claims that chicory tastes like a rusty nail. Fine, as long as he eats his chicory without a word of protest, even if he still finds it disgusting.

The taste of a rusty nail. This reminds me of those giants who would eat bicycles at the fair when I was a child. I tell Grégoire. One of them even attempted to eat a car, a Juvaquatre. Grégoire asks me if his mother – the giant's mother – was aware that her son was trying to eat a Juvaquatre.

60 years *Monday, 10 October, 1983*

My birthday. Why do we celebrate the decades so extravagantly? Mona gathered together the whole crew. Will there be as many people at my funeral? According to Ti-Joe, the reasons to celebrate are twofold: every ten years is both a burial and a rebirth. "You were at the end of your fifties, and now you are at the beginning of your sixties," he says, raising a glass to my health. "A kid in your new decade. Long life to you!" A pretty good way of seeing things. Blow out your sixty candles, young man, you have been reborn for another ten years!

60 years, 10 months, 6 days *Thursday, 16 August, 1984*

The crunching of gravel beneath light-hearted footsteps that I heard in the garden of the T. Hotel around one o'clock this morning. Mona asleep against me. This crunching is one of the soothing sounds of my life.

61 years, 7 months, 2 days *Sunday, 12 May, 1985*

Yesterday afternoon I took Grégoire to see *Greystoke*, an nth version of Tarzan. Grégoire was ecstatic and I was struck by the following scene: Lord Greystoke, Tarzan's senile grandfather, is dunking his shaving brush in a mug of black coffee before spreading the "foam" on his face. I tried doing the same thing this morning. The result was quite satisfying! The pores contract under the coffee's astringency and the aroma of coffee lasts for about twenty minutes. Like baby's skin scented with coffee. Mona loves it. She thinks I am becoming more and more refined.

61 years, 7 months, 17 days *Monday, 27 May, 1985*

Stupid accident. Whit Monday. We were having tea at Madam P's, an old friend of Mona's deceased mother who is about to turn one hundred and two. A neo-Victorian house. Tea was served outside under a plane tree that had grown smack in the middle of a tennis court! The image is even more striking because around the tree, the tennis court (which is a clay court) continues to be maintained as usual: watered, flattened, the lines duly drawn in chalk, as if nothing had happened. Drinking tea under this tree is like walking into a Magritte painting. The game consists in not acting surprised around the old woman. But if ever some indiscreet person questions Madam P on the matter, she answers: "What do you expect? My men are dead, no one plays any longer, this tree grew there, you simply must accept what has forsaken you along with what falls to you." So. We were sipping our tea when a dog burst onto the property. The old woman saw it out of the corner of her eye and took offence. "Who is going to get rid of this animal for me?" Then the accident happened. I jumped to my feet, raced towards the dog waving my arms and yelling, but an invisible obstacle at the height of my forehead stopped me in my tracks. My two feet flew up and I fell flat on my back, my hand and my skull violently striking the ground. For a few seconds I was dazed, with a burning pain across my whole forehead when I came to; and then I was blinded by a sheet of blood. Mona tended to me, wiping me off. Explanation: the obstacle was a wire stretched a bit above eye level, the remains of an old fence that used to surround the tennis court. Then I notice my hand. My middle finger, sticking up vertically from my palm, is pointing to the sky. It cannot be put back in place. A piece of myself out of alignment. "It's nothing," says Mona, "you just broke a finger." In the hospital, the astonishment of the doctor on duty when he sees the range of damage: "What on earth happened to you?" Difficult to explain in just a few words: the tea, the tennis court, Magritte, the dog, the old woman, the wire, in other words, the biggest disaster in the history of high-society tea. Tetanus shot (the wire was rusty), eight stitches on the top of my skull. "Did someone try to scalp you?" An X-ray of my skull, a pyramidal bandage to hold the ice pack against the bump, an X-ray of my hand, not broken, the twisted finger put back in place (a bit brutally), splint and bandage.

Later, Mona asks me what got into me that made me leap up like that.

"I think I was a bit bored."

"That wire could have decapitated you."

61 years, 7 months, 22 days *Saturday, 1 June, 1985*

At the end of *Greystoke*, during a Christmas Eve celebration, the old lord is killed when he slides down the castle staircase on a large silver platter that he is using as a toboggan. As a child, he would hurtle down all the stairs, starting from the nursery, on this same silver platter. But he is too old now, and can no longer control his trajectory; he kills himself rounding a bend. His head strikes a heavy wooden pillar. Tarzan is despondent (so is Grégoire). The old lord was the victim of an attack of childhood. And this is what must have happened to me yesterday when I suddenly tried to play at frightening that dog. Very often, the child will leap up inside me. He overestimates my strength. We are all subject to these attacks of childhood. Even the oldest among us. Until the end, the child wants to reclaim his body. He doesn't give up the fight. These attempts at reappropriation are as unforeseeable as raids. The energy I expend at these moments comes from another era. Mona gets scared when she sees me running after a bus or climbing a tree to pick some fruit that is out of reach. "It's not the fact that you do something like that that scares me, it's that one second before you do it, you weren't even dreaming of doing it."

61 years, 7 months, 27 days *Thursday, 6 June, 1985*

They removed my stitches. The scar forms a pink halo around my skull, as if, according to Grégoire, someone had "opened it to see what was inside". Later in the afternoon, Mona grows alarmed by the way Grégoire is walking. She points to him through the window, playing with Kopek in the yard. The kid is arrhythmic, dislocated, slowed down, as if he were disoriented. The dog seems impressed to see his master walking crookedly. Panicked, I race outside: Then Grégoire says, pointing at my scar, that he is Frankenstein's grandson.

61 years, 7 months, 29 days *Saturday, 8 June, 1985*

Because any unexpected obstacle surprises me (this morning it was some dog shit on which I was afraid of slipping as I left the bakery; this evening it was that extra step as I was walking down the stairs on rue Villiers de l'Isle Adam), I walk along with frightened little steps. Slowly, very cautiously. I am jumping ahead to my old man's gait. It's the reverse of my attacks of childhood. The worried old man I have not yet become is warning the bold child I no longer am. And where is the present in all that? It is entirely wrapped up in this awareness.

62 years, 20 days *Thursday, 31 October, 1985*

I eat and drink with my right hand, but I smoke with my left.

62 years, 23 days *Saturday, 2 November, 1985*

Because of a shoulder destroyed by arthritis, Etienne has given up archery these past years. He was very good at it. He didn't practise it as a competitive sport, but rather alone in his barn. "I felt *whole*," he said. Do you miss it? "Yes and no." He explained to me that, even if he can no longer pull back the bow, he still has his sense of aim. Perfect aim: a brief sense of accuracy. "Take that salt block, for example," he says. "If I had a bow and arrow, I wouldn't miss it." And he shows me in the clearing next to us a cube of white salt attached to a beech tree to attract the roe deer. "The tree is twenty-seven steps away," he specifies. I verify this: exactly twenty-seven steps. In his barn, his gestures had become so precise that Etienne could shoot with his eyes closed. His position facing the target, the angle that his arm made with his torso, the tension of the string evaluated by his fingers and then communicated to his muscles, his breath held at the right moment, his mind empty of everything except the mental image of the target – all this, and so many other parameters, including his indifference to the result as some sort of feat, all contributed to his ability to aim. And, when all these factors came together (which was rare, he said), "I would let go of the string with the assurance that my arrow would hit the bull's eye." And it was true. He didn't take this for an exploit, but as the manifestation of harmony. "As if the heart of the target and I were one." It is a sensation he still feels from time to time. The cohesion of these gestures, so often repeated, the perfect mastery of the body during that one second, created a mental certainty that survived them: perfect aim. No need of a bow and arrow any more.

"Nor of a target?"

"Yes, yes, the target remains, but it can be anything. That block of salt or anything else. For just one second I was both myself and that target. A whole."

He laughed an apologetic little laugh.

"You must think your cousin a crackpot, no?"

No.

62 years, 29 days *Friday, 8 November, 1985*

This morning, I forgot my bankcard code. And not only the code, but also the mnemonic technique I had concocted to remember it. And the way my fingers should move on the keypad. I was dumbfounded in front of the cash machine. Completely shook up. Try again? How? No memory. Not the slightest trail to follow. As if this code had never existed. Or worse, as if it existed somewhere else, in a place to which I had no access. Panic mixed with fury. I remained on the pavement in front of the machine, not knowing what to do. Behind me, people were growing impatient. The machine spat out my card. I said, I think it's broken. What shame as I said these words, as if I had felt obliged! I moved out of the way, keeping a low profile. I had lost everything:

memory, dignity, self-control, maturity. I was completely dispossessed. This code *was* me. I sent the driver away and decided to go to the office on foot. Fury and shame caused me to walk quickly. I crossed the street against the lights. Cars honked. Impossible to calm myself down. Impossible to see the event in its proper light: a power cut, with no long-term consequences. As I write these lines (the code came back on its own to take its rightful place in my memory), I cannot find the words to describe the state of terror into which this short span of forgetfulness plunged me.

62 years, 1 month *Sunday, 10 November, 1985*

The sudden disappearance of data once known: bankcard code, door codes to friends' places, telephone numbers, first and last names, birthdays, etc., are crashing into me like meteorites. It is the shock more than the forgetting that shakes my entire planet. In short, I cannot get used to it. On the other hand, I am not surprised at all when I can answer the questions on those radio or television game shows to which I listen distractedly. Grégoire: "So you know *everything*, Grandfather? You really remember *everything*?"

62 years, 4 months, 5 days *Saturday, 15 February, 1986*

Hairdressers. When I was young, they did not massage your skull. They scrubbed your head roughly before giving you a crew cut, which a glue stick called Pento kept stiff until the next haircut. (Actually, now that I think of it, Pento came later, in the early post-war years.) In any case, the profession has become more feminine, that is, more refined, and now as they wash your hair, nimble fingers have started to massage your scalp. A moment of sheer abandon when, if the masseuse is good at her job, all your dreams become possible. I even think I murmured one day, on the verge of ecstasy: Stop, please. "Don't you like to be massaged?" the young woman asked innocently. I think I mumbled: Yes, yes, but no. When I say "innocently" I don't believe it for a second, because if I were a young woman massaging men's scalps, these gentlemen, subject to my dexterity and whose position in the chair prevents from glancing at their fly that starts to bulge beneath my fingers, would amuse me a great deal. Wonderful occasions for a good laugh among girlfriends. Perhaps they even have contests to relieve the boredom of their long days. "What about your guy? How many seconds did it take for him to get a hard-on?"

62 years, 9 months, 16 days *Saturday, 26 July, 1986*

All morning long, I've been extremely anxious. And Grégoire is bearing the brunt of it. I almost jumped when, at the market, he asked me on the verge of tears if I was angry with him. What face was I showing to him? What reproachful expression was I wearing? What hateful mask? And for how long? In fact, what face do we make whenever we make a face? And what face to we make when we are not making one? We exist behind our faces. The child sees a mirror on the face of an adult. And in this instance, the mirror was reflecting back to Grégoire the image of his own mysterious guilt.

"What did I do?"

"What did you do? You did something to deserve a nice ice cream. Would you like vanilla, chocolate, strawberry, pistachio?"

"Hazelnut!"

Okay, two hazelnut ice creams, please.

From anxiety to guilt . . . I told all this to Mona and she explained to me that the verb *culpabiliser*, to feel guilty, entered the French language in 1946. And the verb dé*culpabiliser*, to free oneself from guilt, in 1968. Ah, when History tells its own story.

62 years, 9 months, 17 days *Sunday, 27 July, 1986*

Another person can cure our anxiety, provided he or she is a total stranger and is somewhat indifferent to us. There is not a single work day when I cannot defeat my anxiety. As soon as I walk through the doors to my office, the social man overtakes the anxious man. I am immediately receptive to what other people expect from me: attention, advice, congratulations, orders, encouragement, jokes, arguments, reassurance . . . I become an interlocutor, partner, rival, subaltern, good boss or bogeyman; I embody the very image of *maturity*. This role has always got the better of my anxiety. But those who are close to us, our family, get the worst of it every time, because they are, precisely, our family, the constituent elements of who we are, the propitiatory victims of the brat whom we remain for our entire lifetime. Grégoire bore the brunt of this the other day.

62 years, 9 months, 23 days *Saturday, 2 August, 1986*

When I mention, rather often, my anxiety in this diary, I am not talking about my "soul", I am not even talking about my psychology; I am, more than ever, staying with the body, that fucked-up bundle of nerves!

63 years

Friday, 10 October, 1986

I was having a pee in a café on the rue Lafayette. The light went off right in the middle of my business. Twice. On the basis of what average age did the people who installed the timers calculate how much time a pisser would be allotted? Is it possible that I have become so slow? Could I ever have been *that* fast? Damn the youth culture that affects even the production of these pee timers, the automatic light timers in stairwells, and the lift doors that close more and more quickly!

63 years, 1 day *Saturday, 11 October, 1986*

Yesterday, after my birthday dinner, I spent a few moments alone with Etienne in my library. He told me something in confidence that leads me to believe we spend our lives reading other people's faces without ever having the code to decipher what's written there. He said that when Marceline's face wants to express nothing, her fallen features glue her lips together in a pout completely devoid of kindness. He sees there – on the face of this woman reputed to be so gentle! – a fleeting but genuine image of nastiness.

"This is, in any case, what I notice these days," he adds. "But it is precisely a *lack of expression* that I interpret, because it occurs at those exact moments when Marceline isn't thinking about anything. Other people would probably see another face. I react as if Marceline's features, which expressed nothing but sweetness the day me met, now show me, whenever they are relaxed, the unsuspected depth of a temperament without kindness. (Pause.) In truth, what I see on my wife's face is the result of a certain number of *my* resentments accumulated over the years and that have recurred often enough to draw the portrait I see of her today. In other words, it's purely a construction of my own mind, the result of an inconspicuous ageing of the couple. (Another pause.) And what about me? What expression do I wear when I have this feeling? I must not be a pretty sight! In Marceline's eyes, my face must be singularly different from the Prince Charming face it was for her when we were young."

I am very moved as I listen to Etienne . He has never stopped being the scrutinising teenager with whom I loved to discuss things when we were at boarding school. Today, two vertical wrinkles are permanently etched on his old forehead. Two wrinkles of pain. Suddenly he asks me: "Am I talking nonsense? Have I become stupid?" And his eyes express a sort of dizziness. "It's my mind, you know. It's not working very well."

63 years, 1 month, 12 days *Saturday, 22 November, 1986*

What will I do with my anxiety once I retire? No more employer, no more employees. Who will fight off these ontological brambles when I am deprived of all those people who are so necessarily indifferent to me?

63 years, 6 months, 9 days *Sunday, 19 April, 1987*

Marguerite scraped her knee when she fell on the gravel. I cleaned her wound using Violette's technique: I screamed so that Marguerite wouldn't. She didn't feel a thing but once she was bandaged, as if she doubted from now on that I could ever take advantage in any way of this objective fact, she said with a tad of fatalism: "You know, Grandfather, I think you are slightly nuts." And Fanny agreed.

63 years, 6 months, 11 days *Tuesday, 21 April, 1987*

With Marguerite's calf in my hand, I had the intuition that this chubby little child would grow into a tall, slender young girl.

63 years, 11 months, 7 days *Thursday, 17 September, 1987*

Ophthalmoscopic examination at Dr L.M.'s. She tells me I have the beginnings of a cataract, and it will progress over the next twelve or fifteen years until I will need an operation. For the moment, I don't feel it at all; I see as clearly as ever. "You have time," the doctor says. "And these days, the operation is really nothing, almost a formality." (The fleeting image of Aunt Noémie in her little apartment on rue Chanzy. Afraid of becoming blind, she practised walking with closed eyes. When she finally did go blind, she could no longer walk.)

63 years, 11 months, 10 days *Sunday, 20 December, 1987*

What got into me to take Fanny and Marguerite to the Musée de l'Homme? They were curious about everything and asked me all sorts of questions that pushed me to the limits of my knowledge. But last night, Fanny had a terrible nightmare: "I don't want to die! I don't want to die!" She had visions of one of the skeletons in the exhibit. "He crawled into my bed!" Terror and enuresis. Personally, I found these skeletons to be rather poorly maintained; the dust that had accumulated on their ribs and in some of their joints perhaps emphasised their funereal character.

When I was Fanny and Marguerite's age, I was not frightened by skeletons. The one in the *Larousse Encyclopedia*, with his pals the muscle cut-away man and the circulatory system cut-away man were my classmates. My father and I spent long morning hours in their company. And my favourite skeleton was Papa's: his hollow temples, his bones easily perceptible beneath the mica of his skin. No, I had no fear of skeletons.

64 years, 1 month, 11 days — *Saturday, 21 November, 1987*

As I was going to get the results of the blood tests that Dr P. had ordered, I realised I had never mentioned in this diary the particularly humiliating ceremony that opening the envelope represents for me. This oversight says a lot about the shame I feel at that moment of sheer terror. If the people in my office who think I am responsible for their careers could see me then! Ah, it's great to be the fearless big boss, guardian of the morale of the troops! A youngster bending over an envelope with the fear of a mine-clearing expert in his guts. An anti-personnel land mine that I have to defuse each time. One day or another the envelope will blow up in my face. Please find enclosed your death sentence. There is no enemy like the enemy inside you. Once the envelope is slit, my gaze immediately turns to the first two lines: white corpuscles and red corpuscles. (Phew! Perfectly average, not a trace of a serious infection.) Then I jump directly to the bottom of the last page, to the prostate indicator, otherwise known as the P.S.A., a fetish number for men in their sixties. 1.64! 1.64, when last year at the same time it was 0.83. In other words, it has doubled. Sure, it's well below the upper normal level (6.16), but still! In one year! So, if the trend continues, next year it will be 3.28, the following year 6.56, and, in a short time, a cancerous explosion and metastases all the way to the folds in my brain. The bomb is indeed there, invisible and set to go off at the appointed hour. And what if it were not only my prostate? Even if I am mistaken in my exponential calculation, what am I supposed to think about my blood sugar level? Because there is sugar, too! Blood glucose level: 1.22 g/l compared to 1.10 g/l last year (already higher than the norm!), and it has been constantly increasing for years. So: diabetes is in my future. Daily injections, blindness, amputation ("the 'poor man' is in such a 'bad way'") ... Although it could be creatinine that is attacking me: it's well above the acceptable level, so I must envisage kidney failure and dialysis for the rest of my days. A blind amputee on dialysis: what a charming prospect. And I am supposed to open this envelope with a smile on my face?

64 years, 6 months, 4 days *Thursday, 14 April, 1988*

Difficult landing at Vancouver airport. Broken landing gear, skidded off the runway, the passengers literally head over heels, an avalanche of luggage, panic and pandemonium, etc. I got out of the whole mess uninjured and, I have to say, was not overly afraid. How do we manage, cowards that we are, to trust our lives with complete peace of mind to things (planes, trains, ships, cars, lifts, roller coasters) over which we have absolutely no control? No doubt the number of other users silences our fears. We give ourselves over to the intelligence of the species. So many skills contributed to the construction of this aircraft, and so many critical minds trust their bodies to it on a daily basis, why shouldn't I? Add to that the statistical argument: we are much less likely to break our necks piled up in there than when we cross the street. And then, there is also the appeal of fate. We don't mind entrusting our destiny to the whims of engineering. Let's let the innocent machine decide my fate rather than my cells, every one of which is suspected of malignancy. From now on, I will check the results of my blood tests when I am eleven thousand metres up in the air, passing through areas of turbulence, if possible in a blazing aeroplane.

64 years, 6 months, 5 days *Friday, 15 April, 1988*

Still, I retain the memory of a conversation I had with B. P., a flight test engineer, who has spent his life testing aircraft. "You have to be totally out of your mind to get on one of those things," is basically what he said. "You know what we do when a plane vibrates to the point of breaking up in the air? Well, we destroy it and we rebuild the same one, in exactly the same way, and this one, who knows why, does not vibrate. As for me," he concluded, "each time I get off an aeroplane with the other passengers, I don't say to myself that I have arrived, but that I have survived."

64 years, 10 months, 12 days *Monday, 22 August, 1988*
In Pliny's *Natural History*, I learned that during a fight, badgers hold their breath so as not to smell the wounds their opponents inflict on them. This reminded me of the exercise I did as a child, holding my breath as I walked through nettles so they wouldn't sting me. It was Robert who taught me the trick. I tell this to Grégoire. All he can manage to answer is: "That's your badger side, Grandfather."

64 years, 10 months, 14 days *Wednesday, 24 August, 1988*
Grégoire is busy reading *Tom Sawyer* and picking his nose. His nostrils? They are Injun Joe's cave. His bogeys? The treasure hidden there. Like me, all his life he will associate the pleasure of picking his nose with that of reading.

64 years, 10 months, 20 days *Tuesday, 30 August, 1988*
Pliny writes that the Romans were forbidden to cross their legs in public, which takes me back some sixty years. I am wearing shorts (but perhaps it was Dodo?) and Papa is not yet completely rotted on the inside. We are having guests for tea. Sitting in a chair, I cross my legs like all the adults around me. Maman shouts: "That's just not done!" In bed at night, I repeat the experience and realise that my little cock gives me pleasure if I move it back and forth with the tip of my fingers between my crossed thighs.

Ti-Joe, who is so small and who, physically, has never been particularly robust, always amazes me with his muscle power, rapidity, precision, and his cunning of a wildcat. Yesterday afternoon when we were out walking with Fanny and Marguerite along the Seine, a seagull was amusing itself by brushing us with its wings. Once, twice, then a third time. Ti-Joe raised his left arm and grabbed the bird in midflight. Clean break of a trajectory. The bird had a shocked look in its eyes. (A real cartoon shock: Gasp!) "Look at this beauty! She hits on you over and over and she thinks there will be no consequences!" Ti-Joe rubbed his nose against the beauty's beak, then showed it to the twins, who stroked its back. Then Ti-Joe let it go. The gull flew away, a bit dazed but not wounded. We continued our stroll, talking about certain jokes, all of them very physical, that Ti-Joe had played on me when he was a child. For example, this one, when I was about the age the girls are today: Marianne and I were flirting, in Briac, when Ti-Joe suddenly began throwing figs at us, screaming: Death to the Krauts! Long live the Resistance! (Summer of '43.) A lightning ambush. By the time I had run to Lulu's fig tree to retaliate, he had hit me in the eye, the forehead, the jaw, and vanished. No more flirting with Marianne. I was so sticky that I was attracting wasps, of which she was deathly afraid. I had to scrub myself from head to toe and stuff my clothes in the washtub. At the end of the season, figs are both dense and soft, and the impact makes them explode like a hand grenade and splatter their juices in every nook and cranny. Not to mention the seeds in your hair. And those scraps of figskin that stick to you like bleeding flesh! A stoning with figs is similar to the tarring and feathering of men in the American West. My revenge was terrible. Like a Nazi's, to tell the truth. The cold, repressive measures of the Occupier. I stockpiled my munitions, I captured Ti-Joe when he was least expecting it (he was going to take milk to the Douviers), I tied him to the Peluchats' plane tree and told him – in German! – that he was sentenced to die. He shouted: Long live

France! And, while I was shooting him, he remained as stoical as Hans Christian Andersen's brave Tin Soldier, which I had read to him the previous evening. That's because he believed his torment would not go beyond his execution, poor boy. Once I had turned him into a jar of jam, I untied him and plunged him into Douvier's drinking trough, then scrubbed him from head to toe. He was much less stoical this time around! Hygiene was not his strong point and the family was not fussy. The water was so cold, and the victim's teeth were chattering so much that even the torturer felt vaguely remorseful.

"You didn't like to wash when you were little?" Marguerite asks.
"Me, little?" Ti-Joe answers, rising on his tiptoes, "I was never little!"

64 years, 11 months, 16 days *Sunday, 26 September, 1988*

Etienne curses those orthodontists who make the most beautiful girls wear braces until a ridiculously advanced age. He gets really angry, which happens more and more frequently.

"Look at these grown girls with their metal mouths! And they accept this, the idiots! Fucking teeth-straighteners! If they served some purpose, that would be different! But they're just a fashion! And there's a huge market for them! Ah, the good old nineteenth century!"

"What does that have to do with teeth?"

He looks daggers at me.

"Prophylaxis, old man! My maternal grandmother, you know, the famous Aunt Clothilde, the colonial governor's wife – she was born in 1870 – well, she cared for lepers in Somalia. One day, it was in 1927 or '28, I must have been four or five, she stuck the putrid stump of a leper's hand under my nose and calmly said to me: 'You see, Etienne , if you keep sucking your thumb what will happen?' *That* was preventative medicine in the nineteenth century. All in all, it was less brutal than braces and at least it made for a good story."

On the same subject, during the same conversation, Ti-Joe is also furious:

"It's not dental devices that parents are putting on their teenagers, but chastity belts! Haven't you noticed that parents force this horror on their kids as soon as their hormones kick in? That device guarantees sexual calm for families! You can't smooch with barbed wire in your mouth! It's nothing but castration! The poor kids don't even dare look at themselves in a mirror. The worst of it is the tenderness the parents feel when they see the remnants of childhood on those mutilated kissers!"

*

NOTE TO LISON

Deep down, my darling, I find it amusing that I kept this diary my whole life. Which doesn't mean that I find the diary itself amusing.

7

65–72 YEARS OLD

(1989–1996)

I should have kept a diary
Of everything I have forgotten.

65 years, 9 months, 2 days *Wednesday, 12 July, 1989*

I sliced my thumb as I was fixing a flat tyre on Grégoire's bicycle. The inner tube having been duly patched, I was putting the tyre back in the wheel rim when the screwdriver slipped, slicing my thumb like a crayfish. Blood everywhere and horrendous pain. One of those pains that go straight to the heart. Because it was Sunday, Grégoire suggested we go to see his friend Alexandre's father, who is a doctor. The doctor greeted me amiably and then set to work. "Nothing serious," he said. "The tendons are intact. But you will need several stitches." Fine. Because Alexandre was not at home, Grégoire thought it would be "interesting" to watch *me* being "patched up" this time. The good doctor takes out a syringe to give me an anaesthetic injection. I refuse, saying we are in a hurry, people are waiting for Grégoire at the starting point of a race on which his career as a cyclist depends. "Are you sure? On an open wound? Fingers have a lot of nerve endings, you know!" It's okay, I say. The doctor pricks me a first time, draws the thread through, pricks a second time; the third time I faint. That'll teach me to want to burnish my image as a heroic grandfather in front of young Grégoire – who had absolutely nowhere he needed to go. If he hadn't been there, I probably would have accepted the anaesthetic.

On the way home, Grégoire tells me about his decision to "grow up to be a doctor." When I ask him the reason behind this sudden calling, he answers: "Because I don't want you to die." Of course, his answer goes straight to my heart, where it eases the beating of my thumb. (Or, more accurately: it goes straight to my thumb, where it eases the beating of my heart.) Oh, how happy is the adult who can recover from any pain or illness thanks to the genuineness of a child's affection! Thinking back on this tonight, my joy turns to sorrow, that same sorrow Grégoire will feel at my graveside, and he will curse the powerlessness of his profession.

At his age, I also felt responsible for one person's eternal existence. I did not want Violette to die. Despite rumours of her imminent demise – "The way she drinks, she won't last long!" – Violette could, thanks to the vigilance of my love, lay claim to immortality. Her varicose veins, her weight, her damp, fleshy lower lip, her rosacea, her shortness of breath, her dry cough, and what Maman called her "noxious stench" did not bode well for her longevity. But this is not how I saw her. Violette was the powerful body in whose shadow my own body had become flesh. I had grown up under her fragrant wing. My desire to live was born from her fierce will to exist; my furious longing to vanquish my fears was nourished by her courage; my need to build my muscles owed everything to my desire to impress her. Thanks to her, thanks to her *gaze*, I had ceased being the ghost of my father. I no longer knocked into the furniture, no longer drowned in my own shadow, was no longer afraid of mirrors: she turned an evanescent boy into a tree-climbing monkey, a fish of the deep, a cheetah on my bicycle. I was her "strapping young lad" who had overcome his fears, who could dive from the top of the rocks and who no longer trembled when he held a living fish in his hand. Even in her absence I would sometimes impose difficult tasks on myself, just for the glory of her esteem: petting a dog that was infuriated by a chain; going to amusement parks where bumper cars, terror trains, and roller coasters are so many traps set to frighten you; depriving myself of Dodo's company when anxiety made it most necessary to me. Yes, Violette even managed to get me to admit that Dodo was an imaginary little brother! Violette had authorised me to live; under my protection she would never die! And Violette had died.

65 years, 9 months, 3 days *Thursday, 13 July, 1989*

Thinking back on it today, I realise I owed my desire to go to boarding school to Violette: "My strapping young lad, now that the watercress has grown around the fountain, we'll need to lock you in a box. So that you really study! So that you don't waste your talents! You'll see, you'll like it. You'll fly sky-high!"

65 years, 10 months *Thursday, 10 August, 1989*

Memories of Manès throwing me in the water to teach me how to swim, which neither he nor Violette knew how to do. "Make yourself limp like Albert when he falls off his stool (Albert was the town drunk in Mérac) and you will float to the surface like one of his wine corks." With complete trust in Violette, I made myself limp, and indeed I floated up to the surface, and I reproduced as best I could the breaststroke movements Violette had made me practise, my body suspended on the outstretched arms of that colossal major-domo, Manès. "A frog," Violette would say. "Don't tell me you can't do this as well as a frog?" So I learned to swim by imitating a frog. (Later I would learn how to do Fermantin's conventional crawl.) Manès, throw me in the river! Not near the rushes, I can touch bottom there. Into the deep part! Promise me tomorrow you'll throw me into the deep part! "And why don't you just throw yourself in?" Because I'm afraid to, of course! Exquisite metamorphosis of fear into jubilation: throw me further, higher, again, again! And each time, the vestiges of my apprehension would transform my fear into courage, my courage into joy, my joy into pride, and my pride into happiness. "Again! Again!" Bruno, Lison and Grégoire, in their turn, would shout when later I would throw *them* into the river. "Again! Again!" Fanny and Marguerite shout today.

66 years, 1 month, 1 day *Saturday, 11 November, 1989*

Those holes in my memory that occur more and more frequently: a sudden logjam in the middle of a sentence; bewildered silence when

I run into a stranger who joyously shouts out my first name; embarrassment when I meet a woman whom I loved in the past and whose face means nothing to me now (yet there were not that many!); titles of books forgotten the moment I need to call them to mind; lost objects; promises I made for which I am criticised for not having kept . . . All that, which has always been a problem for me, is very disagreeable. But what exasperates me most is finding myself in the state of wary animal, when I am afraid of forgetting *what I am going to want to say next* in a conversation that has barely begun! I have never trusted my memory. Of course, I remember almost word for word everything my father taught me when I was a child, but today I wonder if this wasn't to the detriment of everything else: names, faces, dates, places, events, books, circumstances, etc. This handicap made my studies and my career more difficult, without, however, anyone's really noticing it – in conversation, I would replace a word I couldn't find by resorting to a circumlocution. This earned me the reputation of being long-winded. Circumlocution makes you talk much more than your interlocutor, just like a truffle-hunting dog that zigzags, nose to the ground, and walks ten times more than its master.

Today, my memory only serves to remind me of its lapses. Remember that you have a bad memory!

66 years, 1 month, 21 days — *Friday, 1 December, 1989*

I slept well, as usual when it rains.

66 years, 2 months, 15 days — *Monday, 25 December, 1989*

Too much to drink last night. Too much fatty food. Which I ate compulsively, talking and laughing a lot. In other words, I ate like a young person. Lison, Philippe, Grégoire and a few friends were there. Mona had surpassed herself. As a result, I had night sweats and was dizzy when I woke up. The whole room was spinning. Especially when I was lying down. Standing, the décor stabilises. But watch out for any abrupt movement! Sitting down or getting up too quickly, turning my head suddenly, and the merry-go-round begins again. I am an unstable axis around which the world turns. What was the name of those metallic spinning tops when I was a child that you would set in motion by pulling a string and that spun on a wobbly metal rod?

66 years, 2 months, 16 days *Tuesday, 26 December, 1989*

A gyroscope! It was called a gyroscope! This morning, the gyroscope is still spinning inside me, but the décor is stable.

66 years, 3 months, 8 days *Thursday, 18 January, 1990*

That brief feeling of dizziness walking on an icy pavement when I am not, in fact, slipping. I first put down one foot, then the other. My arms shoot out to help me keep my balance. Yet, because the municipal sanitation workers have done their job – the icy patch is rough, greyish, made harmless – I don't slip at all. But I need to reach a decent bit of asphalt, in this case, the pavement opposite, to regain confidence in my steps. So, it would seem I am endowed with a "knowledge of vertigo" and, like everyone who thinks he "knows", am prey to false interpretations.

66 years, 7 months, 9 days *Saturday, 19 May, 1990*

Bruno, returning home from the States, is immediately summoned to Grégoire's school. It appears that Grégoire has been an adept of the *fainting game*, a mock-strangulation game that has already resulted in a few victims. The school administration is obviously up in arms. Grégoire and his partners are threatened with expulsion. Bruno, worried, is wondering about the "death drives" of contemporary children in general and of Grégoire in particular. He's taken aback when Grégoire says: "It's nothing, it's really cool, that's all." (The fact that he only sees his father two or three times a year does not exactly make him trust him.) As for me, this story reminds me of the game Etienne and I played at his age. It was, in fact, the same game, except that we did not fake strangulation, but rather suffocation. The end result, however, was the same: staying on the very edge of passing out, or even going beyond it. The game consisted in cutting off the other person's breathing by pressing on his chest while he himself emptied his lungs as much as possible: and he fainted. A delightful feeling of being about to faint, then truly, simply fainting. Once the person who had passed out came to, he would do the same thing to his partner. We adored fainting! Did any adults know about this? Were there accidents? I don't recall any. Today's fainting game, with a scarf, has an ancestor! I gave Grégoire an anatomy lesson: carotid arteries, jugular veins, etc., to explain to him how dangerous the game was. He asked why, if it was so pleasant, it could be fatal. I abstained from answering that the one explains the other. I spoke of the feeling of drunkenness that depriving the blood of oxygen causes, and the very real dangers this poses to the brain. The same effect is caused by deep-sea diving and mountain climbing, both sports that are highly supervised. Once I was alone with Bruno again, I asked him if, when he was his son's age, he had ever played an equivalent game. "Never!" Come on, I said, didn't you play the same tricks with ether, for example? "Stop it, Papa. It's not the same thing at all!" Indeed it was, and I was just as worried then as he is now.

66 years, 7 months, 13 days *Wednesday, 23 May, 1990*

When I told Ti-Joe about Grégoire, including the anatomy lesson, he commented: "Your grandson is lucky to have a grandfather like you!" To teach him about the circulatory system, Manès would have bled a pig. Otherwise, Ti-Joe was not surprised by this fainting game. According to him, suffocating, strangulation, sniffing stain-remover, glue, ether, varnish: all of these lead in the end to alcohol and modern drugs, and are used in the service of an obsession as old as the hills: trying to see if, on the other side of those damn teenage years, there is a light at the end of the tunnel. And, while he was at it, he asked me: "And you, with old age approaching, what is your drug of choice?"

66 years, 8 months, 25 days *Thursday, 5 July, 1990*

We stopped at Etienne and Marceline's on our way down to Mérac. Etienne 's forehead is wrinkled, his eyes stare, his movements are slowed, but he was smiling to see us. To tell the truth, only his mouth smiled, an involuntary smile, a reminiscence of a smile, as if he remembered what it was like to smile once upon a time. On the other hand, he cannot recall Mona's name. He starts sentences that he then ends with "So, you see what I mean?" I see, my old friend, I see . . .

Marceline admits in secret that Etienne 's illness is progressing quickly. He's losing his memory, of course, and is clumsy, but what frightens her the most are his fits of anger whenever the slightest unexpected thing occurs: a misplaced object, the ringing of the telephone, a form to fill in. He cannot tolerate surprises any more, she says; the smallest setback makes him terribly anxious.

The only thing that relaxes him is his butterfly collection. It is the fortified camp where the last troops are resisting. "Come and see my *Parnassius Apollo*." Once again I am struck by the disproportion between his enormous fingers and the delicacy with which he handles the very fine velvet of his victims. Before leaving us, he said to me in secret: "Don't tell Marceline, but I'm a goner." And he adds, pointing to his skull: "It's my head."

66 years, 10 months, 6 days *Thursday, 16 August, 1990*

"Emissions," says Mona, stuffing the boys' sheets into the washing machine. Nocturnal? I ask. "And diurnal," she jokes, adding a pair of sticky socks and two pairs of boys' underpants glazed with sperm.

Oh, yes. They invented the handkerchief for snot, the spittoon for saliva, toilet paper for stools, portable plastic urinals for urine, and fine crystal for Victorian tears, but nothing specifically for sperm. So that whenever a male reaches puberty and discharges anywhere that his urges incite him to, he tries to hide his infamy with whatever is at hand: sheets, socks, washcloths, dishcloths, handkerchiefs, Kleenex, bath towels, dissertation drafts, newspaper, coffee filters, anything and everything, even curtains, bathmats and carpets. Because the well never dries up – so numerous and unforeseeable are the boys' urges – there is no way to cir*cum*navigate the mess around here! It's ridiculous. A receptacle for sperm should be invented immediately, and offered to every boy on the very first day he ejaculates. The event would be ritualised, and it would be the occasion for a family celebration. The boy would wear his jewel on a chain around his neck as proudly as he wears his Holy Communion watch. "And he would give it to his fiancée on the day of their engagement," added Mona, who thought my idea was a good one.

66 years, 10 months, 7 days *Friday, 17 August, 1990*

Until very recently, the word "pollution" in French referred either to the profanation of a sacred place, or – and especially – to involuntary nocturnal emissions, or wet dreams, otherwise termed *spermatorrhoea.* The choice of precisely this word "pollution" to designate the destruction of our natural surroundings by toxic products dates from the 1960s, the height of the great industrial fucking-up of the environment.

66 years, 10 months, 9 days *Sunday, 19 August, 1990*

That doubt I had as a teenager: would I become a man? In the summer, plane tree leaves were my sperm collectors of choice. Not very practical, however.

66 years, 10 months, 9 days *Sunday, 2 September, 1990*

The summer holidays are over for the children. They have left us drained. Literally: two empty wells. Just the sight of the energy they expend between sunrise and sunset fatigues us. Their bodies are perpetually expending energy, whereas ours are now heading towards economising it. In a mere two weeks, they have exhausted our supply of vital energy. These kids are cutting our lives short, I say to Mona.

And we collapse onto our bed, inert. Where did that inextinguishable desire to create the next generation go? I am as limp as a rag and Mona is as dry as a dust storm.

66 years, 10 months, 24 days *Monday, 3 September, 1990*

I realise I have said nothing about the waning of our desire over the years in this diary. It is not so much a matter of wondering how long it has been since we last made love (magazine fodder), but of how our bodies managed to shift smoothly from perpetual copulation to the simple delight in our body heat. This gradual extinction of desire doesn't seem to have led to frustration, except that some of our outbursts of temper can perhaps be blamed on the fact that our bodies no longer speak to each other sexually. We would make love several times a day during the first months we were together; we did it every night when we were young (with the exception of the last months of Mona's pregnancies, and we continued to do so for at least two decades (as if it were inconceivable for us to fall asleep with one outside the other), then less often, then almost not at all, then not at all. But our bodies remain entwined, my left arm around Mona, her head in the hollow of my shoulder, her leg across mine, her arm on my chest, our naked bodies in their shared heat, breath and sweat mixed together, the scent of a couple . . . Our desire has run its course beneath the scented shelter of our love.

67 years, 3 months, 2 days *Saturday, 12 January, 1991*

Coming home from the Vernes', I broke a tooth. No doubt about it: my upper left molar. My tongue goes to feel around, identifies a suspicious ridge, comes back, returns, yes, that's it, the Matterhorn in my mouth. This tooth had already undergone a root canal. Chicken breast, courgettes au gratin, blueberry tart, dull conversation: there was nothing in all that on which to break a tooth. This is the *real* beginning of old age. A spontaneous break. Broken nails, hair, teeth, hips: we are turning to powder inside our bags of skin. The iceberg breaks off from our pole, but noiselessly, without that groaning of the glaciers that disturbs the polar night. Ageing means witnessing this thaw. He melted away, Maman used to say about a sick old man. She would also say, "He took off," and the child I was would imagine an octogenarian taking flight at the end of an airport runway. Violette used to say about someone who had died: So-and-so has left us. I would wonder where he'd gone.

67 years, 3 months, 15 days *Friday, 25 January, 1991*

Speaking of teeth, I was supposed to have lunch with J.M.L., my protégé during my final years at the Ministry. Disappointment: he couldn't make it. And he sent us this apology: "Having been savagely attacked yesterday by a dentist who ran off with my four wisdom teeth, I am sorry to say that I will be unable to come to lunch with you today, even to eat porridge. Distribute my share to the poor and drink a toast to my memory."

That lad was always a hothead (having all your wisdom teeth pulled out at once!), but he accepted the consequences with panache. He was a diplomat who was straight as an arrow, the only one of his kind as far as I know.

67 years, 4 months, 13 days *Saturday, 23 February, 1991*

When I am lying on my side, in a certain position that through experience I am able to get into without a problem, I can feel my heart beating deep inside the ear on which my head is pressing with all its weight. A gentle, regular hissing sound, a reassuring piston, whose company has been soothing me since I was a small child and which does not completely drown out the whistling of my tinnitus.

67 years, 9 months, 8 days *Thursday, 18 July, 1991*

One of Grégoire's favourite pranks: I'm walking down the hall when his hand, thrusting out of some hiding place, blocks my way, waving a photograph of me. Of course, I jump. Grégoire's conclusion: "Poor Grandfather, you are so ugly that you scare yourself!" Our ritual requires me to follow him, catch him, and take my revenge by tickling him until he cries for mercy. Once that's done, I look at the picture. Each time, I am struck by the same thing: the more recent a photo is, the harder it is for me to recognise myself; if it is old, I recognise myself immediately. That last photograph was taken and printed by Grégoire himself two weeks ago. I have to reimagine the scene in order to recognise myself (quickly, of course, but none the less it is a reimagining): Mérac, the library, the window, the yew tree, the afternoon, the armchair and, in the armchair, me, listening to music. "Judging from your tragico-melancholic face," says Grégoire, "it must have been Mahler." So, you can guess what kind of music someone is listening to by the expression on his face? "Of course. When you are listening to Penderecki, you look like an abandoned Rubik's cube."

67 years, 9 months, 17 days *Saturday, 27 July, 1991*

Spent three hours in a lounge chair reading a detective novel and I cannot get up without leaning heavily on the armrests. Stiff, aching hips. For a few seconds, I have the feeling of being stuck in ice. From now on between the world and me lies the obstacle of my body.

I can picture Uncle Georges during his final years, sitting in his armchair talking about any old thing, his eyes sparkling, his hands like two dragonflies, exactly as when he was forty or fifty. But as soon as he would stand up, we could hear the creaking of his knees, hips and back. Seated, a young man; standing, a hunched old man grimacing with pain and from whom emanated a faint odour of urine in the end. He retained till his last days a very gracious aptitude for taking things *lightly*. "With age," he would say (quoting I don't know whom), "our rigidity shifts."

67 years, 9 months, 18 days *Sunday, 28 July, 1991*

Where does *my* feeling of permanence come from, though? Everything is deteriorating, but the joy of existing remains constant. I was thinking about that yesterday as I watched Mona walking in front of me. Mona and her "queen's bearing," as Ti-Joe says. During the course of the forty years I have walked behind her, naturally her body has grown heavier and has lost its elasticity but – how can I express it? – it has grown heavier *around her way of walking*, which has never changed. I always experience the same pleasure watching Mona walk. Mona *is* the way she walks.

68 years, 8 days *Friday, 18 October, 1991*

One of Ti-Joe's protégés, an ex-legionnaire with one leg (thanks to the Algerian War), comes to see him on crutches. What happened to your artificial leg? Ti-Joe asks. The man beats around the bush. Ti-Joe is patient and learns, after an elaborate story, that there was drinking, a marital spat, and that the wife, after one too many beatings, left him, taking the artificial leg with her! "And what conclusion do you think," Ti-Joe asks me, "my legionnaire drew from all this?" (Hmmm . . .) "Well, this: 'Obviously she still loves me, don't you think, if she split with my artificial leg.'" Instead of concluding that the man was an idiot, Ti-Joe deduced that we all have an insatiable need to be loved.

68 years, 3 months, 26 days *Wednesday, 5 February, 1992*

Aching ankle. Went to see a rheumatologist, who told me to see a podiatrist who, after having examined my feet, stated: "Naturally you don't know how to dance?" I confirmed this. "Nothing surprising about that; the sole of your right foot is resting on only three points (which she indicates) rather than on its entire surface." And so my inability to dance, which I have always attributed to my lack of "embodiment", is reduced to a simple matter of mechanics. I hear myself explain to the podiatrist that, even so, when I was young, I boxed, I played tennis, and that I *excelled at dodgeball*! The preposterousness of these words causes such a clamour inside me that I don't hear the podiatrist's answer, which was probably technical. Me and my dodgeball! (Oh, Violaine!) Why on earth at sixty-eight do I still want to be taken for a *dodgeball* star, when everyone else has certainly forgotten about the very existence of this game? Later, I think about this and I picture myself in the school playground, playing this terribly fast game with its brutal rules: dodge, intercept, trick, kick, stay alone on the field, and still destroy the opposing team, undergo the fire from both sides at the same time, so agile, so combative, tireless, oh! A *purely physical* joy! Such exaltation! Every dodgeball game was a rebirth for me. And this rebirth is what I am celebrating when I brag about having been a dodgeball star!

68 years, 7 months, 20 days *Saturday, 30 May, 1992*

I caught Grégoire masturbating red-handed, he with the illegal weapon in his hand, I with the doorknob in mine. Both of us were terribly embarrassed for no reason, really. As they say, any desire that the hand does not clasp is but a dream. I was bothered all day by an awkward feeling of having intruded. I was stuck in the mind of a pre-adolescent boy, that formless being pulling itself from childhood by the dick. This evening, I turned the attic upside down until I found the Game of the Goose of Defloration that Etienne and I had invented in boarding school. I challenged Grégoire to a game. He beat me hands down. As he was about to arrive at square 12 ("When he finds your dirty underpants by chance, your Uncle Georges congratulates you: You have become a man"), he smiled at me gratefully. I gave him the game.

68 years, 8 months, 5 days *Monday, 15 June, 1992*

Walking alone yesterday in the Luxembourg Gardens. A woman, still young, shouts my name joyously, asks me how Mona is, kisses me on the cheek goodbye, and goes on her way. Who was she? Then this evening as I was leaving the Vieux-Colombier theatre, I could not come up with the two or three decisive words I would have needed in the critical sparring match between T. H. and me. When I was looking for the car in the Saint-Sulpice car park, I got off the lift on the wrong floor, went up, went down, turned in circles. What's wrong with my brain? I am surprised I haven't written more about this forgetfulness of mine that has poisoned my life. I must have thought it was a matter of my psychology. How stupid of me! The phenomenon is as physical as can be. It's a question of electricity, a bad connection between mental circuits, a few synapses that are no longer doing their job as transmitters between the appropriate neurons. The road is cut off, the bridge has collapsed; you have to take a 25-kilometre detour to find the lost memory. As if that weren't *physical!*

68 year, 8 months, 6 days *Tuesday, 16 March, 1992*

I should have kept a diary of everything I have forgotten.

68 years, 10 months, 1 day *Tuesday, 11 August, 1992*

Fanny, who has just turned eleven and who has a greater sense of boredom than Marguerite, asks me if the time passes as slowly for me as it does for her. At the moment, seven times faster, I answer, but it changes constantly. She objects that "from the point of view of the clock" (*sic*), the same amount of time is passing for her as for me. That's true, I say, but neither of us is a clock, which, in my opinion, has no point of view whatsoever. And I gave her a little lecture on subjective time in which she learned that our perception of duration is strictly a function of the time that has elapsed since our birth. Then she asks me if *each minute* passes eight times faster for me than for her. (Ouch, this is getting complicated.) No, I say, if I spend the same time at the dentist as you spend playing with Marguerite, some minutes will seem much longer to me than to you. Long silence. I can hear the wheels of her little brain spinning to reconcile the notions of contingency and totality and I notice that the wrinkles between her two eyes caused by thinking give her the same expression Lison had at her age. Finally, she suggests the following: Let's watch the big hand of the clock together "to force time to pass at the same speed for both of us." Which we do, giving to this shared minute the silence and solemnity of a commemoration. And it is a commemoration, because this whispered conversation reminds me of the lectures in "minor philosophy" that my father would whisper to me sixty years ago (yesterday, in other words) in the tick-tocking of this very same clock. The minute having elapsed, Fanny kisses my cheek and, before running off, says: "Grandfather, I like being bored with you."

69 years *Saturday, 10 October, 1992*

Dinner with a small group for my birthday. "My birthday" is a childish expression that we drag along with us until we blow out our last candle.

69 years, 9 months, 13 days *Friday, 23 July, 1993*

I had forgotten that Montaigne had a bad memory:

> Memory is a faculty of wonderful use, and without which the judgement can very hardly perform its office: for my part I have none at all . . . And when I have a speech of consequence to make, if it be long, I am reduced to the miserable necessity of getting by heart word for word, what I am to say; I should otherwise have neither method nor assurance, being in fear that my memory would play me a slippery trick. But this way is no less difficult to me than the other; I must have three hours to learn three verses . . . The more I mistrust it the worse it is; it serves me best by chance; I must solicit it negligently; for if I press it, 'tis confused, and after it once begins to stagger, the more I sound it, the more it is perplexed; it serves me at its own hour, not at mine . . . If I venture in speaking to digress never so little from my subject, I am infallibly lost . . . I am forced to call the men who serve me

either by the names of their offices or their country; for names are very hard for me to remember . . . and if I should live long, I do not doubt but I should forget my own name . . . It has befallen me more than once to forget the watchword I had three hours before given or received, and to forget where I had hidden my purse . . . ; I turn over books; I do not study them. What I retain I no longer recognise as another's; 'tis only what my judgement has made its advantage of, the discourses and imaginations in which it has been instructed: the author, place, words, and other circumstances, I immediately forget.

And cited by Montaigne (Terence, *The Eunuch*; I, 2, 25): "I am full of holes; I leak at every point."

70 years, 5 months, 2 days *Saturday, 12 March, 1994*

Yesterday, at A. and C.'s place, we were wondering if W.'s cancer wasn't perhaps psychosomatic. Everyone agreed. Yes, yes, of course, unhappy retirement, his wife's illness, his daughter's divorce, etc., everyone was in agreement until young P., the eldest son of our hosts, stopped the conversation dead by saying, "W. will be very reassured to learn that he is dying of a psychosomatic illness. That's so much less distasteful than dying of colon cancer!" Upon which young P. left the room, slamming the door behind him.

I think I understand the boy's anger. Without contesting the fact that our body expresses in its way what we cannot manage to put into words – aching shoulders *signify* that I'm carrying the weight of the world, Fanny's stomach cramps *express* her terror of maths – I clearly see how "everything is psychosomatic" can be annoying for P.'s generation. It stigmatises the same primness that disgusted me at his age. When I was young, the body simply did not exist as a subject of conversation: you could not talk about it at meals. Today, it is tolerated at the dinner table, but under the condition that the body speak *only* about its soul! Implicitly surrounding this "everything is psychosomatic" is the old idea that our bodies' problems are the expression of our character flaws: the high blood pressure of the highly strung; the lethargy of the overweight; the inevitable Alzheimer's of the misanthrope... Not only do people fall ill, but they are responsible for their own illnesses! What are you dying from, old chap? The bad things you have done to yourself, the little deals you made with the devil, those ephemeral benefits you got from unhealthy practices, in other words, from your very nature, which you tended poorly and did not respect properly! It is your superego that is killing you. (In other words, nothing new since the time of *Les Liaisons dangereuses* when smallpox allowed Mme Merteuil's soul to be visible on her ravaged face.) You are dying, guilty of having polluted the planet, eaten whatever you wanted, lived through an era without having changed it, closed your eyes to the health of the world to the point that you neglected your own! The entire system, which your laziness covered up, has attacked your innocent body and is killing it.

For if this "everything is psychosomatic" points to the guilty party, it is in order to better celebrate the innocent. Our body is innocent, ladies and gentlemen, our body is innocence itself, this is what this "everything is psychosomatic" is shouting! If only we were *nice*, if only we behaved *properly*, if we lived a *healthy* life in a *controlled* environment, not only would our soul be immortal, but our bodies would be as well!

This is the long diatribe I deliver in the car on our way home with the passion of my rediscovered youth.

"Maybe," said Mona. "But don't leave out the fact that P. never misses the opportunity to make his parents look like idiots."

70 years, 5 months, 3 days — *Sunday, 13 March, 1994*

Ladies and gentlemen, we die because we have a body, and each death is the extinction of an entire culture.

70 years, 8 months, 5 days *Wednesday, 15 June, 1994*

"We've met before," Grégoire's elderly philosophy teacher tells me during the parent–teacher meetings I attended to collect all the praises being heaped on my grandson. Really? "Yes, I tortured you when you were young," he says with a friendly smile. And then I recognise him: Dr Bêk's nephew! The one whose enormous hand stifled my screams forty years ago when his uncle was tearing out my polyp. Since the beginning of the school year, Grégoire has been praising to the skies this "absolutely fantastic" philosophy teacher. The fact that he turns out to be a Senegalese giant never entered into Grégoire's description, since it had no philosophical bearing on the subject. Monsieur F. taps on his nostril and says: "Today we put people to sleep for that kind of operation, but it is still just as inefficient. Your grandson also speaks a bit nasally, but this doesn't prevent him from being an excellent philosopher."

71 years, 5 months, 22 days *Saturday, 1 April, 1995*

Back from the hospital where Grégoire and I have been to visit Sylvie. She recognises us, but without really *focusing*, it seems. "Grégoire," she says softly, and it lacks reality. He is her son, she knows it, it is her son's name, she remembers it, her voice is gentle, but the image and the name don't reach her, don't meet. "It's as if everything appeared blurry to her," says Grégoire, adding: "In fact, she herself seems blurry, as if she were walking next to her body, don't you think, Grandfather?" When Sylvie first fell ill and Grégoire would give me news of her, he was already saying: "Maman is not entirely 'clear'," or else, "Things are better today, Maman is 'clear'." I see a faint smile flicker across his face when Dr W., ushering us into his office, tells us we are going to "clarify" things.

71 years, 5 months, 25 days *Tuesday, 4 April, 1995*

Thinking about Sylvie last night (she should be out in a month), the word "unhinged" that Maman used when she would complain about me came to mind. The word caused an impression of vertigo and vagueness in me. At bottom, this diary will have been a perpetual exercise in "clarifying", avoiding the vague, keeping the body and mind "hinged" . . . I've spent my life "clarifying".

71 years, 8 months, 4 days *Wednesday, 14 June, 1995*

A massive invasion of the common body on the 91 bus at the Gobelins stop. When I get on at the Montparnasse stop, the bus is empty. I take advantage of this unhoped-for solitude to lose myself in a book and am barely disturbed by the passengers who, from one stop to the next, begin to sit down around me. By the time we reach Vavin, all the seats are occupied. At Gobelins, the aisle is packed. I notice this with the innocent selfishness of someone who, having found a seat, enjoys his reading even more. A young man sitting across from me is also lost in his book. A student most likely. He is reading Fritz Zorn's *Mars.* Standing in the aisle next to the student, a large woman, about sixty years old, winded, carrying a shopping bag stuffed to the brim with vegetables, is breathing loudly. The student lifts his eyes, meets my gaze, sees the woman and spontaneously gets up to offer her his seat. "Please sit, madame." There is something Germanic in the young man's politeness. Standing straight, tall, with a stiff neck and a discreet smile, he is quite distinguished. The woman doesn't budge. It seems to me that she is even glowering at him. Pointing to the seat, the young man insists. "Please, madame." The woman gives in against her will, or so it seems to me. In any case, she doesn't say thank you. She moves in front of the empty seat, but does not sit down. She stands facing me, her shopping bag in hand, but remains standing in front of the empty seat. The young man practically bends over backwards to insist again. "Please do sit down, madame." At this point, the woman speaks. "Not right away," she says in a stentorian voice. "I don't like it when the seat's too hot!" The young man blushes. Her words are so stupefying that they prevent me from going back to my reading. A quick sidelong glance allows me to see the other passengers' reactions. Someone stifles a giggle, someone stares at his feet, someone else conspicuously looks out of the window ... In other words, people are *embarrassed*. Then the woman leans over to me and says, with her face a few inches from mine, as if we were old friends: "I'm waiting for it to cool down!" All of a sudden, people are staring at *me*, waiting for my reaction. It then occurs to me that at this precise second all of us form a body on the 91 bus. A body that has been educated the same way. A single body whose backside cannot stand the heat of a seat warmed by other backsides, and that would prefer to throw itself under the wheels of a bus rather than admit it in public.

71 years, 8 months, 5 days *Thursday, 15 June, 1995*
Without our upbringing, there would be no humour.

72 years, 2 months, 2 days *Tuesday, 12 December, 1995*
Some illnesses, by the terror they instil in us, have the advantage of making all the others bearable. The propensity for imagining the worst in order to accept what we already suffer from is the frequent subject of conversation for people of my generation. Just yesterday, at dinner at the Vernes', talking about T. S.'s diagnosis: "We were afraid it was Alzheimer's! Thank goodness he is simply depressed!" Phew! Honour has been saved. T. S. will still wind up nuts, but no one will be able to say that Dr Alzheimer got the better of him.

I am laughing on the inside, but cannot exclude myself from the bunch. I would rather die than admit it, but the threat of Alzheimer's (and of course I'm thinking of Etienne here, whose condition has deteriorated) terrifies me as much as anyone else. Still, this terror has its advantages: it distracts me from what is really affecting me. My sugar levels are worrisome, my creatinine levels are off the scales, my tinnitus disturbs my hearing more and more, my cataract makes everything I see blurry; I wake up every morning with a new pain. In other words, old age is advancing on all fronts, but I only have one real fear: the fear of Alois Alzheimer! So much so that every day I force myself to do memorisation exercises – my family thinks this is some erudite pastime of mine. I can recite entire sections from my beloved Montaigne, Don Quixote, my old Pliny, or the *Divine Comedy* (all in the original, mind you!), but if I forget a meeting, misplace my keys, don't recognise Monsieur What's-His-Name, trip over a first name or lose the thread of a conversation, the ghost of Dr Alzheimer immediately appears before me. No matter how often I remind myself that my memory has always been unreliable, that already as a child it played tricks on me, that this is the way I am, nothing changes. The conviction that Alzheimer's has finally caught up with me defies all reason and I see myself a short time from now in the last stages of the illness, having lost contact with the world and myself, a living thing that does not remember having lived.

In the meantime, they ask me to recite a poem during dessert, which I do once they have properly pleaded with me. Oh! they say. *You* have nothing to fear from Alzheimer's disease!

72 years, 7 months, 28 days *Friday, 7 June 1996*

Frédéric, a doctor and professor of internal medicine, and Grégoire's lover, complains that he cannot go out for dinner in town without being bombarded with questions from his dining companions about their health. Not a single evening when half the guests don't cadge diagnoses, therapies, opinions, recommendations for themselves or their families. It exasperates him. "For as long as I've been practising," he says, "in fact, ever since I was a student, no one has ever asked me what interests me when I'm not playing at doctor!" And so he hates going out. If it weren't for Grégoire, Frédéric would remain cloistered at home because . . . (and now his hand slices the air above his head), he's had it up to here! According to him, mealtime turns the doctor into a shaman. Seeing a doctor eat and drink like everyone else makes him seem friendly; he becomes the witchdoctor to the tribe of hypochondriacs, the ladies' guru, that exceptional doctor – he's so human! – whom they met at so-and-so's house, don't you remember, dear? Whereas in the hospital, says Frédéric, "in the eyes of these same people, and I mean the *same* ones, I am first and foremost a doctor aspiring to be a hospital director and suspected of swelling the cost of the nation's healthcare in order to increase the size of my Porsche collection. When we dine together, however, I become the quintessence of humane medicine, respectable and competent. If you are a surgeon and someone meets you at a friend's house, he will follow you around like a little doggie all the way to the operating table and will warmly recommend your scalpel to his other friends, because doctors share a trait with jam: your family's is always the best! When I see my medical students slaving away in the emergency room, I feel like yelling: 'Get the hell out of here, forget your patients; go eat in a restaurant! That is where careers are made, not in hospital wards!'"

Frédéric gets riled up all by himself for a good part of the meal, then, as he is leaving the table, with a mischievous, malicious glance at me, he asks: "And what about you? Are you in good health? Take advantage of me while you can!"

72 years, 7 months, 30 days *Sunday, 9 June, 1996*

Grégoire's homosexuality. Despite my being broadminded ("being broadminded", such a narrow expression!), my imagination remains obtuse in matters of homosexuality. Although I can accept it in principle, my *body* cannot conceive desiring someone of the same sex. Fine, Grégoire is a homosexual, he's our Grégoire, he can do whatever he wants, the question of his sexual preferences is not an issue, but Grégoire's body being satisfied by the body of a man, that is what the mind of my own body – if I can express it this way – cannot conceive. It's not a matter of sodomy. Mona and I have not turned our noses up at it, we've enjoyed a good "tossed salad", and what a lovely young boy she made! But precisely, she was not a boy. I contemplate, as I fall asleep, Grégoire's homosexuality . . . Or rather, I stop contemplating it, the mystery unravels, it becomes the very material of the slumber that absorbs me.

72 years, 9 months, 12 days *Monday, 22 July, 1996*

Alone in the garden, I look up from my book, distracted by the singing of a bird that I regret being unable to identify. The same is true for almost all the flowers around me, which I cannot name, for a few trees as well, for most of the clouds, and for the components that make up this lump of earth that I crumble with my fingers. In all this, I cannot name a thing. The farm work I did as a teenager taught me almost nothing about nature. True, the point of it was to develop my muscles. The little I used to know I have forgotten. In sum, I have become civilised and educated to the point of having no basic knowledge! The bird that distracted me from my reading is singing in the silence of my ignorance. In fact, it's not so much its singing I'm listening to as it is the silence itself. An absolute silence. And suddenly, this question: Where has my tinnitus gone? I listen more attentively. It's just as I thought: no tinnitus, only the bird. I cover my ears to listen inside my skull. Nothing. The tinnitus has indeed disappeared. My head is empty; it buzzes a little under the pressure of my fingers, like a barrel against which I might have placed my ear. The barrel is completely empty. Empty of sound, which thrills me, and of all basic knowledge, which dismays me. I take up my scholarly book once again to empty myself out even more.

72 years, 9 months, 13 days *Tuesday, 23 July, 1996*

The tinnitus returned, of course. When? I have no idea. Last night, it was there, whistling away during my insomnia. It is almost reassuring. These small problems that terrify us so much when they first appear become more than our fellow travellers, they become *us*. Once upon a time, this is how village life designated each of us in all simplicity: the goitrous man, the hunchback, the bald man, the stutterer. And in the classroom when I was a child, the pupils called each other: fatty, cross-eyed, gimpy, cloth-eared . . . The Middle Ages considered these shortcomings to be simple facts and turned them into proper names: Gross, Crooke, Short, Beake, Hopper are still in use today. I wonder with what name medieval wisdom would have baptised me. Old Monsieur Whistler? No doubt. You know, the one who has a whistle inside his head! Accept yourself for who you are, Whistler, and live up valiantly to your name.

72 years, 9 months 14 days *Wednesday, 24 July, 1996*

I was thinking again about that bird I couldn't identify when these lines from a poem by Jules Supervielle came to mind:

And from where the woods once stood
A bird's song will rise
That no one will identify,
Or place, or even hear
Except God who, listening,
Will say, "It's a goldfinch."

I think it is from the collection *Gravitations*, and is called "Prophecy". But my bird, the real one, what was *it* called? Tomorrow I'll ask Robert.

72 years, 9 months, 16 days *Friday, 26 July, 1996*

For a while now, a flood of flatulence. An irrepressible desire to fart comes over me without warning. I'm surprised to find myself *coughing* as I fart in the childish hope that the sound of my cough will hide the sound of the fart. Impossible to know if the strategy is working because the explosion of the cough in my inner ear is louder than the outside detonation. This precaution is in fact pointless: in general, I am surrounded by people who are so civilised that they would rather die than denounce my bad manners. And therefore, no one bothers to be concerned about my cough! Savages all!

Ti-Joe, who is amused by my confession, offers me one of his jokes in exchange. As often with Ti-Joe's very physical sense of humour, this joke leaves in its wake a trail that takes as long to dissipate as the scent of a fine Chanel perfume.

TI-JOE AND THE FOUR OLD FARTERS

Four old friends get together. The first one says to the three others: When I fart, it makes a terrible noise and spreads an awful odour. The second one: Mine makes a terrible noise but no odour at all. The third one: Mine makes not a sound but the stench, my friends, the stench of it! And the fourth one: Not me, not a sound or a smell. After a long silence and a few sidelong glances, one of the three others asks him: So why do you bother farting?

72 years, 9 months, 27 days *Tuesday, 6 August, 1996*

Come on, man, be brave! What is the precise nature of the unformulated questions I have been asking myself about Grégoire's homosexuality? That is the real question! I was thinking about it this afternoon as I was watching Grégoire and Frédéric picking raspberries. Grégoire gave me the answer himself after dinner, once he had swallowed the last piece of raspberry crumble. While we were taking a stroll in the garden, he held me by the arm and told me he knew *exactly* what I was thinking about. "You are wondering, Grandfather, which one of us is top and which one is bottom." (The grandfather is slightly dumbfounded.) "It's completely natural, you know; everyone wonders the same thing about homosexuals." (Moment of silence.) "And because you love me as much as I love you, you are wondering if your favourite grandson takes all the necessary precautions against AIDS." Indeed, this is the bottleneck where all my concerns have accumulated. As a result, I release a flood of questions that must torment so many poor folks who don't dare ask a soul about it all. For example, is saliva a risk factor? And blowjobs? Can you catch AIDS from giving a blowjob? What about haemorrhoids? Gums? Do you take good care of your teeth? Does frequency of sex matter? Number of different partners? Are you and Frédéric faithful at least? "Don't worry, Grandfather," Grégoire tells me. "Frédéric didn't leave his wife to cheat on me with another man! And as for me, I am as resolutely monogamous as you are. As for top or bottom, it varies, according to our mood or how it's going, sometimes one and the other in succession." Another stroll around the garden, and then he offers this more technical explanation: "As for *why homosexuality exists*, what a vast question, Grandfather! Let's remain on the surface, okay, and simply say that only a man can really satisfy another man. Think of a blowjob, for example, from a strictly technical point of view: you have to have experienced the benefits of it yourself in order to give a really good one! A woman, no matter how talented she is, will only ever know half the story."

Late that night, the two of us are sitting by the fire: "In fact," he confides in me, "you are the source of my two vocations. I became a doctor because I didn't want you to die, and gay because you took me to see *Greystoke*. That beautiful naked boy in the trees was my archangel Gabriel!" But you were only eight years old! I say to him. "Yes, and I was precocious in that area as well!"

Still later that night, when we're talking about medicine in general, I tell him the story of how Violette died. His diagnosis: phlebitis. Violette had become more and more out of breath, her varicose veins were swelling, physical effort had become harder and harder, and that afternoon a clot must have migrated from her legs or her groin to her lungs, where it blocked her breathing. "Your Violette died from a massive pulmonary embolism, Grandfather. You could not have done a thing – not you or anyone else."

For the first time in sixty years, as I thought about Violette's death, I managed to fall asleep in peace.

8

73–79 YEARS OLD

(1996–2003)

When do we stop telling people how old we are?
When do we start telling them again?

73 years, 28 days *Thursday, 7 November, 1996*

My conference in Brussels ended in a completely unexpected way. Two claws grabbed me by the ribs and crushed me until the pain took my breath away. I must have turned white. Frowns appeared on faces in the audience. It took all my willpower not to double over and to remain standing behind the lectern, which I held on to for dear life. When I caught my breath again and recovered my train of thought, it seemed to me that my voice had gone down an octave. I tried in vain to make it rise again, but pain was depriving me of the air I needed to do so. I concluded as best I could in a strangled voice, then left the room. I did not go to the dinner and, as soon as I got back to Paris, called Grégoire who, on Frédéric's advice, sent me to get an ultrasound scan of my bladder and kidneys. My bladder was distended and my kidneys had doubled in size. This was caused by my prostate; as it swelled, it compressed the urethral canal so much that it became as thin as a hair. Since my urine no longer flowed at the necessary speed, my bladder swelled like a goatskin until it lost all elasticity and my kidneys retained the liquid that my bladder could no longer eliminate. I will need a more specific diagnosis, which requires a cystoscopy. This consists of shoving a camera down your urethra to inspect your bladder from the inside, Grégoire explains to me. The idea that my dick can be penetrated by anything is totally terrifying to me. To get fucked in the cock! I had to take two Xanax in order to accept what Grégoire described as an "exploratory necessity." But it sounds like a Chinese torture! This duct must be as sensitive as a high-voltage power line! "Don't worry, Grandfather, we'll give you a local anaesthetic, you'll hardly feel a thing." Anaesthetise my dick? How do you anaesthetise a dick? With a shot? Where? Inside? Not on your life!

I didn't get a wink of sleep.

73 years, 1 month, 2 days *Tuesday, 12 November, 1996*

Yesterday morning, I underwent this cystoscopy, feeling more dead than alive. Yet I was sufficiently in control of myself to follow with interest the path of the serpent-camera through my penile duct. It wasn't all that painful. I could definitely feel it advancing, as if someone were crawling inside me. I thought of the subway in Fellini's *Roma*, of the buried marvels that the camera was going to discover as it violated the sanctuary of my bladder. The radiologist had a bit of trouble locating the entrance. Several times the tip of the camera bumped against what I imagined was the outer wall of my bladder, without being able to go in. "Oh, well, we are going to have to make this a tad wider." (There are all kinds of doctors – those who minimise, those who exaggerate, those who say nothing, those who reassure you, those who scold you, and the one who explains everything to you. They are all "simply human, like everyone else", guided by their knowledge and their temperament.) The camera finally managed to get through and the doc said: "Look, we're inside your bladder." It was nothing like the Fellinian marvels buried beneath Rome; a quivering ultrasound picture, indecipherable to my inexperienced eyes. "Oh, good, it's not in such bad shape. Just distended." Once the photos were taken, the radiologist withdrew his camera: "Hold your breath." The feeling of its being torn out of me surprised me more than the penetration I had feared so much, as if my organism had already grown accustomed to that prying eye at the end of its tentacle. In the afternoon, the surgeon came to see me. Operation on Friday at 3.00 p.m. They will widen my urethral canal by trimming my prostate a bit, and provide me with a catheter for the time it will take for my bladder to regain both its elasticity and its functionality. "Don't worry, it's very common, I do ten of them a week," the surgeon said.

73 years, 1 month, 4 days *Thursday, 14 November, 1996*

I have lived through these past three days like a deferred conscript. I have given up observing my body, now in the hands of the medical profession, so that I can freely experience those small joys offered to it that make life worth living: a delicious pigeon tagine in which coriander, golden raisins and cinnamon spread all the way to my cerebellum; the cries of children echoing in the courtyard; the darkness of a cinema where I would not let go of Mona's hand ("Illness has always made you more sentimental," she tells me); and, on the footbridge of the Pont des Arts, a sunset worthy of a postcard. The amazing translucence of Parisian air! Paris never manages to smell entirely of benzene!

73 years, 1 month, 5 days *Saturday, 15 November, 1996*

I came out of general anaesthesia feeling rested. No worries about what's next. Not that what's next isn't worrisome, but this is one of the virtues of being in the hospital: because the hospital deals only with the body, we can take advantage of this to put our brains on hold. In other words, no point in mulling things over, all the more so because I am not in any pain. The catheter is working instead of me. A feeling of well-being. "It's when they take it out that the fun really begins," my roommate remarks. We'll see, I say. "I know what I'm talking about. This is the third time I've been back. This damn operation never works for long." We shall see. "Indeed we shall."

On the other hand, my roommate's story attracts my attention. It is not completely true. He didn't come back a third time for the *same* operation. The first time was for a transurethral resection of the prostate, like me, exactly; but the second time was for the total ablation of that truffle after cancer was suspected. (Why have I always thought of the prostate as a truffle?) The third time, it was for something else entirely. He had barely left the hospital when, following the instructions of his doctor – Don't change any of your habits, Monsieur Charlemagne (his name is Charlemagne). "Do everything like I did before?" Everything like before! So he goes hunting, exactly like before. "It was 15 September, the day after hunting season opened. I wasn't going to miss it!" His hunting partner – it was his brother-in-law – tripped, his gun fired, and Monsieur Charlemagne was peppered with small shot where his prostate used to be. He tells me all this laughing. I laugh with him.

"In any case, when they pull out the catheter, the fun really begins."

"We shall see, Monsieur Charlemagne."

"Indeed we shall."

73 years, 1 month, 8 days *Monday, 18 November, 1996*

I don't like having visitors when I'm in the hospital. Just as I would have hated them at boarding school, and just as I will turn them away if I am ever sent to prison. The promise of a minimum of well-being lies in the impermeability of our universes. I am alone in the hospital among other solitary souls who make poignant companions. No visitors, then, except for Mona and Grégoire, of course. And Ti-Joe, who made me laugh when he told me the story of Louis Jouvet who came out of the hospital after a prostatectomy. The waiter at the café where Jouvet used to have his morning coffee kindly asked how he was doing. Since the waiter was a stutterer, the dialogue went something like this: Muh . . . Muh . . . Monsieur Jouvet . . . .wha . . . wha . . . what is the p . . . p . . . pr . . . pro . . . prostate? And Monsieur Jouvet drops these words from on high: "The prostate, my boy, is when someone pisses the way you speak."

73 years, 1 month, 17 days *Wednesday, 27 November, 1996*

For the second time in my life, I left my body in the hospital. Yesterday, before I was released, they thought they would be able to remove the catheter, but my bladder refused to function. I had what the nurse on duty called an "obstructed bladder." The expression is well chosen. My bladder is in fact totally obstructed, like a tightly closed fist. It refuses to release the least little drop, and the pain, staggering, radiates through my entire groin, all the way to my knees. It makes me double over on an incandescent ball of nerves. My eyes wide with surprise, soaked in a freezing sweat, almost unable to speak, just hiccupping that I was in pain, I folded in half over my pubis, breathless from this drizzle of molten lead. "I told you so; their thing never works," said Monsieur Charlemagne.

Once the catheter was put back in place, the pain disappeared like magic. "You'll need to keep the catheter in for a month or two to give the bladder time to get its strength back." Sigh.

73 years, 1 month, 18 days *Thursday, 28 November, 1996*

So. Out and about with the catheter. It starts at my bladder, comes out through my penis, runs along my right leg and ends in a urine pouch taped above my ankle. You empty the pouch when it is full. Approximately every four hours. As simple as that. How amazing, after all, is the elasticity and insensitivity of the urethra! I, who was so afraid of the camera's entering this minuscule duct, now realise that an entire electric train could fit through it.

But the main thing lies elsewhere: the main thing, of course, is the function – *urinating* – which I thought I controlled; it has obeyed my consciousness for as long as I can remember, was expressed by my needs, and satisfied whenever I chose; from now on it is freed from my willpower, reduced to itself. My body empties itself out as soon as it is full, that's all. A cycle that is completely independent of my will. And, below my calf, that pouch, which I empty using a spigot (the same sort of spigot you find on a cubitainer). How many times have I heard the word "humiliation" used in this instance? "You know, he is wearing one of *those devices*." Usually a silence of bashful commiseration follows, or sometimes an amusing bit of bravery: "If that were me, I would shoot myself!" (Oh, the heroism of the healthy!) In these conversations, the word "device" modestly stands in for "piss", "blood" or "shit". When people speak of a "device" each person thinks of the encounter between the patient and his matter. The revolting return of the repressed. Everything that people spend their whole lives trying to hide or silence is suddenly there, in a pouch, within reach and within eyesight. Disgusting. Yet I don't feel particularly disgusted, humiliated, or diminished. Would I feel more so if the people around me were aware of my condition?

73 years, 1 month, 21 days *Sunday, 1 December, 1996*

When it comes down to it, I am a daily witness to the breathing of my kidneys.

73 years, 1 month, 28 days *Sunday, 8 December 1996*

Last night, an accident at the As' house, where we were having dinner for the first time. An inopportune crossing of my legs unplugged the damn thing. My left foot knocked the tube out of place. Everything started dripping along my right calf and a puddle formed around my foot. I pretended to let my napkin fall, dived under the table, sopped everything up, and plugged it back in. Quick as a flash. Have to be careful about that from now on. As I was leaving, I swiped the napkin. (All in all, it's better to be remembered as a napkin thief than as the guest who pees under the table.)

73 years, 2 months *Tuesday, 10 December, 1996*

All around me people are talking about illnesses. "You can't possibly understand, you're never sick!" One of the advantages of this diary is that it has spared everyone from knowing the state of my body. My friends and family have reaped the reward of better moods because of this.

73 years, 2 months, 2 days *Thursday, 12 December, 1996*

I am a clepsydra.

73 years, 2 months, 4 days *Saturday, 14 December, 1996*

My skin is irritated by the small sticking plasters that hold the catheter against my thigh. It's getting infected. I moved the sticking plasters to different spots several times, then switched the catheter to the other leg. As a result, both my legs look like a junkie's arm. I've got to find another solution.

73 years, 2 months, 5 days *Sunday, 15 December, 1996*

I solved the problem when I saw cyclists going by on the Champ-de-Mars in their tight cycling shorts. Tomorrow I'm going to run out and buy a pair that will act like a second skin. The catheter will automatically be stuck against my thigh: no more sticking plasters.

73 years, 2 months, 7 days *Tuesday, 17 December, 1996*

It works. The Lycra holds the catheter against my skin. Mona laughs when she sees me. "My handsome cyclist!" I have the rump of an otter. I bought the shorts in a sports shop with a young salesman in visibly great health. We had a difference of opinion. I realised too late (from the weight of my ankle) that my pouch was full. I had to empty it. So I asked the young man where the gents was. He answered: No public toilet. I said it was urgent, and he repeated: No public toilets. As I was turning away without insisting, I heard him conclude: Each to his own shit.

I walked towards the shoe section and, all the while pretending to look around at eye level, I emptied the contents of the pouch in a green hunting boot with a tan leather flaps and tips. Very chic.

73 years, 2 months, 10 days *Friday, 20 December, 1996*

At the brasserie where I invited the lawyer, a Maître R., to celebrate the outcome of some business in which she had defended my interests,

I offered her, as is proper, the bench while I took the chair. She is young, intelligent, cheerful, radiant, charming. Since we no longer had any reason to discuss the matter that had allowed us to make each other's acquaintance, the conversation quickly turned more personal. And very soon – how can I express it? – very soon I managed to forget the damn catheter between my legs, my age, and even, what's worse, our age difference. Until the moment when the young woman, shifting ever so slightly on the bench, revealed our two faces next to each other: hers, across from me, fresh, young, glowing, milky, rosy; and mine in the mirror – runtish, wrinkled, yellowed, old. Fresh apple, old prune.

73 years, 2 months, 11 days *Saturday, 21 December, 1996*

As I reread this, one of Ti-Joe's more refined jokes comes to mind:

> Two bums sitting on a bench see a very pretty young woman pass by. The first one says to the other:
>
> "You see that girl there? Well, yesterday I could have had her."
>
> The other guy: "Do you know her?"
>
> The first guy: "No, but yesterday I had a hard-on."

73 years, 2 months, 16 days *Thursday, 26 December, 1996*

Tomorrow they will remove my catheter. Should I expect another obstructed bladder? The surgeon's answer to this question kept me up all night: "I hope not. Wearing that thing for a month is already a feat; I don't know what else we could do!"

73 years, 2 months, 17 days *Friday, 27 December, 1996*

So they took it out. If the word "suspense" means anything at all, I swear I experienced one of the most "suspenseful" moments of my life. Will it or will it not start working again, this bladder of mine? It hesitated. An odd (imaginary?) feeling of a balloon smoothing out its wrinkles as it inflates. A faraway pain that increases with this expansion, a harbinger of the pain of an obstructed bladder. The pain increased with the pressure. It started to radiate inside my thighs. I held my breath. My forehead started to sweat. "Breathe!" cried the nurse. "Stop tensing up like that, relax!" Attempting to empty my lungs, I could only empty my nostrils. My eyes filled with tears. Then my foreskin inflated and the dam suddenly broke, sending into the basin a stream of urine tinged with some leftover blood but as thick and heavy as a horse's piss. "You see," observed the nurse. "You can do it if you put your mind to it!"

I would love to spend some time in every hospital in France in order to study the language used to speak to patients.

73 years, 3 months, 2 days *Sunday, 12 January, 1997*

Ups and downs these past days. The bliss of no longer having that thing between my legs is greatly reduced by the fear that it will have to be put back. Therefore, a constant inspection of my flow. Quantity and intensity vary. Once or twice a really strong, solid stream that resounds joyously at the bottom of the bowl and is accompanied by the exultation of a young lad in full possession of his faculties. The rest of the time, a mediocre little fountain.

73 years, 7 months, 10 days *Tuesday, 20 May, 1997*

Brutal encounter with a street lamp this morning. I was walking near the Sorbonne. Radiant sunshine. On the opposite pavement, a group of college girls was joyously greeting spring. They had come with their breasts, which were living a life of freedom beneath their buoyant blouses and for one of the girls, they were blossoming from the low neckline of some sort of vest. Oh, such a lovely lorry driver! As I walked, I looked at them, thrilled no longer to be in a position to desire any one of them. A kind of pure wonder and delight. The street lamp paid no attention to this. It clobbered me as violently as if I had been a dirty old man hypnotised by his prey. I fell backwards and practically fainted. The young women came to my rescue. They sat me up, then brought me to a pavement café. The street lamp was still resonating in my skull. I was bleeding. They wanted to call an ambulance. I refused. They went to buy some disinfectant and some bandages in a nearby chemist's. I was able to contemplate to my heart's content the breasts of the one who, leaning over me, was bandaging me up. "You really don't want an ambulance?" No. They called a cab that didn't want to take me because of the blood on my shirt. I phoned Mona and ordered a cognac for myself while I was waiting for her, then a *menthe à l'eau* and two coffees for the young women to thank them. "Are you okay? Are you sure?" Yes, yes, don't worry, I've only been attacked by a street lamp, after all. Polite laughter. They left shortly afterwards. We had absolutely nothing to say to each other. What could we have talked about? The street lamp? Their studies? They probably had little interest in any of that. About Romain Gary's suicide, after he had become impotent? Or about Buñuel's relief, on the contrary, when he finally felt liberated from his libido? The women went back to their classes, and I ordered another cognac, in honour of Buñuel. If the Devil had offered him a new sexual life, he said, he would have refused and asked him instead to strengthen his liver and his lungs so he could go on drinking and smoking his fill.

73 years, 7 months, 11 days *Wednesday, 21 May, 1977*

Since when have I convinced myself that I no longer desire women? Since my prostate operation? Since I can no longer get an erection? (Well, just barely . . .) Has it been even longer than that? Since meeting Mona made me monogamous? The fact is I never "cheated" on her, as they say. And because I didn't cheat on her, I very rarely desired anyone else. We satisfied each other, in every sense of the word. And it lasted. But with age, as Mona's desire waned, did it go without saying that mine had to vanish as well? Did the fact that she no longer wanted to imply that I no longer could? The wisdom of a common body in a sense? Indeed! It's only a small step from "I cannot anymore" to "I no longer want to." But that small step must be taken with eyes closed. Hermetically. If we open them even the slightest bit on the way, they will show us, beneath our feet, the fathomless precipice of *no longer being*. Hemingway, Romain Gary and a host of anonymous people threw themselves into the precipice rather than continuing down that path.

Well, desire or not, I have one eye closed and half of my face is swollen, which doesn't exactly make *me* an object of desire.

73 years, 7 months, 12 days *Thursday, 22 May, 1997*

Ti-Joe: "I could never have been monogamous. If I had had to introduce *my* wife to someone, I would have had the feeling of exhibiting my penis."

73 years, 7 months, 14 days *Saturday, 24 May, 1997*

Had dinner at N.'s son's house. It had been planned for a long time. The young man wanted to thank me for a favour I had done for him. Already postponed it once, impossible to put it off again, even with my face beaten to a pulp. Which, by the way, no one mentioned all evening. Even though, God knows, it is a sight to behold! A three-dimensional rainbow. This sort of injury becomes more and more colourful as it heals. Every shade, from dark to light, shows up. I'm now entering the period of flamboyant purples and hepatic yellows. My eye socket, saturated with dead blood, is almost black. But no one around the table makes the slightest allusion to this masterpiece. There's no discussing the gentleman's mug. Fine with me. Still, during the second half of the evening, the question of the body (and what one makes it undergo) caused a completely unexpected counter-attack. Lise, the Ns' youngest daughter, who is usually so talkative according to her mother, so quick to charm the guests by enumerating her grievances against her parents ("not true, my darling?") did not open her mouth during the whole dinner. Not to utter a word or to swallow a single mouthful. When the table was cleared, the kid disappeared into her bedroom, and her mother lost no time telling us the worst as she whispered: "Our daughter is anorexic," a diagnosis that her husband calmly took down a notch: "No, no, not at all, my love, our daughter is simply being a pain in the arse, and so are you." The wife has a choking fit, a marital spat ensues, decibels rise, until Lise, bursting out of her room, screams that she has had enough, enough, "eeeeeeee-nuff" and her mouth, open wide from this confession, exhibits a pierced, tumescent tongue with a little steel ball trembling like a tiny bubble of mercury. Horror of horrors! "What is that, Lise? What do you have in your mouth? Come here this instant!" But Lise locks herself back in her room. Her mother, scandalised, is less worried about her daughter's tongue than about what kind of people her daughter is associating with. Then a certain D.G., a lawyer who is from the same generation as my hosts, directs the conversation to the question of the influence of others.

"Tell me, Geneviève, are you wearing a G-string?"

"I beg your pardon?"

"A G-string. You know, one of those little string panties that the Brazilians have nicknamed 'dental floss bikinis'."

A silence ensues, one that is all the more eloquent because the mistress of the house, if one can judge from the smooth way her skirt falls across the impeccable divide of her two hemispheres, must be wearing a G-string, and to great effect.

"And did you ever wonder," continued the lawyer, "where this influence came from, because everyone in your circle is *so* irreproachable?"

Silence.

"Because, if I'm not mistaken, G-strings were, at the beginning, a prostitute's tool, no? A work uniform, like a kepi. How is it that today they are so very common in the best families? Where did the *influence* come from?"

As the conversation turned to the adverse effects of globalisation, Mona and I discreetly took our leave.

73 years, 7 months, 15 days *Sunday, 25 May, 1997*

So many guys with three-day stubble at last night's gathering of forty-year-olds! Such strange times we live in, the least adventurous possible, with all the insurance agents, corporate lawyers, bankers, communications advisers, computer programmers, small-time investors, all employees of a virtual world, all so sedentary and overweight that they could easily fall through the floor, their brains pickled in their corporate lingo, but every one of them looking like an adventurer returning from some expedition, just come back from the Ténéré Desert or climbed down from Annapurna, at the very least. The G-string serves the same purpose for young Madame N., more upright, I could swear, than my deceased Aunt Noémie. In other words, fashion as ironic statement. And as for their children, tattooed and pierced, they are, literally, branded by these disembodied times.

74 years, 4 months, 15 days *Wednesday, 25 February, 1998*

Dinner last night at the Vs'. The appalling taste of one bite almost made me spit it out on my plate. I was prevented from doing so by the private conversation I was having with the man of the house. So I swallow it whole, without analysing it. Just then my interlocutor noisily spits out his own mouthful, crying: "Darling, how awful!" And Darling confirms it: the scallops have gone bad.

74 years, 5 months, 6 days *Monday, 16 March, 1998*

At the end of my conference in Belém, Nazaré, my interpreter, places her hand on mine and lets it linger there, two fingers beneath my shirt stroking my wrist. "I'd like to spend the night with you," she says, "and if possible the three remaining ones before you leave." Her proposition is so natural that I am barely surprised. Honoured, but not surprised. And touched, obviously. (Nonetheless, after a few seconds of reflection, reasonably stunned.) Nazaré and I worked together to advertise this conference, she paved the way for it, rounding up activists, and filling in everywhere for an enthusiastic but deficient organisation. In São Paulo, Rio, Recife, Porto Alegre, and São Luis, she managed to spare me from most of the official dinners and instead took me to places she chose, introducing me to musical and philosophical circles that she wanted me to get to know, and now her hand was on mine. Dear little Nazaré, I say to her (she is all of twenty-five), thank you, really, but it would be a total waste of time, the decades have made it impossible for me. "That's because you don't believe in resurrection," she objects. It's also because the scalpel has done its work there, my desire is dead, I am monogamous, I'm three times her age, and over all these years of no practice I've stopped basing my identity on my sexuality, and she would be bored in my bed and I would miss my old self in hers. These objections are so unconvincing that a room is waiting for us before I've finished listing them. "Let us slide," she says, taking off our clothes, and it is definitely a sliding that occurs, silk on skin, slowness on slowness, naked woman on naked man, and caresses so sweet, so light that time, heaviness and fear all vanish. Nazaré, I say, without conviction. "Monsieur," she whispers, dotting my neck with minuscule kisses, "no more lectures now, there is nothing more to teach or learn." And she gently kisses my chest, my stomach, and the underside of my penis, which doesn't stir, the fool, but I don't give a damn; you are free not to play with us, old thing, the tiny kisses are reaching my inner thighs where Nazaré's tongue is opening the way for her face while her hands slide beneath my bum, and I arch my back and my fingers lose themselves in her amazing head of hair, while her tongue sizes me up, her lips swallow me, and here I am in her mouth, with her tongue beginning the slow work of enveloping me, her lips doing their sculptor's back and forth, and I am blossoming, goodness, yes, modestly but nevertheless . . . Nazaré, Nazaré, and I am getting harder, goodness, slowly but surely, Nazaré, oh Nazaré, whose face I pull towards my lips while we roll around each other, Nazaré who opens to welcome me, Nazaré, in whom I enter as if returning home, slightly timid, it has been so long, immobile first on the threshold, this will never last I say to myself, "and don't tell yourself that it won't last," Nazaré whispers in my ear. "I love you, monsieur," and here I am, penetrating completely our shared home, the original house, slipping into its moist, pliant warmth, still growing, confident now, time abolished, to the extent that I can see the explosion coming from afar, and I take full advantage of its ascent, I can hold it back, enjoy the promise of it, feel it climb and contain it still, before it bursts forth at last. "There you are," says Nazaré, holding me tightly in her arms. Yes, here I am, resuscitated, a second coming . . .

74 years, 5 months, 7 days *Tuesday, 17 March, 1998*

Rereading what I wrote last night, I am thinking about the role of direct-object personal pronouns in erotic descriptions: her tongue sizes *me* up, her lips swallow *me*, her tongue envelops *me* . . . It is not about modesty (I can confirm that it is really a matter of my balls and my dick), nor a question of style (well, perhaps simply a clue in regard to my incompetence as a stylist), no, it is definitely the sign of an identity that has been recaptured, rediscovered. Here is man in the fullness of life, whatever he says once he has sobered up: the *me* is *I*. The same is true for the metaphors I used to designate Nazaré's vagina: *in whom* I enter, *the original house*; it is about her that I am speaking, her identity as a woman.

74 years, 5 months, 9 days *Thursday, 19 March, 1998*

Nazaré's black skin, its unfathomable chromatic depth, the browns, ochres, blues, reds, the purple-violet that surrounds her vagina, the fleshy pink of her tongue, the rose-blond of her palms. I never know which shade my gaze finds so marvellous, from what depths it rises. To look at Nazaré's naked body is to dive into her skin. For the first time I realise that mine is merely a costume of the surface. Nazaré's smooth skin, with its pores so tiny they become imperceptible, is the skin of a wet pebble; her dresses dance on it with each step she takes. Breasts, buttocks, stomach, thighs, back: all of them are so dense that her body seems to be energy itself. Nazaré's eroticism . . . As I complain that I cannot resuscitate each time (far from it!), "Monsieur," she says, "you are limiting sex to the . . . grand finale." There follows a feast of peripheral caresses, a profusion of novel embraces that Nazaré's orgasms applaud. Nazaré's breasts are two islands on the milky surface of our bath: let me introduce you to my emerging countries. Nazaré's taste of pepper and honey, her amber scent, her gravelly voice, the explosion of her afro in which my fingers lose themselves. Nazaré's philosophy: Not bad, I say to her, at the height of my ecstasy. "You mean very good!" she responds. "Absolutely marvellous!" And she makes me realise that the understatements and euphemisms used by us Europeans as if they were the height of culture actually reduce our faculties for enthusiasm and stunt our tools of perception; our *style* has got the better of us and we are perishing because of this. Nazaré's tender sense of humour: Oh! Monsieuuurrr, she purrs, in a long, sleepy sigh; and I desire no other name than this mocking one. Nazaré's tears as I was leaving, without a single feature on her face moving at all: silent tears sliding on the smooth stone of her cheeks. And the hollow that remains in my chest from this treasure held so tightly against me.

74 years, 5 months, 15 days *Wednesday, 25 March, 1998*

I who, when I was with the lawyer, Maître R., was so sensitive to the contrast between our two faces ("young apple, old prune"), I who celebrated the death of my sexuality when the young student with her swaying breasts was bandaging me, who thought my operation had sounded the death knell of my erections, and who now only count in decades, I cannot manage, when I think of Nazaré, to imagine us from the point of view of our difference in age. What would happen if I were to have an out-of-body experience and some moral authority were to force me to look at my ancient flesh against her young body? Would the sight be grotesque? Scandalous? Would I look like a dirty old man? A sort of miracle is preventing this objectification. "You don't believe in resurrection," whispered Nazaré. From now on, it's a done deal. What the resuscitated feel I now know: it's the arrival of this exultant body, a blending of all ages.

74 years, 5 months, 16 days — *Thursday, 26 March, 1998*

It will be easier for me to die now that I have been resuscitated.

74 years, 6 months, 2 days — *Sunday, 12 April, 1998*

"Well," Ti-Joe says to me from his hospital bed, "you began life in the body of an old man, it's only fair that you end up in that of a youngster." And then, he adds with a sputtering chortle, "Colloquia have always turned out more cuckolds than scholars!" We laugh, he chokes, the nurse who brings him his pills scolds him. "This is how they *treat* me," he says after the nurse has left the room.

75 years, 1 month, 17 days — *Friday, 27 November, 1998*

Ti-Joe died this evening. He said his goodbyes to me yesterday, forbidding me to come today. "Don't complicate my death . . ." Each time I visited him, I could see the progress of his illness and the ravages of the treatment; they turned this wiry, dark-skinned man from the South of France into a whitish thing, bald and pigmentless, bloated like a puffer-fish, his fingers swollen with the water his kidneys could no longer eliminate. Unlike most of the dying, who shrink, he became too voluminous for his own body. But neither the illness (lung cancer that had spread everywhere) nor medicine and its morals ("If only he hadn't drunk and smoked so much, monsieur!") could get the better of his cheerful disdain that respected death and took life for what it was: simply a captivating stroll. Before I left his room, he signalled me to come close. His mouth against my ear, he asked me: "Do you know the story of the wild boar that refused to leave its forest?" His voice was nothing but a breath, but it still conveyed the same fun-loving fatalism and – how can I explain it? – a clear sense of his interlocutor.

THE STORY OF THE WILD BOAR THAT DID NOT WANT TO LEAVE ITS FOREST

He was an old wild boar, you see. More from your generation than from mine, really old, with empty balls and worn-down fangs. He was turned out of the herd by the young ones. Suddenly the poor thing finds himself all alone in the forest, feeling stupid. He hears the youngsters making hay with his females. So he says to himself he should leave the forest, check out other places. Except he was born under these trees, and spent his whole life there. "Other places" make him scared shitless. But when he hears the young sows expressing their contentment, it does him in. He makes his decision on the spot. I'm leaving! Off he goes, head lowered, ploughing straight through bushes, groves, thickets, copses, brambles, until he comes to the edge of the woods. And what does he see there? A field basking in sunshine. All green! A phosphorescent marvel! And in the middle of this field, what does he see? An enclosed pen! A completely square pen! And what is in the pen? An ENORMOUS pig! So big and fat that it overflows the pen, like a soufflé rising out of its mould, get it? An enormous, totally pink, perfectly hairless pig, already a ham! Flabbergasted, the old wild boar calls to the pig: "Hey! You there!"

The fat ham slowly turns its head towards the boar.

The old wild boar asks it:

"So, was your chemo very hard on you?"

75 years, 1 month, 28 days *Tuesday, 8 December, 1998*

A few days before Ti-Joe died, I called his "best friend", J. C. (As far as friendship was concerned, Ti-Joe still used childish categories.) The best friend told me he would not visit Ti-Joe in the hospital. He preferred to hold onto the image of his "indestructible vitality." Such vile tactfulness that would abandon us all on our deathbeds! I despise friends in spirit. I only like flesh-and-blood friends.

75 years, 9 months, 6 days *Friday, 16 July, 1999*

Scattered Ti-Joe's ashes over le Briac, as he had requested, from the top of that beech tree where, as a child, he had taken the baby crow (this was Grégoire's idea). As I watched my grandson climb that tree, whose trunk must have tripled in size, for a moment I saw myself once again climbing up to Ti-Joe's aid. Now it was the cut-away man from the *Larousse Encyclopedia* who was hoisting himself from branch to branch. But gracefully, without that stiffness that *exercising my will* always gave me, and that Ti-Joe used to make fun of. Carried by the wind, his ashes first came together, then scattered, then came together again, then banked like an aeroplane before exploding in the sky. Ti-Joe gave us a starling's farewell.

75 years, 10 months, 5 days *Sunday, 15 August, 1999*

My bladder woke me at two in the morning. My laziness resists until laughter coming from downstairs motivates me to get up. Grégoire, Frédéric and the twins are playing the Game of the Goose. Fanny protests that an evil spell is preventing her from moving ahead. Frédéric sniggers as two sixes speed him to victory. "Look out, here he comes!" Grégoire exclaims pointing at me, and they all lie down on the game, pretending to hide it from me. "It's a secret," Marguerite yelps, as if she were still a little girl. "You're not allowed to see it!" At first I thought it must have been the Game of the Goose of Defloration that I had given Grégoire at the start of his adolescence, but it's worse: it's a Game of the Goose of the Hypochondriac that he created when he was on night call. From atrocious illnesses to abominable illnesses, the players all end up on Death, the last square that finally cures them of their fears of getting sick. "Would you like to play with us?" Fanny asks me. (And I admire the use of the polite conditional in a young girl of her generation.) They give me three free turns to start. I pick a multiple sclerosis card, which allows me another turn. (That's the rule of the game: the sicker you are, the more you get ahead.) "Tomorrow we are going to play Seven Families!" Marguerite states forcefully. The seven families in question are forty-two illnesses one could easily do without. (In the Cancer family, I ask for prostate cancer; in the Bed family, I ask for genital herpes; in the Doctor family, I ask for Parkinson's, etc.) "Let's all relax here," says Grégoire with a smile. "No matter what you get, the last square is the same for all of us!" Apparently, the little girls – who are not so little anymore – adore the game.

75years, 11 months, 2 days *Sunday, 12 September, 1999*

The day before he died Ti-Joe gave me back ten years of my life, saying: "I've even caught up with you in age." The oldest one is the one closest to the exit.

Same day, 5.00 p.m.

I'm writing this drinking tea. I've given up coffee ever since my operation. I have the impression that tea cleanses me. A sort of inner shower. You drink one, you piss out three, Violette used to say. Perhaps one day I'll switch to hot water, like Aunt Huguette near the end of her life.

76 years, 2 days *Tuesday, 12 October, 1999*

Speaking of Aunt Huguette who had her "sour stomach", or Maman, with her "acidity", do people still use these expressions? And that woman who would make a three-quarter turn every five minutes so that the bismuth could coat her entire insides . . . This way of thinking of herself as a barrel made everyone around her laugh. Yet in many ways we are not much more than containers. Mona is taking medicine for osteoporosis that she needs to ingest with a glass of water in the morning before eating. After that, she must *absolutely* remain standing for half an hour without going back to bed, because the potion could destroy her oesophagus like lye. So, containers we are and containers we shall remain. Nothing more. As an aside, today bismuth is considered poisonous, its use totally forbidden by doctors.

77 years, 2 months, 8 days *Monday, 18 December, 2000*

Woke up this morning with a pain in the metatarsophalangeal joint of my ring finger, as if I had spent the night boxing with a wall. This is the finger that was bent back ten years ago in Madame P.'s garden. The usurer is demanding his interest.

77 years, 6 months, 17 days *Friday, 27 April, 2001*

My nights are interrupted by pressing, unproductive needs. Miction impossible. (Nice title!) How many times? as my confessor used to ask me. How many times? asks my urologist today. The former would threaten me with a slew of Our Fathers and Hail Marys, the latter menaces me with another transurethral resection of the prostate: no choice, you've got to do it. "It won't make you twenty again, but your nights will be better." Granted, but what will become of those dreamy moments I allow myself on my unproductive king's throne? During those hours of the night when the need to pee wakes me, I don't imagine my bladder stretched like a goatskin, but fossilised like the shell of a sea urchin, a limestone shell that I empty as best as I can, with my little finger under the tap, opening a valve without pressure. Slow emptying of myself. To compensate for this, images of an old donkey abandoned in the middle of a meadow come to me, and the donkey moves me sweetly. Or else I think about the scandal when Manès' neighbours from Marseille allowed that spring to dry up. It was a spring whose free flowing would rock me to sleep. Its sound should be classified with those other calming sounds: footsteps on gravel, the wind in the vine arbour, Manès' grindstone . . . (Manès would spend the early hours of the night sharpening his tools with a grindstone and an anvil, and I also liked the staccato notes of the anvil, which came in pairs: ting-ting, ting-ting). So the spring of those people from Marseille went dry. Moss started growing there and perhaps, upstream, some sort of muddy adenoma. In the end, nothing but a silent and brownish trickle of water, then a few drops at a time, then nothing. To Manès' great fury – who perhaps had blocked it up himself.

78 years *Wednesday, 10 October, 2001*

Lison, Grégoire, and the twins gave us a video projector and a dozen films, including some of my favourites: Ingmar Bergman's "Wild Strawberries", Joseph L. Mankiewicz's "The Ghost and Mrs Muir", John Huston's "The Dead", and "Babette's Feast". Ah! "Babette's Feast"! Who directed that movie? Gabriel Axel! Fanny whispers to me. Well, glory be to Gabriel Axel. It has been a long time since a gift has given me so much pleasure. Which makes me wonder why I didn't buy one myself. When Mona opened the package, my joy sprang out of the box with the projector. I was surprised to realise I was waiting for night to fall with the impatience of a child. When we had finally stretched the white sheet across the wall, I experienced the same excitement I felt when Violette would set up her magic lantern on the pedestal table in the living room. Mona and the children let me pick the movie, and I chose "Wild Strawberries", the film about the ceremony for Dr Isak Borg. I was shocked that I remembered his name! Eberhard Isak Borg is traveling with his daughter-in-law Marianne to the cathedral in Lund, to be awarded the degree of Dr Jubilaris. He is seventy-eight years old, like me! That detail, of course, I had forgotten because when I saw the film for the first time I was not even forty. Seventy-eight. Obviously I began to study the face of this old man (who appeared much older than I), looking for the wrinkles we shared, recognising in him some of the same slowness of gesture as mine, or those half-smiling expressions that become so aloof with age, but also those sudden bursts of life brought about by desires that are still intact (for example, the desire to take his car to go to the ceremony when he already has his aeroplane tickets), or that cheerfulness that the three young hitchhikers whom he and Marianne pick up bring out in him – entirely comparable, that cheerfulness, to the joy I get from the chaotic presence of Grégoire, Marguerite and Fanny when they come for holidays, their pranks, their squabbles and their hilarious reconciliations . . .

I was absorbed by what was happening on screen when something else caught my attention, which had nothing to do with the movie but rather with the projector. Mona and I were sitting next to it. It's a black box into which you insert a DVD through a slit, and the machine does the rest: projection, sound, focusing, cooling the motor, etc. Placed in the middle of the living room, the machine projected the image on a sheet four metres in front of us, a huge black-and-white image, old-looking because the film is old, but sufficiently clear so that I wasn't thinking about my cataract. I was listening to old Isak and his daughter-in-law Marianne, attentive to their dreary argument – a conflict of temperaments and generations – when suddenly I wondered where the sound of these voices was coming from. It seemed to be coming from the screen, where we could see the characters speaking. But that was impossible, because the sounds were emitted by the projector next to me on the table. I looked at the machine: there was no question that the voices were coming out of this black plastic cube, fifty centimetres away from my left ear. But as soon as my eyes returned to the sheet, all the words once again found the mouths that appeared to be speaking them! Amazed by the power of this illusion of sight and sound, I tried to watch the screen without listening to the projector. Impossible. The voices continued to come from the Swedish actors, over there, on the sheet stretched out four metres in front of me. This observation plunged me into a sort of primitive ecstasy, as if I were witnessing the miracle of ubiquity. Then I closed my eyes, and the voices returned to the belly of the projector. I opened them again, and the voices returned to the screen.

In bed, I thought for a long time about this dissociation between the actual sound source and the characters speaking to us from the old sheet. I was starting to perceive an illuminating metaphor in this when I fell asleep. This morning when I woke up, all that is left is an impression . . . It is as if whatever my body expresses is heard far in front of me while I am keeping a silent record of it here, sitting at this table where I am writing.

78 years, 4 months, 3 days *Wednesday, 13 February, 2002*

"Why doth one man's yawning make another yawn?" This question was asked in the sixteenth century by Robert Burton on page 218 of his *Anatomy of Melancholy.* Without providing a satisfactory answer (Burton attributes this contagiousness of yawns to "spirits"), his question takes me back forty years, to those amusing physiology experiments I carried out when I was bored during particularly insipid meetings at work: I merely had to pretend to yawn to see the entire table start to yawn. I thought I had made a discovery, but not at all. Our physical existence is spent clearing a virgin forest that has been cleared thousands of times before us. From Montaigne and Burton, we get a book, but how many unrevealed discoveries, uncommunicated amazements, and surprises are kept to oneself? All those men, alone with their silence!

78 years, 6 months, 14 days *Wednesday, 24 April, 2002*

I might as well admit it to myself: after some too-copious meals, the coughed fart has a tendency to transform into a veritable anal breathing. Inhaling of gas for four or five steps, exhaling for the next for or five, with the regularity of breathing. This pearl necklace is not always as silent as my social status, my natural refinement, and my ancestral dignity would like. A little cough is no longer sufficient to drown it out, so I am obliged, if someone is with me, to speak in long sentences with an enthusiasm that is meant to conceal this gloomy counterpoint.

78 years, 11 months, 29 days *Wednesday, 9 October, 2002*

Grégoire, who had invited himself to my birthday party, called me to tell me that chicken pox, which he caught while on duty in the hospital, has him stuck in bed. "Chicken pox at twenty-five, can you imagine that, Grandfather? And you've been saying all these years that I'm advanced for my age! You should see me. I look like a colander! An exceptionally gifted colander, granted, but a colander nonetheless!" His voice is not changed, perhaps just a bit husky, and for the first time I wonder if my affection for him isn't due to the reassuring musicality of his voice. Even before it broke, when he was just a child, Grégoire had the most calming voice imaginable. Did we in fact ever see him angry?

79 years *Thursday, 10 October, 2002*

My heart, my faithful heart. Not as sturdy as it used to be, of course, but oh how faithful! Last night, I did a very childish thing: I calculated the number of my heartbeats since I was born, that is, on average, seventy-two beats a minute multiplied by sixty minutes per hour, multiplied by twenty-four hours a day, multiplied by three-hundred-sixty-five days a year, multiplied by seventy-nine years. Obviously I can't calculate that in my head any longer. So out comes the calculator. Almost three billion heartbeats! Not counting leap years and those times my heart beat faster from emotion! I placed my hand on my chest and felt my heart calmly, rhythmically beating out the beats that remain to me. Happy birthday, my heart!

79 years, 1 month, 2 days *Tuesday, 12 November, 2002*

Our Grégoire died. The day after his last phone call he went into a coma. At first Frédéric had thought it was varicella encephalitis, from which one can eventually recover, but no, it was something much worse: Reye's syndrome. It occurred with the chickenpox and caused devastating liver failure. According to Frédéric, the syndrome was probably triggered by Grégoire's having taken aspirin, some of which Frédéric later found in Grégoire's pocket. He must have wanted to bring down his fever by taking aspirin, not knowing about this very rare side effect. When Frédéric made him admit it in intensive care, there was already nothing anyone could do. Mona and I came as quickly as we possibly could. At first, we didn't recognise him. Despite the presence of Sylvie and Frédéric, a mad hope led me to believe for just a second that there had been some mistake. This yellow, waxen body, riddled with pustules from the top of the forehead to the tips of the fingers could not be my grandson's. I thought about one of those films in which the Egyptologist, struck by some curse, is mummified in front of the burial site that he has just profaned. But it was really Grégoire on that hospital bed, my Grégoire. Squinting, I managed to focus my eyes in such a way that the atrocious realism of the pustules was erased and I found my Grégoire once again, whose body still expressed some playful grace, even now, lying in this yellow fog. When Grégoire plays tennis, he first plays at playing, he mimics the tennis champions we see on TV, and while his opponent is laughing as he recognises the person Grégoire is imitating, Grégoire scores points and wins matches. The opponent, exasperated in the end, asks him to be serious, for Pete's sake, damn it, or else leaves the court throwing down his racket, like W.'s son did three years ago. This is how – he must have been ten or twelve at the time – I had taught him to play because this is how, I told him, when I was young I would play tennis, that very refined game that had become, thanks to television, a duel between emotional brutes. I didn't want Grégoire to give in to the ridiculousness of athletic movements. God, how I loved that child! And how my pen is seeking in vain to elude his death. What injustice causes us to prefer one human being to so many others to such a degree? Did he really have all those wonderful qualities that my love attributed to him? I could find two or three defects if I look hard enough, no? If he had reached my age, what horrible habit would he have shrivelled around? Even the best must rot! If I'm writing nonsense here, it's simply to fill the silence in which Mona's mute grief has abandoned me. What is Mona thinking about, suddenly overcome with domestic frenzy? Is she thinking, as I am, that Grégoire would still be alive if Bruno had sent him to us that summer when all the kids had chickenpox? If Bruno had accepted that natural vaccination? But you had to be willing to take risks to do that, and Bruno stopped taking risks very early on. The children were naked, they couldn't even stand the contact of a thin shirt. When one of them would whine too much about the itching, all the others would blow together on his or her tiny spots with their translucent heads and then stroke them very, very gently. I think Lison is the one who invented this game. The children embodied the eight winds of Venice, except there were only seven of them because Grégoire was missing, and he would have been the marvellous laughing wind in that game, and he would be alive today! It took Bruno two days to get back from Australia. He arrived just in time for the funeral. Grégoire's body could not be preserved any longer. As I hugged Bruno, I noticed he had gained weight. Fat on his biceps. His cheeks were puffy from jet lag and grief, his face closed. He did not greet Sylvie, who against his advice had chosen a religious service. Family awkwardness. No one spoke much. After the ceremony, at Lison's, the twins were crying in each other's arms without saying a word, Sylvie was soliloquising about nothing, how worried she had been as a mother, and how Grégoire knew how to tease her about her fears – "Don't you remember, Father, you also used to make fun of me!" – short sentences that she released into the surrounding sadness. Frédéric stood off to the back, terribly present in his double solitude as homosexual and unofficial widower, and Lison stood next to him, on principle and out of friendship, and then I realised that Frédéric and Lison were almost the same age, in other words that Frédéric could have been Grégoire's father. All Grégoire's doctor friends came, and they made fun of the priest's homily. Religious funerals serve to confirm the respective convictions of both believers and nonbelievers, to turn the arrows of grief back on the priest, and to transform each and every person into a critic who speaks with authority in the name of the dead person and assesses the portrait the priest painted of the dead person; and the dead person, actively participating in this theological debate, and whom one judges to have been either fittingly extolled or roundly insulted, becomes a little less dead; it's like the beginning of a resurrection. Really, when it comes to creating an *ambiance*, there is nothing like God.

79 years, 5 months, 6 days *Sunday, 16 March, 2003*

How grief causes our bodies to suffer! For three months after Grégoire died, I abandoned my body to every possible danger. I was punched in the face in the metro (Mona insisted that we stay in Paris to spend a little time with Marguerite and Fanny); on boulevard Saint-Marcel I was almost run over by a car – and the driver squashed a rubbish bin as he swerved to avoid me. Back at Mérac, twice my car rolled over, and I wound up in a ditch, my car a write-off, my forehead split above the eye, and finally, one afternoon when I was gathering mushrooms, I lost my footing on the slopes and tumbled down to the highway where cars were speeding by in both directions. "If you really want to kill yourself," Mona said to me, "let me know ahead of time so we can either do it together or I can go on a trip." But there was nothing suicidal about this combination of factors, just a mistaken evaluation of reality, as if I had lost all sense of danger, any apprehension, any specific desire at all, as if my consciousness had abandoned my body to chance. My body put up with whatever I was doing without thinking; in fact, it was surprisingly resistant, almost invulnerable. I left our building and let my body cross the boulevard without looking right or left, and that driver braked as hard as he could, skidded, knocked over the rubbish can, and my body went on its way without my mind even noticing. In the metro, my hand simply and automatically pushed away the hand of the young drunkard who was annoying the woman sitting next to me; I didn't notice that he was reeking of alcohol and that in fact his attitude towards the young woman was not even particularly aggressive – more like an awkward tender gesture. But my hand pushed his away the way one swats a fly, without paying it any attention, and my temple barely felt the boy's fist land on it; my eyes realised that, with the blow, they had lost their glasses, which the woman sitting next to me returned to me once my attacker had been calmed – "Your glasses, monsieur, they fell." Nor did I see myself driving my car when I started to look for my shopping list in my jacket, leaning over the back seat; I had simply forgotten I was driving. I turned around to look for the list, in a car that no longer had a driver and that naturally wound up in the ditch. And during all these events, I don't remember being the least bit afraid, even when I saw my body falling on the highway that afternoon when I was out gathering mushrooms, not even when I saw my broken left arm waving around independently of my elbow: no surprise, no fear, no pain; simply a state of noticing, so that's what's happening to me, okay then, as if life weren't offering the slightest meaning to my grief-stricken brain, as if Grégoire's nonexistence was affecting all the events, freeing them from any hierarchy, removing all significance from them, as if Grégoire had been the logical principle behind everything and that with him gone life had literally lost its meaning, to the point where my body was drifting along alone, without the aid of my judgement.

"Let's go to Venice," said Mona. "We need to take our minds off all this."

79 years, 5 months, 17 days *Thursday, 27 March, 2003*

Venice. Slipping away from his mother, a little boy plants himself in front of me and, chin raised, announces: "I'm four and a half years old!" Later in the afternoon, at a drinks party at the Alliance Française, an old benefactress of the place comes up to me and practically shouts: "Well, I just happen to be ninety-two years old!" When do people stop saying how old they are? When do they start doing it again? For my part, I have never stated my precise age, but I say things like "now that I am an old man," expressions I cannot hold back and that, as soon as I've said them – with a casual smile – fill me with fury and shame. What is it I'm looking for? For people to feel sorry for me because I am no longer what I once was? To be admired – look how spry I've remained in any case? To make my interlocutor sense his inexperience as I pose as an old, wise man, and because of this I know much more than you? Whatever the case, this lamentation (for a lamentation is what it is, by God!) reeks of fearful incontinence. I slip away from my mother to plant myself, chin raised, in front of this sturdy forty-year-old: "Hey, I'm seventy-nine and a half years old!"

79 years, 5 months, 20 days *Sunday, 30 March, 2003*

Those two old people (the man with his arm in a cast) pretending to be blind in Venice as they try to re-experience the feelings from their youth are the grandparents of a dead man who would have enjoyed this game. Look at them, listen to them laughing in this liquid city, just like they did fifty years ago when they were celebrating their young love. They have aged a thousand years.

79 years, 5 months, 25 days *Friday, 4 April, 2003*

Acqua alta. A rising tide of tears. Sunk up to our thighs in Seven League Boots, Mona and I are wading in the very material of our grief. Sometimes a pump empties a house of its water and it's like the massive cascade from a cow in a meadow.

79 years, 5 months, 29 days *Tuesday, 8 April, 2003*

But really, we are fine here, Mona and I, we are happy, we are shamelessly exploiting that animal contentment of being together that has always consoled us about everything. We are going on pilgrimages to all those hiding places where we made love when we were young and the memory of Grégoire plays no part in this. His death is so deeply buried beneath Mona's face that not one of her features expresses grief. As for me, I stride across the docks, the bridges, the squares, sniffing the air like an old puppy.

79 years, 6 months *Thursday, 10 April, 2003*

Unfortunately, we have to believe it when we wake up to reality. The tightness in my throat is telling me: Grégoire is dead. Grégoire no longer is where I obstinately remain. Grégoire isn't gone, he didn't leave us, he is not *deceased,* Grégoire is dead. There is no other word.

79 years, 6 months, 3 days *Sunday, 13 April, 2003*

Pasta, risotto, polenta, *zuppa de zucca,* minestrone, spinach, antipasti, ham sliced more thinly than tracing paper, mozzarella, gorgonzola, panna cotta, tiramisu, gelati: everything the Italians eat is soft. As a result, so is my shit. In Venice, you can toss your dentures into the Grand Canal, old folks! You've made it!

79 years, 6 months 8 days *Friday, 18 April, 2003*

To express the idea of softness in all its shapes and sizes – psychological, sentimental, tactile, alimentary, sonorous – Italians say *morbido.* It's difficult to imagine a more radical false cognate for the morbid state in which I wake up every morning!

9

DYING

(2010)

When one has kept a diary of one's body for an entire lifetime one cannot deny oneself the description of dying.

Dear Lison,

Here we are again, after an interruption of seven years. After Grégoire died, I lost all interest in observing my body. My heart was elsewhere. I began to miss all my dead at once. Deep down, I said to myself, I never got over Papa's death, or Violette's, or Ti-Joe's, and I will never get over Grégoire's death. With mourning as my sole education, I developed a solitary and wrathful grief. It is difficult to determine what the people we have loved take from us when they die. In addition to the warm and safe place of affection, the faith in feelings, and the delights of complicity, death deprives us of reciprocity, it's true, but our memory compensates as best as it can. (I remember that Papa would sometimes whisper . . . Violette, when she wanted to console me, would always say . . . Ti-Joe, when he told a story . . . When Etienne and I were in boarding school . . . When Grégoire laughed . . .) Our dead weave our memories with the life of their bodies, but these memories were not enough for me: it was their bodies I missed! The materiality of their bodies, that absolute otherness; that is what I had lost! Those bodies no longer populated my landscape. My dead were pieces of furniture that had created the harmony of my house and now they had been taken away. And how I suddenly missed their physical presence! And how in their absence I suddenly became absent to myself! I missed seeing them, smelling them, hearing them, here, now! I missed

Violette's peppery sweat. I missed Ti-Joe's gravelly voice. Papa's pale, pale breath and Grégoire's joyous bodily reality: I missed them all. In my moments of clarity, I wondered about which body I was speaking. What body are you talking about, for God's sake? Ti-Joe was a spider with a very shrill voice when he was five, before he became that mischievous companion, dark and huge, with his tobacco hoarseness. So which Ti-Joe are you talking about? As a child, Grégoire was as heavy as an anvil in his bath before his muscles became so delicate and his gestures so graceful! And yet, it was definitely Gregoire's body, Ti-Joe's body, Violette's body that I missed, their *physical* presence. Papa's body, his bony hand, and his cheeks that were so angular. Once upon a time, my dead had bodies, and now they no longer do: this says it all, and I miss those unique bodies utterly. I who had barely touched them while they were alive! I who was reputed to be so physically unaffectionate! Now it was their bodies I was crying out for!

There followed a few fits of mild insanity when I became their ghost: the hand with which I reached for the sugar bowl, for example, and the two fingers I dipped in it were the perfect embodiment of Grégoire's gesture when he would put sugar cubes in his coffee, his exact gesture when he would pick out one cube between his index finger and his middle finger – he never used his thumb. (Had you noticed this detail, Lison?) I had been reduced to these brief fits of being possessed: For just an instant I became Grégoire putting sugar in his coffee, Ti-Joe laughing, or Violette jelly-kneed on the rocks. But oh how I would have preferred to see that gesture! And hear that laughter! And once again yank away Violette's folding chair! God, how I missed their company and how I now understood that word: *company*!

For months and months, I let myself be carried along by these waves of grief. Your mother couldn't help me; she must have felt even more alone than I. If I still took care of myself, it was out of sheer habit. Showering, shaving and getting dressed mechanically. But I wasn't present for anyone. Absent and grumpy. It became obvious in the end. You grew alarmed. "Papa is becoming gaga, subject to senile temper tantrums! Grégoire's death has destroyed him completely." You begged Mona to take me back to Paris, as much for her sake as for mine. Fanny and Marguerite got it in their heads to try to take my mind off things. They made me go to the cinema with them. "Don't tell us you haven't seen anything since Bergman, Grandfather! You can't die an ignoramus! Have you seen "The Hours" by Stephen Daldry? Don't worry, it's a film for your generation; it's about Virginia Woolf!" Mona advised me to listen to them. I was in dire need of being with young people, according to her. Why not? I do like your twins, Lison – Marguerite who has your red mane of hair and Fanny who wears your frown below her tiny nose. The twins have grown into women. Young, magnificent women. And so alive! In the metro, whenever a boy tried to chat them up, they would play the fool: "We can't, we're with our grandpa! Right, Grandpa, we're with you? He's taking us to the cinema!" All this said in perfect unison, and in shrill little voices. Two splendid women of twenty-five! My role was to acquiesce, with a sad little nod. The boy would get out at the following stop; it never failed. The twins showed persistence: two or three films a week. Yet I had to give up the cinema sessions. I was letting myself be overwhelmed by the images. My dead were suffering from them. The actors were stealing my ghosts from me. To take but one example, when I walked out of "The Hours", I was obsessed with Ed Harris's emaciated body. There was no more room for Grégoire's. I could only see Ed Harris, his scrofulous chest, his bright eyes and that thin smile in the scene where he falls out the window to end his attachment to life. I had been possessed by an image! Grégoire was ejected by the first actor who came along! "The Hours" was the last film I went to see. The twins misunderstood why I stopped going. I heard them arguing about it: "I told you so, you are such a fool. That story about the gay man who turned yellow from his illness obviously reminded him of Grégoire!"

In the months that followed, I dragged my dead around the Luxembourg Gardens. I would sit down in one of those slanted-back armchairs designed so that old men cannot get out of them. I would let my eyes wander above my newspaper, looking at the people who meant nothing to me. The apathy of old people is no joke, you know! I wanted to shout to the young people in the Gardens: Children, I don't give a royal damn about your very contemporary existences! And those mothers with their pushchairs, I don't give a hoot about them either! And what's in the pushchair is as indifferent to me as this article that claims to enlighten me yet again about the future of humanity! I couldn't care less about humanity, if you only knew! I am the epicentre of its cyclonic indifference!

That's where I was in my commemorative existence when, one spring afternoon (why do I bother to specify the season? I didn't give a damn about the seasons either), the present once again burst into my life. And gave me back to myself! In just one second! Resuscitated! Farewell, my dead. This is how we live, by disappearing and resurrecting in succession. And this is how the twins and you will get over my death. So, that afternoon in the Luxembourg Gardens, sitting in one of those impossible armchairs, I had opened my newspaper out of habit (be careful, Lison, of the daily routine: buying *Le Monde* not to read it is a harbinger of senility), when my gaze fell upon a woman passing by and whom I recognised instantly. Immediate presence of my past! A woman my age with a lumbering yet determined gait and tensed shoulders: a feminine mass that held firmly to the ground. The kind that nothing can stop. Her shape was as familiar to me as possible; it seemed like yesterday. I only saw her from the back, but still I called out her name:

"Fanche!"

She turned around, cigarette in her mouth, looked at me without surprise, and asked:

"How's your elbow doing, my petard?"

Fanche, my wartime sister! Here, now, unchanged despite the centuries! Moving more slowly, yet unchanged! Twice as big, but unchanged! Fanche unchanged in my eyes. I recognised her the very second she appeared, despite my hopeless memory. I wondered when I had last seen her. At Manès' funeral, I believe. Forty-eight years ago! And all of a sudden here she was in front of me, not having changed a whit. Forever Fanche. She leaned over my newspaper and asked me what I was reading, then screamed out the headline: "Agriculture Without Farmers!" Two or three people walking by turned around. She was on fire. She was shouting at the top of her lungs. "All those small subsistence farmers sent to populate the slums of the entire world by huge agribusinesses and who are committing suicide en masse, don't you see, my petard! In Africa, India, Latin America, in South East Asia, and even in Australia! Even in Australia! And with the complicity of all the governments, everywhere! A planet without farmers!" She knew all the facts by heart, recited to me the acronyms of all those agro-anthropophagic companies, among them a huge French consortium whose entire board of directors she knew. And she shouted the names of its members, one by one, including the name of a certain senator who must have heard it from the open window of his office overlooking the Gardens. "It disgusts you, too, doesn't it, my petard? I know it does. I've read your work, you know, and I've listened to you." And she cited my lectures – all of them! – and most of my articles and interviews. "I've been following you forever, from a distance but very closely, if you know what I mean. I like what you say, you know! I almost always agree with you." I heard her enumerate all my positions on this and that, the occasional surges of my capacity for indignation that she mistook for constant vigilance. "I didn't realise you were also interested in bioethics. What you said about the rights of women regarding surrogate motherhood really touched me! Surprised and touched me!" Her eyes shone, she was looking at me as if I'd spent my entire life tracking down the denial of justice wherever it reared its ugly head. No matter how I tried to tell her that she was exaggerating my virtues, that already when we were young I had been in the Resistance simply by chance, that it had been years since I had protested on any front, that my faculties for rebellion had been completely blunted, and that I had been drowning in mourning, she paid absolutely no attention. She ignored everything I said as if she hadn't heard me, and she listed a number of scandals that it was our urgent duty to denounce. "Not in the name of the good old days, my petard, but *like* in the good old days, the days of the National Council of Resistance, when we made the right of everyone to provide for the needs of his or her family a constitutional value. And it is precisely this right that is being threatened more than ever today!" She harangued me. I listened to her and sensed I was going to capitulate; her shining eyes were giving me a clear conscience! In other words, Lison, as you know, I capitulated. I got up like a young man, tore myself out of that fucking armchair, and I followed her. She had just opened the valves to a flood of new blood. "Together we are going to do some salutary venting, my friend! And people will listen to us, believe you me! Especially young people! Young people need mentors! Their parents don't inspire them. They are looking for Old Wise People.

And that's one more reason why we should not let Old Fools have the last word!"

I followed her. I let her have access to all my files. I kept her records up to date, refined her investigations, carried her briefcase, and during those last years I worried more about her body than mine. Today, when "clean living" is the only way to go, when the sole flag flying above our heads is the flag of "prevention", Fanche smoked like a chimney and drank like a sailor, ate on the run, and worked so hard that she would fall asleep at her desk. I would say watch out, Fanche, slow down, at this rate you'll never make it to a hundred. "No, my petard, if we have to go, might as well go out with a bang; it's fine to begin *piano*, *piano*, to look before we leap when we are starting out, but the way to end is full steam ahead, without worrying about our old carcasses. Acceleration is everything; we are not soft-landing missiles; we are cannonballs of consciousness launched on the ever-steeper path of our lives. Whether our carcasses can keep up or not is their business."

So we left our carcasses to themselves and concentrated on the health of the world. You know the rest, my darling: conferences, symposia, opinion columns, lectures, meetings, high schools, middle schools, planes, trains, an endless supply of words from two old things with long memories and lively consciences. Me, the guy with his files (no more memory lapses!), Fanche, the woman who loved to debate. Amazing how fashionable she had become! Our adversaries speculated about the imminence of our demise. "Those old fogies won't be around to bug us forever!" "I can tell by your face that you are hoping I will die before I answer you," Fanche would say to those who were impudent enough to argue with her one on one. She managed to get anyone who could think and anyone with a sense of humour on her side. Hot-tempered people found her even more hot-tempered;

impulsive people thought she was more impulsive than they were. I tried to get her not to shout too loudly – I thought it only muddled her ideas. But her shouting was the result of both her temperament and her deafness. It was easier to fight against the latter. Mona and I stuffed her ears with the proper little hearing aids, which improved her hearing and increased her fieriness tenfold, because then she was able to hear the whispers of the enemy in question and no one could speak behind her back anymore. She pulled a generation along in her whirlwind. The twins, who took care of our logistical support, scolded me for having hidden from them this combative great-aunt. During this time, your Marguerite gave birth to Stefano, and Fanny – I suppose the result of being a twin – gave Stefano a twin cousin, Louis. My great-grandsons! And you a grandmother! And Mona a great-grandmother! In exchange, however, a few more deaths were added to my list, among whom Fanche herself, who passed away three weeks ago at the Pitié-Salpêtrière Hospital. Her last words were, "Don't look so sad, my petard, you know full well that we all wind up in the majority."

*

86 years, 2 months, 28 days *Thursday, 7 January, 2010*

I haven't opened this diary since Grégoire died. So it has been seven years. My body has become as indifferent to me as it was when I was very young, when imitating Papa was enough of an embodiment for me. My steps grow shorter, I am dizzy whenever I get out of bed or out of a chair, my knee locks, a vein collapses, my prostate has once again been planed down, my voice is raspy; cataract operation, floaters now along with my tinnitus, dried egg yolk at the corner of my lip, trousers harder and harder to put on, the fly I forget to zip, the sudden fatigues, the constant napping: all this is routine now. My body and I are at the end of our lease as indifferent roommates. Nobody is cleaning house anymore, and that's just fine. But the results of my last medical exams are hinting to me that now is the time to take up the pen one last time. When one has kept a diary of one's body for an entire life-time, one cannot deny oneself the description of dying.

86 years, 2 months, 29 days *Friday, 8 January, 2010*

Ever since Frédéric began making me have blood tests every six months, opening the envelope has lost much of its suspense. He reads the results and together we take note of the fact that this or that remains within reasonably high norms, which is the lot of people my age. "You are a perfectly presentable old geezer!" The day before yesterday, however, one number set me thinking: And that red blood cell count, isn't it a little . . . ? "It's nothing," Frederic said. "You're just a bit tired, you're as good as a forty-year-old who overdid it a bit the night before. Your friend Fanche tired you to death and sapped your morale, that's all. Get out of here now, I don't want to see you for another six months, unless of course Mona invites me to dinner in the meantime."

Such is my relationship with Grégoire's widower. And indeed Mona invites him to dinner from time to time. She enjoys his blunt humour. When she asked him why so many heterosexuals become homosexual when the opposite is quite rare, he answered coldly: "Why continue to live in hell when you can have access to paradise?"

86 years, 5 months, 8 days *Thursday, 18 March, 2010*

Exhausted. When it's time to go to bed, I imagine our stairs like a cliff. Why did we perch our bedroom up so high? For a few days now, my right hand has been hauling me up to this summit. With each step, I pull the railing towards me, whispering "heave-ho!" to myself. The fisherman's net. I climb back on board. A little heavier each night. Good catch. I cannot pause for a moment because all eyes are on me from below. Mustn't worry the children. They always saw me climb this staircase with ease. Once on the landing, out of sight, I lean against the wall to catch my breath. Blood is beating in my temples, my chest, all the way to the soles of my feet. I am no longer anything but a heart.

86 years, 8 months, 22 days *Friday, 2 July, 2010*

Seems as if I was right to worry about my red blood cell count. I can see this in Frédéric's eyes after he has read my last results. "Do you feel particularly tired these days?" he asks. Out of breath especially when I climb the stairs. "Not surprising. Your haemoglobin is down to 9.8. Are you bleeding?" Not that I know of. "Not from the nose or anywhere else?" He asks me to get more tests done. Is it really worth examining this carcass? "Don't argue with me, do what I tell you!" One more blood test, as it happens. Then and there. With the same results. Except for one detail: I am not vitamin B-12 deficient. Ah! So much the better, I say. "What do you mean so much the better; this is not at all good news. It could indicate that you have resistant anaemia." Resistant to what? "To all treatment," Frédéric answers, annoyed. For a moment, he has forgotten his patient: he is lecturing a disappointing student. How can anyone, at my age, not know what resistant anaemia means? An angry silence follows. I can sense he is beating around a foul-smelling bush before I hear him say: "We are going to have to do a myelogram." What's that? A bone-marrow biopsy. And puncture my spinal cord? A needle in my spine, never! He looks at me, astonished. "Who's talking about your spinal cord? No one ever touches the spinal cord. What *are* you talking about? You think we are going to go through your sternum, your mediastinum, your heart, your aorta, to go suck out your spinal cord?" Frédéric, you're the one who talked about marrow, no? "Bone marrow! That has nothing to do with your spinal cord!" He can't get over it. So much ignorance is suffocating him. An ignorance that, for his pedagogue's soul ("He's a remarkable teacher," Grégoire used to say), is synonymous with indifference. "Don't you know *anything* about your body? Have you absolutely no interest in the subject? Is it a *terra incognita* to you? You race around the planet to watch over the health of the whole world, but you leave your own to doctors? We're talking about you here, for God's sake, not me! About *your* body!" Another silence. "Forgive me," he grumbles. Without being able to keep from adding: "You and your damned refinement!"

86 years, 8 months, 26 days *Tuesday, 6 July, 2010*

Waiting for the myelogram. Scheduled for this afternoon. I asked Frédéric to describe it precisely to me. You stick a trocar in the patient's sternum and suction out some of his bone marrow to be biopsied. So, now I'm viewed as some sort of marrow bone! I asked to see the trocar. It's a hollow needle made of strong steel, a few centimetres long, with a sort of hilt to prevent it from penetrating too deeply. It resembles one of those stilettos that Renaissance courtesans would use to bump each other off on the sly. The operation itself calls to mind Dracula's countless deaths. They are proposing to stick a stake in my heart, no more, no less. The stake is called "Mallarmé's trocar." What does it have to do with the poet? The only thing I think I know about Mallarmé when it comes to medicine is that he is said to have died while acting out the symptoms that had caused him to consult the doctor in the first place. Such a ludicrous death. As if the true murder occurred during its re-enactment.

Of course, Frédéric's comments regarding my indifference to my body made me smile. It would be amusing to hand him this diary! Although he is not entirely wrong: I never thought about my body as the object of scientific curiosity. I did not try to find its secrets in books. I did not put it under any medical surveillance. I let it have the freedom to surprise me. In this sense, yes, I chose medical ignorance. In any event, how would doctors feel if we came into their offices knowing all they know, mastering their diagnoses? They had wanted to guillotine Condorcet so that wouldn't happen. Frédéric cannot have forgotten!

86 years, 8 months, 28 days *Thursday, 8 July 2010*

So, the myelogram. Local anaesthetic. After having more or less reassured themselves that my carcass could withstand the shock, the doctors stuck Mallarmé's trocar in my chest. Staggering blow. Careful not to fracture the sternum! My ribcage bends but does not break. Fine. The surgeon – who is also one of Frédéric's former students – explains to me kindly that the hilt of the trocar prevents it from piercing the bone through and through. So I will not be impaled to the operating table. So much the better. (Etienne 's butterflies . . . his precious collection of butterflies . . . I would always frown when the needle pierced them. "But they're dead!" Etienne would say. I would cringe anyway. An atavistic terror of impalement. So now comes the aspiration of my bone marrow. Here we go, says the doctor. The piston rises. "It'll be a bit uncomfortable," Frédéric warned me, "but at eighty-six," he added with suspicious cheerfulness, "a person sees less clearly, hears less well, can't pee as far, has less muscle tone; everything has slowed down, *ergo* one suffers less: it's the young kids who suffer during this examination." He was wrong. This pain retained all its youthfulness: horrific. A wrenching pain. The marrow screams with all the fibre of its being. It does not want to leave its bone. "You okay?" my torturer asks me. Yes, I say, a tear running down my cheek. "Good, then back I go."

86 years, 8 months, 29 days *Friday, 9 July, 2010*

This morning it felt as though my chest had collapsed. Short breaths. More dead than alive. Our soul is in our bones. I was torn from myself and the pain goes on. I've stayed in bed, and am writing on a tray. I am thinking about the euphemism "uncomfortable" that doctors use when they speak to us about pain. Not that irreparable pain that pours forth from our body and that is always surprising, incalculable, always our own, but that predictable, ordinary pain, that post-operative pain that doctors themselves inflict on their patients. Packing, probing, pulling out the probes, Mallarmé's trocar . . . Will it be painful? asks the patient. A bit "uncomfortable," responds the doctor . . . Yet they have had plenty of time to try, danger-free, all these "uncomfortable" procedures on themselves (that's the least they could do), but they never do, because their teachers never did, nor their teachers' teachers. No one ever made the doctor enrol in the school of pain he inflicts. And if you even bring up the subject, they call you a softie.

86 years, 9 months, 6 days *Friday, 16 July, 2010*

As expected, the results are not great. My haemoglobin levels have gone down again and it turns out that my marrow is full of blasts, cells that prevent the production of other types of blood cells, red or white. So, "blasts". (Everything has a name.) My marrow is full of blasts. A petrifying invasion. The factory has shut down. Production has ended. No more globules. No more fuel. No more oxygen. No more energy. From now on I am drawing on my blood capital. Which is rapidly disappearing along with my strength. This evening I got stuck halfway up the stairs. Mona has decided to set up our bed downstairs, in the library. "It's only temporary," she says to the company at large. And she and I exchange a definitive smile.

*

NOTE TO LISON

> Your mother as she leaves our library: the way her body undulates as she manoeuvres through the narrow doorway. I can confess it today: if I never wanted to move that one piece of furniture, it was so I could enjoy that feline movement of hers. (An eighty-six-year-old feline! You can imagine, my dear daughter, how Mona hypnotised me!) I realise all of a sudden how a "normal" diary would have presented an entirely different image of our couple. Our conjugal annoyances with one another, the calculating that her silences forced me to do, that mysterious distance she maintained between you and her; in other words, her opaqueness would most likely have dominated the whole thing. You

would have had to read reams and reams about the nightmares of "communicating". But not in this diary of the body. The body's point of view is completely different. I loved Mona's to the point of celebrating it. If the decades got the better of our sexuality, what remained of Mona in Mona never cased to thrill me. As soon as she appeared in my life, I cultivated the art of looking at her. Not simply seeing her, but looking at her. Making her smile just to see that smile's dazzling rapidity; following her in the street without her knowing it just to perceive the almost imperceptible levitation of her gait; watching her daydream when she was lost in certain repetitive tasks; contemplating her hand placed on an armrest, the curve of her neck bent over a book, the whiteness of her skin as it became slightly pink in the warmth of her bath, the mark of her first crow's-feet, and her vertical wrinkles that came with age, like the memory of a masterpiece sketched in a few lines. In other words, now that I've kicked the bucket, you can move that piece of furniture to widen the doorway to the library.

*

86 years, 9 months, 8 days *Sunday, 18 July, 2010*

Poor Frédéric. He came this morning (on his birthday!) to my bedside to carry out the unbearable part of his profession: to deliver his prognosis. No matter how you go about it, once a patient is past a certain age, you are delivering a death sentence. I made his task easier for him: So, Frédéric, how long do we have? It was a communal "we"; after all, he is my doctor. One year with chemotherapy, six months without. More or less. We thought about the advantages and disadvantages of chemo. After all, it is a consumer good like any other. Six months more of survival is not nothing, but with an exhausting aplasia, the loss of what remains of my hair (that's okay), possible vomiting, and the guarantee, more or less, that my old blood will have the strength to regenerate itself without blasts. The vomiting, which Frédéric considers a mere trifle, resolved the matter. I despise vomiting. That turning inside-out of oneself like a rabbit skin always filled me with shame and fury. So I will not risk it. Mona does not deserve for me to leave her when I'm in a bad mood. So, no chemo. But there is another solution: a blood transfusion. It would give me a real boost. The benefits of it would last until the next transfusion, if a next one were possible. As for the end, the real one, whether I choose chemo or transfusion, the choice is already made: fate will decide if I will haemorrhage because of a drop in platelets, some infection or other, for example, pneumonia, caused by lack of white blood cells ("pneumonia is the old man's friend," the English say), or the slow, cachectic process of dying, bedsores and all, in a hospital bed deprived of Mona's company. I would prefer the banality of a heart attack in the middle of the night. To die in my sleep would be the perfect end for a guy like me who, throughout his life, has cultivated the art of falling asleep.

86 years, 9 months, 12 days *Thursday, 22 July, 2010*

Blood transfusions go well with the image of Dracula. Here I am in a hospital bed, being filled drop by drop with someone else's blood. I would have preferred to fly away at night, drunk on having bled dry three duty nurses, but vampirism has lost its charm since it's been legalised. And then, I don't have any teeth left. Drop by drop, then. To help me pass the time, Marguerite offers to stick her iPod earbuds in my ears. She has loaded it with Shakespeare and Mahler. No, no, my little darling, I don't need any diversions, I've never had a blood transfusion before, you see, and so I want to hear the drops fall and watch for every improvement. "We have a surprise for you," says Fanny. "Maman is going to come get you. Don't say we told you! Surprises give the most pleasure to the people doing the surprising!" Maman? Oh, Lison! Lison has come back from her tour? Early? Should I also be expecting Bruno to come by? All this smells of an endgame.

The transfusion turns out to be slow, lulling. My resurrection will not be instantaneous. It required three days from the best of us. Silly ideas floating in my half-sleep, my brain playing lazily with itself. That word "blast" comes back to me. I thought it designated shock waves. But no, "blastos", those deadly cells, blasts. An invasion of cockroaches on my bookshelves . . . they lubricate their wings with the blood of my books and out come their antennae . . . Can you see those blasts?

86 years, 9 months, 15 days *Sunday, 25 July, 2010*

In passing, the words of that musician – Lison's ephemeral companion – who died of an overdose and whom Mona had asked to describe "very precisely" the effects of a hit of heroine. He thought for a long time before answering in a gentle voice (I have never known a boy so thoroughly lacking in aggressiveness): "A real hit? Ah! It lets you understand everything! It's like being rocked in the arms of God." Well, this is the effect that this blood transfusion has on me. A newborn babe in the arms of God. How else to describe this powerful return of life in in old, bloodless body? A genuine resurrection. With something innocent, brand-new about it. An *improvement*, that means nothing! They tell you a transfusion will bring about some improvement, but I don't feel an *improvement*. I feel alive! Alive, lucid, confident and wise. In the arms of God. With, nonetheless, a slight desire to descend from them and climb the stairs back to our bedroom. Which I did last night. Our bedroom, my desk, my notebooks; I filled the preceding pages, and wrote my notes to Lison. Because obviously these past days I have not had the strength to put one word after the other. I merely took a few notes. Resurrection! But let's be clear: I haven't been reborn in my twenties. They are dead, and after them the six decades that followed. No, I am being reborn to myself, today, at my age, and yet I am new. Healing without the convalescent antechamber, without learning how to live again. In other words, I'm high! A hit!

86 years, 9 months, 16 days *Monday, 26 July, 2010*

Until the end, we are the child of our body. A disconcerted child.

86 years, 9 months, 19 days *Thursday, 29 July, 2010*

This morning, I could hear laughter from my childhood as I was shaving and looking at that protruding ear I never had fixed – and about which I am writing in here for the first time! I had complained about it to Papa. He'd asked me what I found to reproach this ear with. Not being like the other one, I said. "And what do you find so extraordinary about the other one?" His answer made me laugh. Then, Papa started in on his speech about symmetry: "Nature despises symmetry, my boy; she never shows such a lack of good taste. You would be surprised by the *expressionlessness* of a perfectly symmetrical face if ever you were to come across one." Violette, who was listening to our conversation as she arranged a bouquet on the mantelpiece, added her grain of salt: "Do you want to look like a pair of candlesticks?" This time, Papa laughed, that whistling laugh of his final weeks . . . He had left to live the same amount of time as I have today.

86 years, 9 months, 21 days *Saturday, 31 July, 2010*

In the restaurant where we were celebrating my resurrection, I congratulated Frédéric on his choice of donor: an exceptional vintage, that blood! He exchanged a glance with Lison. Mona and I understood the tacit thought circulating between the minds of two caring people: let them enjoy their exaltation; the beneficial effects of the transfusion will dissipate soon enough.

86 years, 9 months, 22 days *Sunday, 1 August, 2010*

Fanny burst out of the shower naked. "Oh, sorry!" she said. Once my astonishment had passed, I thought back to the terror I experienced one night when I was about ten: going into the bathroom to brush my teeth, I came upon Maman getting out of her bath naked. Surprise or fright had made her turn towards me. She was facing me naked, a blurry silhouette in a cloud of steam. I can still see her heavy breasts and her thin body (which now seems to me to be a very young woman's body), her skin made rosy from the warm bath, her mouth open, wide-eyed, stupefied; then the mirror above the bathroom basin behind her misted over. I let out a cry and quickly shut the door. I went to bed without brushing my teeth, prey to a truly holy terror. Though at the time, I knew nothing about Diana surprised in her bath and Actaeon devoured by his dogs. That night, Maman did not simply check from afar if I had gone to bed; she came to kiss me on my forehead and twice said, "My little man," as she ran her fingers through my hair.

86 years, 9 months, 23 days *Monday, 2 August, 2010*

Nonetheless, to think that a skeleton is the symbol of death when our bones are life's very principle! The brain that cogitates, the heart that pumps, the lungs that ventilate, the stomach that dissolves, the liver and kidneys that filter, the testicles that provide for the future: all these are mere accessories compared to our bones. Life, blood, platelets, the mute *aliveness* of the marrow of our bones!

86 years, 9 months, 29 days *Sunday, 8 August, 2010*

Scandal! Little Fabien, who is seven or eight and great friends with Louis and Stefano, farted during Mass. During the silence of the Elevation, to top it off! The children are completely unsettled by this. I found them in the middle of one of those big discussions necessitated by the primary preoccupation of childhood: finding a correlation between the causes their little world produces and their effects on the adult galaxy. Obviously Fabien "should not have"; that emanation from a body in the home of the Holy Spirit "is just not done". But Fabien "didn't do it on purpose"; his father was "wrong to scold him in front of everyone" and the punishment he doled out was "awful": poor Fabien must stay at home this Sunday afternoon, even though he has been invited to Louis' birthday party. (In truth, Fabien's father is a young chump whose glacial religious enthusiasm is as irrational as my atheism. His child is as translucent as a centipede brought up in a sacristy. It's a miracle that he can fart.)

Since they saw I was listening to them, Stefano and Louis asked my opinion – as an omniscient great-grandfather – about farting. And it's not easy to give one's opinion when one has been mired for years in the problem of one's own "coughing farts". But I waded right in. I told them that it was hazardous to our health to retain our farts. "Why?" Because if we let our bodies fill with gas, children, we will fly away like hot-air balloons, that's why! "We would fly away?" Yes, and once airborne, if we were to make the mistake of farting – and it's bound to happen because you can't hold your farts in forever – we would deflate and crash down on the boulders, like the dinosaurs did. "Really? That's how the dinosaurs died?" Yes. They were constantly told that it was impolite to fart so they held in their farts, held them in, held them in, and the dinosaurs swelled and swelled and swelled so much that of course they wound up flying away, and when they were forced to fart, the poor things, they deflated and crashed down on the boulders, every last one of them. (The boulders made a big impression.)

86 years, 10 months, 6 days *Monday, 16 August, 2010*

The kids left the day before my second transfusion. Bye, Grandmother! Bye, Grandfather! If these children don't question the fact that they will see us again, it's because they have always known us. When we are children, we don't see the adults around us getting older; what interests us as children is growing up, and adults don't grow up, they are crystallised in their maturity. Old people don't grow up either. They have been old since the time we were born. Their wrinkles guarantee their immortality. In the eyes of our great-grandchildren, Mona and I have been around forever and as a result we will live forever. Our death will be all the more striking to them. Their first experience of fleetingness.

86 years, 10 months, 9 days *Thursday, 19 August, 2010*

The second transfusion does not have the charm of the first. Its effects – just as tonic – will not last as long. Just knowing this fact spoils my euphoria.

86 years, 10 months, 13 days *Monday, 23 August, 2010*

Watching Lison making up our bed and Frédéric writing my prescription after a blood test, it occurred to me that one has to grow very old oneself in order to watch others grow old. It is a sad privilege to see time ravage the bodies of our children and grandchildren. I have spent the last forty years seeing mine *change*. That sixty-year-old man with his yellowing hair, spotted hands, scrawny neck, who is starting to detach from his own skin, is no longer the Frédéric with a plump neck and agile fingers with whom Grégoire fell in love. And Lison hardly looks anything like Fanny and Marguerite, who race down the stairs, promising to come next month to "pamper" me. And those two marvellous young women, as splendid as they look, have already lost that pneumatic density that allows Louis and Stefano to bound from room to room.

As far as clothing is concerned, they all wear jeans, trousers that have been universal, unisex and intergenerational for years. But jeans are a cruel indicator of passing time. For men, jeans empty out with age; for women, they fill out. A man's back pockets deflate on an arse that has melted away to nothing. The crotch becomes crumpled, the fly hangs loose; the young man no longer lives in his favourite jeans, an old man has replaced him, overflowing only above the belt. The mature woman, for her part, pathetically fills out her jeans. Oh, the fly is like a swollen scar! In my day, we wore the clothing suitable to our age. Babies had their bloomers, little boys had their shorts and their sailor collars, teenagers their golf trousers, the young man had his first suit, of soft flannel or tweed with padded shoulders, and then, finally comes the three-piece suit, the uniform of social maturity that I will soon be wearing in my coffin. Bruno used to say, "Once you were over thirty, you all looked old in those suits." It's true, the three-piece suit aged us prematurely, or rather, it aged instead of us, whereas today both men and women age in their jeans.

86 years, 10 months, 14 days *Tuesday, 24 August, 2010*

Ah, but the indomitable youth of those who are twenty or thirty years younger than us! And the early childhood that is still visible on our old children. Oh, my adorable Lison!

*

NOTE TO LISON

Do you remember, Lison, the book that had horrified Fanny and made Marguerite laugh so much? It was by García Márquez. That summer Mona was reading Márquez to the girls at siesta time. I think it was *One Hundred Years of Solitude.* I don't really remember. But I remember that reading! The story went something like this: On Christmas or her birthday, every year a young woman receives a gift from her father. The father lives far away for some reason but is very punctual when it comes to sending the gift, a huge trunk filled with unexpected presents that thrill the children. (It must be Christmas, now that I think about it, because I remember the children's joy.) One year, the crate arrives a bit before the usual date. The same sender, the same addressee, but a little mistake in the date. The family rushes to open the crate in their impatience: surprise, it contains the father's body! Putrefied? Mummified? Stuffed? I can't remember at all, but it is the father's body, no question about it. Fanny is horrified: "That's disgusting!" Marguerite is ecstatic: "That's fantastic!" Mona is very pleased with the results: "Long live magic realism!" And you, as usual, were drawing the scene in one of your sketchbooks. Tell me, Lison, isn't this the same trick I'm playing on you?

Honestly, I would not turn over in my grave if you chucked this whole thing in the fire.

*

86 years, 10 months, 29 days *Wednesday, 8 September, 2010*

The nurse who measures my disappearing platelets curses my veins. They have been called upon too often, so they have hardened or are hiding. She looks for other ones, on the back of my hand, at the top of my ankle. Bruises, scratches, scabs . . . "So you're scratching yourself as well! Look at that!" How about injecting me with a pint of heroin, I say to Frédéric to tease him. My reputation is screwed anyway, just look at my arms! And it would be so easy for you; you'd just have to pick the lock on the hospital pharmacy! The poor fellow gets angry again; he protests that he is not a dealer and accuses me of confusing heroin with morphine: "Your typical mix-up! Heroin and morphine are not at all the same. Really, you are . . ." He looks at me, shakes his head, and suddenly bursts into tears. Come, come. Sobs. And he leaves the room. I, too, would have lived in anger if I had seen my patients die. Including those who got better and then, in the end, died anyway. Improvement and then – dead people. Every day of your life. There are grounds for being angry at the dying. Poor doctor! To spend one's life repairing a programme that has been conceived to fuck up. Other people write *The Tartar Steppe*. Frédéric is his own masterpiece.

86 years, 11 months, 1 day *Saturday, 11 September, 2010*

Everything that I have not written down in this diary becomes obvious to me as I annotate it for Lison. Aspiring to say everything, I said so little. I barely touched upon this body that I wanted to describe.

86 years, 11 months, 4 days *Tuesday, 14 September, 2010*

The closer I get to the end, the more things there are to write down and the less strength I have to do so. My body is changing hourly. It disintegrates more rapidly as its functions slow down. Acceleration and deceleration . . . I feel like a coin about to stop spinning on itself.

86 years, 11 months, 27 days *Thursday, 7 October, 2010*

Finally finished my notes to Lison. Writing exhausts me. The pen is so heavy. Every letter is a steep climb, each word a mountain.

87 years, birthday *Sunday, 10 October, 2010*

One last time, the *Larousse* cut-out man in the edge of the mirror. Next to him, I am Job on his pile of manure. Happy birthday.

87 years, 17 days *Wednesday, 27 October, 2010*

No more transfusions. One cannot sponge off humankind forever.

87 years, 19 days *Friday, 29 October, 2010*

Now, my little Dodo, it is time to die. Don't be afraid, I'll show you how.

TRANSLATOR'S ACKNOWLEDGEMENTS

I would like first to thank Daniel Pennac for his time and patience in answering my questions one long afternoon that slid gently into evening. Thanks, too, to Christopher MacLehose for offering me this book to translate. My thanks as well, and as always, to that miraculous human being and my fellow translator, Donald Nicholson-Smith, for the hours we've shared over the years (and the martinis) discussing the world of words; and my heartfelt gratitude to Dominique Buchan, copy-editor extraordinaire, who caught my omissions, polished my prose, and asked really, really good questions.

Lines from *The Essays of Montaigne, Complete*, by Michel de Montaigne, translated by Charles Cotton 1986, ed. William Carew Hazlitt, 1877 (Project Gutenberg).

Lines from Boris Pasternak's *Doctor Zhivago*, from the translation by Max Hayward and Manya Harari, first published by the Harvill Press in 1958, reproduced by permission of Random House Group Limited.

The verse taken from Jules Supervieille's "Prophecy", in Gravitations (1925) in a translation by William Louis-Dreyfus and Molly Peacock

Alyson Water

DANIEL PENNAC was born in 1944 in Morocco. He was a teacher before becoming a writer of books for children and a series of hugely successful humorous novels. A continued interest in education and social affairs led to his book *The Rights of the Reader*, and thereafter to *School Blues*, for which he won the Prix Renaudot. His books have been translated into more than thirty languages and are read all over the world.

ALYSON WATERS is a translator of modern and contemporary French literature. In 2012, she won the French-American Foundation Translation Award for her translation of Eric Chevillard's *Prehistoric Times*. Waters has received a National Endowment for the Arts Translation Fellowship, a PEN Translation Fund grant, and several residency grants. She teaches literary translation at New York University and Columbia University.